POLLY ANDREWS

She was the "brainy kid" who skipped three grades in school. She was the ambitious career girl who longed to become a lawyer. She was pert, energetic, talented and single-mindedly determined to escape the dream-infested, poverty-ridden, miracle-wishing, absurdly pretentious lifestyle of her family.

To succeed, all she had to do was make a simple, practical choice—between a man who could offer her everything and the "nobody" she loved . . .

WORLD BY THE TAIL

An enchanting chronicle of the fortunes and misfortunes of an unforgettable family . . . An enthralling novel of love . . .

To Mommy From Susan
X-mas 1974
Merry Christmas

WORLD
BY THE TAIL

Marjorie Holmes

WORLD BY THE TAIL

*A Bantam Book / published by arrangement with
J. B. Lippincott Company*

PRINTING HISTORY
*Lippincott edition published April 1943
Bantam edition published September 1972
2nd printing
3rd printing*

*Bantam Books are published by Bantam Books, Inc., a National
General company. Its trade-mark, consisting of the words "Bantam
Books" and the portrayal of a bantam, is registered in the United
States Patent Office and in other countries. Marca Registrada.
Bantam Books, Inc., 666 Fifth Avenue, New York, N.Y. 10019.*

PRINTED IN THE UNITED STATES OF AMERICA

TO
MY MOTHER
AND
FATHER

This book was written in a spirit of tenderness and tolerance for a kind of people whom the author happens to know and to love. But it is primarily a work of fiction and must be so judged.

CHAPTER ONE

THE MOONLIGHT CREPT into Polly's room like a timid scullery maid staggering under buckets of silver. It mopped a shimmering effervescence across the rugless boards of the floor and the tipsy walls that were mostly ceiling. Then, careless of the eerie cleanness it had wrought, it tracked immense shadows back toward the window, where it spilled a radiant puddle upon the sill.

In the center of that puddle sat Polly, hot-cheeked and tight of throat, with her fine little chin cupped in her hands and her great eyes stormy. This was not her first tragedy. Her imp of truth popped out and reminded her of that. No. By the time you are practically nineteen you have sobbed through many tragedies. But this was climactic. Final. The last time, she thought violently, knocking small frantic fists against the ledge, Dad will ever shame me!

Nine days from tonight she would be gone. Scuffing the earth of childhood from her fleeing feet, shaking off poverty and foolish pretendings as she'd shaken the drops from her body after her lonely last swim. That pig-tailed runt, Polly Andrews, who had skipped grades in school and been allowed, cruelly, to finish at fifteen; that determined drudge who, in addition to beating and bluffing her way through the impoverished local college, was also the moral and financial family prop—for her at last, escape.

"Me, a lawyer!" She whispered the words in a catch of breath and heard the muted laughter of the devil who mocked all that she did. "Of all idiotic things for the family to produce!" It was like galloping across the field and cheering for the wrong team. For all their existence the Andrews family had known an embarrassing intimacy with lawyers. Lawyers representing grocers and coal companies had been their most faithful correspondents. Lawyers issuing those impressive documents called judgments. Lawyers pleading and exhorting them to pay.

Sam Andrews pronounced them "The crookedest sonsa-bitches alive, don't you know they are? but good-hearted too." They were, rather—notarizing his patent papers free of charge; advising him not to sue this party or that who had produced articles similar to his shimmy kitty or collapsible lamppost; presiding over those signal deals when, after weeks of exciting conferences, the papers would actually be signed for the sale of his gum dispenser, his fly paper holder or refuse box. Presiding over—and pouncing on the lion's share.

Trotting home intoxicated with the joy of his genius, he would wave the check for five hundred, seven—once it had been two thousand—and proclaim, "Crookedest sonsa-bitches alive, lawyers, but where'd we be without 'em?" Then after the money's quick melting away for back bills, rent, new clothes, movies, ice cream, beefsteak, and the running down of a job, he would sit sometimes with a re-mote sadness on his ruddy little fat man's face.

"Crookedest sonsabitches alive," he would sigh.

So when Polly had gone to work for one of them, he had advised, "Make him teach you how to beat the general public too, kiddo. You could study law right there in your spare time."

With the infinite superiority of sixteen, Polly had sniffed. No musty small town law office for her, thank you. When George Walcott sneaked off for his daily golf, poker, or murky story session in the back room of the bank, she worked on her poems. Or she would sit drawing, with deft, untutored fingers. These talents would be her en-trance to that mystic but vitally real realm, Getting Some-where. The world by the tail with a downhill pull, as Sam would vulgarly put it.

George Walcott, stomping in one day, had surprised her at them. "Poetry, painting!" he snorted. "Like those fly-by-night schemes of your dad's. No money in things like that. Here, you study law!" And he had thrust a case book into her unwilling hands.

She despised him for all that he represented: Stolidity and lack of imagination. The right to press a buzzer and know that she must bounce to do his bidding. To dictate nasty, nagging collection letters to harass harmless souls like Sam. She loathed his moustache and his big stomach and his belchings, and the way he spat toward—and generally missed—the wastebasket. But oh, cursed actuality, he was right! Without money you were nothing. And to get money you had to grab for something sure. If Dad had had a profession what mightn't he have done with his vast store of ideas and dreams?

But it was not George Walcott who lured her from her muses. It was Jud Masters, an evangelistic youth who one day strode into her hot office prison with a stack of magazines under his arm. He found her lettering, quite fancily, a poster announcing a forthcoming Kiwanis Kweens bazaar.

"Say, not bad, not bad!" he boomed cordially. "How'd you learn to print so good? Shucks, I took art three years and can't do much better myself."

"You studied—art?" Polly gazed up.

"Oh, I've fooled around with it, but what I'm really taking is pre-leg' at the U. Say, that's where you oughta be!" He sat chummily on her desk, huge and beaming with collegiate enthusiasm, swinging his two-tone shoes. He was the grandson of a rich Iowa washing machine baron, but —even as his grandfather before him—said to be determined to work for everything he got. Hence the magazines.

This was in the late twenties, before Dale Carnegie's win-and-influence salesmanship had been popularized; Jud Masters had the same idea—in reverse. By the time he had Polly's subscription (17¢ a week, two-dollars less than the newsstand price) she had his life story, told with a curious admixture of self-deprecation, an occasional humbly cynical, oddly appealing little wink. He too, it seemed, was a frustrated artist of many talents, having been high school class poet, Macbeth in the annual Shakespearean play, and even a musician of no mean skill.

"But shucks, what does stuff like that get you? Law—there's the gold-plated ticket to success! You oughta take a crack at it yourself. You could pick it up here in your spare time and then come down to the U. and polish off."

Polly was meekly acquiescent. Impressed, she gulped. When he had gone pounding down the steps, she sat taut with hope and wonder, gathering up her old dreams of artistic accomplishment and patting them fondly even as she shoved them over to make room for this new grim and jubilant truth. She would right the score with lawyers. Right it for herself and for Sam, for Mom who had to carry in the duns and toss them dramatically into the stove; for the whole heckled Andrews clan. She would use George Walcott, his books and his clients and his few stodgy brains, climb over and beyond him to a pinnacle of greatness that not he, or any Gem Lake lawyer, had yet attained. She would study law.

"Oh, Lord, please!" she prayed desperately, this night of her grief. "Let me go away, really study now, leave behind the shabbiness and the worry and—and the stupid awfulness of things like tonight!"

She covered her face with her hands and cried passionately, but briefly. Then she bent and wiped her nose on her cotton pajamas and sat brooding out at the quietly comprehending night.

Directly below the screen stood her cherry tree, its small leaves glistening like pieces of silver. For six years she had looked down upon its blossoms, its lip-red fruit, and in winter its sharp-twigged nudity. It had watched her cry and exult, talk eagerly to herself and the stars in the jumble of confidences and pleas that were her prayers. It knew all about her, and never told.

Back of the cherry tree squatted the garage, a friendly shack, which probably knew too.

The house next door might have known, but its windows were blind. It was the immaculate childless bungalow of an elderly couple, the Flannigans. They arose and quarreled at dawn, spent the day puttering about starched flowers, an untrod lawn, and a garden so clean that the terrified weeds fled to the neighbors. At sundown the

Flannigans were abed with nothing more exciting to dream about than the righteous memory that they had snatched Ramey's ball when it bounded across their Line.

Often, on moonlit nights, Polly's imp made her want to throw stones at their window and yell, "Get up, you crazy old loons! Don't you know you're headed for the grave? Get an eyeful of the lake all crusted with stars before you rot!"

But only to crouch at your window on such a night was almost as bad. You had to do—something. Go swimming—do something—or go mad. And she had sprung up, snatched off her clothes, and still fumbling with the straps on her suit, sped downstairs, up cindery alleys and across the park. It was a night of enchantment, when Frey and Freya, Summer and Beauty, walked hand in hand. And yet there was an overripe quality about it, a hint of mellow bursting and decay. Even the water, for all its dissembling sparkle, was "green" Polly discovered when she had plunged into the cold wash.

She swam nonetheless, to the diving tower, and dragged herself up to lie listening to the music, feasting upon loneliness, and dreaming with a kind of poignant nostalgia of going away. Gem Lake's cheap little public dances wouldn't matter then, or its cruel stupid boys who saw only Jean.

She had come to brood, to be miserable, and so when the man's head came over the ladder she was vaguely annoyed. It was a very curly head; the curls were tight little crocheted balls in which drops of water winked. He wasn't tall, but he had an athlete's triangular figure. His nose was a right triangle too upon the square lines of his face. His lips were thick, like cushions, giving a negroid touch to the otherwise clean precision of his profile. He was considerably older, Polly decided—twenty-six or so at least. Having observed all this in her swift, intense way the usual flashback of self-consciousness followed and she looked away.

"Hello." He dropped to the boards, panting a little. "Boy, is that water green!"

Jean would have had a quip, but Polly, hugging her knees at the end of the springboard, could think of nothing to say.

"I hate to disturb your reverie, but if you don't intend to dive, would you mind—?"

"Oh!" She scrambled up, hastily retreated. "Sorry."

"You needn't be. You looked like a water sprite perching there," he said. And with a terrific thumping jar, he dived.

So he was one of *those*—Polly thought. Well, his dive wasn't as smooth as his line.

"That was awful," he acknowledged, upon his return. "Maybe it's sour grapes and maybe it's just that I don't like swimming in scum, but I think I'll hit for shore." He stood for a minute, wet flesh quivering from the chill night air. Music from across the lake came throbbing in a kind of jungle beat. "Sounds like a good band tonight."

"Cato's."

"They are good. I'd go if I knew someone to ask."

He stood looking down at her and her heart crashed in her ears. A man like this—to be asked—to vaunt a smooth older man like this in front of Jean—!

"I'm Dan Scott from Crescent. I don't suppose you'd care to go?"

For a second the temptation was sweet and terrible. Then she remembered that he might think it strange if no one else asked her to dance. No, not here. Never so long as she stayed in Gem Lake could she make that change.

"If I'd wanted to go I'd have been there," she claimed, a trifle desperately. "Instead, I decided to come for this farewell swim."

"Farewell?"

"Yes. You see, I'm going away." Saying it aloud made it more miraculously true, somehow. "To the university."

"Oh, a succulently green little freshman?"

"Hardly. Post-graduate work. In law."

"But good Lord, you don't look over twelve!"

"I'm almost old enough to vote," she lied.

And suddenly, from the habit of years of camouflaging, pretending, she was off on a whole pack of lies. She'd worked, for the fun of it mostly, in a law office while going to the rickety little college just up the hill from home. Studying law had intrigued her, partly because her father (she made him sound casually genteel) had once had aspirations for the bar. Now she was going to the U. to tat up the loose ends of her knowledge, and have a good time.

"I take it these local brawls don't interest you much."

"Well, they do seem rather adolescent sometimes. My kid sister doesn't think so, but then she lives for dancing. She's a beautiful dancer—plans to take it up professionally. My brother Ken—he's an actor—likes the Casino too. Personally, I can't see why."

"That's because you're the wise one of the family."

"Too wise, maybe!" she said in a sudden disconsolate burst. As impetuously as she had begun this Andrews fantasia, she was repelled by it. She had sensed some quality in this man sitting beside her, something so honest and decently generous in his utter lack of doubt, that she was ashamed of herself. "Sometimes I think the only wisdom that counts is the wisdom of just being glib and gay and—and not giving a damn!" She turned to him. "Do you happen to know that story about Kvasir—the man who was so wise he drowned in his own wisdom?" He opened his mouth, but before he could reply she raced on impatiently. "The dwarfs put his blood in jars to keep. Sometimes I feel like that—as if my blood's been canned, put up in fruit jars with the lids on tight. As if the real me can't get out!"

He threw back his head and laughed. Then he said soberly, "If you'll forgive me, you've forgotten something. The dwarfs mixed honey with that blood. If you've got sweetness in your blood nothing can suppress you completely."

She stared at him, astonished. She had been so blithely superior in thinking that he wouldn't know what a Nordic folk tale was.

"I'm a Norseman on my mother's side," he explained. "Besides, I just happen to like myths."

Myths! Polly felt her skin crawl.

But when he insisted upon taking her home she hadn't the courage to refuse. She waited in his car while he went into the boathouse lockers to dress. She had a sense of shock when he came bounding up the steps, whistling softly, twirling his keys. He looked even older in the good light suit and panama hat—like a young married business man. Feeling suddenly naked and unformed, she shrank down into the seat.

They drove past the shaggy campus of Vista College. Its three humble buildings were like tired old men asleep in the moon. Thank heaven she lived in a good neighborhood, Polly thought. The house, with its L-shaped, vine-muffled porch, its bay windows and turrets and scrolls, gave an impression of shabby gentility as they approached.

"Well, good-night, thanks for the ride." She hopped out, ready for a quick scuttle to safety. But Dan followed her to the porch.

"That's no way to say good-night." He caught her hand as she bounded up the sagging front steps. Her head was on a level with his when he turned her around. "Please?"

"No! No, I—"

Leaning a little forward, he kissed her, gently, but competently with his full firm mouth.

Then the dread thing happened—the squeak of the screen and Sam's blasting bellow, "Polly! Get in here and be damn' quick about it!" Sam, squat and bare-chested, the moonlight glinting on his bald head; Sam, the faithful little watchdog, anxious to show off his most ferocious bark.

"Gee, I didn't mean to cause any trouble," Dan apologized, both to Polly and the menace at the screen.

"Well it don't look very Goddamn' good to the neighbors, this lollygaggin' half the night!" Sam trumpeted righteously. But they heard his wicked chuckle as he rattled shut the door. Dad, the maddening, the incomprehensible.

"Whew! What—was all that?"

Polly bit a hole in her cap; the rubber tasted good. "Dad's—erratic. And after all, I am in a bathing suit."

"I hadn't thought of it like that." He held tight to her hand as she turned to go. "When will I see you again?"

Polly glanced uneasily toward the screen. Had Dad gone padding off to bed, or did he still lurk in the shadows? "Never," she said fiercely. "I hate second meetings!"

"But tonight's been practically perfect."

"All right, so maybe it has. So why go messing it up?"

He returned her gaze, half frowning. "Hey, look—brilliant little women attorneys shouldn't take life so seriously as all that."

Above his secret amusement, was he being gallant, now that the shabby seams of truth had popped through? She plunged, head low, across the porch.

"See you tomorrow," he called after her. "Kvasir!"

Polly crept into the hall and quickly up the open stairs. She peeled out of her wet suit and left it, a dark circle on the moon-scrubbed floor. In her faded cotton pajamas, she crouched by the whitened sill. Never had she been more grateful for her room—or more anxious to leave it.

CHAPTER TWO

WHEN THE ANDREWS family moved into the House by the Lake, nobody else wanted the hot-cold slope-ceilinged back room. Sam and Lydia naturally took the only downstairs chamber, the better to hear their children coming in at night. It was assumed that the girls were to occupy the big room at the head of the stairs, while Ken and Ramey would shove their stuff into what was left. But the Lake House not only boasted a *bathroom*, a double parlor, and three bedrooms—there was still that many-angled cubicle jutting off to the back. Polly pounced upon it. She had always longed for a place where she could prowl around at night without Jean's petulant whine, "Aw, come on to be-ed!"

The first three children of Sam and Lydia Andrews had been born in the White House. But three years was a long time for them to spend in one place, and every first of March thereafter found them shivering in the excitement of clambering onto the dray and riding forth to the New House. Then that first shrieking, exploratory romp, banging open the doors of closets, yelling, "Oh, looky, a cubbyhole!" or "Gosh, a sink!" their voices echoing in the emptiness that preceded the lugging in of their vast amount of junk. And then the cozy shock of discovering that familiar bedsteads shoved into place, a worn old rug

10

unrolled, dishes unpacked and set upon the table that always fed them, could transform this mysteriously barren, curtainless house to Home.

Each brief sojourn bore some titular association—the Bedbug House, Shunk-by-Shunk's House (their landlord had been an old German who raged, "I seen ya carrying my wood out of the barn shunk-by-shunk!" but their lips had been blue with the cold and not a coal company in town would give them any more credit), the White Rat House (where Sam had undertaken to raise the little creatures and once impishly turned them loose at choir practice), the Pink Peppermint House, Jordan House, and Here.

Here represented a goal toward which they had been groping these many years. It was Modern. The smell of leaking gas, the sound of a dripping faucet, reminded them pleasantly that they had arrived. No longer need they cringe when it was their turn to entertain Ladies Aid, or be apologetic about having people stay all night. True, in no time Lydia was complaining about not having hard wood floors, and Kenneth and Sam argued just as vehemently about taking care of the furnace as they had about building fires in the heating stove. But Polly was happy. She had her own room.

With the money she earned Saturdays clerking in the variety store, she bought wallpaper (a pattern of violets entwined with buttercups) and pasted it on, alone. With cans of orchid, yellow and black enamel she attacked the more promising pieces of Grandpa's furniture, which Lydia couldn't bear to sell after her father's death. A somber wooden bed became flamboyant in a coat of orchid, its scrolls and carved pine cones leaping into a blatancy of yellow and black. The same color scheme was used on a wobbly chest of drawers and a commode which she turned into a desk by knocking out the door which had once hidden a chamber with a crochet-covered lid.

The others caught the smell and the spirit of paint. Iron beds and plain varnished dressers in other bedrooms blossomed forth in shiny coats of blues and greens. Everybody was elated at the transformation and wondered why they'd never thought of it before.

Jean finally wheedled Sam into buying that essential equipment for dating, a davenport and chair. He held out a long time, cursing good-naturedly, but when he did give in he told Lydia to pick out a rug too. When he got home on week ends he sprawled luxuriously, rubbing his bald head against the furry velour nap, and admitted it was " a damn sight better than those old rockers that made your bones ache." In time a radio followed; a lamp and a clock won playing Bingo at the Casino; a cheap piece of tapestry which Jean had brought home from a trip to Des Moines; Polly's Christmas presents of pictures, pillows, and smoking stand. Only one luxury from the old days accompanied these newcomers into the parlor. That was Lydia's huge mahogany piano, scratched and marred from so much moving about, but still as regal and solid as it had been on that memorable wedding anniversary when Sam had helped lift it down from the dray, gritting his teeth with its weight and panting, "S'prise!" The sheet music bought at the same time, *Where the Black Eyed Susans Grow, Beautiful Ohio,* and *Lonesome, I Guess That's All,* lay dogeared in the bottom of the bench, tunes that none of them would ever forget.

They dubbed that territory lying beyond the hot air register, the Swell Room; while the more humble adjoining portion, covered only by a worn linoleum and containing Grandpa's knobby old secretary and a home-made bookcase and library table, became the Plain Room. The dining room held the cluttered sewing machine and the round table with its thick leg branching off into four gnarled feet. The kitchen was large enough to eat in, and although the kitchen table had never been large enough to eat on, they still crowded around it.

They talked of buying the house, if Sam's latest traveling job lasted and they could get their debts paid. Sam said, "A damn' shame, don't you know it is? The money we pay out on other people's places. Why, we could've had a place of our own a long time ago for what we've sunk in rent."

They talked and talked and went on paying rent to the old landlady, Mrs. Henniper, who called weekly to whimper, "You ought to make your boys mow the lawn a little oftener, don't you think? And I wouldn't let the young ones dig those caves in the backyard."

A breeze strayed up from the lake and slipped cool fingers through Polly's short damp hair. It carried the winy smell of overripe summer and a crisp smoky hint of the hurrying autumn. She drank it deep into her lungs, every sense quick to this nostalgic potion brewed of things she would leave behind—lake and fish and rock and sand, a boat's gentle knocking against a swaying dock, the cold stroke of water that washed your heart's pain clean. For a moment an overwhelming sadness gripped her.

Then she was alert, nostrils dilate, like a colt with ears laid back. For something else came riding the wind. Music, no longer a dim far-pulsing. "Good-night, good-night, I'll see you in the morning. . . ." The last dance at the Casino. She clapped her hands over her ears, but still it strained through.

And she could see them there. Jean, a fleet-legged nymph, fluffy head tilted back, long lips apart for her bubbling dance-night laughter. Her picturesque little nose would be wrinkled, her eyes, flirting up, bold and secret. Jean, the younger, and ignorant—and wise. And Kenneth, nonchalant, insolent, thrilling girls when he flicked away his cigarette and honored them with a dance. They hated each other, those two. Had hated each other from child-hood, cordially and without compromise. Yet between them was a bond severing Polly from their world. They were popular. Popularity had been born in them, just as ambition had been bred into her very bones.

Kenneth lived upon his popularity, ate it as gluttonously as he wolfed down slice after slice of bread and coffee at breakfast. It had come to him early, warming his blood. In the fourth grade he had discovered, beneath the grime, a handsome face. Cautiously he even tried combing his hair, with results so pleasing that he risked the taunts of his sisters to have Mom cut off the top of an old stocking for him to wear to bed at night.

Lydia warned the girls to be respectful, so they snickered only in private. It occurred to them that a brother coveted by the girls in big houses might bring those girls to their own backyard. That worried them some though. There was always so darn' much junk around. An old boiler hanging on a nail, the wash' machine squatting on the porch, cans tossed blindly from the back door, the smelly rabbit hutches, the bag swing drooling straw. They tried to clean it up—Jean for almost an hour once, Polly day after

day, week after week, fighting to overcome cans that kept
flying, weeds that kept thriving, ashes that came on forever.

She knew that Kenneth faintly despised her for being
a smarty and a drudge, but she was inordinately proud of
him. "That's my brother, the good-looking boy coming
now," she would boast to new girls and be grateful if he
granted her a nod of recognition. To spare Sam's wrath,
she lugged out garbage and staggered in with coal when he
forgot. Once when he forgot his paper route she trudged
around town, sneaking up to porches, piping, "Paper!" and
running like fury lest a dog or an irate customer be lying
in wait.

Kenneth distressed her. She felt his disdain as a dull pain
you mustn't recognize. Yet she was secretly confident that
they were kindred spirits. If ever the family was to be
elevated to higher planes, it would be on the wings of their
mutual wonders. Until then his precious prestige must be
jealously guarded.

Kenneth spent as many hours as Sam and spasmodic
home chores allowed in the swell homes of Gem Lake.
The mecca of swell kids. For his inclusion he traded his
wit and his looks, his ability to play the piano by ear and
remember the words to popular songs. He was something
of a dictator. The girls palpitated for his favor, the boys
cheerfully ran his errands and lent him their bikes and
their clothes. He called all the mothers "sweetheart,"
hugged them, and brazenly told them what to have for
dinner when he stayed—which was practically always.

To compensate for sometimes having to snub his own
people, he showered them with presents. With the change
left from grocery money he bought cheap perfume for his
mother, toys for Ramey, ribbons, stockings and paper dolls
for his sisters. He loved to be praised for his thoughtfulness
and was infuriated by Jean's caustic perception, "Yeah, but
it was Dad's money got it." He casually charged things,
and when Sam stormed he would wail, "Nobody under-
stands me! I'm just trying to make everybody happy and all
I get is disgrace!" Then Polly would go violently to bat for
him, pleading his case before Sam, or bribing Jean into returning the "present" by promising her half interest in the
doll or the magic lantern she was earning by selling seeds.

Inevitably, he matured. His liberties with family finances

were limited to getting occasional cash on the grocery bill, and then only when he absolutely had to have it for a country club dance, or white flannels to wear in the Monday Club musical comedy.

"Oh, Kenneth, I *wish* you wouldn't do this!" Lydia would plead at the month-end time of reckoning. "It's so hard for me to explain to Dad."

Kenneth's arms would go around his mother. "I know it, honey. But what's a guy gonna do? If I'm going to be in plays I've got to wear what the script calls for. Of course if you and Dad don't want me to go with the right outfit, be in the shows—"

"No!" Her gray eyes would be large with rebellion. "We don't want to hold any of you kids back. You can do those parts better than anyone in town. Only it does seem as if they could at least provide the costumes."

"Or a decent job so I could earn my own," he would snort, rising to pace the room with swift, agile grace. Turning, his step was abrupt and beautiful. The cherubic curves of his childhood had narrowed. He was lean of face and body, tall, cut with some fine and delicate chisel that had been used in carving his mother and her profligate brother, Uncle John. He had the same good longish nose, high cheekbones and deep-sunk eyes; the same strong white flash of teeth and defiant thrust of chin.

"These darn' merchants won't hire a town kid. If they've got a job they give it to some new guy. But you tell Dad I'll pay him back."

Kenneth was a comfort to his mother. Affectionate, generous, and such a good boy, she always declared. Sam, however, failed to see wherein Ken was such a paragon. "Those Goddam' girls running after him have ruined him," he said. "Why in hell don't he get out and *do* something? He ain't earned a nickel since he was born."

And that constituted Sam Andrews' notion of a ruined son.

It did not bother Ken greatly that he was seldom able to get jobs or keep them. He had worked briefly for the poultry house, the canning factory and done typing for a teachers' agency. His loathing for routine duty expressed itself in being late, being sick, and being bored. He found but one pleasure in being a breadwinner. It furnished him with a repertoire of anecdotes with which to entertain members of the Do-Nothing Club which met at the Checker-Board Confectionery.

"Move over, you mugs, and make room for some honest chicken dirt," he would order, sliding his white overalls into a booth. He would then launch into an account of the eggs he had scrambled and the hens he'd slaughtered, mimicking the big Swede chicken picker, the battle axe in the office, the boss and the boss's wife. He had a flattering audience harharring as long as he chose to talk. Finally he would yawn, stretch, stamp out one cigarette, mooch another, and saunter home, vaguely content, vaguely troubled. He was well liked everywhere, well thought of nowhere. His lip curled. This damn' town. Sometime he'd get out and show 'em he could really act!

He was usually in a bad frame of mind by the time he reached the L-shaped porch with scrolls. So, as he mounted the steps he whistled, playing the role of laborer wending his weary but cheery way homeward. He pulled Ramey's hair fondly, kissed his mother, asked for the mail, and snarled in offending modesty at Jean, who was trying to kick the chandelier.

He was scrupulously clean, hauling steaming kettles of water upstairs to bathe for a maddening time before every dance. When he was not working, his date money came from his mother, Polly, or his girl friends. Sam, with incalculable inconsistency, railed at him or tossed him a five-dollar bill.

Toward Jean Polly had long felt an unease and a guilt. As if she were somehow responsible for whatever torments Jean suffered—if Jean suffered. Despite her frequent tantrums, her violent heel kickings and impudent tongue, there was about her a cool secrecy, as if, after all, this would soon be done and forgotten.

But Polly couldn't forget. Nagging scenes out of the past made it necessary to do things for Jean, pay for her tap lessons, buy her clothes, defend her before ever-suspicious Sam. There had been the time Lydia, after hours of drill, had hurled an arithmetic at Jean, screeching, "Why *are* you like this? Polly could have seen it! Polly could have done it!" Polly went taut with resentment; pity was an agony in her throat. But Jean only shrugged and trotted upstairs to bed. And when Polly crawled in beside her, Jean wriggled free of her caress, yawned short her speech of condolence. "Oh, go tell it to the rabbits," she said. "I wanta get some sleep."

Once Jean came home with a caustically flippant account of how the teacher had invited the class to ridicule her spelling. "I shouldn't of told," she sighed worriedly as Sam stomped off to bawl out the school board and Lydia had hysterics of tenderness. Unwanted third child though she was, disappointing in all but such dubious accomplishments as dancing and boy-charming, theirs alone was the privilege of maltreating her.

To punish her for her craftiness in evading work, they shoved onto her every errand distasteful to the others.

Yet even in cruelest little girl days before Jean had learned to avenge and rebel, Polly envied her sister for the way boys showed off for her benefit, chose her for those steal-away-together games which they played hot nights under the stars. Jean was taller, and destined to be beautiful. And Jean was not dumb. She was very, very wise. Polly, panting, disheveled from a wild winning run to base, would hear Jean's cool giggle with a discomfiting sense of something missed. A gap in her learning—as, after skipping second grade, she had found the third graders mysteriously doing multiplication. What was this knowledge, this power that Jean possessed?

Sam knew. "She's gonna be like John's girls if we don't watch her," he warned his wife.

"Why, Sam, she is not!" Lydia protested, shocked.

"Well, she's always reminded me of them. Something about her. And if we ain't careful she'll turn out the same way."

He wasn't aware, nor did he care, that Jean paused at the cupboard, a cup in one fist, the other knotted. Her bright head was tilted, scorn quirked her long red mouth and her narrow eyes. This too they expected of her then, just as they had predicted indolence and slowness in school. Being fast, having to get married! She didn't know whether to laugh or bawl, it was so nuts. She didn't 'specially like boys. They just liked her.

She slammed shut the cupboard doors, hung the damp towel behind the stove, and tramped through the Swell

Room, enjoying her mother's guilty start. Sam, however, reared up boldly over his newspaper. "That's what I said, missy, and I meant every damn' word!"

"Sam!" Lydia shrilled, eyes instantly tear-gleamy. "You don't really think anything of the kind."

"Well," Sam growled, "it don't look very good to the neighbors, that Hobbs kid hanging around like a lovesick calf."

"But it isn't fair to hold those cousins up to Jean!" Jean, bending over Lydia's chair for the customary good-night smack, felt herself clutched against her mother's hard flat bosom. "Jean's going to be a good sweet girl." Then coaxingly, as if Lydia too doubted, "Aren't you, Jean?"

Jean wriggled free. "Oh, sure," she snipped. "I'm gonna be one of those Salvation Army dames and go around with a tambourine getting dimes so we can have something to eat besides eggs once in a while!"

And she pattered off to bed, leaving the enemy fuming. She was too fond of sleep to lie awake nursing her grievances, but she clenched her fists into two hard white balls which lay like undelivered blows guarding her the night through.

Polly fought her sister's battles as valiantly as Ken's, but for a different reason. She longed for Jean's friendship, ached to be included instead of left behind to soothe and lie to troubled parents when, with that merry gypsy, Vee Jordan, Jean would slip off to a dance. It did not occur to these two that she might want to share their escapades. To them Polly was of a different generation. They were just struggling through high school when she was in college. She did odd things like write poetry and get up at sunrise to go walking; and late one night she had taken a notion to swim the lake, just to see if she could. She went unannounced, without even a boat to paddle along, though it was three miles across. At dawn Sol Silverberg, Jewish proprietor of Casino park, spied her bobbing black head and went to the rescue with his launch. "Go 'way!" she sputtered, " 'm—almost—there." And finally, blue and half-drowned, she was spewed upon the sand. The Jew brought her home in his car, scolding violently all the way. "I did it!" she kept retorting through rattling teeth.

"You're nuts," Jean grinned, dropping to Polly's bed

and shaking her head on that signal occasion. "It's you the folks should be losing sleep over instead of me!"

"I did it!" Polly still triumphed. And she had her picture in the paper and it seemed important for a while.

Jean's attitude toward Polly was a gallimaufry of pride, disdain and solicitude. "Here, nitso, try it on," she would invite, tossing Polly the hat she had just legerdemained out of some scraps of old felt. Or what appeared to be a new dress might be dangling on Polly's closet pole some night. "Ain't it a darb?" Jean would ask proudly, surveying her handiwork. "But watch out for the seams, the sewing machine was balky. The jacket's out of some old curtains I found in a trunk in the garage, and the rest's from a skirt that must've been Grandma's. Kid, wouldn't you think Mom would of used up that stuff years ago?"

"But this is simply adorable, Jean!" Polly exclaimed one time. "Why don't you keep it yourself?"

"It's too short. Besides, if you're going to read at Cosmopolitan Club you've got to have the *best!*"

Pridefully together they laughed over the ragbag creation, and briefly they were chums.

On the night of Polly's public appearances Jean would fix her hair and force her to stand face up while she applied deft pats of rouge. She might even say, "Here, Miss Barrymore, wear my coat" (which Polly was still paying for), and Polly would gaily kiss everyone good-by and start the long walk townward feeling very much the pampered celebrity.

None of the gushing matrons or booming business men who allowed her to enliven their gatherings ever thought to send a car. Even after a triumph, when there had been insistent rounds of applause, even then sometimes she must slip down the streets alone. Thus, starting off aglow with anticipation, or scuttling home still giddy from the hot sweet wine of her talent, a car would cut by, perhaps honk, one voice or two call, "Hi, Poll!" and there would be cigarette scent and the smell of gas; spilled laughter, youth skidding by without her. And she would halt suddenly, knowing with terrible bitterness that this was not her night, after all. This was Jean's night, as all nights were Jean's. For Jean was young with a youth that had not been maimed by precocity.

They were playing, *Home, Sweet Home* now. The dance was over. This night was ended, packing up all its unplanned stage effects—moon and lake beat, vine shadows and drama at the doorway, stealing forever down the lanes of the past. Going perhaps as she would go, with defiant joy and thudding throat and pain. The kind of pain that haunted through that song, no matter how pertly they played it. "Be it ever so humble—" Oh, pot-bellied Dad and drastic Mom, imperious Ken and remote mocking Jean—and Ramey of the hay-colored cowlick and crooked, fight-broken teeth. This my home and these my people and oh you God who are but a listening silence, let me go!

She slammed shut the window. It was hot in here and still. A cell. But nine days from tonight—oh, please! surely—wasn't it settled?—of course, and you didn't dare doubt—she would be gone.

CHAPTER THREE

THE SUNDAY MORNING clatter began.

The first time Lydia's voice came hallooing up the stairs, it sounded melodically cheerful. "Come on, kids, it's a glorious morning! And——" coaxingly, "I'm frying pancakes."

There was the thud of bare feet and a shout from Ramey. "Pancakes! Oh, boy!"

"Pipe down, will ya?" Kenneth growled.

The summons from below became a discourse. "Now listen, kids, I want you to get up. I want my whole family in church today. Polly, come on, please. You too, Jean. Dad's folks are coming over for dinner and we've got lots to do."

Polly sat up, yawned, and looked crossly at Jean, who had crawled in with her after the dance. Jean's bright head was plunged deep into the pillow and she was breathing heavily. She was either very much asleep or pretending to be.

"Mother's calling, Jean. C'mon." The lovely bare shoulders didn't stir. "Okay, Mom, down in a minute," she called. Somebody had to be first, and there was no outstaying Jean.

Lydia, Sam and Ramey were just lifting their eyes from the oilcloth as Polly entered the kitchen. At Lydia's

"Amen" Ramey stabbed deep into the plate of thick brown pancakes.

"Here now, don't be a pig," Sam fussed. "Gimme half of those."

Ramey surrendered three of his five.

"Here Mother, you dive in while they're hot," Sam urged, fearful as always that she might be neglected. "Lemme pick out a couple for you. These are dandies."

Polly took the two slightly burned ones on the bottom.

"Say, Liddy, these are swell!" Sam smacked, rolling a chunk on his fork and smearing it in thick store syrup. "You oughta teach these restaurant cooks how to fry cakes. They make theirs so damn' thin you might as well be eatin' paper."

Lydia wasn't listening. "Is Jean up?"

"She'll be down."

Sam sputtered, "Well she better be damn' quick about it. Mother wants all you kids in Sunday School this morning."

"How about you, Pop?" Ramey asked gleefully. "You be there?"

"Don't you worry about me, fella. You just get yourself there."

Kenneth sauntered in, weary but sleek in his gray suit and soleless but spotless white shoes.

"Any chance of me getting a place to eat?"

"Here Kenneth, sit down in my place. I'll fry you some hot—" Lydia half rose, but Sam jerked her back.

"No, by God, you ain't gonna get up and wait on the kids. No damn' sense in them staying up half the night and then expectin' you to wait on 'em when they finally take a notion to get up!"

Polly bobbed up and whisked off her sticky plate. "Here, Ken, I'm through anyway."

He slid into her chair, sat with his elbows on the table, staring moodily out the window. Lydia could reach into the cupboard without rising. She brought forth a clean plate and began to pour coffee over bread. Polly silently fried cakes. There was never much talk at breakfast after Kenneth appeared. The most innocent remark might precipitate a quarrel.

As Kenneth doused cream over his third slice of coffee-soaked bread Lydia remonstrated, "Hadn't you better save some for Jean?"

"Aw, let her get down here with the rest of us."

Sam plunged through the opening. "I didn't notice you hurryin' any."

Kenneth crammed his mouth full, speaking with a distorted grin. "Well Sam, I heard Mom starting on you a good two hours before she got you out. And you couldn't even make it to the table dressed!"

Over an unlighted cigar Sam gazed down upon his shirtlessness. "That ain't my fault. Mama has to sew on a button."

"I must do that!" Lydia gave an exasperated little sigh. Duty, put off until the last minute, had finally caught up with her. "And there's some material for my Sunday School lesson I haven't found. Ramey, go get my quarterly. It's under the library table—somewhere."

Yawning, Ken shoved aside his plate. "Got any more cigars, Dad?"

Sam sighed. "Go look in my vest pocket." Then, to anyone who happened to listen, "Oughta be earning his own cigars. Man twenty-five years old."

"Twenty," Polly corrected, against her better judgment.

"I don't give a damn, he's plenty old enough to have a job."

Hands in his pockets, pulling luxuriantly at the cigar, Kenneth demanded, "Who was that guy I saw you getting into the big car with last night?"

"Dan Scott."

"From Crescent?"

"I think so."

"Yeah, I've seen him at dances. Folks own about a section of land out of Crescent. He sells cars for the Crescent Motor Company. Goes with some swell girls all right, but he drinks."

Lydia looked up quickly from her quarterly. "Who drinks?"

This would finish it. Thus far this morning there had been nothing to quarrel about. "Dan Scott, so Ken says," Polly said angrily. "But don't worry, he probably won't be back—thanks to Dad."

Sam slapped himself on the chest, chuckling proudly. "Hell, I was just havin' a little fun. But I sure scared the socks off him. He lit for home like a whipped puppy. Yes, and I took on that bird that brought Jean in around five o'clock too!"

Polly's devil snorted with wild weeping laughter. Something in Dad's bluster, his exaggerations, struck bluntly to the core of herself. Infuriating though he was, how much she was like him!

She whirled to go upstairs and collided with Jean.

"Good morning to me!" Jean carolled, pulling her pink cotton kimono tight about her hips. "What's all the row?"

"Well, well, well. If it isn't Sleeping Beauty herself!" Kenneth bowed low. "Oh, brrrother! Oh, Rrraymond! Come. Escort the princess to the breakfast table."

Jean made an ugly noise with her mouth. "Horses to you!" she jeered as she flounced past.

An air of tension bound the Andrews family as they hastened Sunday Schoolward in the Chevrolet coach which Sam drove as salesman for the Raven Tractor Company. ("That ravin' tractor man" his offspring called him.) This morning the matter of delegates to the Christian Endeavor convention would be fought to the finish.

"Now Sam," Lydia begged as they neared the recently erected, unpaid-for brick temple of the Lord. "Promise me you won't start anything."

"Hell, I won't start nothin'," he said, ignoring a stop button and thumbing his nose at the cop lounging on the corner. "But they hadn't better try to keep Jean from going or I'll light in and tell 'em a thing or two."

"So that's what you were practicing for when you lit into me last night!" Jean yawned good-naturedly from the back seat. Already her grievance was forgiven and half forgotten.

"Last night nothin'—this morning!" Ramey hooted, trampling his sisters' white shoes in his haste to get out and play catch before being dragged inside.

They emerged, those smartly dressed leading lights of the congregation, the Andrewses. Once a week they preened anew their plumage of prestige. Here they counted. In the language of envious opponents, they "ran things." They never looked or felt so prosperous as when alighting from the Chevy and parading up the sunlit walk toward church.

Lydia was regal in ten cent pearl earrings, a white leg-horn hat that had cost nine dollars, a flowered chiffon dress, and run-over shoes that served for both Saturday scrubbing and Sunday scurrying. For a few hours each Sabbath she shed the frettings that marked the erratic running of her household and became that beautiful, smart Mrs. Andrews who played the piano, led the choir, and taught the Young Women's Class how to be better wives and mothers. To the dowdy she was style, to the uneducated, culture, and to all the group which crowded her chill little basement classroom and embarrassingly refused to budge when they reached the age limit, she was wit, wisdom, and sainted motherhood. Her daughters were secretly amused and rather proud of the way she put it over.

About Sam, however, hovered no synthetic sanctity as he trotted up the steps, dapper in his thirty-five dollar Penney store best suit, traces of powder on his ear lobes, his straw sailor cocked jauntily over one eye. Rather, he was that clowning devil who, though baptized into the brotherhood after years of stubborn resistance, refused to be altered one whit. It was still his privilege to shock and delight the ladies by his antics at sociables, worry his wife and the elders by refusing to take communion or pray in public, and say what he damn' pleased even to the preacher himself. He was that super salesman who could afford to kick in with more than his share, to make up for the poor cusses who were outta work or piddling along on farms or in filling stations. He was Sam Andrews, a helluva good fella.

To Jean and Polly church was but a phase of home, filled with quarrelings and rejoicings, duties agreeable and irksome, people for whom they felt the fondness of habit. And there they too underwent a transformation. They became those dashing Andrews girls, not to be approved of certainly—Jean because of her dancing, Polly because she often uttered ideas that seemed downright heretical—but still deferred to and cordially liked.

Laughing and calling greetings, the Andrewses hastened

through the crowd that swarmed the steps. They were here now (late, as usual) let the services begin.

Jean wheeled gracefully to the platform and announced the first song. Lydia struck a chord, the assembly arose and vocally attacked. "The fight is on, oh Christian *soljers!*"

Polly titillated to the song. It might have been the theme song for years. From the days when Church had been a white frame shack on the corner and Grandpa Saunders had sneaked them sips of grape juice when communion was passed, her most vivid memories of church were its squabbles: The blood warming, exciting elections, with people getting mad and quitting; the splitting up into factions and going to war; the chips on the shoulders, the whisperings, the feuds over preachers and funds. She had long wondered—and shocked and grieved her mother by asking—where Christ hid out during all this.

Slyly watching, Polly found little in her mother's religion that she wanted. It gave Lydia no serenity with which to meet the week's woes; only a few friendships and the stimulus of bake sales, church suppers, ladies' aid. Worship for the Almighty was not its prime factor; it was merely an ancient corroded excuse for organizing. Nor was it a smooth-running, well-managed organization either, but a constant hubbub of a business forever striving to make or get money. All this under the banner of Right. All on the March to Zion.

Today Jean stood decoratively upon the platform, high-heeled, bare-legged, her tiny waist accented by a broad belt, a petite hat perched on the back of her head so that a basket edge of curls framed the slender flower of her face. At first she tried moving her hands in time to the music, but Lottie Kessler's indifference to mere rhythm made that rather ridiculous, so now she concentrated on following Lottie with the rest, focusing on that thin emphatic figure an expression of rapt admiration.

Lottie was a tall gaunt girl well into her twenties, whose firm conviction it was that only the pure in heart should see God, or be permitted to serve him. Since she had joined the church too late to claim her rightful post as song leader, she went ahead and led anyway. From the back row. Her extraordinary soprano voice elbowed the

crowd aside and soared in triumph above its timid war-
blings, forcing them to cling desperately to the high notes
which she held with such vehement ease, dragging them
panting behind her on those passages she decided to sing
fast, or holding them firmly in their tracks, word by word,
note by note, until she deigned to release them.

"And now I'm going to ask Lottie to sing the last
verse by herself," Jean interrupted the battle song to coo.
"The rest of us will just help along as best we can on the
chorus." And though there was a quirk of amusement on
her face as she sat down, her fists were hard white knots
in her lap.

Lottie was Jean's rival for the coveted trip to Des
Moines. Unsullied if rather mature maidenhood versus a
chit of a girl who ran to dances and had dates every night.
Lottie drew a deep breath and gave the words her all:
"And face to face in *stern array* . . . the *right* and *wrong*
engage today!"

Polly fidgeted. Sam leaned over to whisper, "Jean was
a darn' fool to do that." True. Jean had handed Lottie her
campaign song.

Now they chimed in. "If God be for us, his banner o'er
us, we'll sing the victor's song today!" But Jean, they
knew, was licked. Poor Jean, she did so want to go. She
—they felt uneasily—needed to go.

The congregation leaned forward. Superintendent Tom-
linson was clearing his throat, pulling at his wilted collar.
He was a teacher in a neighboring consolidated school,
gray, bespectacled, always ill at ease. There was enough
money in the treasury to send one delegate to Endeavor
conference, he announced, and—since Jean Andrews had
gone last year—it seemed to him—that is, some people
thought—well, that someone else should go this time.

Despite Lydia's frowning headshake, Sam spoke up
from the rear. "Sure but that way you'll never get any
trained workers like if they go regular and graduate.
Where'd our schools be if kids had to take turns going?
We'd never have any teachers, even good for nothin'
ones like you, Tommy!" he joked pleasantly, slapping his
foot and looking around for approval.

Mrs. Kessler, a tiny squeak-voiced woman, bobbed up
at that and fought valiantly for her Lottie. "Well if that

conference in Dez Moinz is for developin' Christian character how much good's it goin' to do if we spend our money sendin' young folks that just go for the good time they git out of it? Now reports come to me, and I ain't the only one, that some of the delegates, and I ain't mentionin' any names, just tore around all the time they was there, havin' dates and goin' to the amusement park, and they couldn't of learned much Christianity doin' things like that!"

Sam's head jutted forward like that of a fighting cock; the cracks in his ruddy neck fairly sprouted feathers. He was hopping on the pew. "Mrs. Kessler, just *who are you referring to?*"

His adversary blanched, but she set her lips firmly. "I ain't mentionin' any names."

Sam bounced to his feet and strutted down the aisle. His face was ruddy with the joy of battle. He winked at Lydia who sat knotting her handkerchief in silent agony.

"Now listen here," he addressed the nervously delighted audience. "I don't wanta start any trouble, but nobody's gonna get by with insinuating that Jean wasn't a credit to our church last summer. Let the treasury send Lottie if Mrs. Kessler's so crazy for her to go, but no old maid's gonna keep Jean home—because I'll send her out of my own pocket, that's what! And if any of the rest of you appreciate what Jean's done here and want her to represent us, why shell out!"

"I'll help." Simon Griffith's mellow voice came from the back pew. "I haven't much but you'll hunt a long while before you'll find a girl that's as kind and thoughtful to everybody as that Polly Andrews."

"It's Jean they're talking about Simon!" somebody whispered loudly.

"As them Andrews girls. Both of them!"

He wasn't the only one. By the time the classes were stampeding to their places, Sam had collected enough to send Jean without having to dip into his own funds. Which had been his intention from the beginning.

In the hubbub between Sunday School and church both girls darted outside and made a dash for the car.

"I'm going to drive!"

"No, I am!"

Sam, using the recess for a few puffs at his cigar, settled that. "Neither of you are gonna drive. You're going right back in there to church."

"We're just going after Ken," Jean pleaded.

"No, you're not. If he had to hang around downtown during Sunday School by hell he can walk to church!"

They turned back, reluctant to give up this interlude which would make them late and necessitate sitting in the back where they could daydream or read Sunday School papers without Lydia's frowning at them.

Sam sat up front so that Lydia could join him easily when she was through draping the communion table and playing for the choir. Ramey squirmed beside him. Spotting his sisters, he began to wiggle his ears and make faces.

The electric moment for them all arrived when Ken slipped in and took a seat far to the side where a stained glass window set off his profile to striking advantage. Lydia turned around to smile her relieved welcome. She hadn't been sure he would come.

Most of Kenneth's friends attended the Presbyterian church, if at all. No frantic revivals rang under its steepled towers; no flocks of riffraff barged through its Gothic doors. There they would have been rapidly sniffed and eyebrowed out. Here, however, they were given pound parties, offices, and funerals. So often was Lydia called upon to play and take charge of flowers at these last services, and so seldom was there a car to transport her to the post of duty, that Ken called her Trot-Trot, the Flower Girl. She accepted the title with a giggle and the defense, "Now kids, we shouldn't ridicule the work. This sort of thing is what the church should be for."

The preacher today was a Drake Bible student "on fire for God" in the time-honored terminology of the cloth. He was one of a succession of sacrificial lambs offered up by the State Board; for this problem child among churches kept no regular leader long.

Polly pitied these doomed-from-the-start clericals and was impatient with them, irked by the abundance of false analogies, fallacious reasoning, and general hokum that peppered their sermons and pleas for money. She longed to heckle, to deliver stinging rebuttals. They won their debates because their few opponents might be labeled Sinners. The gospel team could get by with murder and it was okay with the audience who sat vague-eyed in the stupor of faith.

She peeped about the big, sadly empty auditorium. There they sat, all thirty-two of them, beaming in placid agreement, or clog-brained or asleep. Sam's chins were folded upon his bosom, he was all but snoring. Mother, fearful of that, was fidgeting. Jean was frankly reading her *Girlhood Days*. Ken yawned and glanced at his wrist.

And, confident that she could improve upon everything yet builded, Polly began to fashion her own church. It would be a simple but beautiful gathering place resembling no temple yet designed. There only those who cared to could come to meditate, to hear a few psalms read and the stories of Jesus, and there would be a background of good music and one picture, a very young Christ upon the wall. It would be on the shores of a lake; they could look to the lake and be sustained. There would be no membership campaigns, no ballyhoo or salesmanship of any kind. No announcements of sociables, suppers or bazaars. (He had been hammering worldly things; ye gods! what was heavenly about a rummage sale?) No passing of collection plates and no pledges. Perhaps by the door a wooden box carved in the shape of a cupped hand. The hand of a poor woman who has washed and scrubbed and tended many children, and at the base, the words, "For those whom you wish to help." Let that be all. Wouldn't people *want* to give if they knew the money would be used for starving babies? She thought so. But who would pay the light bill? She would! She would be a philanthropist who erected and accomplished this new place in which to find faith.

And that was another reason she had to get out and amount to something.

CHAPTER FOUR

PRAISE GOD FROM *Whom All Blessings Flow* finally released them. The Andrews family congratulated the new minister on his inspiring sermon and cut short their usual visiting to hurry home.

"You fool, don't drive so fast!" Sam barked as Ken rounded a corner, in the same breath declaring, "It's a damn' shame, don't you know it is, that guy wastin' his brains on numskulls like those back there. He's a smart cuss, brilliant as hell. But we're about the only ones—us and maybe Simon Griffith, that even appreciate what he's talking about."

They all agreed.

At home the turmoil began. Kenneth insisted on pounding the piano, making it impossible for Polly to dust. Sam strewed ashes and the Sunday paper on the floor. Ramey dragged everything out of the bookcase, looking for his popgun. Jean flopped to the davenport to look at the funnies. Flustered and scolding, Lydia came in from the kitchen.

"Why in hell do we have to have a hullabaloo just because Mother and Chick and Herb are coming?" Sam fretted. "Mother raised eleven kids. She knows how it is."

"She notices her daughter-in-laws' houses just the same.

31

I don't want them to catch me in a mess!" Gone was Lydia's recent poise; now she was filled with dread.

They came long before dinner was ready, Aunt Chick apologizing for Uncle Mac's absence, as usual. And Grandma Andrews, leaning on her cane, creeping up the steps, agreeing in the protracted croak that was like the growling of her stomach, "Ooooh, yes! Yes, sir, that boy needs to get outdoors when he can, I say, cooped up in that old bank all week—if he enjoys his golf let him run along, I say."

Chick had been the baby of the family. She had taught school and saved up considerable money until sentiment against prosperous married teachers forced her to retire. Now a plump stylish forty, she dabbled in real estate and took care of Grandma. Polly and Jean admired and resented her. She had watched them grow from babyhood without giving them so much as a bracelet or a cast-off dress.

Uncle Herb, the enormous bachelor from Cedar Rapids, lumbered up the rear. He squeezed through the door. His thick lips curled about a cigar, he spoke out of the corner of his mouth, his ripe sonorous voice filling the room with the geniality of the politician.

"Well, well, if it isn't my two beautiful sweethearts, Jean and Polly!" He hugged them, one against either side of his protruding belly, down which cigar ashes were drooling. He plunged a fat paw into the pocket of his shabby pin-striped trousers and greeted Ramey with a handshake which left that lad wide-eyed.

"Whimminy-jizz, Unc'! Gee, thanks! Lookit Mom, a dollar!"

He was the eldest and the favored son. Grandma doted on him. Bragged on him almost more than he bragged on himself. In her eyes he was a great man, associated intimately with "big deals" which smacked of gold mines, oil wells, vast enterprises of real estate and invention.

Lydia took his dusty derby and forced a bright, "Happy birthday, Herbert."

"Now don't let him talk you *in*to anything," she warned Sam, who had followed her into the bedroom and was scrambling through the dump of papers in his dresser drawer. "Makes me tired, the way he always tries to run you. Just a big bag of hot air, that's all he is. And for heaven's sake don't *tell* him anything!"

She sighed in exasperation, for already Sam's face was aquirk with but one temptation—to talk. Talk with bombast and effect to equal that of a dominating older brother.

"Here, Sammy, here now, come, sit down!" the pompous voice was summoning. "I've got something tremendous that I'm going to let you in on." Big lips kissed the words loudly. "Yessiree, it's tre-*men*dous!" He lowered himself to the davenport, and squatted there like a great bullfrog. Plump little brother frog joined him, and the two sat chug-aruming and croaking loudly.

The others paid Grandmother the compliments she loved. Her blue eyes sparkled like the comb of brilliants in her frosty hair. She was eighty years old and stooped with fat. She had a firm little nose and a chin which fell to her bosom in folds of rose petal skin. About her gray satin shoulders was a shawl of lavender wool.

"Ooooh, you dear kiddies, I've had such a lot of dear kiddies, Lydia, but they go away, they go off and don't come home but once a year and some of them not then." She shuffled into the kitchen where they had hoped she wouldn't come, dabbing a fluff of lace at her eyes and groaning that guttural of misery, joy and bitterness of which she was so oddly composed.

Lydia gestured to Jean to get the potatoes peeled. "Yes, but they've got to go, we can't keep them always!" She was shouting, as she always did in times of stress. Then proudly, somewhat defiantly, "Polly's leaving for law school next week!"

Grandmother turned her sharp sprite eyes toward Polly who was swiftly shredding lettuce at the sink. "Ooooh, what's the use? What's the use of it anyway?" she chanted. "Just a waste of time, I say—books, reading. Lydia, Polly, you two, you're just alike." The little eyes, peering out through layers of rosy fat, were atwinkle. She bragged to the doctor, the judge, all her illustrious callers, how Sam's wife and daughter had read every book in the public library, but she enjoyed baiting them.

"Now me, I didn't go only to the sixth grade, all we had in them days, but me, why I know as much as anybody in town!" She touched the white aureole of her hair vainly. "I didn't have to go away to learn, I married Granddaddy and had babies, lotsa babies!" Tears began to trickle down the meandering channels of her face. "But I tell you, Liddy, when they go to college they don't have babies! Look at Chick. All she thinks about is business and that damnable bridge! Oooh, what's the use? What's the use, anyway?"

"There's lots of use." Lydia's tone was respectful but vehement. "It's—it's broadening to read and study."

Half-sobbing, the old lady gazed down the satin-covered mountain of her body. "Broadening, eh? I've only read one book in my life, Uncle Tom's Cabin, it was, and I could of written a better one myself, and I ain't exactly narrow."

You are! Lydia raged, though her mouth curved politely. You are narrow and bigoted and fat and old and foolish. And then the spurt of anger died as she saw that her husband's mother was weeping in earnest, when with horrible clarity she realized that some day she too would be fat and old and foolish, weeping for books unwritten and unread.

Dinner was finally ready. Lydia called, "Come on now, bring chairs to the table." There was confusion getting seated. Kenneth spoke in a sharp undertone to Ramey, who went sullenly upstairs to wash his hands. Lydia asked the blessing, a quavering self-consciousness in her voice at praying before her godless in-laws. They stirred, lifted their eyes and fell to. The Andrewses were hearty eaters. Uncle Herbert said again and again, "My but this is delicious, Lydia. I just must have more chicken." Coyly, "Dare I?" He smacked his lips and spilled gravy on his chest. His toupée, yellowish for years, was greening at the edges.

It was while the girls were serving Lydia's inevitable jello and devil's food cake that they saw Uncle John in the doorway. A two days' growth of whiskers silvered his skeletonic face. His blue overalls and shirt were clean but ragged. "Oh! Why—why—why I didn't know you had company, I didn't mean to intrude. I—I—I—" He whipped off his cap, clutched it in trembling claws. He had the deep-gouged eyes, the rapier nose, the outthrust chin of Lydia and Kenneth.

Lydia sprang up, flushed, garrulous with embarrassed welcome. This was her brother whose girls had "gone wrong," who had drunk his life away. "Come on John, sit down, you know Sam's people, sit down! Girls!" her voice shrilled. "Bring another plate."

"No, no, I'll eat in the kitchen. Yes, I know Sam's folks, how are you?" He bowed, swept through the dining room, the whiskey aura in which he perpetually moved lingering after. Sam snorted and went on eating. Lydia wiped her moist upper lip.

Jean heaped his plate while Polly darted to get him a magazine. He distressed them too, coming always at unexpected and inopportune times, but he seemed closer, more their own blood than Dad's corpulent blustering clan. He could sing until the piano danced and people clear to the lake paused to listen. He read gluttonously, anything, everything, wolfing down print as he engorged food.

When he had finished, he wiped his mouth on the back of his hand. "That was a good story, that first one. I hear y-y-you are going away, Polly, to be a lawyer, that's good." And he was gone, sneaking swiftly out the back door and up the alley, putting on his cap as he went.

It was past three o'clock when everyone else had finished, the elders flatulent and groaning, the youngsters jittery with impatience.

"Has he gone?" Lydia whispered anxiously, coming into the kitchen where the girls were clearing up. "Oh, why does he act that way? The idea, eating out here, leaving by the back way like a convict!" She cleared her throat fiercely and blew her nose. Her eyes were hot. "It only makes it harder for me, as if my own brother wasn't good enough to associate with Dad's high and mighty outfit!"

Sam trotted in, curious, eager for conflict. "Beats hell he had to come today," he said, disappointed at failing to find the object of his scorn. "Girls, get at your dishes. Don't think you're going to leave 'em for Mama."

"What's it look like we're doing?" Jean snapped.

They sailed in, recklessly stacking glasses, carrying wobbly piles of dishes to the sink. Vee Jordan came in via the back door, grabbed a towel and helped them to a clattering finish. As they passed through the Plain Room they had to stop and speak to Aunt Gert and Uncle Glen, who had just come. The air was blue with smoke. The inevitable political argument raged.

"Hoover, hell! He ain't to blame. It's these chain stores—"

"Why good God! Do you mean to sit there and tell me—"

Lydia was seated uncomfortably on the piano bench. Her eyes enviously followed the girls' flight upstairs. She too would escape if she could.

As they wheeled the turn in the landing they could hear Sam's voice bragging above the rest, "Yep, Jean's a looker all right and don't think the college boys don't know it. Went to another frat dance last night and I suppose from now on—"

The bathroom door clapped shut behind them. Jean slyly flipped open the floor register so that Sam's voice echoed on into the untidy, rust and paint stained room. "Guess we didn't do so bad on our girls. Take Polly f'rinstance—"

"Sam's sure going strong today," Vee grinned. She was perched on the bathtub, black shingled head thrown back, every brown elfin feature alive with amused listening. "His lies should be good!"

"Law school next week, what d'you think of that now? In a way it's too bad though, she goes with such a swell fella. Name's Dan Scott. His folks are the richest farmers in Crescent County, own three or four sections of land."

Vee raised an eyebrow in comic incredulity. "Boy, he *is* dreaming 'em up! Where'd he get the inspiration for that one?"

Polly turned away, began to vigorously, blindly brush her teeth.

"Oh, he brought Poll home last night," Jean said, kicking shut the vent with a pointed toe. "And he's coming back today, ain't he, Polly-woggy?"

Her air of companionable interest, mildly congratulatory, a little proud, was no camouflage for the look of pleased expectancy in her eyes. Confidently she moved to the mirror, caught up the snaggle-toothed, not too clean comb and attacked her cloud of snapping curls. "What time d'you say he's coming, sissy?"

It was then that the knob rattled, that Lydia called, "Girls! Let me in." They unlocked the door, she crowded the little room, breathing hard from the stairs and her excitement. "There's someone down there for you, Polly," she said. "I think it's that man Ken was telling us about this morning—that Dan Scott!"

CHAPTER FIVE

"I DIDN'T DARE ask him in for fear Dad might say something," Lydia panted on. "Now Polly, you know I don't want you girls going with boys who drink."

"Why Mommy Andrews," Vee hooted, providing the swift essential antidote. "Dan doesn't touch the foul stuff. He's a shirt-tail relation of a shirt-tail relation of ours in Crescent and they just rave about what a good guy he is."

"Sure," said Jean, one hand on the knob, "Ken's got an idea everybody from Crescent bootlegs or drinks. C'mon, Vee."

Polly said desperately, "Jean, wait. May I wear your white sweater and skirt? I've spilled toothpaste on my dress!"

"Now Polly, you know I just got that outfit cleaned. I'm saving it for conference."

"Sure I know, I paid for it!"

"Now girls, if you're going to quarrel neither of you leave this house! I tell you I can't stand it, I'm under enough of a strain as it is. Jean, let Polly wear your things." Lydia slammed down the stool lid, sat on it, and began to peel off her hose. "Here, Polly, you've got a runner, trade with me."

They exchanged swiftly while Jean swept across the hall. The stockings were damp from Lydia's feet. They had to be folded under at the toes and they ballooned a little at the ankles, but Polly was grateful. Dear, inconsistent Mom.

"Gee, Mother, you always come through," she said impulsively. " 'Member the old coins?"

Lydia smiled and stood up, stamping her shoe on. For years her hobby had been to save odd coins, convinced that some day they would be worth a fortune. But along had come Sullivan's Tent Show, and they were broke, and Lydia, unable to bear the wistful longing in her children's eyes as the music wagon went by, had rushed home and divided the box among them.

"Yes, I guess there's nothing I wouldn't do to make you kids happy. Maybe I'm too lenient, I know Dad thinks so. He may not like this, but if Vee says the boy doesn't drink—" She was tapping her gold tooth doubtfully. "I don't know, really, I just don't know."

Jean returned, a black dress over her arm. "Here, wear this."

It was last year's. Dresses were shorter now and Jean was taller. It wouldn't do, Polly saw with angry anguish, and said so.

"Yeah, Jean, let her have the white outfit," Vee agreed. "That makes her look like Old Mother Hubbard or somebody."

"Now everybody keep their undies on." Jean dropped to the floor. "All I've got to do is hem it up." Her needle dived, swam in long swift strokes while she ordered, "Stand up straight, runt, we don't want scallops."

Lydia sighed her benediction. "I'll go back down. Maybe you had better invite him in, Polly, after keeping him on the porch all this time. I'll warn Dad to be good."

Jean snipped the thread with her teeth, then whirled her sister around, surveying her critically. "Slip shows in back, better hitch it up. There's a safety pin on my dresser. Use my lipstick and put on those red earrings, but *don't* climb on my bed to look in the mirror, there's a clean spread on."

"I won't," said Polly humbly. "Thanks, Jean."

She watched Vee and Jean flit to the stairs, heard their heels tapering lightly down. A sheer little flag of Jean's laughter floated up from the porch.

Polly stood very still for a moment. Last night there had been Dad. Today there would be—Jean. The final

ignominy. And to watch the inevitable mesmerization before Jean's curiously elusive charm, to hear Dan Scott say
indifferently, "Well Poll, I'll call you up sometime" and
know that when next his voice came over the wire it would
be brotherly, casual, asking, "Say Poll, is Jean there?" was
something that, for a moment, she thought she could not
face. For she had been swayed by that man. The thought
that he was downstairs now shattered her feeble defenses
of independence and ambition, chilled her blood, made her
throat go dry. She covered her cheeks with her hands.
My God, I'm scared!—she thought. Scared of—of I don't
know—what!

They were framed by the black boundaries of the screen
door as she ran down—Dan, perched on the porch rail,
Jean's golden fairness, Vee's Indian darkness flanking him
on either side. Dan's head jerked up. He tossed away his
cigarette and was on his feet.

"Hello, Polly."

"Hi. Sorry I kept you waiting."

"Oh that's okay, I've been entertained."

"Would you like to come in and meet the folks?"

"I was hoping somebody would ask me. That paternal
ancestor of yours sounded highly interesting last night!"

Polly studied him, alert for some sign of ridicule.

Lydia hastened to them through the smoke. She was a
trifle effusive, but Polly was proud of her. She looked a
club woman with her graying hair so nicely waved, the
pearl earrings, the rather good black dress. "Sam! Sam,
come here a minute!" Lydia called in her loud, her breathless voice of strain.

Sam looked up from a grotesque three-legged chair, the
like of which had not been seen by man or beast. Its back
was an ordinary crutch, split at the base to sprawl into two
narrow legs. Its center, upon which Sam's bulk was precariously perched, was a leather triangle, supported by a
metal prop. Sam's hands were folded and he was beaming
fatuously upon his audience, like an amateur magician
who, to his own surprise, has just produced the rabbit
from the hat. He lifted a fat paw and wagged it at Dan
calling, "Hi Scott, you young devil you! C'min here and
have a look at this contraption!"

Polly had a shriveling sensation. Oh no, Dad, no—please no inventions this time!

Lydia said, "Oh, that's right. You—you've met Polly's father."

Dan winked at Polly. "Last night, I believe." He crossed into the Swell Room and shook hands. "How are you, Mr. Andrews?"

Sam bounced up from his unique throne. "Fat and sassy in spite of waiting up half the night for you to bring my daughter home, damn ya!" His shirt collar was limp and undone; gray hairs curled up about his turkey-red gullet. He slapped himself on the chest, chuckling, "And don't call me Mister, call me Sam—all the girls' fellas do."

"Now Dad, introduce Mr. Scott around," Lydia prompted, beaming anxiously, impatience on her voice. She glanced apologetically at Polly.

It doesn't matter, Mom, don't look so stricken, it doesn't matter. I'm going away. Rave on, Dad, you sad, you silly!

"Meet Polly's grandmother, Scott, prettiest woman in the state of Ioway!"

Grandmother wiped her eyes. "Oooh, ain't he nice lookin' though? Yes indeed, I say, I like your looks young man." The old pink goblin face jutted forth. "Can't you keep her from leaving though? Can't you now?"

"I'd certainly like to."

Polly stood rigid by the bookcase, smile riveted, stubby fingers gripping an unseen pencil, busily writing shorthand on the centerpiece.

"Yep, prettiest woman in the state even if she did raise eleven kids. All her girls won beauty contests—here's one of 'em right here even if she is fat now—my sister, Mrs. Maclean—"

"Mrs. Maclean?"

"How d'you do, Mr. Scott."

Polly was a little ashamed, a little angry, at feeling grateful to Aunt Chick for her poise, the flash of diamonds on her fingers, her lace and georgette and misleadingly cordial opulence. Oh well—she thought, with a compensatory snigger—this is the only way I'll ever share it!

"The girls were lookers but the boys were smart," Sam prated on—"and bald headed!" He ducked his chins against his Adam's apple and waggled both thumbs ludicrously at a ruddy, sweat-pimpled dome. "Even Herby's bald under that toopy. He never got married and had a bunch of kids to feed, so he could afford a toopy. That's Herby, that little fella over in the corner."

Uncle Herbert sputtered at Sam's revelation. "How'd y'do, how'd y'do, you don't mind my not getting up, do you son? It's so hot—my, my, it's positively torrid!" His great sonorous chung-a-rum—his long slender hands with the seal rings and synthetic diamonds, dainty upon slim frog knees between which the mountainous belly protruded, white-vested, ajangle wtih lodge emblems—"What business are you in, my boy? Automobiles, eh? Fine, fine, but if you're ever interested in a really good proposition get in touch with me. My firm is always interested in young blood and what we have to offer is the coming thing. Here's my card, you can contact me either at my office or my club."

Dan thanked him, gravely studied the card which read: *Herbert Arthurby Andrews—Rat Poison,* and pocketed it with only the suggestion of a smile.

"Never mind Herby's rat poison," Sam said—and now Polly knew what was on the card and wished to die— "here's something bigger'n you ever dreamed of, Scott." Sam rattled his odd chair fondly. "Ever see anything to beat that? Now watch careful and I'll show you how she works." He turned his back. After a few seconds of clatter he arose, looking very pleased, and faced them leaning upon a now fairly normal crutch.

"Now looky here," he demonstrated, crooking one leg and vaulting across the floor. "I'm a cripple. I've walked downtown and I'm tired. I look around and I don't see no place to sit down."

Ah, the weary cripple, sad-mouthed, grotesque! There was a clawing in Polly's throat. With viciously gripped ghost pencil she wrote a shorthand prayer on the centerpiece.

The chairs were, indeed, all occupied. Aunt Chick was telling the women how to make sensational new lamp shades—"Just a coat of shellac and then you sprinkle the beads on"—Herbert had flourished forth some papers and appeared to be deep in a scowling study. Jean and Vee swung in and began shuffling through the sheet music on the piano—*Ramona, Chloe, Sonny Boy.* "Dream train,

please carry me back, dream train, stay on the right track."
Vee was learning the words in a torchy undertone, leaning over Jean's shoulder as she knelt on the piano bench.

Dan Scott, Sam's only attentive spectator, stood with his
brown flannel-coated arms folded.

"Nobody gives a damn about a poor cripple, so here's
what I do." Balancing on an armpit, Sam fumbled with
the paraphernalia in the center of the crutch. "Well I
can't seem to get at it right just now." He planted both feet
on the floor, leaned his chair against the wall, and after
further gyrations with the screwdriver, the little seat
flopped forward.

"There now!" he beamed. "See how steady she is. Safe
as your own bed and just as comfortable. Come sit on it,
Scott, try it."

"Oh Dad!" Polly cried out. "He doesn't want to sit on
that thing!"

"He most certainly does!" Dan stamped his cigarette into
a tray and obligingly crossed the room. He sat upon the
silly little chair, feet apart, testing it with shifting move-
ments of his hips. "Why it is strong, isn't it? This is a very
ingenious device, Sam."

Startled, quickly defensive, Polly stared at him. But he
didn't seem to be making fun of Dad!

There was but a tag end of the day left, and that a blowy
thing of swaggering waves and ruddy sunset and mudhens
riding like rowboats at anchor. The lake, the boats, and
the mudhens fled past them. Below them gritted the gravel,
occasionally shrapneling up to ping! against the body.
Behind them trailed their white feather fan of dust.

And now they swerved sharply onto the concrete, a flat-
rolled arm reaching forever across the hills. Here the car
leapt, seemed to stretch out beneath Polly, who was driving. Here the wind became cold fists pummeling her face,
pinning her lashes back against the lids. This was like
swimming, when water washed away all but the feel of pull
and power and cold. A deletion of self with its myriad
puzzles, motion; a blessed loss of identity, animal and good.

"Beat my record to Sioux City," Dan said, "and I'll buy
you a flower."

She became aware of him, an oblique slope on the seat beside her.

"Oh, but we can't go clear to Sioux City!"

"You little winged Mercury, we're nearly there."

Her foot left the accelerator. Her hands loosened their grip and the car swerved toward the ditch. Dan sprang to attention, with a swift sweep of arm brought it back in line. "I'm sorry," he said, "I didn't mean to startle you or take over!"

"I wish you would. I'm fast but not thorough. I missed the Crescent turn, didn't I?"

"Miles back. I'm glad."

She stretched her cramped fingers and leaned back against the soft leather of the seat. The hills were burrowing down snugly now into a velvet darkness. Lights yellowed in farmhouse windows, and lanterns began their lone-eyed swing to barns. It was a long way to the city, and she didn't know him really; she wondered uneasily if they shouldn't turn back.

With Dan driving she learned what speed was. They sang up a slope toward a white steel bridge that framed the landscape like a picture. Farms and little towns moaned by in blurs of light. Once Dan turned to her, asked, "Think this'll take the lids off?"

"The lids? Oh—the *lids!*" Polly hugged herself and shivered deeper into the seat. "It should!"

"Yeah. Yeah, it should. But somehow it doesn't always. At least not for my brand of bottled-up blood."

Polly looked at him questioningly. He settled behind the wheel, his eyes straight ahead but narrowed, introspective. "I hadn't thought much about it until after I left you last night. Then, for some reason, it got to bothering me that I'm not as far along as a man of my age—I'm twenty-eight—should be."

She said nothing. He was spoiling the picture of the prince—at least of a successful young business man—somehow.

"For too many years now I've done too many things. Sold haberdashery, a nice gentlemanly gentleman's job where you get no place fast. I've worked on a road gang, bummed my way to Cuba and back, been maintenance engineer for the county—that sounds nice, but it means you drive a grader and use a shovel. I've even jockeyed cattle to market, like those poor devils up there."

They were swerving past an increasing number of stock trucks, hump-back monsters with red eyes, exuding musky odors, earthy and of the farm. Their headlights gleamed on white noses thrust through palings, they heard gruntings and squealings and dolorous moos.

"But didn't you specialize in college?"

"I didn't go," he said with direct honesty. "I didn't even finish military academy. At one fell swoop my folks had a fire, a crop failure, and my oldest sister died. By the time we were in the clear again I was so much older than the other kids I didn't have the nerve to go back. I'm the only uneducated member of my outfit, but that never seemed to matter. I read a lot, do whatever there is to do, and don't mind admitting I've had one hell of a general good time. I haven't been consciously frustrated, bottled up. But now—" His eyes touched her briefly and went back to the road, "like your too wise Kvasir, I can sure feel those lids!"

But—you had to go to college, Polly was thinking. You were nothing nobody, unless you went! It was her one belief. To be persuaded otherwise now would be to doubt the whole premise of her frantic strugglings. And yet she still felt annoyingly humble before him; as if his very candor had relegated her to some lower class which looks up craftily for some toehold by which it can cling to self-respect. Though he was sorry he hadn't gone, it was evident that he attached none of her impassioned significance to going; that his was the kind of safe, established background where culture is inbred. This despite the fact that his folks were, incredibly, farmers. Polly, whose conception of farming people had been distorted by a clan of miserly, ignorant and arrogant country cousins, was confused.

She was more so as the evening progressed. Dan bought her the promised flower, a white gardenia, dewy in its cellophane envelope—the first she had ever seen, much less worn. They dined in hushed elegance at what seemed to her a fabulous hotel, with Dan ordering lavishly and paying her preposterous compliments across the snowy cloth. They attended that dazzling pleasure palace, the Orpheum theatre, and bought candy in a fairytale shop.

Finally, they danced at a rainbow-lit roof garden with an orchestra from Hollywood and lounges of such velvet magnificence that Polly felt superior forever to the Casino, that crêpe-paper decorated barn at home.

Once Dan asked, "You wouldn't like a little drink, would you? It's quite easy to get here."

"Oh, no," she said, startled. "I don't drink."

"Good girl. I wouldn't either if you were going to be around."

He impressed her village-bred inadequacy with his casual air. He was forever leaping to open doors, pull back chairs, hold wraps, and he had a gallantly flattering little bow that Polly traced to his mention of military school. Money dripped through his fingers like water. Altogether, he must have spent fifteen or twenty dollars on her, Polly calculated uneasily, but with an awed sense of importance. Why?

And who, what was he, actually, this truck driver, farmer, salesman with the speech of a poet and the manners of a prince? He baffled her, vaguely angered her by the very gallantry which made her feel so miserably gauche. She felt somehow as if she must punish him for being simply what he was—a nobody with the airs of a Louis XIV. (That bow!) Only the truly great should have the right to make her blush and stammer like this. But when she met them (and suddenly, gloriously, all tonight seemed to her a hint, a promise, a preview of the really marvelous things she would some day know) she would be beyond such stupidities. She would have been metamorphosed into a creature of commanding poise and charm; she would be great, herself.

Surely!

She leaned her head back upon the seat and passionately implored the stars that were streaking overhead, a mad far multiplication of light. She could feel Dan looking at her.

Presently he asked, "Asleep?"

She shook her head. "Just dreaming."

"About going away?"

She nodded.

The car thrummed on. Plowed earth and roadside grasses sweetened the breath of the cool night air. A creek flashed briefly into being and plunged off through a pasture where kneeling cattle slept.

"Polly, since it can't do any good it won't do any harm so I may as well tell you. I'm in love with you."

Polly sat very still, her body tensed. She was waiting for the car to slow down, for him to turn off onto a side-road. She was on guard, but not afraid; she was even amused at what now seemed the goal of this extravagant evening from its beginning.

But nothing happened. The little farms and country towns, now decently dark, asleep, continued to wing past them.

"You don't believe that, do you?" Dan asked.

"I'm not quite that dumb."

"All right, don't. I said it wouldn't do any good to tell you. But maybe you'll believe this—because after all you could take me up on it. I wish to God you weren't so smart or so ambitious, although I suppose that's partly why I love you, because you're different. I wish you weren't going away. I wish you'd stay home and marry me!"

CHAPTER SIX

THE TELEPHONE WAS ringing. A dull insistent shrill, piercing the steady drum of rain. Reluctantly Polly wrenched herself from a sweet vague dream, a kind of happy incredulity in which she had slept all night, and pawed up to the surface of consciousness. It was like treading water to stay there, listening for the heavy pad of Dad's feet, the gruff groggy bark of his "H'lo!"

The silence was a live thing prowling the house. The rain beat the roof with an urgent sound. Was everybody dead down there? The call might have been important, so early this way. Or was it early? They always overslept on Mondays, especially when it rained. She'd be late to work. Dad should be out on the road.

Now came the familiar stomp, the annoyed, " 'Lo! Yeah, this is him."

Lately the company had taken to calling at inopportune times, using some slight pretext to check on Dad's whereabouts. Sometimes his expense sheet said Cleghorn, when really he had driven home to be with Lydia. "Oh hell," he always grinned in self-defense, "what's it to them where I sleep as long as I get the orders? I'm high man all the time, ain't I?"

It must be late! He was so meek. He wasn't saying much. Only, "Yeah. Yep, I guess I see. Awright, I'll be in.

Mind if I bring my wife? Oh. Oh—so that's it. Well, awright. 'Bye."

Silence. Then stomp stomp to the stairway and a bellicose roar. "Kenneth, you get down here and be damn' quick about it! You won't get out and do a damn' thing but by God y'ain't gonna sleep all day. Polly, see if you can get Jean up. You too, Ramey!"

Polly leaped from bed. The wind had keyed its pitch to a dread moaning noise in the bedroom below. Mom was crying. Dad had been called to Omaha, she reasoned quickly; Mom was crying because she couldn't go along. That—had to be all!

For an instant, from habit, she wriggled her toes in the cool dark pool that sloping boards and an open window often drew beside her bed after a rain. Then with angry haste she dried them on an old slip which she tossed into the closet. You were not a princess with a footbath beside your bower. You were a scared girl whose dad might be losing his job and you mustn't be late and lose yours!

Jean's pink boudoir clock said a quarter of nine as, hooking a brief plaid skirt, Polly raced past. The ornate wall clock in the Swell Room pointed to a silent permanent seven (it needed winding), Ken's Ingersoll wrist watch tocking loudly on the dining table averred it was ten to eight, and the alarm clock lying on its face beside her parents' tumbled bed stood for six-thirty. The only way to ascertain time in this house was to take an average or ask Central. Polly darted to the telephone and was informed that it was eight-fifteen.

"I won't have time to eat, Mom," she said, ignoring Lydia's red eyes. "Don't put a plate on for me."

"Hell fire!" Sam sputtered from the kitchen table. "George Walcott ain't God or nothin', you can't go to work without your breakfast, you'll be sick. Pour her some coffee, Liddy."

"Yes, please, Polly," Lydia urged in a quavering voice. She set down the chipped and stained blue coffee-pot, grabbed a piece of torn sheet from her apron pocket and blew her nose. Her head was high, her eyes large, her mouth grim as she announced in a tone of stark finality: "Dad's been called to Omaha!"

"Yeah," Sam grunted, "it's come. The boys been

gettin' laid off right and left. They let Rathburn go last week and he's done damn near as good in his territory as I have in mine. I'm next, that's all, it's just been a matter of time, just a matter of time."

Polly hacked an orange in two with a dull knife. "Oh, Dad, you've been saying that all summer!" His exaggerations, his predictions of ruin, futile in staving off their demands for money but upsetting them all—where did they get him anyway?

Lydia's voice rose to a chant of despair. "But it was that snotty Benedict calling. He said to—come—turn—the car in!" Her lip was trembling. A tear trickled down her nose. "Oh, it's not *fair!* Why is it nothing lasts for us? Just when we think we're going to come out all right, live decently like other people then—then—!" She covered her face with her hands; the horrible discord of her crying filled the room.

Polly put an arm around her, helplessly patted the heaving shoulders in the faded housedress. "Don't cry, Mother," she said, though her soul was sick with alarm. "We'll come out all right. Dad's never let us down yet." He wouldn't dare. Not now!

Jean came in, yawning audibly. "Criminee no! He'll probably talk 'em into a raise and a new car, won'tcha Sambo?" She kissed the top of his bald head. " 'Member the time you thought the feed company was gonna can you and instead you talked 'em into changing their whole bookkeeping system just to make your checks come on the fifteenth?"

Lydia's sobbing changed to laughter. As she blew her nose she smiled tremulously. "It'll be all right. It's got to be! But—but if it isn't, Dad will get something else, so don't you worry, Polly, you won't have to stay home and feed us."

Polly gave a little start. How accurately Lydia had plunged the dagger of her own fear home. "All I'm worried about now is being late!" She snatched up an orange half, bit into it as she darted through the house toward the closet tucked under the stairs.

"Beats all hell," she could hear Sam grumbling. "Can't even siddown and eat breakfast."

Beats all hell—she thought, holding the orange with

her teeth and groping into the dark closet—but it beats losing a job, you little boy Dad you!

By jumping and grabbing, she was able to dislodge an old felt hat from a clutter of boxes, rags, and old magazines on the shelf. Jamming it over one ear, she knelt to feel about on the floor for some oxfords once tossed into these caverns. Her hands touched something big, sharp-cornered and tinny, and impulsively for an instant she hugged it. Then she must haul it forth to be sure Ramey hadn't peeled off the precious stickers.

It was a homely, scratched and dented green thing, ex-harbinger of a vast collection of Fuller brushes which Sam had briefly lugged from door to door. Because canvassing seemed to him a degrading pursuit for a traveling man, he hadn't sold any brushes; in fact, he had been forced to buy the lot himself when the company threatened suit. (The kids had a marvelous time with the samples, riding the longer-handled ones for horses, wearing dust mops and whisk brooms for wigs and tails.) Now the bag was glorified by three gold pennants which had been sent to Polly with her entrance papers. She felt the need to see their shining assurance this morning.

She was still crouching there when she heard the step on the porch, the rap on the screen. "Dan!" She scrambled up, frantically stuffing the orange into her pocket. "Where did you come from?"

He came in. He smelled just bathed and shaved and toothbrushed, of cigarettes and damp fabric and rain. He looked at her steadily for an instant, then kissed her lightly on the mouth.

"Where are you going?" He motioned his hat to the bulging briefcase and squat traveling bags that stood beside her case.

"Nowhere. Not right now. Oh yes I am too—to work. These are Dad's. He's going to Omaha on—on a business trip."

A wild yell from the landing spared her further explanation. The bannister shook and squealed as Ramey mounted and slid down. He was naked except for a pair of shorts in which he had obviously slept; his back was very brown and not clean. Still astride the newel post, he grabbed Dan's hand and wagged it up and down. "Hiyah, palsy-walsy!

Howsa-bouta ride to Scout camp, huh? Howsabout lettin'
ole handy Andy himself drive that wagon of yours?"

"Ramey!" Polly ordered in a voice low with shame,
anger, and pity for this changeling who didn't even own
a pair of pajamas. "March right back upstairs. The idea!"

"Yeah, imbecile," Kenneth echoed, sauntering down.
"Summer's over now, they say you gotta wear clothes
when you go to school. But don't march. Back. Your pants
are splitting." He lifted a finger in casual salute to Dan.
"Hi Scott, glad t'see you. I'll be gladder if you can spare a
cigaroot."

He plucked two from the pack Dan extended, dropping
the second into his white shirt pocket. "For my coffee and
market page," he explained. "A man can't study his in-
vestments when he's out of smokes." He swung on toward the kitchen.

Polly laughed thinly. "You have to know how to take
Ken. He's a—a born actor, and I guess they're all pretty
unpredictable." She caught up her purse. "I'll have to
leave, I'm late."

But a voice was already bellowing from the kitchen,
"Hey, you young son of a sea cook, what d'ya mean hanging around here practically before we're outta bed? C'mon
out and have some breakfast, damn ya!"

Polly felt faint. Cracked oilcloth, handleless cups, corn
flakes, burned toast, and Mom's boiled over and over
coffee . . . "Yes, Dan, won't you stay?"

"No, thanks. I ate at the hotel. I stayed over to see a
prospect this morning. At least," he grinned, "that was
my excuse."

Sam trotted in, stuffing his shirttail into his trousers.
He'd been careless about that button again. Polly averted
her eyes, hoping Dan wouldn't notice. Her hands, rammed
deep in her pockets, tore blindly at the orange peel.

She said, "Dan's eaten, Dad, and I'm terribly late—
he's going to take me. 'Bye."

"Hold on, hold on, I gotta ask this tramp why he ain't
out workin' this time of day. You birds that hang around
my girls gotta prove you can feed 'em!"

"I sold a car before eight o'clock," Dan said. "Does that
qualify?"

Sam refused to be impressed. "Nope. Gotta do better'n

that." He kicked his briefcase fondly. "I could show you orders in there that'd make your eyes pop. Money's tight, no doubt about it, but I pry it loose some way. I been high man out of the Omaha branch ever since I went with this company. They pay me good too. Two fifty a month and all expenses ain't bad, is it?"

Oh Dad, let's not lie! Not now—not so near the end. Or was it? Maybe they were calling him in today to— to raise his pay, or to put him in charge of some of the other men, as he was hinting to Dan. Now he was fumbling with that trouser button. Let it go, Dad. let it go! Was there a grim little droop to his mouth, a sad anxiety in his eyes, or were those ghosts of her own fears? It's all right—she thought in a wrench of pity for him. Lie if it helps. Maybe, oh please God, maybe it's true!

When the door slammed behind Dan and Polly, gloom clutched the family in firmer grip. Ken and Jean argued over the cream and jabbed each other with their elbows as they sat at the crowded table. Ramey was railed at for hogging the bacon. Halfway through the melancholy crunching of her cereal, Lydia slammed down her spoon.

Her glaring eyes subdued them. Ramey mumbled, "Gee, Mom, I'm sorry." Kenneth patted her hand, urging, "You'd better go back to bed, Mother, you're tired."

Lydia's face was contorted, her fists clenched. "Dad's losing his job for all we know and this *beastly* day, but you don't even think about me! You'd stand beside my casket and quarrel!"

"Jean wouldn't," Ken sneered. "She'd be off to a dance."

"Aw Ken don't," Ramey begged wretchedly. He felt his mother's moods keenly.

Jean shrugged and hopped up. "Guess I'll go help Dad get canned."

She found Sam by the bedroom window, trying vainly to thread a huge needle. "For God's sake, Jean, where's all my socks?" he complained.

"Mom threw 'em away, I guess. I heard her raving about how messed up your drawer was one day. Here, gimme that."

Sam sat down on the bed, crooking his stockinged foot in readiness for the needle. "Yeah, I should have someplace else to keep my papers. And I don't suppose the socks were worth mendin'."

"You could run the lake through the holes. Take off that one that needs fixing."

"Hell, I ain't got time for fancywork. Just sew around it and tie a knot."

"That's why you haven't got any decent socks now. If they were darned once in a while they might last."

"Now don't you criticise Mama." Sam peeled off the sweat-stiff stocking. His toenails were neatly trimmed but black; grime encrusted his ankles. "She's got an awful lot to worry about, don't y'know she has? You kids running around the way you do and me not able to get a nickel ahead and always thinkin' from one day to the next we'll be out of a job. This time it sure looks bad, damned if it don't. So don't you kids go makin' it hard for her, y'understand?"

"Well if Ken would just keep his trap shut—"

"Oh sure it's all my fault," Ken agreed sarcastically from the doorway. He was enveloped in an enormous autographed and cartooned slicker which he'd borrowed from Hap Hilton two years ago and had always been intending to return. His head was sleek and hatless. On his hands were a pair of pigskin gloves, on his feet gray eyelet shoes that were a veritable sieve for the rain. "Gimme a dime, Dad."

The request unleashed Sam's own champing devil. The idea, him a man grown asking for dimes like a two-year old! Let him get out and earn his own dimes. By God he was going to have to from now on when the checks stopped comin' in!

"Oh ring off," Ken said wearily, "we all know your act. You're gonna get fired and we might as well start packing for the poorhouse. Lord knows we hear it often enough!"

Sam yanked his shoelace so hard he broke it, said, "Damn!" hopped up and bounded after. "Wait a minute, don't go off naked!" He flipped Kenneth a quarter. "Don't you realize it's storming, boy? For Christ's sake put on your hat!"

"What hat? Course if you want to get me one—"

"I'll get you one all right! I'll get you that huntin' cap

down in the basement, it'll at least keep your ears dry! And lookit them shoes." Sam's voice dropped to a grim hush. "Of all the son of a bitchin' foolishness it was buyin' shoes like that. Not a damn' thing to 'em. Hardly enough leather to cover your foot, and how much did they charge you for 'em?"

"You mean how much did I charge them for 'em!" Ken looked up from his pipe to grin.

Sam grinned too before returning to the fracas. But Lydia, scraping egg plates, blew her nose, wiped her eyes, and began to lower the locks of rebellious silence behind which she hid after hysterical outbursts. She resented the way the family was taking this hideously familiar thing. Lightly or with fretting they faced the imminence of Sam's being jobless without turning in awe and sympathy to her, the protagonist in this ever more bitter tragedy. About her all things had revolved in younger years. Then Sam had come humbly, apologizing for his failure. Then too the children had trod on tiptoe, sorry-eyed and distressed, bringing her little presents and pillows for her back. Now all they did was fight.

"Put on my overshoes," Sam commanded, "they'll at least keep your guts from floatin'!"

Lydia winced. Ken snapped, "Wouldn't I look just too lovely?" and opened the door.

He decided, however, as the water sucked coldly through his shoes, that sometime he would dig out the galoshes and the hunting cap and that old broken black umbrella. The guys at the Checker-Board would get a big holler out of seeing him walk in in that.

Meetings of the self-styled "Do Nothing" Club were not his real excuse for going. The gang's adulation was not worth the price of soaked feet and a dripping nose. He realized that he could turn back at the corner, to guess out banging tunes at the piano, or crawl into his snug pile of ragged blankets and real old love letters and detective stories until he should drop to sleep. But he, like Polly, was a mechanical thing, wound and set in motion by desires too powerful to subdue, so that he moved forward, a lean slant figure against the big strength of the wind, suffering, unwilling that he should go, but going, nonetheless.

Nothing much awaited him downtown. Only a hope. A chance. He went first to Steve Rankin's shine parlor and spent the quarter for a can of tobacco, a candy bar, and a *Billboard*. He sat in one of Steve's chairs for a while, munching the candy and reading, while Steve ran a floor broom around, picking up cigarette stubs. The windows wept. Occasionally there was the slap-slap of Steve's rag, voices. Ken didn't look up. He was lost in a carnival world.

At length he snorted, rushed to where Steve was scraping up gum, goosed him and with the magazine still in his hands, rushed out onto the street.

George Walcott was dictating to Polly when Kenneth slammed into the outer office and took possession of the typewriter. "Hurry up and get through with my stenog!" Ken called, rolling in a letter-head and beginning a rapid two-fingered poking. "This is important."

"More important that a half-million dollar estate suit, I suppose," Walcott growled. "I'll be tickled to death if some fool show ever hires you, just to get you out of town."

Polly glanced anxiously into the fat pink face of her employer. She was never quite sure when he was amused by her family, when disgusted or downright angry. To her relief a grin crawled beneath the fuzzy black caterpillar of his moustache.

"Here," he said, tossing a pack of cigarettes onto the desk. "Take these to the pest and maybe he'll shut up and let us get some work done."

She carried them obediently into the next room, but her neck was hot with embarrassment. "Ken, I wish you wouldn't—" she began in timid undertone.

He ignored her. "Thanks, George!" he yelled. "Someday you'll be braggin' you knew me."

As Kenneth answered ads he combined imagination with truth in stating his theatrical experience, justifying himself with: "I'm as good as any of those professionals. It's their break to get me. I can act!" He daydreamed extravagantly as to what he should do if he should one day actually be hired, yet he only half believed in his dreams, and he was totally unprepared when, toward noon, Polly summoned him to the office telephone.

"It's Mother. She says there's a telegram for you."

"Hollywood, no doubt," he informed Walcott, languidly trailing the receiver to his ear. *"Hello*, gorgeous, don't you know you shouldn't bother me at my office?" Then he was leaning forward, young face tense, the corners of his mouth jerking. "Aw you're kiddin'," he said again and again. "Well, for Lord's sake, well I'll be——! Why of course I'm going, don't ask me how, I just am!" And he was smacking kisses loudly into the transmitter.

For an instant he stared out the streaming windows, then to Polly's astonishment he grabbed her and kissed her: was challenging Walcott in gleeful little thrusts, yelping, "Congratulate me folks, I gotta job!"

"Out of his head," Walcott said, backing off.

An excited hope was thudding in Polly's throat. If this were Ken's chance—if he too got away—! She kowtowed frantically to all the saints: Oh make this thing be! More to be prized than gold, yea than much fine gold, a chance for Ken! She could lash her way to the top somehow, but Ken must have the help of destiny.

Now Ken was serious, tersely volunteering the facts. The Bordgren Musical Shows had summoned him to Pittsburgh to do "sort of juvenile leads" at a starting salary of forty dollars a week. He had to let them know right away. With shaking hands he lit a cigarette, paced the floor in long, agitated strides. "I've waited twenty years for this and now it's a laugh. Just a big laugh. I haven't got a penny to go on. What'll I use for train fare? What'll I use for wardrobe?" He beat his fists together, stamped out his cigarette, ran a hand through his hair.

"Oh Ken, control yourself," Polly said impatiently. "Use your head. Think of something!"

"I suppose you'd hitch-hike!"

"I certainly would."

"Better check up before you light out," Walcott warned. "Might be a gag. No company'd be crazy enough to hire an amateur like you."

"No," said Kenneth, unoffended, "it's from them all right. I wrote last week and sent my picture." Suddenly his chin jutted. He aimed a finger at Walcott. "You!"

"Me what?"

"You can stake me. You're helping Polly."

"That's just it, I've lent her all I can spare. Besides,

she's the only member of your tribe I'd trust as far as I can spit."

Kenneth argued, beat at that beefy wall of resistance for an hour. At last he and Polly set off for home, Polly panting little speeches of encouragement to which Ken didn't even reply. She knew wretchedly that he somehow held her accountable for the fact that George Walcott refused to help him. All the years of her superior determination lay between them. She could hear the bitter sound of his thoughts: Here strides thwarted genius while a brainy little drudge gets the breaks! And she knew that she could not set him right because to do so would only vaunt herself—an insulting thing to one who accepted his own greatness with such indolent assurance.

"I'm sorry, Ken," she said finally as they approached the porch.

"Sorry! A lot of good that does. If you were really sorry you'd do something about it."

"Why—" and she was suddenly afraid, "why you know I'll do whatever I can."

His smile was cold, almost malicious. He opened the door, stamped on in ahead of her. "You've got some money," he said.

CHAPTER SEVEN

THE FAREWELL PARTY at the church was like the stickers on the old sample case. Proof that she was going. And now she stood misty-eyed in a hand-linked circle singing a plaintive *Blest Be the Tie That Binds,* and though she sniggered as Ramey whispered, "Cheese," her heart was full to bursting as she saw that other eyes were wet with affection, and that Lydia's were great haunting holes.

After wild wonderings and reasonings at home they had decided that of course Ken was leaving too! Sam had been called in for a promotion and would come home with a new car. What idiots they had been to doubt before. Maybe he'd even come shining and purring back to the curb tonight in time to take them all to the church parlors for this occasion which—s'prise, dear brethren—could now be a twin farewell.

Only Ken had balked at the prospect of two hours of Musical chairs, Winkum, coffee and cake, and gone off to a dance with Snooky Glynn. Nevertheless, they had babbled the impressive announcement of Ken's offer to join a big eastern theatrical company at a fabulous salary.

"Yes, I guess I have just cause to be proud," Lydia smiled tremulously at the excited congratulations. "All I've asked for my children is that they be sweet and good, and faithful to the church, but if they have talent too I don't want to restrain them from what they want to do."

Your soul soared. Not only were you about to fulfill predictions long made of you, but Ken, of whom the world was skeptical if fondly tolerant—he too! And if dimly below the ecstasy and the first sampled ache of nostalgia, your devil muttered portents, you ignored him. You dared not listen.

Toward ten o'clock Polly came out upon the wet and glistening steps. Furry white rags of cloud had wiped the faces of a few young stars and sponged off the moon. Only the still damply shining walks and the tingling scent of after-rain testified to the day's torrent. She stood breathing of the night and listening to sounds of departure: Children whimpering as they were wakened and hauled into wraps. Scrape of chairs and the clack-clack of their folding; the gradually thinning din of voices as people pattered down the steps calling, "Got a ride home? C'mon, always room for one more!"

Go to your beds now, kind, homely, often exasperating people. Live your little lives and the Lord love you. How scant your hopes, few your demands, and futile my pity for you. But oh sad, sad that all of you cannot be as I, as Ken and I, who go forth to find something better!

A big low car swung to the curb. The door banged and Dan came up the walk. "Hi, Polly, I've been combing the town for you." Then with his curious way of making elaborations sound simple and earnest, "I might have known I'd find an angel at church."

For a moment she didn't answer. For, looking down, she saw in his eyes an echo of something she heard, and did not want to hear, within herself. Not her secret Loki's taunting gibber, "Y'won't go, won't go!" but akin to it—"Don't go, Polly. Please don't go."

"They've had a farewell party for us," she said, coming down to him. "Ken and I." And it was suddenly a triumph to be able to tell him the news of Ken. "Naturally," she laughed, "he couldn't be bothered coming to a gathering in his honor."

(Actually, at the moment, the Casino dance was being interrupted with fanfare to announce that their very own Kenny Andrews would leave on the morrow to make his

Broadway début. Take a bow, Kenny boy! Better still, come up and render a little ditty with the band. And Kenneth was vaulting the platform with smiling ease, ordering, *Blue Skies,* feeling already the professional about to lay the yokels in the aisles; but worrying: Dad's got to let me have the money; even if he has to borrow it he's got to get it some way!)

"But that's great, Polly," Dan said. "When's he going?"

She swallowed. "As—soon as he can make arrangements. Tomorrow or the next day."

"How about you?"

"I hope to get off this week-end."

"Then we haven't much time to lose, have we?"

Jean and Vee came scudding down the steps, light coats over their arms, wise child faces eager. "Well if it isn't Daniel! Just in time to take us to the dance."

"Yeah, for gosh sakes, Dan," said Vee. We're stranded."

Dan looked at Polly. "Do you want to go?"

"Not to stay," she said. Not to stay, hunched in lone agony along a wall while he danced with them. To be his humiliating responsibility as they were flung from partner to partner, scrambled over by those hatefully snubbing sleeks who were nothing, nothing, yet could damn her to oblivion. No, she wouldn't dare stay.

"Polly's not so keen on dances," Jean said in her light confusing lilt that was half affection, half contempt.

They circled the lake to Casino Park. Jean and Vee laughed the then wickedly new, "If you can't be good be careful!" before whisking off.

"How will they get home?" Dan frowned, backing out.

"Hoof it. In other words, take a chance on catching a ride, which they're sure to."

Dan drew a long breath and shook his head. "Gee honey, I'm glad you don't stag dances," he said.

And suddenly she was too. Suddenly, astonishingly, she knew she had nothing to fear from Jean.

They drove idly down the quiet streets of town. Dan turned between the twin stone pillars guarding the graveled lakeshore drive, and along it their tires crunched. The lake was spread like a breeze-ruffled skirt, rustling with the sound of a thousand hidden petticoats.

All this Polly had possessed always, gluttonously, but

tonight it seemed changed in some wondrous new way. Were things simply more than ever hers now that she was about to forsake them? Or was this appeasement for that gripping dread that she might not go even yet? She shuddered. If only you could keep your dreams. If you could only arrest the hour that might blast or even fulfill them.

As they stopped before the park she said, "I almost wish tonight needn't ever end."

"And how!" said Dan.

"But it will. You can't stop time. You can't even comprehend it. A moment's gone before you get your teeth into it; suddenly it's an hour later and you're somewhere else, doing something else, without realizing what's happened to you at all."

"I realize what's happened to me," Dan said quietly.

"Right now we're here. In a few minutes we'll be up in the park. It's so strange."

He leaned over and kissed her. "This isn't," he said, and opened the door.

Their heels echoed hollowly on the steep up-sloping walls. "It's bothered me ever since I was a little kid," she said. And as they sat on an iron bench atop the hill, she tried to explain: You were swooping now high, now low on a scratchy bag swing, then suddenly uptown in freshly whitened shoes on Saturday night, or munching popcorn at the Sunday afternoon band concert or on your knees on the corduroy seat of the old chugging steamer, leaning out and trying to catch foam in your fingers. You were four or twelve or nineteen, in a car, a house, a train, eating breakfast which suddenly was supper, putting on new shoes which were immediately old ones; and only at rare intervals did you see what you were about, eat, drink and savor the moment, clutch it into startled senses before it slipped mysteriously off into the deaf-and-dumb stagger of living.

"Then there was a game I called *What-if?* What if I'm the only person in existence? What if I'm an experiment and the world is a mirage to test my reactions? What if there is no actual earth and no one else at all?"

"There's no one else as far as I'm concerned," said Dan.

"Dan, you weren't listening!"

"Every word. You little monkey, one night you've got

bottled blood, and the next you're wanting to eat time!"

"You think I'm crazy, don't you?"

"I think you're lovely. Listen."

Laughter, the twanking of a ukulele and a lusty voice trying to sing *Ramona* floated up from one of the docks. "I'll kisshyoo, caresshyoo, and bless th' *day* y'taught me t'caare!" Plink, plink, plink. "I'll alway re*mem*ber th'rambling rose y'wore in your haair!"

"My page seems to need singing lessons, but he stumbled onto the right song. Isn't that the show we saw?" Leaning, Dan snapped a prim, spicy geranium from its stem and placed it gravely in her hair. "Mona."

For a long moment they just sat, hands locked, looking at each other. . . . "And dread the daaawn when I awake t'find y'gone!" nasaled the baritone on the beach.

"That's it," said Dan. "That's why the passing of time scares me too now. I don't want to wake up and find you gone."

"But suppose you don't," Polly said uneasily. "Suppose you should find me on your hands."

"I'd consider myself so lucky I don't dare even think about it. But I'm not wishing for that because I know how blame' bad you want to go. I just hope you'll be happy, that it's what you really want."

"Oh, it is! Don't you think I'll be a successful lawyer?"

"Probably. But I didn't say successful, I said happy. You haven't chosen law with your heart, but with your mind—because it represents prestige, now haven't you?"

"Yes," she admitted. "I guess so."

"Actually you're a whole lot more a poet and an artist than a lawyer—it's evident in everything you do and say."

"Things like that never get you anywhere."

"They might. At least you'd be doing what you were really cut out to do."

She stared at him a moment, amazed. He knew all about her.

"But it's too late to change now."

"I know, and I shouldn't be getting you upset. After all I'm a great one to give advice."

"You could amount to something yet, Dan," Polly said.

"I could if I had you." Then he said, "No, strike that

crack from the record. C'mon, let's go back to the car.
There's something I want to show you."

Polly thought, when Dan first threw back the blanket
in the back seat, that he was trying to announce that he
too was leaving. And it didn't seem particularly nice of
him to vaunt his own good luggage, after seeing that
shabby old sample case of hers.

She regarded the three sleek gray squares politely.
"They're very handsome. Like you. Where are you going?"

He handed her the smallest one. "You're awfully stupid
for anyone so smart. Do you demand an abstract of title,
or do I have to come right out and say they're yours?"

"*Mine?* Oh, but good heavens I couldn't! Not—not this
soon."

"Look honey, they didn't cost me much. My cousin
has a luggage shop, he let me have them for practically a
song. Besides, money burns my pockets, it would just go
for something else anyway."

That was right, Polly reasoned. In some ways he was
dismayingly like Sam.

Dan opened the small one and placed it on her lap. And
blinking down upon those silver brushes and gleaming
crystal bottles, Polly marveled in half shamed awe: My
first hairbrush! My first all-to-myself comb and mirror
and—things. "You must want me to go," she said
brusquely because her throat hurt and she could think of
nothing else.

Dan kissed her. "Sure I want you to go. But I also
want you to come back. Suitcases are like round trip tickets
—they work both ways."

This was one of the nights when Polly dreamed of the
Pink Peppermint house. Month after month for years she
had awakened chilled and shaken from its specter. Sometimes she saw Mama pregnant, big with Ramey there,
hunched in old coats by a cold stove; she was staggering
in again from the windy barn, lugging a bucket filled with
wood chips and cobs scraped up with her bare hands. Or
she and Jean would be scrooching under the covers as
Ken and another boy swaggered through on their way to
his room. And the rusty heating stove with its clumsy pipe.
That long closet where they had thrown things until the
door would scarcely open, or if it did you got a landslide

of trash. And the smelly oil stove gummed with years of boiled-over candy.

Tonight Dan sat on its steps with her. Ramey screamed in his carriage and Dan produced pink peppermints to pacify him in the manner of Grandpa Saunders, long since dead. And Dan was saying, "We'll have the world by the tail with a downhill pull, Mona. Stay and marry me."

She was awakened by a terrific banging on the screen downstairs. Dimly in the distance came the wail of the departing Flier. She sat up, relieved to be rid of her dream, to see that it was almost daylight. Blackbirds were noisily aswarm in her cherry tree. Again, more thinly, came the last whimper of the train. And she thought with a shock: Dad's home. He didn't drive. He came on the Flier.

She got up and padded barefoot down the hall, peered, desperately hoping, out the window. The street was wrapped in a chill gray slumber. No car stood at the curb.

CHAPTER EIGHT

SAM ANDREWS NEVER knocked. He grabbed a door and shook it. If that failed to rouse a response, he stomped up and down, kicked the sill, and pounded with the flat of his hand.

"Sam!" Lydia whispered, pattling to the door in bare feet and nightgown. "You'll wake the neighbors."

"Hell, it's time to get up, ain't it?" he asked with vast show of cheer.

Lydia peeped anxiously past him into the street. There had been no sound of brakes or slamming door, only the dismal whistle of the departing train. "How—how are you, Sam? Up all night? I'll bet you're tired."

"What've I got to be tired about?" He smelled of cigars. The *Saturday Evening Post* was stuck in his pocket as always, and for an instant Lydia, and Polly who stood on the landing, told themselves that perhaps, even yet—

But now Ramey came galloping, bleary with sleep but shouting, "Hiyah, Pop! Wheresa car? Wheresat new car?" Though Lydia frowned at him, he yanked back the curtain. "Golly, where's our Shivy? Pop, ain't we got no more car? They lay you off, Dad?"

Sam's control broke. "Oh, pipe down, will you? Yeah, Liddy, I got laid off, but we don't care, do we? The whole damned outfit can go to hell and I told 'em so. Polly, how about some breakfast? I'm hungry as two bull pups!" He grabbed Lydia, gave her a little spank. "Wait till you hear the scheme I got up my sleeve! We'll be making more money inside of ninety days than you ever—"

Polly patted his arm as she slipped past into the kitchen. The world could end. You went through the same motions, you lit the gas, got out the usual skillet of cold, crusted grease, reached blindly into the cupboard for the sack of eggs, but the world could end. What did you do when it came roaring and booming about your ears? Awake now and coldly aware, you just—fried eggs.

Ramey snatched up the square green parcel Sam had put down and shook it. "Oh boy, candy! Rattles like choklits. Yeeowzah! Choklits!" He looked cross-eyed and patted his bare stomach. "Hey Sambo, kin I open it? Kin I, Mom?"

"Hold on there!" Sam said. "That's for Mother. C'mon Mama, cheer up. I brought my sweetie some candy. Let's go eat."

Lydia was striving valiantly to restrain the flood of tears. "I'm glad you're back, Sam." She forced a smile to her quivering lips. "I've—worried about you." Suddenly it was upon her, the vast despair. She covered her face; dry sobs shook her.

"Now, now, Liddy," Sam said, taking her in his arms. "I know it's tough, damned if it ain't but we'll be all right. You ain't heard my new idea yet! Why you'll be ridin' in a Packard inside of a year, know that?" He sought Ramey with tired eyes. "Go get Mama something to put on, she's shivering, she'll catch cold."

"I'll be—all right," Lydia choked. "I'm just a b-big b-baby! And I was going to be so brave!"

"You're the best damn' beautiful wife in sixteen counties. I wouldn't trade you for the best lookin' waitress I ever met," vouched Sam. Still joking and patting, he guided her toward the kitchen. But a pall of silence fell as they sat down.

Then, just as the rising sun spread in shining sweep across the table, Jean wriggled in. She paused, took one look at the funereal group, and burst into song: "Goodmorning to *you*! Good-morning to *you*! We're *all* in our *plac*es, with *sunshiny fac*es—!"

They snorted reluctantly. Then they were chuckling, ramming each others' thumbs into butter, snatching turns at the three cereal bowls. Briefly they were united by an utterly unreasonable bliss. It was as if Sam had returned from one of his long ago trips to New York to sell a patent and had come home with presents for all and his pockets full of money. Ramey was permitted to open the candy, which he did with a shout of triumph. They sat dipping into it as they listened to Sam quote what he'd told the big guns about the slipshod way they ran their business. They thrilled to his account. Dear Dad! Swell Dad! And the new scheme of his, like all his inspirations, seemed a surprisingly practical if somewhat comical contribution to civilization.

"It struck me on the road when I was driving down. Now looky here—Polly, get me a piece of paper, will you? Wait, this envelope will do. Now look. Here's a cow."

Ramey hunched over his shoulder. "Looks more like a jackass to me!"

"Well the principle is the same. Polly can draw me a good cow for advertising purposes when we get started. The main thing is the tail, and I can draw that. See—all summer the cow keeps his tail busy switching off flies. Now there's a funny thing about cows, sump'n I bet even the dumb farmers don't know. A cow never hits himself with that tail. If he did it'd be like getting stung with a whip, hurt like hell, get the idea? Now! Since the cow keeps his tail in motion and don't ever hit his own hide, why couldn't a fella coat that tail with some kind of fly goo so the cow could actually catch the flies that're bothering him?"

"But Dad," Jean hooted, "think of the poor tail!"

"A cow ain't got much feelin' in his tail. But tell you what—we could make a little sack out of fly paper strips and fit it right over the tail. Then he can pick off flies in absolute comfort, maybe rid the country of 'em, cut down disease, produce more milk, who knows?"

"But that's so—simple!" Polly objected.

"That's what makes it good. Lookit the mouse trap, the safety pin. Laugh, damn ya!" he grinned in good-natured defense, slapping Lydia's knee, "but just you wait. This'll be the biggest boon to the farmer since tractors. T'hell with tractors! Ain't that right?"

Lydia sighed. "I know, Sam, but wouldn't it be safer to try to get on with another company right away?"

"Oh, I'll have another job inside of a week, but there's no harm in figgerin'. It'll take a little capital. I think I can get Doc Courtney in on that end of it. He's a bird that ain't scared to gamble, don'tcha know he ain't?"

Ken came in, step quick, face anxious.

" 'Smatter boy, you sick?" Sam asked. "It ain't noon yet!"

"Aw cut the comedy, I'm not in the mood for it this morning." Kenneth dropped to the place Polly had vacated, shoved the plate aside. "I don't want any breakfast, I've got too much on my mind. Has Mom told you I'm going east to go on the stage?"

Sam set down his cup. "God, you are sick! In the head."

"Oh, Kenneth," Lydia wailed, "couldn't you wait? Dad's tired, he's terribly worried, couldn't you wait?"

"Wait! I can't wait! They'll get somebody else if I don't wire back by noon! I've got a million things to do."

"Hold on there, hold on, don't talk to Mama in that tone of voice!"

They glowered at each other, father and son. And thus, in a tangle of nerves, Ken produced his telegram. There was a moment of taut silence as Sam perched his glasses atop his nose and began a scowling perusal of it.

Ken leaned forward. "You've got to let me have a hundred dollars," he demanded. "I know you've lost your job. I know all the excuses you're going to hand me, so save your breath. But I've got to go and you've got to help."

"Help?" Sam yelped. "How can I? I ain't got it! The rent ain't even paid. I ain't even got a car now and still I've got to make a livin' for Mama and you kids somehow." He shook his head. "Nope, you're crazy to even consider it," he reasoned with stern good sense. "What'd you use for costumes?"

"Wardrobe," Kenneth corrected indignantly.

"Besides, you couldn't get by with professionals. They'd see you're just a green kid from the sticks and you'd be stranded. No, Ken, you stick to the minstrel shows and home talent."

He had touched off the bomb of Ken's pride. "So that's what you think!" Kenneth shouted. "That's all the faith you have in me! I get the chance of a lifetime to go out and make good like you've always nagged me to, and you sneer, you call me just a green kid!" Tears began to stream down his nose. He beat his brow. "Nobody's ever understood me! Nobody!"

"Oh, Kenneth, Kenneth," Lydia pleaded, rising to comfort him. "Don't say that! We love you—we—we do understand!"

"You maybe, but nobody else in this family, this town, the whole world! I'm just the town loafer, that's all I am. A guy nobody'll help." His voice shook with self-pity. "But Polly—everybody helps Polly all right, she's that smart Andrews girl that's going places, thanks to everybody's help. Me, all I ever get is kicks in the pants!"

Polly stood rigid. Unfair, unfair this of you, Ken. We've all helped you, you've lived off of us. Unfair! Oh, I'd like to be rid of you, to give you a push if only not to have to make excuses for you any longer, but I can't. It's my chance now against yours!

. . . Or was it? Dad out of a job. Jobs scarce and Dad not young any more. You had to have a car to even get a job these days and Dad hadn't a car. Winter coming on. Jobs even scarcer in winter. A roof over your heads. Fuel. Warm clothes.

All this beat in her brain as she sat staring at the typewriter that morning. Mr. Walcott was out of town and she had time to think this thing through. Toward noon she fed a letter-head into the machine and batted out a few terse phrases. She was grateful for that partial scholarship which she hoped they could grant her again—later. Meanwhile, would they please remit her entrance fees and room deposit. Regretting that circumstances over which she had no control had altered her plans, she was, respectfully—

She made a mess of signing her name. It was hard to see.

The family tempest was still raging when she crossed the porch an hour later.

". . . the lake, I tell you!" Ken's voice lashed out wildly. "I'm going down to the lake!"

Polly quickly shut the door, stood against it, a tiny figure in an open-throated white blouse and plaid skirt, a nondescript brown jacket over her arm. "Oh Ken, hush!" she cried out. "I heard you clear up the street. People are sitting on their porches listening!" And was instantly sorry, for he whirled and she saw that his face was haggard and tear-streaked.

Ken wouldn't actually kill himself. He threatened to too easily and often. But this time there was something pathetic about his crazed determination to make them think so. This was not a matter of a dance, a car, a girl friend. This concerned the only thing that had ever been vitally important to him.

Sam hunched glumly on the piano bench, a gargoyle of resistance. Jean, on the davenport, was placidly sewing up a runner. Ramey tagged his brother's pacing feet with forlorn anxiety, muttering, "Aw, Ken, aw bub, aw Ken, don't worry!" Lydia, Polly knew, would have retired to the kitchen to cry.

"Let 'em listen!" Ken wept.

Polly's devil howled. She put a hand to her throat as if to choke down the imp's pained laughter. "Suppose *you* listened for a minute. Go wire them you're coming. You can have my fifty dollars."

Jean looked up and emitted an eloquent sigh of relief.

"You're crazier'n hell," Sam barked. "Crazier'n hell."

Ken's refusal was dramatic but not too definite. He couldn't take it, she needed it herself. No—he might as well forget his opportunity and go on being nobody. Besides—fifty wasn't enough.

"Well it's all I've got. Mr. Walcott hasn't given me any cash yet. Now he won't need to. I've changed my mind. I'm staying home."

"I'll need fifty dollars' worth of clothes alone," Ken worried, ignoring her announcement. "It'll take some to get there and to live on till I get paid. No," with angry despair, "I guess I might as well forget it!"

"Yep," Sam agreed doggedly, "y'might as well."

"Oh Dad, borrow fifty some place," Jean urged—for

she was courting visions of peaceful slumber with no Ken to be cussed out of bed.

Now they all turned upon Sam. Polly led the argument. Here at last was a chance for Ken to become self-supporting, couldn't he see that? Lydia entered wailing, "It's not fair for you to make this sacrifice, Polly, but you can keep up your law studies here, you've at least got a job, while Ken—if only Dad wouldn't be so obstinate!—Kenneth could get his start!" She glared at her husband. "Honestly Sam sometimes I think you don't even love Ken, that you *want* to hold him back!"

An expression of hopelessness touched Sam's face. He got up and reached for his hat. "I'll go see if I can borrow a hundred dollars from Uncle Mac," he said.

Now suddenly they were silent. Fused each by his own little flame of guilt, they sorrowfully watched Sam tramp to the door. Sam's head was low. He trotted down the walk and across the parking before he halted, as if jerked upright by the realization that there was no car there.

"Poor guy," Jean said. "Poor old geezer."

"I'll make it up to him!" Ken vowed. "I'll pay back every cent and more too. You folks are gonna be proud of me some day, Mom. It'll be worth all this. I'll build you a home on the lakeshore, you'll have any darn thing your heart desires, you and Dad!"

"How long d'you think it'll be?" Ramey asked in all seriousness. His eyes were wistful. "I'd sure like to have a bike."

Kenneth left Gem Lake that night. A small but admiring group had gathered in the smelly depot to see him off.

Ken had deferred to his father by wearing his old cleaned and pressed gray suit on the train, but he was already the swaggering actor in a new belted topcoat and snapbrim hat. His shoes were new too, pointed and black and shiny. On his hands were yellow pigskin gloves (smelling slightly of benzine), and beside the bench where his people sat in a stiff visiting line, stood his lone piece of luggage. It too was new, and Polly was trying miserably not to look at it.

Lydia's eyes followed Ken up and down the station. "Waiting—a mother's destiny," she said as if to herself.

"We wait for our children to be born, wait for them to come in at night so we can lock the doors and go to sleep, and then—then we wait f-for trains to take them from us!" She pressed her handkerchief tight against her trembling lips.

Polly patted her.

"She's comin'!" somebody yelled.

Ramey jumped down from the scales and came running. His sisters and Vee stood up, and to their astonishment Ken casually bent and kissed them.

"Gosh!" Vee gulped, pretending to swoon. "Will I have something to tell my grandkids!"

Ken grinned engagingly, gave her a spank, and turned to his mother who clung to him, crying softly. Only Sam, the blasé traveler, still sat, vigorously chewing gum. "Keep your shirt on," he said to the commotion about him. "Ain't even time for it yet."

"Just a freight," came the confirming word, but Ken said nervously, "Maybe we better go on out to make sure."

The freight rumbled by on a side-track. Loaded dray carts lumbered through the crowd. Ramey laid his ear to the tracks, though his family ordered him to get right back up here on the platform, he wasn't two years old, was he? "I heard it!" he claimed. "I could hear the tracks shake."

Now they heard it too, a shrill knee-weakening banshee warning. They saw its lone yellow eye swelling, glaring down upon them. They smelled the acrid smoke and the steam chuffing out in fat white side-whiskers.

And suddenly, as one, they were afraid for Kenneth. Afraid and envious. They all wanted to climb aboard and go too. And they all wanted to scuttle home, together in quarrelings and laughter, never, never to part one from the other.

"Well Mom, g'bye," Ken said, kissing her again. She clung to him with frantic tightness now.

Their throats were choked. They could think of nothing to say. Only inadequate, "Now you write." "Good luck." "Write and let us know how you get along."

"Speech!" a wag from the Checker-Board yelled.

Somebody else took up the cry, adding, "Three cheers for Kenneth Barrymore Andrews!"

They were only trying to be gay in their loyalty, not giving him the raspberry, but Kenneth scowled and muttered, "Aw dry up!" There was now no shrinking back to the security of fancy. Sick as he was, sick with fear and dread, the world watched, the train was waiting.

Sam crowded up, blowing his nose and holding out a hand in which were crammed two cigars and another ten dollar bill. "Here, costs a hell of a lot more to travel than you think for."

"Aw Pop, y'better keep that."

"No, you take it. And if things don't go right out there, why you let us know and we'll get you back some way."

Kenneth's chin shot high. "Don't worry about that," he said. "I'll get by."

Oh, brave and cocky Ken! Oh, frightened but determined!

Ken picked up the suitcase, his heels clinked up the iron steps. He turned, flashed a final smile, waved his hand in the manner of movie stars to his public.

Polly felt a touch upon her arm. A voice said, "And you're next." She looked up into Dan's eyes, full upon hers.

The train glided away from them, at first slowly, then more rapidly. The lighted cars flashed by, filled with people, none of them knowing, none caring that Kenneth Andrews had joined them. Kenneth Andrews, the actor.

The rest turned to go, but Lydia stood as if transfixed, her great shadowed eyes straining after the tiny red and green stars that fled down the tracks and at once winked off into the darkness. A plaintive *whoo-whoo—whoo-whoo!* shifted back, like a last good-bye.

Sam put his arm around her. "Don't cry, Mama."

They turned, started slowly down the platform, bending a little together.

Dan asked, "Your folks have a way home, haven't they?"

Now it was begun, the questioning, and for an instant Polly hesitated, tempted to speak the truth. Clean and bitter. Shameful—but simple. She drew a deep breath. "No, it so happens they haven't," she said. "Dad was offered a good deal so he—he up and sold the car! Of course," she added brightly, "he'll get another one right away."

"Of course," said Dan. "Say, maybe I can pick up a bargain for him."

Polly was taken aback. She hadn't thought of that.

"Let's take them home, shall we?"

"Dad'll probably take Mother to the movies to cheer her up."

Yes, they were turning townward at the corner. The bright lights had beckoned. They sniffed popcorn. At first mournfully, then with a kind of grudging cheer, they would munch from tall butter-streaked sacks and watch from middle to back and front to middle whatever picture happened to be on. Senseless, without direction, like their lives. They would emerge disgruntled at not having gotten full measure of satisfaction for their dollar; and to compensate, spend another dollar at the Greek's and go home at length philosophizing under the stars.

A frantic impulse to run after them came over Polly. She longed to comfort them. And she wanted to shake them, scold, "Children, children, don't you realize winter is coming?" She shivered, as if already feeling its chill breath at her throat. No, run along, have your little hour of forgetting, for winter is coming and winter is hard. And it came over her appallingly, that all the diligently pawed-away earth beneath her prison bars had slid back and now lay packed harder than before.

"Why so sad, honey?" Dan asked, as they walked toward his car.

"Oh, I guess it's just that there's always something depressing about a train."

He halted abruptly, announced, "Then if you feel that way about it, let me drive you to Iowa City when you go!"

For a vacant instant she stared at him. Then she muttered "But Dan I—I'm not going. It's all been changed." There—the lock was sprung. Now you dumped your little box of carefully planned pretendings in his lap, fast, fast, one atop the other before he discovered how puny each was.

"For one thing, Mother's so cut up about losing Ken right now that I haven't the heart. Then I've been wondering if I'm really ready for the *U*. There's plenty I don't know, stuff I can dig out here with George W. another year. Today he asked me something about the enforcement and effect of equitable decrees and I just looked blank. 'Woman,' he warned me, 'how do you expect to buck stiff competition down there if you don't know that?' It—it's got me worried." She looked at Dan anxiously. He gave no sign of doubting, so she raced on, tackling the hardest part.

"And to complicate matters, Dad's decided to quit being a wage slave and work on a new idea. It looks pretty idiotic at first glance, but several men with capital are interested in it, and until it materializes I'd really like to be around to put in my nickel's worth." (I sound like Alice Adams— she thought. Only Dan isn't an Arthur Russell. He hasn't any future either. I haven't even—that to compensate.)

They swept down the street in Dan's long, powerful, once rakish, car. Dan's curls were shining. He had never seemed more mature, handsome—and remote.

"So you're not going?" he remarked at length.

"No—" and she despised the too glib, too gay sound of her voice—"here I am!" *On your hands,* added the malicious little Ratatosk within. *But for God's sake don't— don't feel you've got to be chivalrous about it, just because you committed yourself.*

"You could take me home," she said.

"No, let's drive around a while, then pick up your folks."

But something was wrong between them. Not once did he say, "I'm glad."

At length they parked near the theatre. People came to the car to tell her good-bye. And she must gather up those tawdry excuses to flaunt them again while Dan listened with a kind of gallant credence. Though he knew now. Any fool would know!

People finally began to trail out of the picture show. Polly had hoped to go straight home, but Dan asked her parents and the gleeful Ramey to join them for refreshments at the Checker-Board.

"Okay, if you don't care how much we eat," Sam grumped. "Gotta stoke up for some damn' lean days ahead." And in confidential undertone as they all trouped into the little toastily scented shop with its fatuous signs

of the era, NO SPIKING, and its babbling crowds—
"Polly tell you I got laid off? Yep, it don't make a damn'
bit of difference how good a record you got, when they
clean house they clean house, and you can starve for all
the big boys care." Man to man now, sidling into a booth
and rapping the table for service—"You know of any
outfits where an old war horse like me can get in harness
again, Scott? I'd be willing to take less than I been getting
but they'd have to furnish me a car."

Her shame, now openly revealed, was like a cold,
brazen nakedness. She sat bitterly silent, pretending she
didn't care.

From courteous acceptance Dan turned to earnest sharing. "Not right offhand, Sam," he said, frowning as he
peeled open a new pack of cigarettes, "but I'll keep my ear
to the ground. As a matter of fact it's twice as hard even
to sell automobiles these days."

Ramey blew bubbles in his ice cream soda so that it
gushed all over the table and a waitress had to be summoned to mop up. Lydia kept them while she dramatized,
with gestures and many interruptions from her son, the
entire story of the picture, concluding with a sudden eye-
dimming. "That new actor, Frederic March I think his
name is, reminds me *so* much of Ken!"

"Y'know, I've noticed that resemblance too," Dan said.

He was equal to anything, even to an interest in the cow
which Sam was drawing on a paper napkin and Sam's
accompanying lecture on flies. It was almost midnight
when, to the relief of Smiley Davis, the proprietor, they
started home.

"Now no stayin' up and muggin' till morning," Sam
warned as they stood in the hall. He dragged forth his
watch. "Go on Scott, beat it. I give you just sixty seconds
before I start shootin'!"

"Po-oll!" Jean's voice trailed down from the stair top.
"Can I take one of your new suitcases? You let Ken have
one." She pattered two steps down in bare feet and pink
silk pajamas before darting back. "Oh m'gosh, didn't know
you were down there, Dan!" Her golden head reappeared,
tilted over the bannister, Rossetti's *Blessed Damozel.*
"Hi, Daniel—in the lion's den!"

"Hello, Jean," Dan called up. "Going somewhere?"

"Christian Endeavor conference, can you tie that? You don't care if my sister lends me her new luggage you gave her, do you?"

"She can do what she wants to with them. They're hers."

"The hell they are!" Sam joked, loosening his belt. "When anything comes into this family it's whoever gets there first and the devil take the hindmost. I'm next on the list just as soon as I get a road job again."

He was still prattling as Dan led Polly onto the porch and into the shadow of the vines. "Oh, my dearest, my very, very dear little fool!" Dan said as he kissed her.

CHAPTER NINE

SAM SALVAGED ENOUGH from his last, mockingly big check to purchase a Model T Ford coupé (dubbed at once the Chicken Coop). In this he toured the countryside, buying chickens for the poultry house which had always put him to work whenever one of his ventures failed. For Sam Andrews could cajole more chickens out of more farmers' wives for less money than any buyer that had ever scoured the territory.

"Yep," Sam bragged, cocking his greasy cap at a jaunty angle, "I can always buy chickens!" And he would pick up the lard bucket which held his two jelly sandwiches, boiled egg and store cookies, kiss Lydia, crack her jovially across the rump, and trot out to crank and curse the vehicle.

Yet each time he returned to buying chickens it was a hurtling backward, an acknowledgment of unaccomplishment. He was like a mechanical monkey continually climbing a stick, pulling himself almost within reach of the gilded knob on top, then slamming abruptly downward. For one five-year stretch he had actually stayed with the company and managed a branch feed and poultry store downtown. Sifts of fine meal and the sour smell of mash and the medley of crowings, the wild wing beat of the caught fowl, the bold dead-eyed blink of roosters in their wire staterooms—these were the children's memories of that period when Dad had been a local business man. Lydia's were of a precious, if false, sense of shelter and permanence. Yet when Sam began to get that glint in his eyes, hers too became feverish; when he began to draw pictures and "figger" on the backs of envelopes, she shared his dreamings. And when he kicked loose his moorings for the daring upward scramble, she watched anxiously, but with never a detaining tug.

To Lydia and the girls this latest retreat to chicken buying was the ultimate in degradation. Dad the dapper traveling man again in overalls, bartering with fat farm women; a noisy rattletrap to ride in instead of the dear shining Shivy, the imminence of eviction from their precious modern house. Polly tried to bury all this in the back of her mind, but the imp of reality dragged it forth. There it was when she went home at night, there it lay when she awoke in the morning.

She closed her eyes and fled from it in a dust of pretense. "See our new chariot?" she indicated to Mrs. Lee, the refined little secretary in the office next door. "Dad bought it as sort of a run-around wreck for Jean and me. We're all using it till he can decide what kind of new car to get for himself."

Lying, despicable pretexts, though the truth screamed itself hoarse every time the Chicken Coop came quaking to the curb and blatted its summons, or Sam tramped upstairs smelling of poultry and lice spray.

Slapping himself on the chest he boasted loudly, "Well Walcott, they ain't a Goddamn' rooster left in the country. How'do Mrs. Lee. Nope, they ain't a rooster from here to Ida county. I bought 'em all today and here's the order book to prove it!" Fluttering the pages of a smudgy pad he would chuckle, "And boy, are the old hens lonesome!"

"Aw hell I was just havin' a little fun," he would defend himself as Polly scolded on the way home. "Might as well let people know you're doin' all right, no matter what line of business you're in."

How could Dad, who nursed such dreams of affluence, have so little pride?

Not to crawl and whimper, but to camouflage; to brag rather than admit.

One October noon, scudding home, she came face to face with the living presentment of her nightmare. It was Old Lady Henniper hobbling off from one of her prying calls in quest of rent. Sight of that hooded, black-shawled witch (rumored to be worth a million) was like catching a glimpse of what they always half expected to see; the old family jinx crawling up out of its coffin.

Here then shuffled the Thing that could sentence them. Five minutes before it had come tapping at the pane: "I *paid* you four dollars only day before yesterday!" Lydia bristled from the piano bench. "I *told* you we wouldn't have any more until the end of the week."

"We-ell yes, but this is Friday and being close, looking after my Birch Street place—they're behind too, awful, it's mighty hard on a poor old woman when people won't pay her and taxes so high—and letting things go to rack and ruin like they do."

"If landlords would keep up the places so they're fit to live in and not charge twice what a house is worth they wouldn't have trouble with their tenants that way!"

"Well I just thought I'd stop by and save the long walk tomorrow." Suspiciously, "You're sure you'll have it tomorrow?"

"I can't promise," Lydia said defiantly. "I said I *thought* so. It's not pleasant being hounded."

The harpy rose. "We-ell, I should think your children would help. It don't look right your daughter graduatin' from college and talkin' law school and you not able to pay your rent. And your boy off making money, he oughta help, and this boy right here—" she wagged her cane at Ramey who had just come in—"he's big enough to work."

"He goes to school."

"We-ell, after school and Saturdays. You, boy, come up and I'll put you to cleaning my yard."

"Sure," said Ramey. And when she had gone tapping down the walk, "Don't cry, Mama. I'll work. I'll go work for her."

Lydia lifted red eyes. "You will not! Not for that old—old *Hela!* She's just a fiendish old walking death sucking people's life blood! She'd probably work you all day and then apply a dime on the rent."

"By golly I bet she would too!" he shouted. "Hey Jean, I'm gonna pay the rent!"

"I'll bet," Jean sniffed.

"Sure I yam! Hey Poll, Old Lady Henniper was just here and we made a deal. I'm gonna pay the rent. A dime every Satur-day keeps Old Henniper away! *Hoo*ray, *hoo*ray, just watch ol' Ramey pay!"

"Oh, dry up," Polly snapped. "Want the neighbors to hear?"

Lydia sighed. "It doesn't matter. They can figure out why she haunts the place the way she has ever since Dad lost his job. They know. They know all right."

"Here's something they don't know yet," Polly announced.

"What, Polly?" the others asked with the eager curiosity that kept them believing in miracles. "What?"

"I've got a new job."

"Where kid—who with—how come?"

"The newspaper." She hauled a bulging notebook from the teetering homemade shelves. "Mr. Buckley wants me to do a column, girl-from-office-window-looks-down, funny little things observed on the street below. I got the idea this morning and asked him this noon. He said to go ahead, give it a try."

"Why, Polly, that's wonderful!" Lydia exulted.

Ramey looked up from picking his toe through a hole in his tennis shoe. "How much they gonna pay you?"

"The magnificent sum of a dollar, per each and every five hundred words. Two, when accompanied by a cartoon if I make the linoleum block myself."

"Sounds like a lot of work for nothing," Jean remarked.

"It'll at least pay for your dancing lessons."

"Yes, every little bit helps," Lydia said. "And you never can tell what a thing like that might work into. It might catch on and—and be nationally syndicated! Why they say O. O. McIntyre had to give his first column away. I think it's splendid, I think you're lucky!"

Polly scowled at a fistful of scribbled notes and sketches. Unreasonably, her mother's enthusiasm irked her. Poor Mom, a surprisingly bright, incredibly stupid child who year after year comes downstairs to find an empty stocking, yet blithely goes right on believing in Santa Claus.

"It's nothing," she said more harshly than she meant to. "Only some extra work to make a little extra money! It hasn't a chance in two million of ever being syndicated."

"No," Lydia echoed dutifully, half apologetically—and this attitude was infinitely more trying—"no, I suppose not."

Suddenly they were gripped into one fierce unit of despondency. They sat filmy-eyed, staring out at copper October. It was one of those moods that bound them together, baffling them, beating down the gaudy bravado they showed the world, so that they felt their frenzied littleness and shared it one with another.

Ramey broke it by pecking out a one-fingered dirge on the piano. Grinning, he peered up from beneath his arm-crook, and mimicked each mournful expression.

"Ramey, you fool!" Jean laughed, jumping up.

"Attagirl!" He rubbed his stomach and let his tongue hang out in simpleton fashion. "How about some dinner, huh?"

"Come on. C'mon everybody. We can't sit around and blubber all day!"

They trooped toward the kitchen where they laid the oil-cloth sumptuously with bread and peanut butter, cold canned beans and coffee. As they munched they laid gay plans to leave Old Lady Henniper in the lurch by moving into one of the new Vernon Heights bungalows, for which Polly was to pay by peddling caricatures of the old witch.

"And she can paint a great big sign with *N. G., LOUSY! IT LEAKS!* on it and Ramey we'll send you down here to picket the place!" Jean declared.

"Sure boy, I'll picket to pieces."

"One thing you can say for Mrs. Henniper though," Lydia giggled. "She's faithful."

"Old Faithful! Erupts every so often!" Ramey guffawed.

It was a grim winter. Lydia was often wild, wet-eyed and cursing with her inadequate, "Darnit, *darn*it! It's not fair. As many years as we've lived in this town and tried to be decent and then the minute we're down they don't give us a dog's chance!"

"Hell, they don't give nobody a chance unless he's got money," Sam said. His lips formed a hard line. His face was expressionless. The Man in the Iron Mask. "It don't matter whether you're a liar or a thief or any kind of a bastard as long as you got the money. That's all that matters. There's no use tryin' to be honest, and by God from now on I'm gonna beat every damn' pup out of every damn' cent I can!"

"Sam, quit talking that way!" Lydia ordered. "You aren't going to do anything of the kind. You know very well there's something to life besides money."

"Not in the eyes of the General Public there ain't. Ain't I bought coal of Nelson and Luddy for years? Will they send us a nickel's worth now? They will not. Well it's their loss if some of it's missing from the yards some dark night. Just wait and see. A man can't let his family freeze to death and damned if I'll burn up the furniture."

"I can just see Dad with a gunny sack over his shoulder," Jean scoffed sweetly. "Wouldn't he look cute trying to squeeze his fat stomach through a knothole in the fence?"

Ramey tagged Lydia into the kitchen where she had retired to cry. His usually animated face was taut with concern. "Mom, say," he mumbled. "Dad was just kidding, wasn't he? He ain't really gonna go steal coal, is he?"

She whirled upon him. "Of course not! Haven't you heard him make that threat winter after winter after *win*ter? You know Dad wouldn't do anything like that! Now get down in the basement and chop up something to burn like he told you to."

"Dad, I wish you wouldn't take on in front of Mother," Polly remonstrated in the Plain Room. "It just makes everybody feel bad."

Sam shrugged and slapped his foot. "Hell," he said disconsolately. "A man's gotta say what he thinks once in a while."

Which was exactly what he always did. The butchers expected his Saturday-nightly, "For God's sake, I said a roast, not dog meat! That's all bone!" He never bought a pair of shoes that he did not examine with a shake of his head and the plaint, "Christ, that's awful to bleed a man five dollars for that little bit of leather. The farmer can't hardly get that for a whole cow." Though to the farmer he would vituperate, "You're the luckiest sons a bitches alive—plenty to eat winter and summer, while us guys in town gotta hustle and plank down dough for every bite, and yet you yell for help."

In addition to his poultry buying, Sam culled chickens, sold for a dollar a gallon a vile smelling lice spray, made four dollars hanging pennants for the Harvest Festival (and spent it gambling at a blanket stand when the festival was in harvest); discovered in an old cook book a formula for a brew guaranteed to cure gappy chickens and sold it successfully until his brother Glen, to whom he had confided the formula, in turn confided it to all Sam's customers. He wrote three hail insurance policies, patented his cow tail switcher, and spent all his Sunday afternoons dictating job applications.

Polly loathed those hours of sitting at the dining room table. The clutter—salt and pepper shakers and a stray spoon left on the tablecloth, Sam's cigar ashes trailing over a saucer, the litter of letters, carbon and typing paper, want ads, and old order blanks.

"Now kiddo, just read that over again and we'll do a couple more and that'll be all," Sam would say.

"But I've read it through three times already. Don't be such an old maid, I'll fix it up when it's typed."

"Well all right, go ahead. Let it go. We can quit if you're tired."

He was not consciously pathetic, just resigned. And his utter lack of expression made Polly despise herself for hurting him—if Dad could be hurt. Despite his bombastic opinions on the dumbness of the General Public, Sam was an enigma, a man behind a wall. He loved to debate hotly on any subject at hand. He was injudicious and knew it, telling his cherished secrets with the mischievous pride of a child. He often cussed himself for a blatting fool, yet on the next provocation he was eager and ready to hint, then to confide. Yet despite all this, he remained a secret and unseen Sam, whom even his wife did not really know.

The night he came home and found Lydia getting supper on the cookstove in the feeble flare of a kerosene lamp, he muttered, "Well I'll be damned!" turned on his heel, leaped into the Chicken Coop and rattled furiously downtown. His tirade was neither eloquent nor original, but it was delivered with all the indignation of a man who feels that he has been deprived of his rights. Still pleasantly aglow with the conviction that he had thoroughly cowed his adversaries, he picked up Polly.

"I been down to the light and gas company," he said proudly.

"Paying what we owe them?"

"No," he grinned. "Jist scolding 'em a little."

"Oh Dad, what for?"

"The damned sons a bitches cut us off."

"Then you did pay them didn't you? If you couldn't, let's go back. I've got enough."

"Back, hell! I had enough in my pocket at the time. Take a look at this." He hauled forth a wad of crumpled bills. "Not a bad day's work, huh, sellin' something somebody else couldn't give away?"

"Well then why *not* pay them? I can't get the point of our family—letting bills go and *go!* Having all the humiliation and trouble of being cut off, refused credit, even when we've got the money. Dad, for heaven's sake—" Her voice rose, "What's the point? Why can't we budget and be systematic and live decently like other people? What's the particular virtue of all the hullabaloo all the time? Where does it get us, anyhow?"

"I'll pay 'em, I'll pay 'em, don't worry. But they can wait till tomorrow. I wouldn't give 'em the satisfaction of trotting down and paying up like a nice little doggy they had scared out."

"But there's tonight ahead of us. What'll we do? Dan's coming down and Jean's got a date. What'll we *do?*"

"Do? Why those guys are good sports. Make 'em take you to a show. That's what I'll do with Mama. Do her good to get out and take her mind off it, don't y'know it will?"

Oh, smart little boy sticking his tongue out at teacher. Oh, eager, vaguely troubled Mother powdering by lamplight and sputtering because she wasn't getting the powder on straight. Oh, wise, brittle, nonchalant Jean holding her lamp aloft as she met her sleek new admirer, Stew Vold at the door, carolling, "The torch bearer! The Statute of Liberty greets you! C'mon in, nit-wit, don't stand there looking dumb and getting chilblains. We got our lights cut off, that's all."

He laughed uncertainly. "You're kidding."

"The heck I am. Think I'd be getting all oiled up with this thing for a gag? Sa-ay, haven't your folks ever had their lights cut off?" It was brave mockery. Stewart Vold was the only rich man's son at Vista, a senior in Commerce, preparing to enter his father's Illinois bank.

"Oh sure, sure," he cooperated, grinning. "I'm black and blue half the time from stumbling around in the dark."

"Well don't go knocking over any of our swell furniture. One good thing—now Dad can't blame you guys for staying overtime and using up too much electricity!"

Why couldn't Polly too assume Jean's delusive mask of brightness? Why had she lied to Dan when he called? Why was she huddled now on the davenport, alone in the big wind-pawed house? Why had she not let Dan come to be with her?

The house was a whimpering mouse in the great cat-claws of the wind. Two cat eyes came blaring out of the night, gliding down upon the house. Mouse-quick, Polly leaped up and blew out the lamp. Heart thudding, she stood rigid in the dark and heard the footsteps on the porch, the knock upon the door. The wind howled. The footsteps went away.

For a long time she stood there. She wished she had let Dan in. She was glad she had not let Dan in. He would think she was off on another date. Why did she persist in lying to him?

Jean crawled in bed with her that night. "Kid, you awake?"

"Yes. I couldn't get to sleep."

"You dummy, whyn't you go with Dan?"

"Oh, he's so swell. I hate having him know about this."

"That's something you gotta get over." Jean planted very cold feet in her sister's back. "I used to let it bother me too. Now I figure if you've got a wooden leg people are bound to notice, so why not call attention to how cute it is?"

"I don't know," said Polly. "I don't know why I keep lying. I guess I've pretended so long I can't stop."

"Well, 'night," Jean yawned, flouncing over and giving her sister the kick that in their code meant "Shut up."

Stewart Vold was cursed as heartily as any of his predecessors, subjected to the usual interrupted telephone calls, front door scenes and sendings of Jean to bed. But privately, peeling the band from one of Stew's cigars, Sam conjectured, "Hope Jean's got sense enough to quit chasin' around and hang onto him. Plentya money back of that bird, and he's got an inventive turn of mind. With his dad's capital he can promote some of his ideas some day and really amount to something."

Stew was a tall, good looking, personable young man with a lopsided grin, droll blue eyes and a cowlick. At his fraternity house and on the Vista campus he was known as The Duke, because of the impeccability of his wardrobe and the long rainbow-hued cigarette holders which he sardonically affected. He could be the life of a party without exerting himself and with no loss of dignity. There was a seeming soberness even to his idiocies, and those serious moments when he lectured Jean, or made love to her, were tinged with a slyly derisive good humor.

He and Jean wrestled, argued with gusto over trivialities, and played many a practical joke on Sam. One night they entered solemnly, Stew's lean, well overcoated back bent with the weight of a gunny sack half filled with coal which they had stolen along the tracks. "There now!" Stew panted, dumping it at Sam's feet. "Don't say I never contributed to keeping the home fires burning."

They presented him with a camp stool. "For when you camp at the door with a shotgun," Stew explained. He devised what he called his Automatic Sam-Waker-Upper, a series of feathers on a wheel which Lydia was to place beneath Sam's chin and twirl whenever Sam nodded in church. Also a Sam-Snore-no-More apparatus to clap over his nose at night. "To keep the doors and windows from rattling and the davenport intact when we want a little peace and quiet."

"Don't worry about that, fella," Sam retorted, chuckling. "I ain't doin' any snoring when there's a damn' Communist hell's too good for in the house with one of my girls."

But though they were all merry, the fact remained that it was a hard winter. Jean, usually all ashine when in the first raptures of a new affair, was much of the time raging or disconsolate.

"I can't go to the Delt dinner dance in that old blue rag!" she would storm, dropping into a chair across from Polly's office desk. "There's a cute black formal down in Tilton's for only nineteen ninety-eight, but it might as well be a hundred for all Dad'll cut loose."

"Jean," Polly sometimes suggested, "why don't you find a job? Then it would be so much easier to have clothes."

"Now Poll, you know how that is! Dad wants me to help Mother."

This was the excuse supreme for Jean's idling at home. Sam liked to consider her a substitute for the maid he'd never provided for his wife. Except for occasional spasms of cleaning or baking the two women accomplished their daily stint with a minimum of effort. Each enjoyed an afternoon nap and many a between-meal cup of coffee. Yet Jean felt complacently justified in the oft flung reminder, "I stay home and do the dirty work so *you* won't have to!"

And now moodily she would conclude, "Guess I'll have to call Stew up and tell him I can't go."

Polly's defenses would collapse. "Oh, you'll do nothing of the kind!" Half angrily, "Go get the dress. Good heavens, somebody has to keep up the family prestige."

She would arrange both for the dress and for shoes to match. Then utterly drunk with good will, she would slip into the drugstore and buy perfume to be presented as a surprise on the gala night. Pride in sending her beautiful little sister off to a college dance to which she herself had not been invited, rose like a flame in her throat.

But the divine afflatus of generosity did not last. In a few days she would be quarreling violently with Jean over the dishes, the Chicken Coop (despicable though it was, it ran) even over the right to use some of the perfume she herself had bought. Soon, when the dinner dance had joined a parade of events no longer important because they were past, she would have to make good the post-dated check for the dress and pay two dollars more on the shoes.

Polly's myriad activities those bleak months were an

echo of Sam's indomitable resourcefulness. She had little time to suffer as acutely as she had intended. Not now, she told her emotions when they clamored for release— later. But by day she was of course too busy, and by night too tired even to study the ponderous case books which she lugged home.

Mr. Walcott had concealed his satisfaction at keeping her by grumping, "Well all right, but don't expect any ten dollars a week like you got this summer. Six bucks is the best I can do, and that's charity, considering what I'm teaching you." But he allowed her to do public stenography in her spare time, persuaded the Kiwanis Club to pay her for pepping up their bulletins, and engineered poster prospects her way.

The chattering typewriter, the sibilant softness of her paintbrush lettering fifty-cent placards, the scratch of her pen as she drew caricatures, the squeaking cut of a jack-knife hacking cartoons out of linoleum to accompany her weekly column—these were the sounds to which her thoughts whispered: Ramey's got to have a new sweater. A good one this time, those cheap cotton things go right through. Poor kid, we thought things would be different for him, that he wouldn't have to go without haircuts and the right school supplies and be shamed and scolded like we were. . . . That awful time Dad went down and bawled out Superintendent Steele for all the Goddamn' extras they made the kids buy. Called the school board a bunch of grafters. Marching past the office on the way out to recess and hearing it and wanting to die. . . . And how Miss Freders patronized Mother when she came to visit school in that shabby brown coat. I still hate Miss Freders! I hope she's married and lives on a farm and has to slop the pigs! . . . Jean's new tap shoes will cost three dollars. Hope Dad doesn't find out, he'll have a fit, but she mustn't stop dancing, she's so good, she might get a break some-time too—Ken might fix it. (And she dreamed it all in elaborate detail, Jean's skyrocketing to fame, Ken's reign as a Broadway star.) We all have talent—even Ramey tooting that second-hand trumpet, picking out tunes. Why can't one of us make good? Thank heaven Ken's at least trying. If only he could help some way. If only Dad could get back on the road. If only I could stop being the family prop!

And she would push back her hair with a scrubby ink and paint stained hand, and for a moment regard the image that arose before her.

Incredible as it seems, he does love me! He wasn't kidding and he hasn't gotten over it. He wasn't glad that night because he knew I was so damnably hurt and he had too much sense to try to comfort me. But he's waiting, waiting for me to get so sick and tired of all this I'll break down and marry him. Waiting—like a vulture! A vulture with kind big claws and an ardent beak that keeps tearing at my liver! I'm Polly Prometheus, bound to my family, and Dan a vulture whose love would consume me but cannot free me!

She laughed crazily, shook her head, and went back to her poster with more firmly gripped brush.

CHAPTER TEN

DAN COULD BE fatal to all that she expected of life. That was the fundamental reason that she fled him, that she seldom answered his letters and warned Jean or Lydia when the telephone rang, "If it's Dan I'm not here."

There was another more immediate reason. His very poise and candor still made her feel shoddy, humble, ill at ease. It seemed necessary to defend herself by exaggerated implications of a refinement, utterly lacking at home. That he knew better only made it more oddly imperative. Though Ramey shouted, "Soup's on!" Lydia called, "Supper's ready" and Sam invited, "C'mon Scott, get your belly up to the bar," Polly would announce half defiantly, "Dinner is served, Dan, won't you join us?" Facing him levelly, daring him to doubt.

Not once did he appear to. He ate fried eggs as if they were oysters on the half-shell and discussed the depression with Sam as something which deeply concerned them both. And the way he combined courteous ignoring with an honesty that was as gleaming as a freshly scrubbed sink, made her the more conscious of her own lack.

When he stormed the office unannounced and carried her off to the grandeur of the hotel dining room, she attained a casual flippancy by prating rudely of her boy friends; rooting her boasts in truth—the sycophantic misfits, the studious and scorned, the dregs from Jean's quaffed cup—but exalting them in the telling, building up an illusion of popularity that was a companionpiece to the picture she wanted him to see of home.

It was absurd of her to play-act with him, the only man destined to love her enough to cherish even her peccadillos; and though she knew this, was miserable and even a little arrogant about it, she was not strong enough to face him without clutching her little staff of pretension. And so, because she loathed her own deceit, she fled.

He was inescapable. He learned the technique of surprising her and was rewarded by her start of welcome. In entertainment he was resourceful and extravagant. He took her to shows, dinners and dances, to an opera in Sioux City and a play in Des Moines. He was forever fathering feasts, steaks and oysters to be shared with the family at midnight (he tied a dishtowel around his waist and prepared them with ritualistic care, himself), concoctions of sweet chocolate, cashews and cream.

When, with blind egoistic zeal, she undertook to write and produce a Christmas pageant for the church, he scolded her soundly, but nightly fought thirty miles of drifted roads to transport her to rehearsals and see that she ate properly.

"Why do you do it?" he asked one night, perched on her office desk and forcing her to take bites out of a hot sandwich he'd brought up from the café below. "You're already burning your candle at both ends, honey, working a dozen jobs into a day. And when I'm not here, dating everybody that pops over the horizon, apparently. Now this. Why?"

"But I can't let them put on another of those song and recitation by so and so things!" She chewed, swallowed, her eyes never leaving the sheaf of papers on her copy stand.

"It's all they expect. They don't mind."

"I mind for them." She ripped the last page from her machine, gathered up the stack, sighed and switched off the hump-backed desk light. There was pain between her eyes, but she was eager for the hour ahead.

She loved her creation. It was pageant, play and musical. It was poetry and grim biting prose. It was as sketchy and hodgepodge as her religion. She had alternated Biblical episodes with their counterpart in the present: Mythical disarmament led by the Prince of Peace, starving waifs fed by philanthropists on whom it had dawned that they must sell what they had and give to the poor, glimpses into an orphanage, a college, a penitentiary. She knew that it was exaggerated, melodramatic, but she still loved it and slaved to turn farmers and ditch diggers into convincing wise men, prophets and potentates; to persuade the Sunbeam class that they were supposed to be cherubs, not demons; to keep peace among the swordbearing Juniors, whose idea of being little Christian soldiers was to jab each other with their weapons; to dissuade her barefooted angels from using red nail polish on their toes. While Dan sat, half amused and concerned in a back pew, she dictated, scolded and flattered. She was touched by the pathetic attempts of the burly men to please her, infuriated by the babblers who wouldn't learn their parts, and in tears over having to use curtains made of sheets and safety pins. The night of the dress rehearsal, she collapsed.

She had had a tooth pulled and the wound refused to heal. She was nauseated from the taste of blood and handicapped by the throbbing jaw. The dress rehearsal was wretched, but she didn't much care. Dan hadn't come for two nights and she despised everybody and wished she were home in bed and could stay there for a month. She dragged on her coat, snapped, "C'mon Jean, for heaven's sake!" reached for the door, saw it blur away and sprawled.

When she came to, her head was against a familiar overcoat. She heard Dan say, "Let's get her to the kitchen and wash that blood off her face."

"Dan, where'djoo—?" she burbled, but her mouth had filled again.

She clung to him on the ride to the dentist's office. She looked up at him while she drooled into a hooked tube and the doctor injected a deliciously hot fluid into her jaw.

"That shouldn't give you any more trouble, Polly," Dr. Courtney said briskly, taking off his apron. "But tomorrow you go see an M.D. There's something wrong with your blood when it won't clot."

"You mean she may have anemia?" Dan demanded.

"Quite likely. But, whatever it is, she is certainly badly rundown."

When they were back at home Polly said, "It's a nasty, weakish sounding word, but don't look so stricken! Lots of girls have it though I never thought I would, not with my swimming and walking miles and the way I *eat*."

"It was partly my dead sister June's trouble," Dan said. He hesitated, afraid to tell her that she ate entirely too little and too irregularly, snatching nibbles of the wrong things. For she would be at once offended, fancying a reflection upon her family.

He substituted a frowning, useless, "Mona, must you kill yourself for people? This play business on top of everything else—it's swell, but how many down there have even the capacity to appreciate it? Where does it get you, this constant burning yourself out?"

Polly cupped her aching jaw. "I don't know. But I have to. There's such a loss otherwise. I hate things going to waste, even ideas."

"You're wasting yourself, Polly. That's worse. Why won't you marry me and let me take care of you? I suppose you're thinking that would be waste too, but at least I'd save you from the demands you make on yourself. I'd keep you alive!"

"Stop looking at me as if you think I'm going to die! I'm not. Don't you realize I can't?" She believed it with naive impudence. "I've got a million things to do yet. The only death would be to know that they won't get done."

"They won't if you keep on at this pace."

She laughed, gleeful, taut with her proven strength. "They've been saying that for years. Keep her back, hold her down, but they couldn't! At school I won every contest, I was cheer leader and put out the annual and was private secretary to the principal and worked downtown besides. Some days I didn't even see a classroom. All the calamity howlers said I'd break, if not then, certainly when it came to college, but I fooled them!"

The blood was pounding in her head, forking hotly in

her jaw. It seeped into her mouth, warm, brackish, and spiced with medicine. She swallowed it quickly that she might go on vaunting herself, molding herself in indurate, shining metal. Look you! Look you! Dare you to clamp the talons of your love upon me? To throttle me with tenderness? I, who have the strength of Atalanta in these ninety pounds!

"I fooled them! I did twice as much there—class to office, office to basketball, basketball to debate, debate to a date—like that all week and I didn't break. I couldn't bear to miss a thing. I can't yet! I know it's stupid and callow, all the things I've done and the things I'm doing, but at least they'll keep me in practice for—for the big things that by golly I'm going to do yet!"

He shook out a white handkerchief and wiped the flecks of red from her mouth. He said, "Mona, dearest, won't you please go to bed?"

She shook her head fiercely. "No. I won't have you think I'm a weakling!"

"I don't think anything of the kind. I think you're sweet and wonderful and almost pathetically foolish to chase so frantically after unimportant things. Honey, for your own sake give up this pageant thing. Come home with me for Christmas, stay a week and rest."

"You don't think my play's important?" she accused.

"Not half so important as you are to me."

"Oh—that! You always come back to that."

"Yes, that. I can't do a darn' thing with you, but I love you enough to keep trying. For your own sake. To save you for the really big things you plan to do."

Ah, this was more like it! "Then you do think I'll amount to something?"

"I don't know, but I honestly hope so, since you want to so terribly. And get this, Polly—I'll help. If I can help now by restraining you I'm going to try, even if it makes you boiling mad. And there may be other ways. I wish to heaven I was rich."

"If you were rich," she told him brazenly, "I'd marry you."

He studied her for a long instant. The wind crawled through a crack and rattled the doors. Upstairs a bed creaked as Ramey turned over, mumbling in his sleep.

"The supreme sacrifice for the family. I know. And that's all right too." He kissed her. "Good-night, gold-digger!"

A prim little forest had popped up and marched the length of Main Street as merchants set out their curbstone firs. At night their lighted necklaces poured puddles of color on the snow. Even the church was resplendent with pine boughs. But at home reigned despair. Mr. Timmet, their grocer, had given his ultimatum: No more food until something was paid on account.

"The old *Scrooge!*" Lydia cursed from her perch atop the old brown chair. She was draping red and green ropes across the bay window. "At this season of *all* times to refuse people credit! There's not an ounce of Christmas spirit in a man like that!"

"And I'll just bet Santa Claus doesn't leave him anything either!" Jean echoed.

Lydia bent and snatched a tattered paper bell from her daughter's hands. "Well it isn't funny!" Her eyes were misty. "Do you realize we haven't an egg in the house? That we're down to our last drop of flour?"

"Hell, she don't care." Sam sat on the piano bench slapping his knee. "As long as she could get Polly to fork over thirty dollars for a toothbrush for Stew that's all she cares. If he was here, damned if I wouldn't ask him to give that military set back, let us get the money on it so we could eat."

It was noon. Polly crossed to the hot air register and shook her coat. Its frost crystals hissed to oblivion on the ruby-topped furnace. Dragon tongues of heat licked at her legs and ballooned her skirt. She turned the draft, scolding, "It's hot in here. We'd better make the coal last." She had bought this ton, paid the light bill, given Jean nineteen dollars for Stew's gift. ("Kid, he's been measuring my finger, I think he's gonna give me a diamond and it'll look funny if I haven't got anything decent for him.") At the moment it had seemed a good investment. If Jean got married—she shrank from that desperation-born thought. Now it was two days before Christmas and she was broke, without even a present for Dan.

Lydia immediately began to shiver, to rub her arms.

"Oh, I loathe being cold! It makes everything so much worse, so miserable. Let's at least be warm even if old Timmet does want us to starve!"

With a rattle of chains Polly reopened the draft. "I don't think we should be too hard on Mr. Timmet. We aren't the only ones that expect favors because it's Christmas, and we did owe him a bill so long it was outlawed, wasn't it? Seems to me he was pretty decent to let us start over."

That was a mistake, for it set Lydia to weeping and Sam threatening to go to the city for a basket, or to pawn Jean's diamond, if and when she got one.

The hall doors rattled warning and Dan stuck his head in. "I knocked and hollered myself hoarse, but there was too much competition! Can you come here a minute, Poll? I can't stay long enough to take off my overshoes and I don't want to track."

She went to him and he kissed her with lips that were rough with cold. "I have to meet a prospect, hon', but I just stopped to tell you my folks are plenty disappointed that you aren't coming at least for Christmas dinner. Can't you change your mind?"

"Nope, she can't!" barked Sam, who had been listening, unabashed. "It's gonna be lonesome enough for Mama with Ken gone. You come put on the feed bag with us, Scott."

"Oh, but Dan will want to be home on Christmas!" Polly shrilled.

Dan winked at her. "Home's where the heart is. Tell you what—I'll come on condition that I can bring something. Do you all like goose? I'll get one from the farm. Ducks too, if I have any luck hunting tomorrow."

Lydia had clambered down from the high chair, smoothed her mussed hair and snatched frantically at papers. Now, the instant he was gone, she flung down the wads of tissue, the snarls of tinsel and string. "Why did you do that?" she demanded in a hoarse choke. "Sometimes Sam I think you haven't got good sense! Now what'll we do? What'll we do for bread and butter and—and cranberries and things?"

Jean sent a holly wreath spinning toward her father.

"Three-ee shots at big fat Santy, folks! Hit the old bloke and you'll win a goose!"

Sam caught it, twirled it on his finger. "Hell yes, if I know that boy he'll bring it all. I ain't gonna have you girls off eatin' big dinners while Mama sits home hungry. Hell, no! Jean gets the idea, don't you, kid? There's more'n one way to kill a goose!"

"It's so cheap," Polly seethed. "So cheap and obvious!"

And as Lydia mourned and Jean laughed and Sam spat back, Ramey dragged forth a string of faded cardboard bells. Hopping on a chair, he fastened them gleefully across the doorway that spanned the register.

JOY TO THE WORLD! they proclaimed, dancing nimbly on the heat.

Sam was right. Dan came the next evening, staggering under his load of food. There was a gargantuan fowl already dressed and in its granite roasting pan. "Mother wanted to stuff it too, but I persuaded her you probably have your own special kind," he told Lydia who was gasping and protesting and wondering privately how in the dickens you stuffed a goose.

There were sacks of carrots, potatoes, onions, winter apples and black walnuts, all he assured them from his family's surplus. "On a farm things just go to waste." There were tall fluffy rolls under an immaculate dishtowel. There was whipping cream and strawberry jam. "I snitched the jam, but Mother insisted on sending the rolls. They're her pride and joy and she wishes them onto everyone." And there were three mallards, their feathers shining, and wild-smelling, their limp green throats dangling from the table.

Sam was viewing the laden kitchen with frank greed. "We'll, looks like us eats!"

"Yes, us eats." Dan hauled Polly against his leather jacket, kissed the tip of her nose. His eyes were hopeful, inviting her to join them in shameless admission of thanks. But she was rigid against him and her nostrils flared.

"You sound as if you were afraid we wouldn't. Lucky you got here before our grocery order was delivered. Now I guess we may as well call up and cancel it."

And she broke from his arms, ran swiftly upstairs to the coldness, good and bitter, of her little unheated room.

CHAPTER ELEVEN

DAN INSISTED THAT she spend the following weekend with his people. There was no valid excuse for refusing, so with excitement and dread she scraped together the funds for a down payment on a new dress. Jean cheerfully did the altering, contrived a jaunty hat from an old one turned inside out, manicured Polly's nails, set her hair, and stubbornly refused to lend her coat. So she must go looking half-smart, half-shabby and about as salmagundi as the Patchwork Girl of Oz, she thought wryly, waiting for Dan.

A blizzard had raged all night and she half-feared, half-hoped he might not get through. But at four o'clock, by the infinitesimal watch he had given her for Christmas, his car blundered triumphantly down the last block. At seven, after devious routings through the deep shining lanes cut by snow plows, they skidded into the driveway of his sister's Crescent home.

It was a long white magazine-cover house, with wreaths in every window, a fanlight over the door, and twin shrubs in squat pails on the porch. "Oh, how lovely!" Polly faltered. "I didn't dream—I mean I didn't know—"

"Not bad, is it?" Dan grinned, frankly proud. "The kind of place we'll have some day, hon'."

She was suddenly breathless with temptation. "But Dan—how?"

He pushed back his hat, scratched his head. "That's right, darnit—how? Oh well, by the time you've got the world with a downhill pull, as Sam says, I'll have it figured out. Kiss me."

He lifted her out, strode with her across the drifts, set her down upon the step. "Kay," he told the woman who opened the door, "this is my darling. She's going to marry me, even if she won't admit it, and I'm going to build us a house like yours, so show her around!"

"Come in!" Kay extended her hand. "I'm delighted, Polly. This is a form of lunacy I've gotten used to since Dan met you."

She was Dan's oldest sister, tall and lovely, all white marble and gold. Her hair waved softly into a heavy coil. She had dimples that mocked the classic lines of her face. There was a lilt running above the depth of her laughter, like a little wave glinting atop a big one. Hearing her speak was like running your hands over velvet. Polly was conscious that her own voice sounded a trifle too loud, too eager to be at home. She wished that she hadn't worn the beads and ear rings, and desperately that Jean hadn't so recklessly whacked off her dress. Kay's simple black gold-zippered gown was rather long.

They went into a long white hall, Colonial in effect. The rug was thick and soft underfoot. There were flowers in tall white vases, and a curved white stair.

Kay said, "Doc's champing for his dinner, so we'll let you put your things in the downstairs bedroom and take our tour later. Here, Polly, let me hang up your coat."

"Man's privilege!" Dan put in at once, helping Polly struggle out of it and placing it upon a hanger. The lining was ragged, the imitation fur collar worn and powder-ringed at the neck. "Look at her, sis, don't you think she belongs on some kid's Christmas tree?"

"Dolls Polly's size go in stockings."

"How do you know? You never put one there."

"No, but I still have ambitions," Kay said with a lightness that belied the ache of fading hope. She was seven years married. "Heavens, what lovely legs! You've played basketball, haven't you? I wish I could wear a frock like that."

She meant it, Polly realized. The Scotts didn't ridicule people under guise of flattery.

Kay indicated powder and an adjoining bathroom. "Now I'll go see about food—if Myrty will let me in the kitchen! She's the local colored girl. I can't afford her except for special occasions and then she browbeats me. If there's anything you need, Polly, ask Dan. These are his quarters when he stays with us."

Polly looked about the room, all copper and cream and brown. There were candlewick bedspreads, a hooked rug, at the windows heavy off-white curtains that looked expensive but weren't, she recognized. Kay must have made them. Kay. Dan. Theirs was an inbred affluence, denying the external. They had substance. There was substance in this room, the hardwood floors, the maple furniture, solid and good—but they did not spurn the humble. They took it gratefully and made it beautiful. Yes, this was Dan's kind of room.

"Twin beds?" she said.

"I only occupy one at a time. But we'll visit here often when we're married."

He stood looking at her. And suddenly she was awake and aware as she had never been before. It was one of those moments when she seemed to burst through the blind sleep of living and savor her surroundings with startled and gluttonous senses. . . . Your hands clutching a satin curve that seems to be the tall post of a bed, the strangeness of a room that is like a stage set upon which you have been magically dropped but for whose act you know no lines. You are frozen, tongueless, appalled, so that it is more like sleeping than waking, more like dream than reality, this reality that is so starkly real! For God's sake what is this place and what are you doing here, anyway?

It was like that, but there was a sharp newness about it. For never, despite all their kisses, had she felt this shock of wanting and being wanted.

Suddenly Dan crossed to her. He kissed her. He was breathing hard. "Now you know how I feel, Mona. How it is. I talk light, I hold back, but I want you. I mean—I want you married to me so damn' bad! And it's the only way I want to want you, do you hear?"

"Yes! Yes, Dan—yes."

"It's not like wanting other girls—though that's all over now—I can't even see anybody else. I want you with the worst kind of wanting of all when it's hopeless. But is it? I mean—oh, Polly—!"

She had a sensation of something breaking inside her. She could almost literally feel the hot spilled blood of Kvasir, hear the sharp crack of the jars.

"Let's—get out of here!" she whispered.

They joined Doc in the library. Kay's husband was a homely little man, big-eared and bespectacled, reputed to be the best and most expensive doctor in Crescent. "Well Dan you sure know how to pick a winner," he declared, pumping Polly's hand. "I can see by the legs on this filly she'll always be first to the post." He raised his voice at Kay who was sidling through swinging doors into the dining room, balancing a tray of goblets. "Now my mare needs more meat on her bones!"

Kay set down the tray. "That reflects on you—you won't feed me."

"How can I when people won't pay their bills?" He sat down and resumed his cigar. "Times are certainly bad. I've never seen people so hard pressed. We are too, for that matter."

A log sputtered bluely in the fireplace, books were inviting stripes of color on the wall. Little boxes of cigarettes and dishes of candy were placed conveniently on low tables about. A sleek white collie drowsed at Polly's feet. She bent and patted his head. Nice doggie. Lucky doggie. Dad had to take Ramey's out in the country and "lose" him. We couldn't feed him and we couldn't buy him a license. Nice doggie. Lucky doggie.

"Yes, times are pretty stringent," she echoed politely.

The youngest sister, Kit, burst in, fragrantly furred, snow-covered, and pealing in a flute-thin voice, "Hey Kay, we're tracking! Haven't you a broom for your porch? Oh Dan, *there* you are. How did you ever make it clear from Gem Lake? And you beat us with only four miles to come. At last I meet Polly! Though I feel as if I know you already. Do you realize he actually raves about you in his sleep? Polly, this is Martin Chase. C'mon in, Martin, you can't track any more than I have. Oh wait, here comes Kay with a broom!"

She slid out of her curly black Persian coat and was lank and tall as a mannequin in the wine wool dress. Her wavy hair was cropped short. She was as lustrous and brittle-sweet as a stick of candy.

Plump, dark Martin Chase said his how d'you do and retired behind the newspaper. He had married June Scott who had died at the birth of their second child. He and his children, Marilyn and Skippy lived with Dan's parents. It was evident, for no good reason except the way Kit fluttered at and bossed him, that she regarded him as her inheritance.

Now Kay rejoined them, followed by a sullen negress in cap and apron, who passed a tray of tinkling glasses.

"Putting on a little dog, aren't you, wifey?" Doc asked.

"Oh sure!" she laughed. "In honor of Polly. Yours is the blue glass, Polly—pineapple juice. Dan said you didn't drink. This is what we call our medical special, thanks to Prohibition, and it's pretty bad."

"Hey, don't forget your reformed brother," Dan said. "Which is mine?"

Martin Chase emerged from behind his paper. His black eyes regarded Polly with sober marveling. "So this is the girl that put you on the wagon!"

"We think it's just splendid what you've done for Dan," Kit piped. "He was something of a hellion."

"Oh, lay off, will you?" Dan said, lifting Polly's fingers one by one as he sat on the arm of her chair. His tone was light, but Polly realized that Dan too was sensitive about his family status. "The only uneducated one," he had said.

"Yo' dinner's all raddy," the maid announced.

"In other words come and git it or we'll throw it out!" Doc mocked, and offered Polly his arm.

Doc whetted his carving knife and glanced down the table. "Two, four, six of us. Now if Glenn and Carol were here Polly could meet all of Dan's tribe."

"With their two demons?" Kit shrilled.

"Preferably without the demons, though I guess F. C. and J. D. are no worse than most boys their age."

Kay informed Polly, "Carol's our other sister." And to

the others, "They probably won't get up this way now until spring, with the roads all so bad."

They were not aristocracy. They were not wealth. They were simply people accustomed to comfort, to a grace of living which made the struggle at home seem doubly grim. To be here was good because here she was warm, well-fed, and all about her was loveliness; but to be here was distress because her chapped hands were not at ease among the glittering forks, because her spirit had been so dulled by disappointment and responsibility that even her glib tongue was dull. She did not belong here. Her place was thumping a typewriter for a pittance that would somehow keep bread and butter and eggs on an oilcloth covered table for a dear and squabbling clan.

"I'm sorry but I don't play," she had to admit when Kay suggested a table of contract after dinner.

"Swell, that lets me out!" Doc cheered, squeezing her arm. "Boy do I hate bridge," he confided. "Let's you and me go to the dance."

"No, you don't," said Dan. "Let's *all* go down to the Armory."

After the dance they were alone. Dan's car was a cozy, spacious cabin, winged with light. They sang down winding paths in a cavern cut cleanly from solid diamond walls. Polly opened a window and let the dazzling whiteness blaze in upon them.

At length, churning down a drifted sideroad, they crept across a bridge and up a lane of tall and clattering trees. Three dogs came leaping, stirring up their own small blizzards. They drove past great white barns and nameless little ones, rimey and ice-whiskered; past a silo and a windmill, shining towers to the moon. At the hill's top they stopped beside a brick house so big, so splendidly modern that to Polly's unaccustomed eyes it seemed the dwelling of a vast pretentious estate.

A woman no larger than Polly herself greeted them in the kitchen doorway; a tiny person who didn't quite fill the crisply starched housedress she wore. She had a thin little face, eager and a trifle shy, beneath a ridiculous gray bob of hair held neatly back by two shell combs. She smelled of honeysuckle and of fresh baked bread. She made Polly think of tissue paper, of elves, of a cool mist that hung briefly over the lake sometimes. Yet this woman was strong. There was a clean competent strength in her fragile flower-stem wrists. Her feet were on the ground in sturdy, unimaginative little black shoes. She had none of the regality that seemed to belong with this massive house, yet in this warm and shining kitchen, in this home, it was evident that she was queen.

Dan's father stood behind her. He was erect and tall, his thick white hair wig-like in its wavy perfection. He wore what must have been a very old black suit and a string tie. "I'm proud to know you, Polly," he drawled with a slight bow. "So Danny, like his pappy, has picked the nubbins of the crop!"

"Kit will show you to the bath if you want to freshen up," Mrs. Scott beamed. "Then we'll have a bite. I know you must be cold and hungry after the drive."

They sat around an immense white-spread table in one end of the kitchen and ate prodigiously of creamed chicken and waffles, while Mrs. Scott bobbed back and forth filling plates and cups. Dan's father remarked that he was "fixin' to hitch up a team and come to meet y'all in case you couldn't get through but," sheepishly—"I reckon I fell asleep on the couch."

"The children were determined to stay up too, Polly," Kit said, "but we promised you'd still be here in the morning."

Mr. Scott chuckled. "Don't be surprised if they expect you to work magic. Danny has them thinking you're some kind of a fairy queen."

Dan's mother turned from the stove. Small though she was, she had a certain lift of chin, an elusive grace that was much like Kay's. "Polly has already worked magic with Dan," she said.

Dan's hand sought Polly's under the cloth, their eyes held. And this was best of all the evening—here where things were cozy as a toasting apple and she was loved. Warmed and welcomed, with her stomach filled and her heart bursting with the gift of these people's goodness, Polly felt that she had come home.

It was very late when Kit led her upstairs and into the guest room. It was spacious and unimaginatively good.

There was an ornate solid oak suite, a good carpet, a full length mirror beveled into the door of the cedar-lined closet where Polly hung her clothes. Built and furnished against time, this house—for people of permanence.

"I hope you're flattered by the spread," Kit said. "It's hand crocheted, Mother's *opus magnus,* used only on special occasions."

Polly admired it. "Goodness, what a lot of work. It must have taken years."

"Nine, I think. She could work on it only between canning and mending and other things."

"My mother reads," Polly said so automatically that her defense was her own surprise.

Kit kissed her. "Good-night. If you need anything I'm just next door."

The door closed. Polly put out the lights and undressed in a sheaf of moon. How soft the mattress and smooth the sheets. She lay wriggling in comfort, treating each hardened muscle to the spongy resilience of inner springs. Ah! . . . But she couldn't sleep. Unyielding slats and a concrete slab for couch had made her too much the small Spartan to adjust her bones to clouds. She got up, remembering the prized spread, and carefully turned it back.

She shuddered happily. There was the muffled thud of a horse stomping in its stall, and the dim mysterious singing of country telephone wires. She leaned out of the window, letting the feeling of excited wonder grow.

This place is mine! she thought jubilantly. Mine because love has somehow made me belong. Mine because tonight I have the power to possess place and time. And she thought: If I could remember how this thing is, how it comes upon me, if I could remember and control it I could appropriate every room of every house I enter, every street and alley, every nook and cranny of the earth! Nothing should ever be denied or taken from me. I could see and own existence, I could have all power!

In a frenzy to impress her memory, she ran her fingers across the smooth wood of the sill, lifted one of the fluttering white curtains to her nose and sniffed hungrily. It was crisp and clean. She wondered suddenly, smiling a little that homely thoughts could tagtail ambitious ones, if ironed sheets and dustless curtains had anything to do with what you were. If perhaps bumpy beds could account for the humps and hollows of your disposition? For Dad's and Mother's erraticism and the moody tempestuosity of all the kids. Maybe she and Jean could have been like Kit and Kay if—well, if they'd only eaten oftener in the dining room!

The sun was bright across her eyes when she heard the door creak and Dan tiptoed in, balancing a huge silver tray. Squat little pitchers were upon it and fragrant smoking things under globes of glass. Startled, she sat up, then scrooched beneath the covers in her clownish plaid purple pajamas which Jean had made.

" 'Morning, sleepyhead." He set the tray on a table by the bed, bent to kiss her, then hauled her up against the pillows which he was arranging with efficient thumping. "Now stretch good. I'll be back in a minute to wash your face."

She felt foolish, embarrassed. But there was about all this something remarkably wholesome, a continuation of the mood that had bound them at the table last night. She perched there, wriggling a little, peeping beneath the lids and sniffing the escaping incense of coffee and ham and eggs.

Dan returned, bearing a steaming cloth, and proceeded to wash her solemnly upheld face. "Now your hands," he said, and she held them out.

Finishing, he said, "There. Oh honey, I've wanted to do this for you so long."

"Wash my face?"

He laughed and shook out a napkin to poke beneath her chin. "No, you goofy little Pierrot. Cook for you, wait on you, make you rest."

Kit entered, snug and lovely in blue wool. "Polly would probably be lots more comfortable down at the table. What a fuss he makes over you! Usually he can't pour himself a cup of coffee, let alone cook a meal and bring it upstairs."

Dan lay across the bed, a cigarette in his mouth. "Okay, Kit, tell her what a lazy wanton I am, but she won't care because she loves me and is going to marry me and have me bring her breakfast in bed all her life, aren't you, sweet?"

Kit arose with an expression that said, "Oh, you make me sick." It changed as Martin Chase passed the door with a shirt in his hand. "Oh Martin, what is it?" she called. "A button?"

"A lot of nerve she's got kidding me," Dan said, "the way she babies Martin."

Feud was apparent, though Dan would be the first to deny it. June had been his favorite sister; to him marriage was indissoluble, even by death.

Dan produced a pair of shiny new-smelling overalls which he had bought for her coming and in the attic they found a pair of boots which had been his at twelve. Bundled to her ears, she galloped outside with the children, feeling like a freshly stuffed rag doll.

They hauled their sleds to the crest of a hill and shot earthward, the wind shrieking at their backs. Dan sat behind her, steering with his feet, deftly skirting logs and ruts, and deliberately dumping them both into a bank below. They fought icicle duels with shining weapons wrestled from the eaves. They dug a cave and huddled in its cozy glister, an Eskimo family snug against the world.

At length, numb, tingling, and with dripping noses, they came in to a feast like something out of Washington Irving, with a bewildering clan of aunts, uncles, cousins, grandparents and babies gathered about the carved oak board of the dining room.

Skippy and Marilyn gabbled, "Didjoo see Aunt Polly slide down that big hill? She wasn't a bit skairt!"

"*You* put them up to aunting me," Polly accused Dan.

"Well," Dan's father asked placidly, "won't you be their aunt some day?"

Mrs. Scott scuttled by, her face radiant with the joy of feeding her clan. "Now Father," she reprimanded, "we hope so, but you mustn't force the child to a public avowal!"

Polly kept her eyes low, struggling to ignore the temptation that had begun at Kay's last night and grown more intense until now it surged in hot beat clear to her toes. They mustn't! she thought. I'll burst. I'll burst from food and happiness and love.

But the temptation had become something she could not shake. It was rooted in her brain, her flesh. It was with her that afternoon as she and Dan tramped the rutted fields for rabbits. I could stay. I could marry Dan and stay. All this land. All this rolling earth— The field was a desolate battlefield now, over which the wind snooped, rattling dry skeletons of the slain, but in a few months the green legions would be on the march once more. . . . These acres of ground with their abundance, that solid, built-for-generations castle of a house—I could belong to it. It could belong to me. Mine, not just for a moment of moonlight sensing, but mine forever through Dan! It occurred to her, and she was somewhat shamed by the thought, that Dan was the only son, the logical heir to take over the land.

Dan had paused and stood searching the little blown trenches with his eyes. He stretched one hand back to her, whispered—"There, down by the fence. You shoot it." He snapped the safety catch and handed her the rifle. She shelled off her mittens, lifted the hard cold weight of the gun against her shoulder, squinted at the sight and fired.

There was the crackling shock of the explosion, a whistling whine.

"Got him!" Dan cried. "C'mon!"

They ran toward the fence. Polly had known an instant of triumph. But now, gazing down upon the quietly bleeding furred thing, she felt sick. She turned and groped for Dan's arms, and he held her and shielded her against the wind.

"Why you little dickens, what's wrong? You're a wonderful shot! And we'll have rabbit stew." She shuddered. He lifted her face and looked into her eyes. "Polly, do you love me?"

"Yes."

"Say it."

"I love you, Dan."

She could feel him tremble. "Lord, I've waited for that so long!"

"I've known it. I've known you were waiting." She tried to recall the old resentment and could not. It was as if those hours of dreams and drudgery at home belonged to some stranger. As if this moment were the apex of a set of hours devoted to the building of her only true and happy self.

"Why didn't you say it before? You've realized it before, haven't you, Mona?"

"Yes. But before I didn't dare. Before I'd seen only one side of you. But now I've seen your people, been in your home. I see all that is back of you, and all—" She had turned and stood with her back against his chest—"all that is before you. I always thought that to marry a farmer would be the final ignominy." She laughed apologetically, but her voice had grown eager. "Until I met your father I didn't know what a farmer was! Why a farmer is a god. He owns things! Living things—all those cattle you showed me, and horses and pigs—good smelly noisy pigs that grow up into hams! He owns fruit trees and grain— and ground!"

She knelt impulsively where the snow was thin and scraped with her fingers to feel the frozen earth. "Ground," she repeated wonderingly. "A lovely big chunk of the world to fence off and keep his family on." She laughed up at Dan, who was regarding her with troubled eyes. "That must sound crazy. As if my love for you is a sort of greed. It's not that, Dan. Only—" and suddenly it was good to blurt it out—"when you've seen your mother shunted around from one rented house to another with never a tree or a back yard to really call her own—well, there's something thrilling about ownership. You'd like to farm, wouldn't you?"

He kicked the crusted snow with his boot, gazed out over the hills on which sunset was spreading a blanket of crimson. "More than anything," he said.

"Well then?" Idiot—warned her old, her secret demon self. What of law school? What of fame, what of fortune? . . . I don't want to be a lawyer, not actually, only for what it represents. I can still work wonders—out here I can do anything!

Dan said, "I can't let you in for it, honey. Lord knows it's tempting, but you're not meant for the sort of work it would entail. I know I could save this place, make something of it, but only by getting rid of the tenants. That would mean buying equipment and working like a slave. I wouldn't mind the work. I'd glory in it if it meant saving the place for the folks. And us." He kissed her with slow new tenderness. "But there's that little matter of capital."

Capital. *Capital?* A familiar feeling of helplessness and loss came over Polly. Was there no permanence anywhere, no stability but that which she must build out of her own ambitions?

"I don't understand," she said.

"Those hard years I told you about once—well, I won't go into details again, but they took nearly everything Dad had. He sold what he could and mortgaged the rest. Our tenants farm on shares and steal him blind. It's all he can do to meet the interest payments." His eyes, squinted against the glare of the dying sun, were roving the hills again. "Now it looks like we're going to lose the place."

CHAPTER TWELVE

KENNETH'S JOB WITH the Bordgren Shows had lasted three weeks. "There's been a bust-up," he wrote home, "but don't worry. The manager skipped out with all the money we've been taking in and no salaries paid. We been drawing good crowds too and I've been going over big. Learned my parts in no time and all the company seem to think I'm an old time actor same as they are even if they do call me 'The Kid.' Anyway all the time we been playing here in Pittsb. I've been getting a big hand when I go on the stage and of course that keeps up the old spirit. Well, to tell you about what I'm going to do next. Honey Dawes, the ingénue on this outfit and a sweet kid too I'm telling you, has asked me to go home with her. Her mother takes care of the wardrobe for the girls in a show that's working up in Chicago where they live and she thinks if we come back there she can get us on. Anyway we're going 'cause we sure can't stick around here. Boyd Gammill, that's our ex-mgr., didn't even pay for the theatre and of course everybody's pretty sore. Now don't worry. I been having a lot of good experience and boy did I ever get the applause like I told you about, and everything's going to be jake. Tell Dad as soon as I can I'll start paying back that hundred bucks."

His letters brought him closer to them than he had ever

been in person. He spoke endearingly of them all, even Jean, and he repeatedly expressed his wish to repay Sam. In a few weeks the prospective job had materialized and he wrote to Lydia concerning his engagement.

"I can hardly wait till the day when I can bring Honey home with me. She certainly is beautiful even if the enclosed pictures don't do her justice. I want to warn you before hand that she smokes, but I hope you won't be shocked because most of the girls here do and that doesn't make her any less of a 'honey' (ha! ha!) than she is."

"Oh dear!" Lydia paused in her reading aloud to wail. "Well, I won't say anything. If she is really nice I don't suppose that makes any difference, but it would be awfully hard for me to get used to a daughter-in-law that smokes." Then with a flash of dimples, "But what would I *do* if she lit up at Ladies Aid?"

"Don't worry, Mom," Jean comforted. "She isn't the first girl Ken's engaged to, and she won't be the last."

In a fortnight Ken had a different job and a different girl. The family became used to his letters written on cheap hotel stationery describing his theatrical experiences, while the pictures of prospective brides rapidly assumed the proportions of a collection.

"Ken should've been a Mormon," Sam grumped.

"Well one thing I will say for Ken," Jean remarked, "the girls usually fall for him first."

And Kenneth, borrowing soap from his landlady, washing out his one white shirt and hoping it would be dry enough to iron before he had to go down to that joint where he'd promised to do a number for a meal, had found out amazing new meanings to Home, Sweet Home.

He had learned many things in his months of trouping: That Dad's abuse was mild compared with that of irate directors; that the repugnant habits of Uncle John were more tolerable than those of an unbathed chorus girl who'd become sick on bad whiskey; that bedbugs are annoying bed-fellows but you can get used to them; that it's best not to bum cigarettes off the leading man—also wise to leave his girl alone; that when you and a dame can just scare up the price of a room between you it's dumb to stand on a street corner all night; that you quickly forgot seeing said girl mending her stepins, and brushing her teeth with cigarette ashes in lieu of that luxury, toothpaste. The more he learned of these things the more ardent became his letters, the more earnestly he assured his mother, "I'm being the kind of boy you want me to be, dear. It's sure been a help to me to of been raised in the church and I'm so glad you were so set against drinking. Nobody thinks me 'upstage' because I don't drink. In fact not as many show people drink as you'd think for. All in all they're a pretty nice bunch of folks once you get used to their ways."

Tears would trickle down his nose as he sat penciling out his nostalgic heart. He would remember the aristocratic old L-shaped porch with scrolls, he would think about his beautiful, popular sisters, his roguish little brother, his jovial eccentric father, his mother—queen of her domicile, woman of God. He would turn with a dry little sob and hold out his arms to the pajama-clad blonde who was frying eggs. And drawing her down upon his knee he would paint word pictures of Home.

"The Home where I'm going to take you some day, Kitty darling."

And Kitty darling, who at sixteen had broken the Methodist heart of her father by running away from bed and board in Steubenville, Ohio, wept too, while the eggs burned, and she wondered if she'd ever be able to convince her folks that Kenneth Andrews was not just a common trouper, but nice-people, like herself.

Ken was quite convinced that he loved and wanted to marry Kitty darling, just as he had loved and wanted to marry Honey darling, Kewpie darling, Phyliss darling, Tessy darling, Angel darling, and all the other darlings in his retinue of adored ones, past and present. He always believed himself the martyred yet loyal lover—a multiple Dante pining for a dozen lost Beatrices, even while bouncing a new one—the last!—upon his knee. Emotionally he was really quite moral. He desired to have a wife and be done with affairs. He had been precariously close to his goal several times but one thing always sorrowfully saved him. He simply hadn't enough money. His darlings were often brave little shoulder-to-the-wheelers who didn't mind, who would rather starve with him in a garret than eat caviar with a stage door Johnny, but Kenneth's un-selfishness prevailed. He refused to subject them to his pre-success tribulations. But sometimes they went ahead and starved in the garret anyway. As Kitty.

Kitty was petite and personable and she knew the ropes. She sang suggestive double-twist songs in a smoky voice (*My First Piece, The Fuller Brush Man, It's a Screwy Town but I Love It!*) using a pair of enormous round eyes, a darting dimple, and a fake but enchanting com-bination of southern accent and baby talk. She got them jobs which Ken couldn't have landed by himself, and as promptly lost them, due to an ungovernable temper and a proclivity for being late for performances, forgetting re-hearsals, and burning holes in costumes.

In East St. Louis Ken realized that he was startlingly close to home. As the week passed and they breakfasted, lunched and dined on sardines and crackers, home's proximity began to prey upon him in visions of roast pork, bologna, and even fresh side meat, at whose smok-ing fat he had once lifted a sensitive nose. Now he con-sidered writing, wiring, no—telephoning would be more dramatic—to announce his return. Even better to stride in some morning, he and Kitty, and surprise them, an-nouncing that here were two of the stage's greatest artists pining for the pastoral life, and broke. He felt sure he could count on Polly to send ticket money and keep the secret of their coming.

Before he could act, however, Kitty zipped in, chortling, "Pack! Pack, sweet!"

"Okay, hand me my red bandana," he said with good-humored sarcasm. "Also a stick." He had pawned Polly's suitcase and his other suit.

"But I got your stuff out of hock. Look!" She waggled two limp bills. "I got us a job. I even got an advance on our salaries!" She was too excited to bother with her accent now.

"How much?"

"Thirty-five a week."

"Apiece?"

"No, silly, who do you think we are, the Lunts? The act!"

Kenneth snorted and gnawed on an empty pipe. He

was thin and threadbare and magnificent, rocking back and forth on his shiny black shoes. A limp tie was knotted carelessly low at the throat of a clean white shirt. Purple suspenders held up his snug, pleated gray trousers.

He teetered and chewed at his pipe to express his scorn as Kitty clucked cheerfully on. He only half heard her, though he had objections aplenty when she paused: In the first place it wasn't enough dough. In the second he bet she didn't get an advance, he bet it was that horse's fanny Joe-boy Beal that had wangled them into the unit and lent her the money, you couldn't kid him. Joe-boy'd been on the make for Kitty—hadn't he quit the same night Kitty did, now hadn't he? Besides—Kenneth clutched his side and made his mouth go grim—he was sick, he thought he had appendicitis.

Actually it was the sardines, and a scarcely-to-be-borne fever of homesickness. He wanted to go home! He wanted his mama!

Kitty petted him to bed, forced him to swallow some slimy castor oil and an aspirin. Then she fed him a steak, thick, brown and bloody, garnishing every bite with flattery.

The show that was Kenneth Andrews must go on! Talent, yea genius such as his couldn't go undiscovered much longer. He must triumph over even physical pain and carry through. She even proved to his satisfaction that she had conjured their advance out of the manager purely on Ken's drawing ability and promise. So he couldn't let her down now, could he?

That did it. He couldn't. They joined the presentation and went to Reading, Pennsylvania, Kitty thanking her lucky stars that Ken was yet too callow to the road to have heard of the town. He was soon enlightened, however. Most of the troupe had been stranded there at one time or another, and they exchanged adventures with jovial apprehension. Kenneth's agitation and his stomach ache returned. Even Kitty's admirable resourcefulness the night it happened as predicted, failed to reëstablish his lust for trouping or cure his hunger for home.

When no pay envelopes were forthcoming and no manager in sight during the last act of the last show that Friday night, Kitty whispered, "If I'm not back in time you'll have to go on alone, sweet boy, I'm getting the sheriff!" And with the flapping tails of her polo coat revealing peeps at her rosy little thighs, she darted out the stage door.

Kenneth, a martyr to the cause of the cast, ad libbed and sang as never before. He smiled, profiled and strutted, winked at the girls on the front row and blew kisses to the balcony. They called him back and he was inspired. He dropped to one knee and "Mammied" grotesquely. He brazenly stripped a cane and silk hat from a brother in the wings and burlesqued Ted Lewis. He Ben Bernied belchingly; he held his nose and Rudy Vallée'd. The orchestra, uncued and helpless, made no attempt to accompany him. They couldn't. They were howling with that rare phenomenon, honest laughter.

Kenneth knew that he was good. Knew it with exhilaration and brave sadness. The show must go on! He was doing this for Kitty. Kitty and his buddies, his pals, the cast. Laugh, clown, laugh! Amuse the mob though your heart be brrr-eaking. Amuse the mob though your stomach be aaach-ing. (Would she get the money? Could he go home?)

It was his greatest triumph. He had four encores. Panting and perspiring, he staggered backstage to receive the plaudits of the company. The company, however, were receiving plaudits of their own of a more vital nature—their money. And whatever gratitude they manifested was for Kitty, who held the sheriff proudly in tow. She had sworn out a warrant and had the box office attached.

"Sure, sure you were swell," Kenneth congratulated her later, hurling socks and his extra shirt into the recovered gray bag. "Joan of Arc herself. All you lacked was the horse!" He whinnied with derisive laughter. "But that don't mean we ain't left high and dry without a job again. And I'm sick of sardines!"

"Sick! I'll say you're sick," Kitty hooted, sure now that she was losing him. "Homesick! That's all that ails you— you *am*ateur!"

Kenneth whirled upon her. "Amateur, am I? I'll have you know I was the hit of the house tonight! I held the audience in the palm of my hand. I—I—ask Jim, ask

Cady, ask any of 'em! Oh, but you wouldn't understand. I'll show you!"

He snapped shut the bag, jammed on his hat. Kitty ran to him, arms outstretched. "Of course you'll show me, sweet boy! I just—just wanted to get in your hair so's you'd get mad enough to amount to something!"

Stoically Kenneth detached her clinging arms. "I'm sorry," he said thickly. "You've meant a lot to me, Kitty. I'll always love you, but now—" He lifted his head as to a vision that only a Galahad might see—"now I've got to go it the hard way. Alone!"

CHAPTER THIRTEEN

THAT WINTER POLLY'S purse was the main source of food (Sam's spasmodic earnings going, naturally, for bills, fuel, cigars, car expenses, and the never-to-be-neglected motion picture show) and she demonstrated to the grudging but necessarily longsuffering clan the potentialities in dry beans, rice, macaroni and prunes. Unfortunately she hadn't always time to supervise their preparation or disposal. There was much surreptitious throwing out when her small shabby figure had safely vanished in the snow. But she was not to be thwarted. She kept bringing in bulky bargain packages of oatmeal and raisins and dented sale cans of vegetables.

"God A'mighty," Sam declared with astonished unreason, "don't spend all you make for eats. Why I bet you got five dollars' worth!"

"Sure I have," she admitted, realizing the futility of the argument, "but don't you see if you get a lot you get it cheaper?"

He shrugged. "Beats all, don't it, Liddy—here we been feedin' the kids for twenty years and now they up and tell us how to do it?"

"Not only *tell* you *how*," Jean reminded pleasantly as she sailed to the sink and dumped out a bowl of gravy to make room for a bowl of beans.

Polly watched the waste with a pang. And the shame of her penuriousness was at odds with her resentment at their criticism. Her eyes moistened with the uncontrollable quickness of Lydia's. Oh, budgetless, planless Andrewses! Dear maddening idiots all, bone of her bone, whose blood her blood. As futile her attempts to reform them as to scoop the lake dry with a little red bucket. She had made about as much progress in her lifelong campaign as Lydia chasing dirt from corner to corner, yet courting Utopia, blithely convinced that there was yet to come a shining hour when all would be a veritable Fensalir of tidiness and brotherly love and bliss.

At four o'clock a hint of dark came down. Toward six she hurried with the mail and listened for the blatant honking at the curb. Her spirits climbed with each step she scampered down. The end of the office day was the end of all exile. Nothing existed but the golden hours of the evening; there was no tomorrow.

Even the acrid odor and noise of the Chicken Coop were good, and though she was always tired she glowed to Jean's and Vee's gabbling. They came for her often. They included her now. They flirted with Dan, marveled openly that she, the little misfit, should have snared him She was too grateful for this interlude of companionship to mind.

To keep gay. To not think. That was important now. To clutch and consume—with bright false interest in their plottings to get to distant dances, their intrigues against other girls, their myriad gossipings and ribald stories and new slang—the core of this late and sudden-found fun. She had not gone ahead. She had cut back to an adolescence she had never known.

And it was vital, all this, for two reasons. She was getting nowhere and she mustn't think about it, mustn't hear the hoof beats of time thudding by. And she must have the protection of her own puerile idiocy against Dan. From his superior dignity and years he looked upon her caperings, the stagged dances, the pick-up dates, with shocked hurt, a jealousy he was too proud to admit, and real concern.

"I thought you were beyond such things," he told her.

"You said you love me. You'd have been willing to go on the farm. Now I can't figure you out."

Yes, but we haven't the farm, don't you see? her devil screamed. We haven't anything but your shaky salesman's job—like Dad's. We haven't a thing. I was a fool to admit I love you. It's dangerous. It—hurts, suffocates, when there's nothing ahead!

And she would spring up from his lap at moments like these and pace the floor, accusing him of possessiveness, of wanting to restrain her. "Why should I be beyond it? I'm not old. You've had your fun, why shouldn't I have mine?"

"Fun," he said bitterly. "With drooling babies! Or cheap rotters, anything in pants. My God, Polly, this isn't what you want."

"No," she muttered wildly, "it's not what I want! I want to go away. I want to get away from the folks, my job, this town and everything in it. But how? Tell me how!"

"I wish to God I could," he said.

Then, quite casually, Representative Paul Pruitt met her at the post office one day, and asked if she would be interested in coming to Des Moines as his clerk during State Legislature. She gasped her stunned assent and a few minutes later pushed out upon the snowy street in a daze. She stood for a minute, shivering in her amorphous old coat, and beaming fatuously at passers-by. It meant twenty-eight dollars a week (a fortune!), short hours, life in her first city, and prospects of an even better job when the session closed. It was too good to be true!

But miraculously it began to materialize. First there was informing Mr. Walcott, who growled and shook his head. Then telling the family, and the ingenuous dashing about of them all to proclaim it to the relatives, the neighbors, and the world. It meant the old exciting scramble of getting clothes ready, mending, pressing, shopping skimpily with her meager funds. And it meant being kind to Dan who came every night now and stayed so late, holding her close with great perturbing silences, and smiling in a way that made his eyes dreadful to see.

The night before she was to leave, Dan took her to a college basketball game. The familiar odors of the big noisy gym stabbed at her. Here so briefly ago she had yelled and sweat with a frenzy that now seemed sheer imbecility. The games that all of them would have given blood to win were lost down the lanes of the past. Forgotten, as tonight's game would be forgotten. Utterly inconsequential, the crazily hammering heart, the maniac yelling, and the agony of defeat or the bliss of victory. And after the gun, one small paradoxically shy figure scuttling through the coupled droves, megaphone under her arm, a glory in her throat and cold palpitant misery in her breast: Would there be anyone to take her home? Oh, damning brand of aloneness after power!

All that, thank God, across a wall she need not climb again.

And yet as though in one crazed farewell, she screamed herself hoarse, leaping to her feet, beating her breast, and hoping with great convulsive pangs that those who had filled her post would invite her down front to lead one last yell.

They did. Chuck, her erstwhile junior partner in bombast, hauled her down from the bleachers at the half. Here was a little lady none of 'em would forget. He wouldn't call her an old grad, she was too young for that —he shook her playfully—but she sure had done her bit for old V. C. And now he heard she was leaving town, faring forth to seek her fortune, to study law wasn't it, Poll old pal? Anyway here she was to lead 'em once again in—well, what would she choose for her farewell holler? The old fight yell? Okay. C'mon now you guys—he bullied the crowd—give 'er everything you got!

She threw her coat to Dan, not looking at him lest she see there the old expression of tender concern: It isn't important, honey, don't do it, please. Or his taut, not-to-be-hidden resentment as Chuck put an arm around her; his woman whom no man might touch. She dropped to one knee and spanked her lap in the familiar fashion. She raised her arms in eloquent supplication.

They stamped and clapped and whistled. They called; "Atta girl, Poll, give 'em the axe!" They demanded that she lead not one yell, but three. They liked her! she realized in childish gratitude. They always had. If only she had known how—apart from fanfaronade and the false cloak of leadership—to meet them on their own ground.

Now it was too late. Feeling rather proud and rather sheepish, she rejoined Dan, who squeezed her hand.

At home Lydia sat listening for the honking which would announce that the game was over. Several times she arose and lifted the shade at the bay window to peer out toward the gymnasium, a twinkling smear of light on the lakeshore. She had never seen a football or a basketball game, but it did not occur to her that she had not. The descriptions which the kids rattled off, the years of sending them forth in a whirl of ribboned megaphones and noisemakers, the parades with bands playing, and these past years of being close enough to catch that baying swell of voices from the gym, gave her a sharing that belongs to mothers of the young.

She felt that she had not only seen games, but participated in them, just as she felt that she had danced and gone swimming and play-acted and driven fast cars, though she never had. From childhood she had been an uncommonly pretty girl with the great tragic glory of eyes pressed deep into a dark flower face, her mountainous burst of smoke-black hair, and her height and bearing of a queen. She had had wit and talent and promise, and but for the poverty of her parents and the brow-beating of four older brothers bent on seeing that little Liddy remained unsullied, she would have been very popular. Girls and young men from the best homes invited her, sought her out. "But I never had a chance," she was fond of recounting. "Mama and Papa were sweet and good, and clean—you should have seen my mother's house! Not a pin out of place. But they were so miserably poor and then the boys drank so and were so terribly afraid I'd have a little fun."

Because she had been cheated, she desired "fun" for her children almost as much as she desired that they be "good." She was a highly sensitive woman with a love for the dramatic who, under the delusion that she lived for her family, actually lived in them.

Thus, when she had walked to the telephone this evening, it had been with the anxious step of one of her

children, and when she turned from it, it had been with a
flaming indignation that Polly's own could not surpass.
"It's not fair! Not fair! If the word of one of our states-
men means nothing what's the country coming to?" she
demanded of the mute black instrument. Then, in a little
anguished moan, "The poor kid!"

She wept, drinking deep of her daughter's hemlock before she must relinquish the cup and strive for calm. And
now she haunted the window, eyes moist and brow
strained, rubbing the gooseflesh from her arms, hoping
with impatience that Polly and Dan would come straight
home from the game.

They walked home from the gymnasium. The glittering
snow crunched beneath their heels. She clung to his big
overcoated arm and sometimes she turned and danced
sidewise, the other hand in his pocket. They bent forward
joyously against the sleepy savage cold.

On the porch they stopped. In a second they would go
in—to thick heat, to rosy lamp glow, but for a moment
of wonder they saw each other's faces in the light of
snow and moon, and their cold roughing lips met and
clung together. They fumbled for each other against the
handicap of heavy coats.

"I'll follow you," he whispered.

And she answered, "You must!"

"Do you love me, Polly? Do you really love me, dear?"

"I love you, Dan! I always will."

For now she was drenched in the panic and joy of departure. He was her man who loved her, and she would
grieve for him, but now at last, thank God, she was going
away!

It was cold and soon they went inside. Lydia dropped
the curtain, turned from the window. "Why, my goodness, I didn't hear you! You must have made so much
noise I didn't hear you come in at all!" she gasped in-
coherently.

And Polly could tell by the deep breathing, the dark
torment of the eyes, that something was wrong.

"Mom, what is it?" she asked. "What's the matter,
Mom?"

"Polly—honey, you've got to try to be brave. There's been a call from Des Moines."

Polly halted, stared at her. Then she whispered, "You don't mean I'm not going?"

Lydia nodded. "Mr. Pruitt. He went down early. He said—his other girl—the one he had last year—was already there!"

"Oh," said Polly in a bewildered tone. "Oh." She stood rubbing her cheek and staring at the drawn blind of the window. Then she was aware of Dan's step, of his arms about her. Somehow his touch unleashed the pain. She could not bear having him see her beaten, humiliated again. She wrenched free, accusing, "Oh you—you're probably *glad!*" Sobbing horribly, she slammed through the doors and ran upstairs.

Dan's hands shook as he lit a cigarette. "I'm not," he said to Lydia, who had dropped to the piano bench. "I can't bear to see her unhappy."

Lydia locked her fingers and cleared her throat. "Neither can I. She's counted so on this. She's worked so hard and had so little. She wants to get away from all of us, Dan."

"She should," he said quickly, somewhat to Lydia's surprise. "But after all this was only a job. She might have been as far from her real objective there as she is now."

Lydia nodded. "Yes, this is probably all for the best. It's all for the best but we can't yet see it—that's what my father used to say. But there is one thing certain," she said vehemently. "Polly will never be satisfied until she's tried her wings, Dan. None of us can hold her."

"We don't want to, do we?" he asked agreeably. Then, with an abruptness that startled Lydia, "Mom Andrews, would you have any serious objection to my helping her get what she's convinced she wants? A chance, at least a year of law?"

"Why—why, I don't know," Lydia faltered. "I'd have to think that over. I wouldn't want her to—to sacrifice her independence. She's got to live her own life."

"I want her to. It's why I offered. Lord knows she'll never get there pounding somebody else's typewriter. I love her, Mom, I guess you haven't any doubts about that, but I'd never ask her for—anything. I'd even rather she didn't know." He smoked thoughtfully for a moment, his eyes remote. "Her emotions are confused enough about me without getting them mixed up with gratitude or a sense of duty."

"I don't know what Dad would say! But then," Lydia added with guilty inspiration, "I don't see that he'd need to know either."

"Well that's up to you. There couldn't be much to object to. Frankly, I'm not making very darned much any more. But I've an insurance policy I could borrow on, and I could begin saving, cutting down in little ways. I should have enough by next fall to give her the extra push to make it possible. I wish I could do it now. I hate having her work herself to the bone the way she does. That and—" he hesitated, smiled cynically, "all this promiscuous dating is what makes girls crack up."

"Now listen here," Lydia defended, "if you have any ideas of tying Polly down I don't believe we'd better even consider it."

"I haven't a thought but her welfare and happiness, Mom. But by helping her a little I may be able to keep her from killing herself."

Lydia's eyes were wet. "You're a fine boy, Dan. I don't know anyone else I'd trust to do a thing like this for one of my girls. I guess you know that Polly won't be ready to settle down for a good many years, and even then—"

"It may not be me."

Lydia nodded. "She's unpredictable. Impulsive, like all the rest of us. And she'll say things that will cut you to the quick—like just a moment ago. But I hope you'll understand it's characteristic of Polly to hurt most those she loves the most."

"I hope so," he grinned. "That's encouragement."

"I'm going up to her now," Lydia told him.

She found Polly crouched on the floor by her frost-crusted window. Leaning forward, she began to scratch her daughter's head, a trick she had used to quiet the children when they were small. "Sweetheart, you're so hot. You'll catch cold in here. Hadn't you better go down now and tell Dan good-night?"

"No, I don't want to see him again!"

"Then undress and get under the covers. I wish you

would sleep somewhere else. It's so cold in here. Come on now."

And presently, when Polly had shivered into her ragged flannel pajamas and lay stubbornly asking, "But why did it have to be like this?" her mother answered, "I can't tell you why. All I know is that it's for the best."

"The best!" Polly scoffed. "To pin on our medals and parade the way all us damn'-fool Andrewses do—they had me lead a last yell at the game tonight—and now to be slapped in the face again, to have Dan see me crawling round and round in the same old hole! It's the second time. I'm running out of lies, I'm running out of pride!" She clawed the pillow, crying wildly. "And—to have had a decent salary, a chance to dress decently for a change!"

"I know," Lydia said helplessly. "It's almost more than I can bear to have you hurt so! But try not to be bitter. These things happen in everybody's life. I remember once I had a chance to go to Humboldt and teach in the town school. I'd been teaching two years in the country and I know it sounds silly to you but I was just as excited over going to that little town as you were about this trip to Des Moines. But when Uncle Nathan and John heard about it they decided it wouldn't be best. Both of them tore around, but oh they were pious when anything concerned *me!* I was just sick, but trouble in the family hurt poor Mama so I just kept still and didn't sign the contract." She looked pensive for a moment, then added, half apologetically, "There was a young superintendent over there I suppose the boys thought would lead me astray. We'd met at a church sociable where I'd given a reading, and he told me I had a lot of talent for elocution—that's what we called it then. He was really anxious for me to teach in his system. Afterward he himself went on Redpath Vawter Chautauqua. So you see—" Lydia laughed, vaguely proud, vaguely humble, a sad amused little sound, "what your old mother had to give up. What—what I might have been!"

"Well," Polly challenged, "was that all for the best?"

Lydia looked baffled. Then she declared, "Why yes, honey, I think it was. Just six weeks later I met Dad! Nobody used the word keen then, but that's what he was—just *keen*. I don't suppose you kids realize it, but your father was a mighty good looking man when he was young. My brothers did everything they could to break us up too," she confided. "But Dad wouldn't stand for it."

Polly emitted a choked giggle. "He wouldn't!"

Now Lydia's voice became annoyed. "I wonder why he doesn't get *home*. He's been downtown for hours."

A bantering voice called up to them then. "Hey, Mom, is my girl coming down to tell me good-night or will I have to come up there?"

"Oh, Lord," said Polly. "We forgot all about Dan!"

Lydia arose hastily. "I'll go down. You ought to be nicer to him, honey."

"I know it. I don't half deserve him."

"Okay—here I come!"

"Don't let him in here!" Polly begged. "I look awful."

"She's in bed, Dan," Lydia protested. "She says she looks awful."

"She couldn't." He was at the door of the cold room. And then he was sitting on the bed with his arms around the thin-breasted girl in the ugly pajamas. "Good-night, princess," he said. "I didn't want to remember you crying, all the way home in that rickety wreck at the curb."

"Oh honey," she blubbered, with her cheek against his hair, "I'm afraid you will. I can't bear to think of you driving so far and maybe having car trouble when it's so cold!"

He produced a handkerchief and mopped her cheeks. "So now it's for me you'll be cryin', you crazy, tender-hearted little meanie."

"Do you have to go back tonight?" Lydia asked. "Why don't you stay here? That is, if you don't mind sleeping with Ramey." Timidly, "He kicks."

Polly stifled a protest. What was Mother thinking of to flaunt that final ignominy of smelly gray blankets and dust? Oh—well! If he were going to despise them he'd have done so long ago.

He was gone before they were up in the morning. She found his note, penciled on the back of an envelope, stuck cornerwise in her mirror: "Sweetheart—you snore! But you're so tired, honey. I am watching you now with your head tucked under your wing. I've got to see a guy early this a.m. in Crescent. (Hope the car starts.) Here's a quarter for a taxi to work since I can't take you. I love you. Dan. P. S. Tell Mom Ramey doesn't kick. At least not a pal."

Polly blew on the envelope thoughtfully, making a sound thin as thread silk. Pinched between her fingers was the hard disc of the coin.

Today she must slink again up the old stairs with the worn rubber mats, the dry brown wads of spewed tobacco and fat white worm butts of cigarettes. She must open the door to the dead, musty clutch of all she had thought squeezed forever from her lungs. She must come crawling in on her belly, begging for the old job. And Dan had arranged it so that he should not see her humiliation.

Lydia was perturbed that Dan hadn't stayed for breakfast. But Sam, manifesting the first symptom of a rancor he himself couldn't quite understand, grumped, "Let him go. It's all a man can do to feed his own family without some *guy* hanging around. Pass the cornflakes, damnit."

Ramey shot one of his surprising barbs of perspicacity. "Smatter Pop, scared he's gonna marry Poll and she'll cut off your allowance?"

Polly pushed back her chair. "Please! Just this morning—"

Lydia scolded Ramey to silence, but Sam went blithely on. "Well it don't look very good to the neighbors if guys get to stayin' all night. First thing y'know Stew'll be movin' in too."

Jean's eyes imped over the rim of her cup as a pounding came at the door. "Sure, there he is now, with his trunk! Ramey, go tell him Sam's on the warpath and it ain't safe to come in."

"It's probably the paper boy," Lydia said. "Makes me *tired,* his coming around practically before we're up like this. Ramey, you go tell him we'll pay him next week."

"Aw jeebers, I always gotta tell him that," Ramey whined.

"I'm through anyway," said Polly. "I've got a quarter."

She went swiftly through the house and into the frigid front hall, took her purse from the table to get the quarter Dan had left. The knob rattled impatiently and a voice barked, "Hey, let a guy in! 'Spect me to stand out here freezin' all day?"

Polly whirled, cried out as much in dismay as joy. The shadow that loomed behind the frosted pane was tall, gaunt, and handsome.

Ken had come back. He too.

CHAPTER FOURTEEN

FROM THE KITCHEN came a scrambling of chairs, a screeching, "Kenneth! Ken!"

There were snowy hugs, Lydia's joyous sobbing, their excited questions: "When'd you leave?" "How come you're home?" "Get fired?" (this from Ramey). And their thoughts—he's older, he's so *thin*. Sharp-featured, sunken-eyed, teeth as fine and white as the edge of a china plate. It was the first time they had ever really seen him and the shock of his familiarity and strangeness made them gape.

"How about something to eat?" He was shaking off his wet coat. "Lord, I'm tired. Sat up all the way. Show closed and I been sick. Appendicitis, I think. Gee it's good to get home! Ramey, you been riding any more goats?"

"Naw, Mom wouldn't let me keep Otto, he ate Mrs. Ashbaugh's rose bushes. But say, I won a gum chawin' contest at school! Our teacher—"

"*Lis*ten, Ramey! Let Kenneth talk," Lydia interrupted. "You don't mean you're going to have to have an operation?"

"Aw I donno'. Maybe it isn't that bad."

"I sure hope not boy, damned if I don't," Sam said glumly. "I donno' how we'd pay for it."

Ken's lip curled. "So that's what's worrying you!"

132

"Of course it isn't!" Lydia declared. "He just got up cross this morning. He doesn't mean it the way it sounded, he's just worried—we've—we've all been so worried."

"Sure, I know," Ken said wearily. Then with renewed cheer, "Gimme some bread and coffee Mom, you old sweetheart you!"

"I will," Jean yawned. "I don't feel like going downtown today. I got a headache." (She had clerked a few Saturdays in the variety store.)

"Now don't go playing off on my account. I'm going to bed."

"Well, well, ain't we important though? Think I'd stay home on account of *you?*"

"Now children, please don't start quarreling the very day Kenneth gets home," Lydia pleaded. "I did hope that maybe now things would be different with us. Separation is so dreadful, it should make us appreciate one another."

Kenneth sneered, "Aw cripes, she'll never change. She don't care. She don't give a darn." Then seeing his mother's eyes film, he grabbed her waist, whirling her around and palavering, "Mom, I haven't seen a chorus girl or the star of the show that could anywhere near come up to you for looks!" He kissed her. "How about that bread and coffee?"

They went to the kitchen, Sam tromping after, torn between vexation and pleasure at his son's return. Ken dropped to the table, hunched over the oilcloth and sat staring at the frosted window, hearing, seeing nothing. . . . So the aristocratic old house was in reality a chilly barn, his regally beautiful mother sniffly, humble, his picaresque brother an annoying blatherer, his two radiant sisters small town girls who wore made-over dresses, and his dad neither amusing nor colorful, only blustering, vulgar. He dropped his high narrow forehead upon his arms.

"Why darling!" Lydia cried, leaving three popping eggs to Jean's disdainful supervision. "What is it?"

"Oh, it's just so g-good to get home!" He drew her down upon his lap, his Adam's apple working. "You don't know what I've been through. Oh, I've been crazy about my work and I been a big hit all the way, but I've missed you so. And now to really be here—"

The coffee choked with fragrant black fury. The fortune

of eggs slicked to his plate. Upstairs there would be hot water and toothpaste and a lumpy but bugless bed where he could sleep forever. Home, sweet home! He doubted if he would ever leave again.

Polly's galoshes plodded through the unshoveled drifts of their front walk and then hurried gratefully down the open spaces where industrious people had shoveled. Her mind plodded and hurried too, planning explanations.

So another dream had come to an abrupt end? Or was any of this waking? Not having a decent car any more, no Ken away in a glamorous world, but home to loaf and borrow and be harassed by Dad. Not boarding a train for a new life, herself. The past that seemed now so poignantly rich, if only with hope, and the wolf-mouthed present—which the dream, which reality? Your feet are now wading, now dashing, and now stamping at your office door, and you are too thickly muffled in layers of some blinding stuff even to discern one footstep from another. You cannot grasp a moment. It is gone before you half have known it, hence all the million moments parading into a mass of experience are stranger things. You cannot tear them apart or mark this regiment from that with any certainty what you are about. After all, you may be walking in your sleep!

So why, she demanded of herself, should anything matter?

But perhaps—her mind snatched at a straw—Ken really was sick but would get back to his work again soon. She tried to believe it, had to believe it to make it sound convincing to George Walcott and Dan and all the countless others who would ask. And she loathed Kenneth for not sticking it out until he should come home triumphant; loathed herself for her role of panderess between the public and the family's prestige; loathed them all and felt for them the fierce loyalty that made lying defenses against a world of casual inquisitors seem so imperative.

There was music in the house again, the bang, thump, stomp-on-the-pedal kind in which the melody was a whimpering wraith struggling to survive the din. There were shuffling dance steps executed with professional nonchalance. There were cigarette butts burning gouges in the piano. There were stacks of scripts and songs, piles of stained towels, tins of cold cream, littered boxes of make-up. As Ken stayed on there was much bickering and squabbling, and there were the old rows with Sam.

Yet there were pleasant aspects to his return. One night when Sam was home and Lydia sick with the flu, Ken volunteered, "Call Vee to come over, and everybody stay home and I'll put on a show for the little family."

They perched on chairs and the edge of Lydia's bed while he spread his stumps of color on the dresser, and with swift hands demonstrated the fine art of make-up. "Now this is how you start," he said, filming his face, neck and ears with cold cream from a flat blue can. "Protects the skin."

"Never thought I'd live to see a son of mine using cold cream," Sam joked. "Did you, Liddy?"

Lydia frowned at him and leaned forward to watch the procedure eagerly. Kenneth was massaging his young flesh briskly, slapping and pinching it. He wiped it dry with the end of a paint-splotched bath towel. Drawing rust-colored stripes across his forehead, cheeks and chin, he said, "I'll show you quite a few things you never thought you'd live to see."

"Don't you call that the ground-tone?" asked Polly, who had studied make-up during a play production course.

Ken turned upon her an offended silence. With dramatic resignation he extended the stick. "Go on, if you know so much about it!"

"No," she gulped apologetically. "I just wanted to know."

Wrinkles of blue, cheek hollows of gray, a dusting of talcum for the silvered hair, a sadly drooping moustache fashioned from crêpe hair, and behold—an old man!

He looked what he was, a youngster made up to portray his grandfather, but they exclaimed with polite impressed awe. Bravo! How does he do it? And so fast, too. They say it takes Lon Chaney hours.

That gave him an inspiration. Now they must turn their backs. His fingers flew. When at length he whirled upon them he was the Hunchback of Notre Dame, the Phantom of the Opera, a tusked and leering monster. "Aaaaaah-ha-ha-ha!"

Lydia said, "Oh good heavens, isn't that awful? I declare, I won't sleep tonight!"

Sam said, "Yeah, it sure is. How d'you do it, Ken?"

Jean hid her face with her hands. Between spread fingers she winked at Vee.

Indifference—Polly thought. Indifference in the face of grotesquerie. And oh ghastly, never to suspect! She sprang up and darted into the kitchen to stir the fudge.

But Ramey was agog. He teased so frantically that Ken laughingly relinquished the illusion of horror to him that he might barge next door to scare and entertain the Ashbaugh boys.

Sam pawed through a tumbled dresser drawer to find the prized red wig which Stew Vold had solemnly presented to him as a jibe at his baldness. Donning it, twiddling his thumbs and making foolish faces, he boasted, "Hell boy, you ain't got nothin' on your old man. Why I'd make a swell actor. The girls'd mob the place when I got an outfit like this on and got up there to sing Seeing Nelly Home or some hot number like that."

"Mob the place getting out!" Jean hooted.

Kenneth tilted back his head, blew a smoke ring toward the ceiling. "One thing sure, you wouldn't have to worry about board—not with all the eggs and cabbage they'd throw you!"

"You should know about that," Jean yawned pleasantly.

The rich chocolate odor of Polly's bubbling candy mingled with that of grease paint. The dresser was piled high with a gaudy clutter—a rabbit's foot and rouge, burnt cork, a powder puff stiff, pink with old make-up, cheesecloth, court plaster, combs—accoutrements of make-believe hobnobbing chummily with Lydia's own parade of lotions, her Mentholatum and imitation ivory comb and brush.

Ken talked now, and that was delightful. Unlike those story tellers who leave cavernous gaps in speech, his tongue kept pace with the growing tempo of his tale. He paused only to laugh richly in anticipation of his climax, stirring his audience to eager, anticipatory laughter too. He told anecdotes of the stage people he had known, coloring their eccentricities with his sweeping brush of imagination. He

described the raid upon a cabaret in which he was singing, and his own escape via a cable which took him
through an old maid's window. (Lord send us a man!
Amen!) He spoke with fond amusement of the mash notes
and presents with which teen-age girls bombarded him—
a pipe, handkerchiefs, home-made candy, and a flask
(this to Lydia's horror, though he assured her he had
never used it).

The wind came wheening and fumbling at the windows,
faintly stirring the worn green blinds. The candy was cut
into thick chunks and passed. Crumbs of it fell to the
floor and into the bedclothes. And Ken's voice spun
about them an enchanted web of devotion. Grand Ken!
Gay Ken!

On her propped pillows Lydia laughed and cried.
Here, captured in grace for one rare night, were those
lives she had brought together—and Vee, who for years
had belonged. And she would lift her arms to pronounce
some great and everlasting benediction which would in-
sure them against the pain and fret and melancholy into
which they were all so often plunged. She would ensnare
this hour forever, knitting them to a cozy unity, so that
they would always love each other, laugh together, and be
glad.

CHAPTER FIFTEEN

YEARS AGO THERE had been born in the backyard of the Pink Peppermint House a little company known as the Andrews Famous Players. Their quilt-walled, clothesline-suspended theatre appeared each of several springs following the departure of their inspiration, the Ben B. Sullavan Tent Show.

The Andrews Famous Players had long since dispersed. And to Ken, their producer, even the annually changing crew of Sullavan dramateers had ceased to be antipodean gods. Glynns and Sullavans were old friends, and since Kenneth had always spent much of his ample leisure time on the porch swing with Snooky Glynn, he soon met and became chummy with B. B., the Big Shot, Gram (Mrs. B. B.) and all the others, whom he nicknamed as brazenly. In return, they called him Cass, the Great Lover.

"Sure I'll make you my leading man," Sullavan had snorkled good-naturedly in response to Ken's fifteen-year-old half-earnest, half-jesting plea for a job. Flicking the ash from his cigar, he added, "As soon as I find a leading lady that won't faint dead away when you take her in your arms."

Season after season Ken had hammered at that grinning wall of resistance. So it had been a secret singular triumph when, under Ben Sullavan's very nose, he had been hired to the distant superiorities of "eastern stock." Boy, wouldn't Ben sweat when Kenneth Andrews became the star that Ben himself might have discovered? Oh well, that's the way the breaks went—Ken wouldn't hold a grudge. And now that he was back, with legitimate experience behind him, he admitted as much to Ben.

"Look, B. B.," he announced, leaping to the running board of the Sullavan Duesenberg when it purred up to the hotel, "I've decided to forgive and forget, bein's how we're old friends. I'm temporarily at liberty and not above a little summer rag opera. Gimme leads at fifty a week and I might consider it."

Ben Sullavan had just received a wire to the effect that his juvenile man could get thirty-five dollars elsewhere, meet it or leave it. He looked at Kenneth Andrews and growled, "C'mon in and we'll try you out as the butler in *The Mistakes of Mabel*. If you can read lines and drive a truck I may give you twenty a week and a commission on the candy."

It was, Kenneth realized with mixed gloom and relief, better than layin' around home with Sam on his neck all the time. A certain compensation too—vaguely sensed —for those lost years of backyard shows when make-up was colored chalk and lamp-black and each Andrews had to be a quick-change artist to carry his several roles.

All the Andrewses except Sam, were overjoyed. "It's just a God damn' waste of time, him chasing around with these shows!" he raged. "Spending every cent he makes to live, not saving a damn' thing and then coming home next winter to live off'n us."

"But Dad," Jean argued (for even she couldn't sleep mornings with both Sam and Ken in the house), "he'll at least be earning his board and room."

"Let him get a man's job and earn more than his keep!" Sam said.

He had not watched Kenneth driving stakes, yanking rope, loading trucks, staggering under sets.

On the opening night, however, Sam was a turkey gobbler in full strut. Against Lydia's wishes he had telephoned "over home" to urge that Mother and Chick attend. "I can get you in free," he informed them, "and it'd do the kid good for you to be there, don't y'know it?"

"I wish you'd never asked them," Lydia fussed as they held their place in the front line before the box office. "They never did take an interest in anything our kids did, even if ours are the only grandchildren that've ever shown an ounce of talent!"

"Oh, they'll be here," Sam assured her somewhat uneasily. He stood on tiptoe, waving and grinning at acquaintances. "I don't see 'em yet but it's early. There are the girls and their fellas." He beckoned and called loudly, "Jean, Polly! C'mon up here. I guess if your brother's gonna be in this you oughta get a good seat! Let 'em through, will you?" he urged the little huddle of farmers and neighboring small townspeople who constituted a Sullavan first night. "Our son's got the lead in this show. He's just back from the east, was on the stage out there. Get up here kids so you can see good."

"Ken should hire you as his publicity agent, Sam," Stew grinned. He was not embarrassed, but amused. And yet beneath his delight in the comic eccentricities of Jean's family he had a growing sense of concern. He was an only child of excellent parentage. There had been a correct and lovely girl at home whom they had always rather expected him to marry one day. Or someone like her. How, he wondered more and more now that he had committed himself, would they take these volcanic relatives? Jean's beauty had knocked him cock-eyed at sight; he had been complete captive to her honest rioting laughter, her scampish acceptance—her almost pride in their lack. But what would his parents think of them, and her? They didn't know about the diamond he had given her for Christmas; a small but excellent stone which sealed his bond with this clan.

Dan laughed and said, "Sam needs a soap box to stand on though, like his daughter here."

"Hold on there Vold, I ain't takin' no sass off'n a fourth rate banker!" Sam sputtered at Stew. And the two of them taunted each other with a new shared camaraderie which ignored Dan, while Polly stood bitterly by.

So cruel, Sam's growing rudeness to Dan—so senseless and unfair. Dan's first fine wardrobe had diminished to two suits which he wore interchangeably now. Dan's car was beginning to look disreputable and to give him trouble.

But to Polly, despite his dwindling resources, he was still above and beyond them all. It maddened her that any should dare to think him less.

Lydia fretted nervously, "It seems like they could have gotten a better place than this. This mud! And so near the stockyards too."

The sweet rank spice of animal and mash was on the air. A switch engine snorted near by. The red and blue scalloped edges of the canvas tent held beads of moisture. It would be chilly inside, for Sullavan's were taking to the road early this spring.

The music wagon finally drove up from its tour of the town and was parked by the tent, where it continued to trill pert new melodies on haunting tongues of the past. Each Andrews felt the sentimental clutch of the music. It took them back to countless springs in innumerable little rented houses; to earnest shoe whitenings, the frantic scraping together of nickels and dimes, and the eager unflagging tentward trek, pushing Ramey's buggy or dragging him along by the hand. Each a would-be Pepys. The play's the thing!

Lydia said, "I wish Ramey was out here with us. The *idea* of preferring to sneak under the tent!" She giggled softly. "But then it's the way Ken always did."

"Lord knows he had to!" Jean laughed.

"Yep," Sam said, for the benefit of bystanders, "never thought he'd be the star of the outfit some day."

"Oh Dad," Polly remonstrated, "after all, this is his first year with Sullavan's—he hasn't such a big role tonight."

She looked anxiously toward the street. The Sullavan limousine was turning in with its traditional entourage of actors. There was a stirring, a craning of necks. Gem Lake appetites were not yet so jaded by radio and talking movies to fail to respond. Here was glamour on the hoof, erstwhile or potential celebrities in the flesh. Wheeler and Woolsey, it was rumored, had once spent a season with Sullavan. And the plump little red-faced comedian who was now steering the tall ash-blonde toward the back used to play supporting roles with Mary Pickford, so Ken said.

"Where's Ken?" Dan asked innocently.

Not heeling gracefully with these others toward the rear, certainly, because he was already in the rear where he had been all day, hustling canvas and assembling properties. None of the Andrewses answered. They were pluming a somewhat disdainful unconcern with the flattering thrill of being recognized by several members of the company whom they had met through Ken.

Secretly and eagerly too, they were anticipating the moment when Ben Sullavan should grandly tell them to go on in. It distressed them that he should be so poky about climbing into the box, stopping to gladhand and backslap other people.

"For goodness sake," Lydia whispered, "I should think they'd want to get started!" Then, with acrid satisfaction, "Might have known your folks wouldn't come."

But suddenly, Aunt Chick and Grandmother were there, fragrant and heavy in their soft winter furs, but wearing smartly veiled little spring straw hats.

"Ooooh, the dear boy, the dear kiddy," Grandmother moaned. "Just like Chick, I say—just like Chick that they wanted to go with this same show when she was young, ain't that right, eh Ben?"

"Well, well, well, Mother Andrews!" Ben Sullavan exclaimed, bending from his red wooden perch and grasping her gloved hand with a great jeweled paw. "And beautiful little Chick herself that you wouldn't let me have! How are you? Go on in. Put that money away! Hattie's at the door. Go right on in, glad to have you!"

The—the big palaverer! Lydia thought, forcing a wan smile as her in-laws waddled in slow magnificence through the roped alleys.

Sullavan was unwheeling his tickets now and starting his chant; the crowd impatiently pushed forward. Sam was bunted a little to one side, though he struggled valiantly and sent up a determined, "Hi Ben, you old devil you!"

Several had bought their tickets and filed by before Sullavan could heed. Then he merely nodded and motioned Sam and Lydia past. They went humbly, Lydia half turning to note with rankled pride that Dan had produced a bill and was paying for the rest.

Ken added the finishing touch to his flash and surveyed it a second like a housewife casting one last approving glance upon her dining table before summoning the guests.

The Japanese parasol upon the floor, the Spanish shawl across the davenport, the fringed floor lamp, the little gifts heaped Christmas-fashion upon a small table where squatted another very ugly, gaudy lamp. Yes, it was a good flash. It should make the candy sell. He swung off the stage and lifted a saluting finger to the electrician.

Out front the house lights dimmed and the footlights sprang up. The orchestra snapped a tune in two. The curtain rolled up its scene of sunset in the Alps to reveal the splendid flash which the audience was allowed to admire a second before Kenneth Andrews came, alert and graceful, from the wings.

There were sighings, nudgings and gigglings wherever adolescent girls were grouped. From down front in the reserved seats his family's faces were eagerly uptilted. A shrill familiar whistle spotted Ramey for him with a group of urchins high and far in the back.

Ken smiled, his teeth like diamonds in the sharp false light. "Well folks, here I am!"

Applause. Whistling. He acknowledged it with a casual wave of hand.

"Gee, you're swell! I guess you know this is my home town. And Ben's home town too, for that matter."

More applause. Lydia's eyes were wet. Sam squirmed a little forward, a chipper half-grin on his face. Grandma was weeping daintily. Aunt Chick sat with pleasant dignity. Jean yawned. Dan and Stew were polite, interested. Aching taut, Polly begged: Ken—Ken, not too thick—not grotesque!

Briskly—"Now folks, as you all know, each and every year at each and every performance the Sullavan Show offers you the finest candy on the market. That delicious confection known as Silver Kisses. Now these boxes of candy sell regularly for twenty-five cents, but we offer you this golden opportunity to buy this rare, expensive and delicious confection for the amazing price of only one dime, ten cents. Now in each and every box you will find a small prize, something to delight the kiddies and the grown-ups. And in some—I might say many—of the boxes you will also find pink slips. Now this is one instance where the old familiar adage 'slips don't count' positive-ly does not apply. For each and every slip entitles the holder to come down and claim one of these valuable prizes you see displayed. *Bed*spreads, *ta*ble lamps, bee-*yew*tiful dishes, silk (he snatched up and exhibited a step-in, then hastily crammed it beneath his coat)—woop! silk—er—shawls!" He draped a fringed shawl fancily about his shoulders and minced across the stage, to the half protesting delight of his audience. He was almost too poetically handsome, too graceful, to play the fool.

"Now the boys will pass among you only once, so have your dimes ready please." He paused an instant for effect, then whooped, "LET'S GO!" and was joined by the waiting venders.

Down the aisles they moved, trays slung over their shoulders, chanting, *"Sil*vah kisses, one dime, one tenth of a dollah. *Sil*vah kisses, thankyew—how many please?" The orchestra began a frantic, jazzed rendition of *Kiss Me Again*. Kenneth's passionate, deep-set eyes swept the audience, halting effectively here and there to stare, to wink, to beg throatily, "Kiss me! Kiss me—again!"

It was grotesque. Ludicrous. Hysterically sad, and funny. Old men howled and plunged into their pockets. Fat women tittered and opened their pocketbooks. Girls of all types and ages, as though hypnotized, fumbled in their purses for dimes.

The little boxes tossed to them were ripped open, the half dozen paper-wrapped candies searched. Lucky ones began to traipse self-consciously down the aisles and Kenneth Andrews must stop his singing to bend over the footlights, check the number, then select and smilingly hand down their prize. "There you are beautiful, a gorgeous dish for a gorgeous dish!" (This to a bespectacled little mouse who returned to her seat proud and blushing.) He was as charming to stodgy old women, some of whom said, low and excitedly, "You're Sam Andrews's boy, ain'tcha? I know your pa well—sold him lotsa chickens!"

And presently, sales lagging, he yelled, "Can't let these beautiful premiums go to waste! Make way folks, here I come!" He hurdled the footlights, snatched a basket and swung forth.

As he came close, caroling his rhythmic, "Anyone *else* ovah heah? Anyone *else* ovah heah?" they could see that his smile was as false as his make-up, that his ardent eyes caressed them and did not see them. But that didn't matter. He was an actor, aloof and great, a youth whose existence was a thrilling one of hotels, restaurants, and travel.

And Kenneth, feeling the growing weight of coins, calculated his commission. He hated selling candy. He felt that it detracted from his stage appearance. But there was good money in it and Gram Sullavan had insisted he was the only member of the crew who could put it over. He winked and murmured, "How'm I doin', Gram?" to Mrs. Sullavan who was taking tickets tonight. She turned upon him the floodlight of her Irish smile. "Kenny boy you're a peach and a prize," she burbled, "but hurry it up, darling, and send Lem back here. I've got to get dressed and you've got to help!"

He swept on, smiling his fixed enchanting smile. "Anyone *else* ovah heah?" Dear Gram. He wondered what she'd have done all these years without him to hold her smelling salts and kid her into calming down before her entrances? Gram Sullavan, who'd been in show business from the time she could walk, still scared as a kid getting up to speak her first piece. Gram, who'd played these same jerkwater towns for twenty-five years, bringing down the house night after night, getting flowers from lovesick boys, and home-made cookies from farmers' wives. Why she knew these folks better than Ben's shifting casts. What'd she have to be scared of? He'd asked her that, hanging around backstage long before he'd had an acting job of his own, and she'd only quaked, "I know it, honey lamb, not a thing, but it's a disease I was born with. I never want to go on and I never want to come off!" And she had laughed richly—a plump little white-haired woman with girlish house dresses which she donned in her room whenever she felt like weeping for the house she'd never had to keep.

Now him—he didn't get scared. His pulses double-timed and he breathed faster, but only with a kind of impatience to feel himself looked at, to hear the ripe clear tones of his own voice. Sullavan still regarded him as a barefoot gate crasher, a home town kid with an idea he could act! Well he'd show 'em. He had a few ideas of his own how the part of Dinky in tonight's bill should be played. Or could be! Of course he'd give Gram a chance, but for the rest—!

"Anyone *else* ovah heah?"

The family watched with proud tension. Kenneth! Brother, son, actor, candy peddler. Ah! Oh Ken, we forgive you now your conceit and hysterics and snubbings and lavish irresponsible generosities. This your night in the old home town! Lay 'em dead boy, roll 'em in the aisles.

He did. Boldly and blithely.

He paced the stage in orgies of grief, he was earnest and intense and so amorous in his leave-taking of the leading lady that even that canvas-toughened star blinked in astonishment and forgot her lines. When the curtain flapped down upon the position-frozen cast in the lobby of Pineway Inn (furniture courtesy Smith's Undertaking Parlors) bringing now to the attention of the audience that: WE EAT AT CASEY'S CAFE, FOR 20 YEARS JOE'S LAUNDRY HAS DONE OURS, and inviting MEET US AT THE CHECKER-BOARD AFTER THE SHOW, it was Dinky whom everybody was hopefully convinced would marry the fair Phyllis, when actually author and producer had intended him only as a rich young simpleton suspected of murdering his grandfather!

"Sa-ay!" Sam sank back, sighing contentedly. "The kid ain't bad, he ain't bad at all! He's good, don'tcha know he is?"

Lydia stirred, frowned at Sam, and looked about, trying not to appear self-conscious. The mother of the man. From her all passion and all greatness. *She* had spoken those lines, paced the stage, embraced the high-bosomed woman with the ash-blonde curls. Her lip trembled. She glanced at Chick, whose fat little satin butt protruded through the back of the chair as she turned to converse with a woman behind her. But not about Ken, Lydia observed jealously. Oh, no! They were talking bridge. Sterile women who consort only with cards, denied and denying rewards like mine! She cleared her throat and said to Dan, "Wasn't that fine?"

"Yes, Mom Andrews, you certainly should be proud."

Now Ken was bounding to the orchestra platform where he was to double at the piano. The instrument shook with the force of his attack; the slaughter of melody blared forth. The violin and trumpet strained thinly to survive, while a yawning drummer who had been reading *Bill Bruno's Bulletin* throughout the first act, tilted back in his chair and beat an uninspired time.

Between acts there was vaudeville: An agonized rendition of *Mama Grows Younger, Papa Grows Older Each Da-aay!* by the general business man and a big-mouthed ingénue with a voice like a jew's-harp; a pair of tap dancers whose frantic feet brought the dust sifting up from the platform; a juggler.

Then on with the show. With murder in a country hotel, a dead man who had gotten up to become his own valet, a hick detective with a G-string and a thee-ry, by cracky! With Gram Sullavan as the Irish proprietress, and the helpless, infuriated leading man trying to win his lady love over the illicit competition of one juvenile, Kenneth Andrews. And Ken in all his shabby glory, stealing the audience, the girl, and the play.

Oh, Ken! Polly thought in a kind of sweet anguish— it doesn't matter! We are the chosen two. We shall be great, you and I. And the pitiful vehicle of his triumph, the flagrant piracy by which he had pillaged his precious sorry loot, the bloated canvas walls—what matter that these were the tongueless tribute to his grandeur? Had Ken been the star of a Broadway success—or so it seemed in the tremendous distortion of her pride—he could have *been* no more splendid, no more the master of his art. She knew with exultation that no company need be too illustrious for him, no height too vast for him to climb; and with a sad and bitter, vigorously denied recognition, she knew that he would never reach his rightful pinnacles.

That would be up to her.

After Ben Sullavan's quiet, homely curtain speech announcing the next night's bill, thanking them all for their very kind attendance . . . after the throat-clogging beat of the ancient theme song, *Good-night, Gem Lake, Good-night,* they stood waiting uncertainly for Ken.

"Maybe he wants a ride home," they justified themselves. And when Chick had told them with that brisk enthusiasm which she could summon so gratifyingly, "You tell him it was just fine, he does mighty well," and Grandmother had wept her praises and the two of them gone,

Sam said in a pleased tone, "Damn' glad they were here, don't you know I am?"

"It does seem as if they could have waited and told him he was good themselves," Lydia said.

"How do we know he's comin'?" Jean asked. "Stew and I don't wanta stand here all night. Ramey, go, you see."

With a whinny of joy Ramey strode importantly toward the rear, two big-eyed buddies in tow.

"He needn't have taken those Ashbaugh kids," Lydia fretted. Then in a sudden benign burst, her voice quavering with a mild, jubilant hysteria, "But then I guess it's all right! I guess Ken won't mind."

The tent was rapidly emptying.

"Damn' cold standing here," Sam said, agitated. "You'd think he'd come."

"Well but he's probably got to change." A few yet lingered who might witness their reunion with Ken. Overhead the rain thrummed. The round black charcoal barrels stationed about the tent gave off a thin and acrid smoke. The little company huddled closer to the nearest one, stretching their hands to the heat.

And now he appeared in swift flowing stride, small brother and cohorts tagging after. "Hi, people." He nodded indifferently to his sisters, Dan and Stew. Then on an abrupt twist of heel, he paused to bark, "Hey you lugs, gimme a cigarette." He took one from each of the two packs offered, purling, "My, my, I just can't make up my mind!" and freeing the smoke addressed his parents. "Look, you folks better go on. I got work to do."

"Work tonight? Hell boy, you're crazy!" Sam said inconsistently. "It's damn' near midnight and forty below zero." Then coaxingly and at the same time bullying a little, "C'mon downtown and eat some ice cream with us. We'll go have a lunch at the Checker-Board, show the town we got a kid that can act. Ain't that what you say, Roberts?" he called loudly and chummily to the leading man who was guiding the leading lady up a near aisle.

"For Lord's sake Dad, haven'tcha got any sense?" Ken railed in an undertone as the man turned toward them a surprised, rather supercilious smile. "What d'ya want him to think I am, a baby that can't get two feet away from his mama?"

"Well," Jean purred, "it's a possibility."

"Now children!" Lydia begged.

Sam's ruddy little poker face was somewhat concerned, though he blustered in a subdued tone, "Hell, what's eatin' you? Gettin' too high hat for your own family or what?"

The actor swung toward the embarrassed, defensive little group nested about his rival. His empty failure of a face glowed with false cordiality. "Hello, hel*lo* all! How are you, son?" gripping Ramey's shoulder with a gloved hand. "And—Kenneth's mother? Charmed! Isn't he the lucky one to have such a family?"

He was gallant to the flattered girls, pleasant to their swains. He spoke to Sam of Ken in fatherly tones. "The boy has a real future. With more experience and a good director he'll be all right. I'll help him all I can."

"He didn't seem to need no help tonight," Sam dared wickedly.

Ken colored, his nostrils flared. He said, "Well, look, I got work to do."

"That reminds me, Ken," said the older actor, "I wonder if you'd move my trunk around to the south side? I'll appreciate it."

"The high-hattin' has-been!" Kenneth sneered when the man had gone. He glared at his father. "But you needn't have rubbed it in, made it any tougher for me than it's gonna be with that guy."

"Hell, I was just havin' a little fun," Sam said guiltily. He turned to his wife. "Well, c'mon, Mama."

Lydia cleared her throat. "Then—then you can't come with us, Ken? Couldn't you come have a lunch with us and then come back?"

"No," Kenneth snapped impatiently, "I wanta get through."

As he turned to leave them Dan attempted to compliment, "You did great tonight, Ken"—and was ignored.

And sick rebellious frenzy was on Polly's heart. Ken, the supremely insolent! The brilliant and careless and cruel. She hated him bloodily, wished for him every human humiliation, every ugly disaster—because she hurt for Dan, who only smoked and knotted his belt and didn't care.

The little company trudged up the aisles and into the night. "Well," Sam sighed, settling his puffy bulk into the back seat of Stew's big new car, "the kid can act, don't you know he can?"

CHAPTER SIXTEEN

FOR A WEEK the ice had been weakening before the fierce onslaught of the sun. Then strong winds had sent it booming toward shore—a dark and lovely sound to be awakened by at night. Now it was piled in jumbled stacks, like macabre monsters cast up out of the water to stare wet-eyed and glistening upon the land. Freed of their burden, the waves swaggered in, destroying themselves with roars of abandon, licking their foamy tongues around strong rock teeth.

"Doesn't the lake smell good?" Polly called to Sadie Williams, the corner spinster, who had stepped onto her porch to get the mail.

Sadie lifted a shrunken nose and sniffed. "Do you really like that fishy odor?" she asked, gliding back into the house.

Polly scampered on toward home, wondering if Sadie had ever lifted ardent letters from the mailbox.

"Why what's the matter, Mrs. Ashbaugh? What's happened?" she asked of the huge aproned figure that blocked the walk. For confusion reigned in the Andrews front yard.

"It's Gee Gee!" Excitement made Mrs. Ashbaugh's voice a bellow. Everything she did was enormous—whaling the last speck of dust from her rugs, baking gigantic angel cakes, presiding over the Woman's Club. "Old Lady

Flannigan took after him with a hoe, told him not to clutter up her yard."

Jean and Lydia were hauling the weeping idiot to his feet, gathering up his bright wind-scattered circulars. "There now, run along and peddle your papers," Jean soothed, straightening his cap. "And water or no water, don't flirt with any more of the neighbors, it ain't healthy."

The runted, ageless, old man wiped his streaming red face on a khaki sleeve. "B-blut I wlastn't flirting, honest!" he whimpered. "I w-was jlust tlelling her about the whlater in the l-lake. The glirls w-wlon't glo with me but I d-don't care. I jlust mlind mly own b-blizness."

"Sure you do, Gee Gee," said Lydia. "Don't tease him, Jean."

"There's Plolly!" George Gloster blubbered excitedly. " 'Lo Plolly, thlere's whlater in the l-lake!" He considered it his special duty to proclaim the annual reappearance of the water to all the town. The lake in all its moods meant much to him. "Everythling's all right whlen thlere's whlater in the lake, huh?"

"You bet it is!"

He staggered on.

Ramey and the Ashbaugh boys darted around the house, big-eyed with excitement. They had appointed themselves spies and were ready to report that Old Lady Flannigan had locked her doors and pulled down her window blinds.

"That Old Lady Flannigan's crazy!" Ramey declared, a cowlick of hair in his eyes. "Why she's crazier'n Gee Gee ever thoughta bein'!"

The three women went into the house. Lydia's eyes were red. She said, "I tell you, we haven't got much, but it makes a person thankful just to be normal, seeing a thing like that." Broom in hand, she sat down on the piano bench and gazed toward the lake.

Jean dropped to the davenport and dissected a scattered newspaper in her search for the funnies. One of her dresses dangled on a hanger from the chandelier. A gray shawl of dust draped the piano. Glancing toward the bedroom Polly saw the bed stripped of its sheets, its striped mattress sagging and ugly. Over the pile of dirty linen on the dresser peeped the green topknot of the mirror. It was noon but there were no odors of cooking. The sun moped behind a cloud.

Lydia roused. She had to get up to mimic Mrs. Flannigan's hoe raising and yelping and the cowering of Gee Gee.

Jean yawned and didn't look up. Polly watched in an agony of pity for Mother in her crude eager demonstration; for the vision of Gee Gee who would always be grotesque and conspicuous peddling his bills throughout an indifferent town. Yet, she wondered, why should it matter if you were grotesque and conspicuous in the face of indifference? Why should she care so desperately lest her own family appear grotesque before indifferent ones?

"I tell you for a minute I was so mad I could've killed that old woman!" Lydia ranted. "The very idea, hurting a pathetic creature like that! But then I think Old Lady Flannigan's almost more to be pitied than George," Lydia philosophized. "She and that old man shutting themselves off from society the way they do. I guess their daughter's burning to death must have been an awful thing to embitter them the way it has."

"Ye gods," said Polly faintly, "is that the reason?"

Jean looked up. "Sure. Didn't you know that? But everybody says they practically drove her to the oil can, fighting with her."

"You mean she committed suicide?"

"Yeah, ain't that dumb? Wouldn't you think she'd of figured out an easier way than that? If it was me I'd go jump in the lake."

Lydia was beginning to stir up dust with her broom. "Well, if you intend to do any jumping it had better be toward the kitchen to get Polly something to eat. I'll go ahead and clean up this house. It's so dirty I'd hate to be caught dead in it!"

"I'm tired," Jean groaned, dropping the paper. "I got a headache. Polly, you can fry your own eggs, can'tcha?"

"Is that all there is? I'm starved."

"There's dill pickles, honey," Lydia coaxed sympathetically. "And syrup. We could have bread and cream and syrup for dessert."

"Unless Ramey's drunk all the milk."

Lydia hung her head like a child abashed at being

reprimanded. "I should have sent Ramey to the store," she scolded herself, "but I declare this morning's gone so fast. Tell you what, I'll send him yet! This is Saturday, we've got time. I'll have him get a pie and some cold meat."

"Oh never mind," Polly said. "Stuff like that's so high at the little store."

Lydia Andrews had put the potatoes on to boil. There, always, was the basis for her meal. Now what? She opened the doors of the built-in cupboard and stood staring idly up at the chaotic shelves. There was something about a cupboard that distressed her—the heterogeneous huddle of dishes, the drooling syrup pitcher standing in a sticky saucer, half-consumed jars of molding fruit, dabs of food that she had conscientiously saved thinking they might be used in some economy dish that she never quite knew how to make.

Lydia wiped her eyes. She sighed. The shelf papers needed to be changed—a messy job. She despised disorder but it was a leech she could not shake off though she tried frantically, trotting about, tossing things out of sight, sweeping at seven o'clock or four. Planlessly, she had a helter-skelter confidence that all would one day be arranged on a neat routine. Meanwhile, she closed the cupboard doors and felt better.

The potatoes were bubbling hard. She turned the fire lower. Gas was so much better than having to build a fire in the range, but it did cost like the dickens. She pushed the thought of gas aside, not wishing to remember that the bill hadn't been paid. Thank goodness Sam's poultry check was due tomorrow. Instantly she felt ravenous. The check always seemed to justify a good meal. She lifted the alarm clock from its face (it refused to run in any other position) and saw that it was almost six. Good. She could probably catch Polly at the office. She scurried to the telephone, humming, "All things are ready, come to the feast. Come, for the table now is spread!" Lifting the receiver from its hook was like lifting the nagging supper problem from her annoyed shoulders. "Just get anything that looks good, honey," she told Polly, and hung up.

A glad anticipation lighted her face. She had come across her old English literature book while cleaning today and her eyes had fallen on, "She was an angel of delight," an old favorite. There were other treasures too to be rediscovered, Browning's *My Last Duchess,* and Milton's *Comus and Lycidas*—she had always loved that. She would wrap up in an old sweater, drag a rocker on the porch and read poetry with one eye on the sun as it sank into the lake.

The screen door slammed and there was a quick smooth step in the hall. Her stomach contracted sharply. It sounded like Kenneth. Big-eyed, she rushed forth.

"Oh, hello John." She tried to keep disappointment out of her voice. "Your step is so much like Ken's that for an instant I thought— Sit down."

The threadbare skeleton whom she had not seen for six months dropped to the piano bench, struck a chord or two, sprang up and paced the room. "Oh. Oh—" the narrow lips twitching, "you expecting him? I heard he was gone. Gone with Sullavan's Show."

"No, I wasn't expecting him, not until next month. How are you getting along?"

"I'm alive yet," he snarled in self-pity, "though it's a w-wonder. Been s-sick all winter and broke, they w-wouldn't pay me, working l-like a d-dog and sick as a d-d-d-dog and Marfacks wouldn't pay me!" Marfacks were distant cousins, a rich, narrow, ignorant, insulting and miserly clan who had taken him in for what little work there was left in him. "I tell you, Liddy, you don't know how it is to be without a home or a person in God's w-world who cares whether you live or fall in the gutter and d-d-die like a tramp!"

Lydia twisted her hands. He was like a ghost come to ruin her party. "Now John don't talk that way! I'm your sister and I care what becomes of you. If only—" She hesitated, still terrified of the domination of her older brother—"things had been—different—"

It was dangerous ground. His drunkenness he carried like a chip on his shoulder, daring people to blame it for his misery.

He whirled, scowling. "People don't understand, they're so righteous, so holy! Sam couldn't ever understand, that's why he won't have me here, I know all r-r-r-right!"

Lydia could not deny this. John's presence made Sam furious, but how could she turn her own brother out without a place to sleep or anything to eat?

"Are you going back out to Marfacks?"

"No, thank God! Bill Murphy thinks maybe he can use me, starting next week. Don't know what I'll do till then. Maybe I can sleep in the park now that it's warm, but the damp air makes my rheumatism worse."

"Now John you aren't going to do anything of the kind!" Lydia's voice was frantic. "You take one of the girls' rooms till then."

"I suppose I'll have to," he snapped. He moved kitchenward with the agile grace of a cat. "Got anything in the house to eat?"

"Polly will be home pretty soon with stuff for supper."

He grabbed three withered yellow stalks of celery from their bowl on the kitchen table. Munching them, he filled two slabs of bread with cold gravy. Sighing, Lydia reached into the cupboard for plates. Through the window she could see the slant gold fingers of the sun still touching the water.

To complicate matters, Sam came in early from work that night, and Stew and Dan came home for supper with the girls. Lydia knew they couldn't help a furtive shame for their uncle, and their loud whoops of welcome touched her. How boisterously brave they had learned to be. How much they had to camouflage. Why this too? She felt guilty, helplessly responsible somehow.

"He ain't gonna stay, is he?" Sam asked, alert and suspicious. He set his lunch bucket—a tin syrup pail— on the kitchen cabinet and rolled up his sleeves as he went to the sink.

"Only for a night or two until he finds a place," Lydia said defensively.

To her surprise, Sam didn't sputter objections. About the corners of his lips there was a familiar twitching. He even began the chipper off-key whistling that indicated he was harboring a secret. Probably some new idea to spend time and money on, she thought impatiently. Well, if it kept him from fussing about John before Dan and Stew, she was grateful to it.

"Yessir," Sam remarked. "Yessiree by hellsky I've got a proposition now that'll have us on easy street inside of a month!"

Lydia's butcher knife paused in mid-air. At once her breath came a little quicker, her eyes hoped; from the architecture of habit she flung up swift familiar castles in Spain. "Oh Sam, what?" she asked eagerly. Then with the fingers of her subconscious crossed, "It's not—not another patent?"

Sam laughed heartily and kissed the back of her neck, scraping it playfully with his whiskers. "Not *a* patent—a whole carload of patents. Maybe two carloads! I'm goin' into the patent business!" He thumbed his suspenders, strutting foolishly. "I'll have you know I been hobnobbing with an ex-State Senator!" He said it again, for the reassurance it gave him. "A Senator!"

"Oh—Clete Parrish," Lydia said flatly. Her lips went thin with disapproval. She drained the potatoes and began to mash them vigorously. "Now you be careful what you're getting into."

"Sure, I know what I've always said about Clete," Sam admitted. "But I've done a little investigatin' and I think that Inventor's Exchange of his is all right. Why he showed me a pack of testimonials that'd knock your eyes out. He's placed quite a bit of stuff on the market for guys like me with ideas but no capital."

"Yes, but those awful fees he charges! Sam Andrews, if you give that pussyfooting crook twenty-five dollars when we need it so bad for other things I—I'll divorce you!"

"Hold on, who said anything about givin' him money? He just showed me how I could make a killin' contacting these backyard inventors and signing 'em up. That whole initial fee's mine—think of it Liddy, twenty-five bucks for every call! And I can do it, too. I know patents and these birds around the country know I know patents. That's why Clete wants me. Half the farmers I talk to ask my advice about patentin' something they've got hid away in a barn someplace, swear me to strictest confidence of course, when half the time it ain't worth a tinker's damn. They ain't a one that comes up to my crutch chair for practicability, y'know it?"

Lydia didn't answer.

"And if I can make 'em pay me twenty-five bucks to soft soap 'em a little, why shouldn't I?"

"Oh, I—I don't know what to say," Lydia wailed softly out of her confusion, her quick perception of what twenty-five dollars a day, possibly more, would mean to them. "It just doesn't seem *right,* taking people's money without guaranteeing them anything in return. Of course," she reflected, "if Clete does sell their stuff—"

"Sure he does! Yeah, he does turn a few deals. Anyway, he tries, and that's all you can promise anybody. Anyway by golly," with roistering cynicism, "might as well beat the other fella before he beats you. We've come out on the short end long enough."

"Now Sam don't talk like that! And—and is it *safe?*"

"Clete's got an air-tight contract. He used to be a lawyer too, remember—and we could have Polly check any hazy points. Nope, Clete knows what he's doin', he's a smart cuss." He gave his wife another kiss. "How about supper, kiddo? I'm hungry as a bull pup!"

Despite Lydia's warning, Sam couldn't refrain from announcing his new enterprise at the table, glancing significantly at his tramp brother-in-law. "Yep, a fella can't expect the world to make a livin' for him," he hinted. "These days a man's gotta hustle and have ideas and know the right parties. Now Senator Parrish says—"

"*Sen*ator Parrish!" John scoffed. "Well ain't we political, though?"

"Yeah, Pop," Ramey asked, stabbing a chunk of steak, "didn't he get deseated or dismembered or something?"

"He did nothing of the kind!" Lydia declared.

Sam wavered between indignation and amusement. "Hell, what if he was? But I don't think so. Anyway he's a bird the suckers go for, and by God I've come to the conclusion that I been on the sucker list long enough myself—'s time I hooked a few too!"

Polly suddenly could not eat. Lydia sputtered, her eyes hot with distress. But Jean laughed and flung one arm around Stew's neck. "You tell 'em Sambo! Suckers!" She was wearing Stew's diamond, but hoodwinking him shamefully when it came to other dates.

CHAPTER SEVENTEEN

SAM ENJOYED HIS new work, for it had to do with something close to his heart, a line he could handle with glib cock-sureness. And he was dismayingly successful. Although the Inventor's Exchange was an organization whose assistance to inventors was mostly hypothetical, it had on rare occasions been the route to market for a post-hole digger, a pneumatic valve, and several gadgets eventually sold through ten cent stores. The testimonials from these singular triumphs grew to such impressive proportions that crass indeed was the shade-tree genius who questioned them.

Sam's approach was psychologically good. A friendly chat about crops and weather. A couple of funny stories. Then when the victim's eagerness became apparent, he casually mentioned having heard of the invention. Kindly but firmly he warned that while he had been interested in the device to the point of making this trip, it might not be quite up to the standard his company required; therefore be it understood in advance that many were called but few were chosen. He then slapped the beginning-to-look-doleful inventor on the back and braced him with another story as they marched to view what would be deemed, after careful examination, a find! With enthusiasm so curbed as to seem the more genuine, Sam sketched its

159

possibilities and drew up the contract. Finally, with hoarded bills or a shakily written check in his pocket, he shook hands all around, gave gum to the children, bragged of his own, told another story, and bounced off down the road leaving them beaming and dreaming.

His unvarying triumphs surged in his throat. His guilt squirmed in his belly. "Damnit all," he told Lydia one night as they undressed, "I feel sorry for the poor cusses, damned if I don't. But then the poor ignoramuses wouldn't get anyplace just sittin' on their tails waitin' for that million. They're tickled to see me drive on the place, don't you know they are?" He flopped over on the bumpy bed, asking as always, "Care if I turn my back to you, honey?"

"No, go ahead," Lydia answered. "Well I tell you I'm in a muddle about it. I don't know which is worse, to take people's money they're actually anxious to give you, or —or not take it and not have any to pay our creditors with." She twisted about, restless with her misgivings. "And it doesn't hurt people to dream. I hate to imagine what our life would have been like if we hadn't always had some mirage to look to over the horizon. Funny— always thinking the next one would be real—wealth and good clothes and a nice home and everything the kids wanted."

"Well now kiddo it ain't over yet! I been figgerin'. Why can't we really start swinging some of this stuff onto the market? Why can't I go to Mr. Cudahy, the big shot packer, with that new meat saw and say, 'Looky here, Cuddy, if this ain't the best damn' saw you ever saw you ain't never seen a saw!' "

Lydia laughed. They rolled over in their comical night-shirts and kissed each other across the barrier of fat abdomens.

Sometimes Jean was drafted into the service of her father. "Now you ain't doin' a damn' thing, come drive for me today. It's tough I tell you, drivin' all day in the hot sun without somebody to spell me off. I ain't as young as I used to be, don't you know I ain't?" This remark would be directed at Lydia. He would frown and rub his legs. "It's getting me, this driving. Wish I had a little ranch where I could raise frogs for market. They's money in that. If a man had a place of his own he could quit hammerin' the roads and rest and raise frogs."

Jean often balked, but Lydia was always willing to drop her housework and go with him, reading a magazine while he made his calls, proudly contrasting her dapper man with a hulking overalled farmer or some greasy mechanic. The second-hand Chevrolet Sam had dealt for seemed a limousine after the Chicken Coop. They had money now for restaurant dinners instead of the paper sack lunches of chicken-buying days. The patent business was certainly more pleasant and profitable. If only—only . . . She smiled and bowed graciously to the gaunt woman in kid curlers who had darted out of the farmhouse and was vigorously pumping water into a slop jar. Ah yes, the patent business was far more pleasant and profitable.

Much as Sam enjoyed the company of his wife, Jean had distinct pragmatic values. "I love to have Mama along and it does her good to get out," Sam confided, "but you're the big help. You turn the trick lotsa times, don't y'know you do?"

"Sure," Jean said, deftly slicing a corner. "Whatcha think I flirted with that dumb looking filling station guy for if it wasn't to get his do-re-mi? I need a new dress."

Sam chuckled. "Well I guess you earned it."

At such moments Jean and her tyrant father felt very chummy. But much of the time they were hotly warring. Jean's engagement furnished no asylum for Sam's constant fears. Jean did not at once begin embroidering doilies or in Stew's absence hie herself dutifully to bed. She simply tossed her ring into the cluttered basket on the sewing machine and sailed off to the usual dance. And when Sam threatened, "Now it's either gonna be one thing or the other—you settle down and stop this chasin' with other fellas or—or by God you'll send that ring back!" she retorted, "Okay, if it means taking the veil at my age it ain't worth the price."

Sam was rebuffed. Grieved. Acutely worried. He wanted her to hang onto Stew Vold. He fished the gem up from a snarl of buttons and thread, stuck it on his little finger and adjusted his glasses. "It's worth a damn' good price if you ask me!" he said, wiggling his hand to catch the sparkle.

"Sure, that's all that's eatin' you—how much money Stew's got!"

"Please try to see our side of it, Jean," Lydia would intervene. "We've told everybody you're engaged. It just doesn't look right for you to step out whenever Stew's back is turned! What—what if he finds out?" She too had sketched hopeful little plans for the family—Jean's settling down, marrying well; Sam's getting enough ahead to go into a business of his own (there *might* be something in raising frogs, silly as it sounded); Polly's getting her chance to go away, thus breaking gently with Dan. Oh why couldn't life ever fit the precise little patterns her mind was forever snipping for it?

There was flaring up of argument, ending always with Jean's angry dash upstairs. Or she would corner Polly to demand, "I didn't ask 'em to blab to everybody I was engaged, did I? They could hardly wait to spill it down at church and over to Grandma's, Dad ballyhooin' about the diamond being a carat and a half and how Stew's president of a chain of Federal Reserve banks and all that BeeYes. If they'd pipe down, quit acting like the public might think he wasn't gonna do right by me or something, I might really *get* married and put 'em out of their misery!" Her little deep-pressed eyes stared out into the blossoming cherry tree. "Only Lord knows what his swell outfit will think of a dumb bunny like me. Or of the folks! But the folks are so crazy for me to marry him they don't even consider that."

Polly hunched on the bed in sympathetic if slightly acrid listening. "They don't want me to marry Dan," she said.

"Well if they think I'm gonna sit home all summer and crochet pillow cases they're sadly mistaken!"

They were. Sadly and definitely.

There was for Polly something of distorted delight in helping Jean make her escapes, in brightly lying and covering for her, despite the fact that she too would have been glad had Jean docilely married, or at least acted as if she were going to marry Stew. It was one way of assuaging the constant blundering wounds that Sam and Lydia dealt her through Dan, a small secret vengeance for their pitifully obvious attempts to steer her toward the very

channels in which she had always insisted her life must
go. She had perhaps too vigorously pointed out her goal;
now they were hell bent to see that she didn't change
it. Certainly not for Dan who had no "future." And all
the while they were in deep dark collusion to hide their
concern. Lydia, at least, was very nice to Dan with a
solicitude that acknowledged his inadequacy; Sam dropping hints about hard times and how "It's a hell of a job
to feed a family these days. A man better be damn' sure
he's got something ahead before he gets too stuck on a
girl, or first thing he knows it'll be twins and the rent to
pay—ain't that what you say, Scott?" Brazenly offered
advice, beneath which ran a fumbling concern. Infuriating
as Sam was—he only wanted to warn them.

Dan would quietly agree. Then Sam, as if recognizing
that by his very admonitions he had himself confessed to
failure, would begin a gasconade of his present partnership. "See what I made in a couple hours' fast talkin'. Not
bad for an old has-been like me, huh? Guess you young
liars ain't got much over us old ones, after all!" And he
would pocket the roll and ask with an arch pretense of
casualness, "How many cars you sell last week, Dan?"

There would surge up in Polly a wild twist of wrath and
pity, making her want to do physical violence to her
father. Run along, gloat over your late, not so fairly won
marbles, little boy, but oh leave Dan and me alone!

"Honey, don't. I can be hurt only if you are," Dan
told her as she perched crying beside him on the hard
rail of the porch. His tone was that one of special lightness he used for the family. And it was true, the pain in
his eyes was not for himself, but for her.

"But I am hurt, and you should be too!" she cried
fiercely.

She resented his calm tolerance; it was as if she must
make him realize the injustice that was being done both
of them. The folks were using every means to get Jean
married to Stew, not because Stew was smart but because
Stew had money. They were just as zealous, though more
cautious, in trying to keep Polly from marrying Dan, because he hadn't. And this maneuvering was grotesque in a
family that had always dreamed its own extravagant way
to wealth. Grotesque too, because neither of the two was

rich. But most grotesque, most touchingly sad and strange and maddening of all because these parents who were like children themselves now strove to guide or haul the girls into those paths which would be best for them, in the manner of conventional parents alert for the welfare of their young!

And not only was it grotesque, it was a ludicrous effrontery to Dan. Barbarous, after all he had done for them this winter—the smoked ham and pails of cream and dozens of huge white eggs he had lugged in, the chickens and pheasants and ducks which he and Sam had dressed together in the basement. Oh, the fool! The sweet, gallantly ignoring fool to sit there so imperviously smoking, claiming he couldn't be hurt.

Paradoxically, at moments like these, she felt a half-savage, half-tender yearning to make it up to him. She flung herself into his arms, this night, and began to kiss him with parted lips, babbling, "Dan—Dan!"

She felt the swift responsive upleap of all his muscles, his quick intake of breath and the sudden hammering of his blood. And then he pulled away and his face, in the spattered moonshade of the vines, was white.

"Polly—don't!" he whispered. "For God's sake, don't."

She smiled at him. Her body, even her brain, seemed dipped in a winy blur, but all her senses were awake, alert, and grasping this flash of time. The harsh cut of the rail behind her back, the moon-painted porch with its goblin dance of leaves, the drenching sweetness of the cherry tree, the sound of cars thrumming by. It was like that night in the bedroom at Kay's—the sudden drowning burst of awareness, the shock of wanting and knowing that she was wanted, despite what he had said.

She said, "Dan listen—I love you. I've never been a smug little priss about things, but I always thought I'd wait, I'd want to wait, that there was something tremendously important about just—waiting. But now I—I don't know!"

He didn't answer. He made no move toward her.

"It would be different if we had any kind of set-up at all," she rushed on, "but everything's against us. Even the folks are against us now. And we love each other. We're—we're all we've got!"

"If you do love me, Polly, don't talk like that. Don't even think about it. Please."

"Don't you want me?" she whispered.

"Want you? My God." He laughed. Then he said, "No, I don't want you. Not like that. I don't dare." He stood up and kissed her lightly on the forehead. "Good-night, you little Kvasir. You'd better go in now or your dad'll be at the door."

CHAPTER EIGHTEEN

POLLY WENT STUMBLING upstairs. She stood on the landing a minute, sobbing under her breath and listening. The folks' bedroom door clapped shut, there was the creak of springs as Sam's heavy body crushed them, then a low drone of voices. A breeze flapped the curtain at the landing window into her face. She clawed it aside and looked out, down upon the car at the curb, at the man who bent, crank in hand, his fist jerking, while there came the taunting rasp of an engine that won't start.

One curl kept flopping in his eyes. He paused to push it back with the angry gesture of a child, and it was then that Polly started back down the stairs to him. He wouldn't take her along. How could he? Perhaps the car wouldn't go at all and he'd have to leave it shamefully here on the street and thumb a ride home. (Dan Scott! He who had first sailed up with such splendor, turning the neighbors' eyes.) But she could at least huddle by— show him and Dad and the whole listening block that whatever his status, he was still her man.

And it was suddenly, miserably, akin to something that had been before. The fierce loyalty. The achingly high head as she had gone walking with boys of genius or nonentity, but misfits, aliens to the kind of men who swarmed around Jean. Even Dan's sweet inordinate idolization put him on common ground with those others who had offered up their humble, utter devotion. Was he not then the superior young god whose choice of her had been such triumph?

She didn't care. He *was* more splendid than other men. Tonight they would elope in a rackety car and be married on nothing. She wept as she ran; she was Lydia now, all eager and desperate with hope and love.

But at the lower twist in the stair she clutched the rail, for she heard the loud beat of the engine. The gears cried out.

She crept back up to her room, cautiously, feeling the surface of wallpaper, knob and sill. This blind pawing back to the safe bleak clutch of her room. Sick-mad as she'd gone at Sam's cursing abuse that had met them again tonight at the door, she was only sneaking with self-detestation back along the same old alleys to her hole. Was it always to be so?

She stopped an instant where the ceiling dipped, shrank before her door, staring in upon the stupid grotesquerie of her painted furniture, upon which an idiot moon smirked in frail white rays. Would she ever actually escape this place, either to follow her dream or her man? Maybe she'd be an old maid, trudging brightly back and forth, back and forth to work rain or shine, joining little business girls' clubs and withering to a husk of all that she'd stormed to be.

Shuddering, she pressed her head against the sill. Dan wouldn't marry her until he had something to offer, or she'd had her chance. He had made that clear in the park tonight.

Under the wide spaces of the trees she had lost the cramping restlessness that had knotted her nerves all day. Feeling suddenly young and exultant, she had run from him, kicking up her heels and snorting like a wild pony.

She had hidden from him in the echoing vastness of the pavilion, in one of the dressing rooms where the celebrities of her childhood had once awaited entrance. The ghosts of the great were in this place—William Jennings Bryan, Teddy Roosevelt, Eugene Field. For those august presences the scrolls and curlicues had been wrought. Now Chautauqua was over. No one would ever follow. The pavilion stood rattling and deserted, rotting away.

Dan's feet crunched on the sanded aisles. She heard him begging, "Polly don't—please honey, don't waste what little time we have like this!"

She sprang across the platform at him from behind, pouncing on his back and uttering a little cry of pain and joy and pity. They went down together in their light clothes, into the sand and dust. "Dan—" she murmured as they bitterly kissed—"Dan, I do love you!"

For an instant he had lain half across her, his face curious in the gray half-light. Then with that brusque little laugh he used so much lately, he hauled her to her feet and brushed her off, scolding softly, "No, Polly—no."

"You think I'm awful, don't you? You think I'm wild and bad!"

"I think you're wild and sweet." His big hands curved her cheeks. They were trembling. "But I won't let you do anything you'd regret. Do you hear?"

She nodded wretchedly. "Dan, if we were married—Oh, I'm so sick of it! So sick of all this. College behind me and nothing ahead, and the folks so mean. If we were married—"

He led her out across the grass to the fountain, and he washed her face and her scraped elbow with a handkerchief which he held in its spray. The bowl was bud-clotted and slimy with moss. The leaping iron nymph had the face of an imp.

"But we're not married, and we're not going to be for a while," he said.

"You've changed. You used to beg me to marry you," she accused. And she could have torn out her tongue at the look in his eyes.

"Sure. I know," he said patiently. "But I had more confidence in what I could offer then. Besides, I wouldn't think of letting you marry me to spite your folks—or to stand up for me."

"It wouldn't be that!"

"It would be partly that."

"You don't want me!"

"I do want you. I want you now. I want you so damn'

bad. But I've promised myself to try and make you happy, and you won't be—not that way. Not until you've had your chance."

So it had been unjust, so hideously unjust, Sam's tirade, his bellowing their private agony for all the street to hear: "Now see here Scott, I'm gettin' damn' tired of you takin' Polly off in the grass along the lake every night! By God you ain't able to marry her and support her and I'll be damned if I'm goin' to stand for this lollygaggin' every night!"

Now Polly became strong with the tigerish anger that had only left her shocked and impotent before. She must rush downstairs and kill her father! Split that shiny little bald skull, bruise and bloody those prune-fat lips, trample that hairy chest and protuberant tummy with her tall wild heels.

It seemed the only possible way to annihilate her own flaccid inadequacy. To mash out the nasty little worm of relief that had crawled through her consciousness at realizing that Dan wouldn't have let her do other than she had done. All to no avail anyway, her dashing after him, tearful and frenzied and sacrificial, begging him to take her away. *But she hadn't gone!* She hadn't defied Sam. Only slunk upstairs to cringe now, beaten and baffled, before her door.

And yet—asked her devil—what do you want? To get away! To get away from here! Of course. Away from them all, even Dan. For he is no longer the impersonation of splendor. He is the grown-shabby spectre of romance. This was not romance you knew tonight—it has stopped being romance long since and grown into something else, terrific and perilous. Need. Blood with earth and a star in it. The stuff of which marriages and mistakes are made.

She went on in, undressed, crying with a spent tiredness. She had resented Dan's waiting for her to weaken, and she had resented his change, his unwillingness to take advantage of that weakening when it came. But now she was grateful, in a sad shamed little way, for his strength.

CHAPTER NINETEEN

SAM SAW LITTLE of Dan now, and denied opportunity for that baiting inquisition which served to reaffirm his own righteousness in matters of family and finance, he turned his bitterness upon Polly, grumbling, hinting, disparaging. However much Dan had done for them, he felt honestly that his paternal rights were being abused.

He could not finger down to the roots of his disturbance. He was incapable of dragging forth to the light of tempered reason his change in attitude toward the debonair Dan who had first come to the house and the Dan who came now, sunburned from going hatless, in an immaculate shirt and excellent trousers for which, however, he had no matching coat. But the source of his agitation was the fear that this man who was no good because he could not make or keep money, might be planning to steal Polly, the mental prize of his crop of children. She who, bearing the seeds of Lydia's greatness, could give back to Lydia the ripe fruit that he, Sam Andrews—who was no good because *he* could not make or keep money —had stolen in stealing her. The wheel of life's mistakes kept turning, but it had to be stopped!

Sometimes Polly flared back, but mostly she steeled herself to ignoring her father while Lydia wiped her eyes and suffered. Why couldn't Dan just—just make his magnificent gesture and then step out of the picture? Why did he have to let Polly keep on *loving* him? Poor Dan. Darnit! Why couldn't he have been rich and successful, able to persuade Polly not to go away at all, but to just marry him and live in a big house on the lake and write poetry?

Lydia's too the precarious task of preparing Polly for what might lie ahead. "Honey, don't be too hurt," she would venture as Polly stared blindly out the kitchen window after a difficult session with Sam. "Things will—work out. I just know they will. You might even get to leave like you planned last fall."

"That's a laugh!"

"Don't be too sure. Dad's doing so well with these patents, we're getting on our feet, we won't have to hold you back again."

"It's too late now. I don't even want to go."

Lydia winced. "That's because you're afraid of being disappointed again," she said, deftly skirting the real issue. "But I—I promise you won't be. Why don't you at least write the university about a job and ask Mr. Walcott for a loan? Now don't tell Dad I said so, but I—I might be able to help you a little myself."

"You?" Polly turned upon her mother a glance so incredulous, so tenderly amused, that Lydia felt with a shock how lightly this daughter, of all her children, must regard her capabilities.

Lydia began to gather up the litter of lunch on the table, her lips trembling in defiant hurt and confusion. It would be hard to deceive Polly. And with her helpless need for blaming someone for her ills, she again illogically fastened her resentment on Dan. He—monopolized Polly so. Shadowed her, couldn't let her alone. He must always be reaching for her, with his hands and with his eyes. When she darted upstairs he hovered about the hall until she came down, looking up with glad relief, as if only in her presence could he begin to live again. It was—strange. (Not the way Stew treated Jean, certainly! Stew with his cool superior fondness, his mocking indifference.) Was Dan engorging himself with Polly before he deliberately gave her up? Could Sam's ugly exaggerations have some foundation in truth? Oh, but of course not! Oh my goodness, what a monstrous— She had no words for that fearful possibility. It simply did not exist for her children. Through church and many warnings she had immunized her offspring from rampaging emotions under the moon. No! No! No!

"Yes, me!" Lydia replied. "I know I'm little more than a moron, that I can't cook or keep house and I believe in old fashioned things like church, b-but n-nobody can say I d-don't love my children!"

"Oh, Mom!" Polly cried, exasperated. She glanced at her wrist. A quarter of one, no time for hysterical heart talks and consolings. She snatched up her raincoat. "Nobody said you didn't love us. You'd do anything in the world for us, but this business of my getting away—how could you help?"

Lydia drew a deep breath to ease the constriction around her heart. "Would you be surprised if I said I'd been saving?"

"Surprised?" Polly laughed. "That wouldn't be a surprise, it'd be a miracle!" For an instant of ecstatic soaring she reasoned the miracle into reality. Those fistsful of bills Dad had tossed Mom all summer, his sheepishly vaunted checks which she endorsed and cashed—why couldn't she have sneaked away a five now and then, or a fifty?

Polly kissed her mother and went hopping puddles to work, weaving an extravagant fantasy of escape. She might claim she didn't want to go, but how small a spark it took to rocket her dreams to the moon!

As she neared town, Dan's familiar car whished around a corner and skidded to a stop at her feet. Heedless of the rain, Dan jumped out and hurried her to the opposite door. (She adored him for not being a window leaner, a "get-in" bawler.) "Where you going?"

"To work—and maybe away!" And she told him of her conversation with Lydia, concluding, "But Mom's saving sprees are about as numerous as Niobe's children, and as short lived. The minute we run short or Ramey wants a ball bat or Jean a new dress she'll trot to the fruit jar. I know, I've been on the receiving end so often myself." She laughed. "Dear Mom, wanting everything for all of us."

Dan looked at her an instant, not smiling. He had spoken to Lydia of this again a few days before, and now for the first time he felt the taste of sacrifice in his throat. "But this time maybe it'll be different. She—talked this over with me the other night. She wants this for you more than she's ever wanted anything." Unaccustomed as he was to dissembling, he found it oddly simple—and good. "It's because I feel so sure of it that I've been pulling strings today myself. What's the sense of selling cars for the Crescent Motor Company when I can be selling them in your town, right under your precious nose?"

"Dan, they've hired you?"

"Sure. They didn't think they needed another salesman, but by the time I got through talking they thought they needed two. Only I persuaded them I was as good as half a dozen."

"And they're paying you accordingly?"

"Well practically. It's commission."

She tried not to let him see how afraid she was. Dad had declared so often, "If they don't think you're worth a salary they don't think you're worth a damn." He would explode when he heard of Dan's change. "If that don't beat hell, givin' up a steady job where he's known for a fly-by-night proposition just so he can tag Polly every step! Well he needn't think he's gonna stay here and *sleep* with her, I can tell him that!"

Dan stayed at the hotel, and when he could no longer afford that, at Jordan's. Polly no longer dared invite him even to a meal when Sam was home, but to Sam's helpless indignation and over Lydia's tearful protests, on Saturday nights she tossed things into a bag and ran off with him.

They would be gone by sunset, roaring past the huddled boathouses fringed with docks, past hot dog stands that tossed a whiff of onion on the air, past the canvasshrouded old city steamer, bobbing at anchor with a weird and melancholy dip.

Back across the darkening platter of the water, town would twinkle into being. Charcoaled against the sky the hill-lifted roofs of the college, the square Presbyterian church tower, the steepled cross of the Catholics, and below these, pricking the trees, the rosy dusk, the myriad little lighted eyes watching them run away.

On they hurtled, through miles of silver darkness. Past occasional splatters of light where a band concert made festive Saturday night. Past it all, known briefly, joyously and with a vast benevolent pity for all who could not be one with them as they tore through the night in their noisy old car, lashed together by the wind and knowledge of the summer's going and their dream of parting which enhanced the hysterically perfect Now.

At last a wide glow in the sky and they were sailing down the old familiar streets of Crescent.

Dan was making little now, but he spent it all with a gallant flourish. Usually they dined luxuriously in a quiet hotel. But often after a bad week they must eat in some smoky, clanking café, and this was oddly sweetest of all, for from this earthy level Polly caught sharper visions of the heights to which she was soon (oh surely this time soon!) to climb. All things seemed radiant, all things possible. She would grip Dan's fingers across the cloth and declare, "You'd make a marvelous lawyer too—your way with words, the direct, straight-to-the-core way you have of looking at things. Think what we could do together! Me to do the fabricating, all the tricky embroidery, and you getting your teeth into the truth. Oh Dan, let's!"

"Hey you little giant killer, one thing at a time!"

"But we could. We could. Nothing's impossible!" She was beginning to believe it, for this very week the pieces had been falling into place. She had had a favorable reply to her application for a position at the university. George Walcott had grumpily admitted that he couldn't, but would, lend her a sum sufficient to make up for the deficit after Lydia produced the three hundred dollars she claimed to have. "Just this year though," he warned her. "If you can't do it in a year, after all I've pounded into your head during the last five you're hopeless." . . . "Oh I can, I will!" she had cried, aching with a gratitude that made her forgive all his harsh stupidities of the past.

Because it pleased her, Dan pretended to share her rhapsodic dreamings. Thus, as they ate or danced, they wrought their fantastic plans, draining each dream with a gluttonous hunger so intense that it began to seem real

even to Dan, who knew better. That instantaneously this
year would be gone and she a succesful attorney and Dan
in school on her earnings. "For we'll be married then,"
she confidently told him, "and you've already done so
much for me."

Married. To be married. It was what they really wanted
as they prowled the streets on their penniless Saturday
nights. They would pause before a dazzling room, a setting
for happiness, couched and tabled and book-studded, with
one good picture, a tall white vase and soft lights and
drawn blinds. Oh tormentingly near and bleakly far this
room, their kind of room! They wanted to have done with
dreaming. They wanted to be rich and successful and
married. Now!

Or they would stand before the jeweler's blazing torments of glassed-in diamonds. They would pause, hungry-
eyed and hopeful while with elaborate care Dan selected
hers. The largest, the most splendid. "Not one you'd have
to have a microscope to see, like Jean's." Since Christmas
Dan had felt a resentment for Stew that he could not
help. He was jealous not only of other men, but bitterly
jealous of what they could do for their girls.

"Why Dan," Polly defended, "Jean has a lovely ring!
And," coaxingly, "I'd be contented with a little one too if
I could have it now."

"No, honey, I haven't the cash, and I'll never give you
anything that isn't mine to give you."

But he bought her other things, blouses, powder, hose
—things she would need when she left. Once when she
had admired a hat, he guided her into the shining velvet
cubicle of shop. "My honey wants a new bonnet, Aunt
Mame," he informed the big-bosomed woman who came
peering at them through her spectacles. (He knew or was
related to nearly everyone in town.) The woman pressed
the stiff buckram crowns down upon Polly's head, exuding
sweet amusing flattery and accusing them of being secretly
married. And as they left, with their bulged-out sack, they
were bound by a new hush of pretending.

These small gestures of providing were precious to Dan
because of his driving, helpless desire to do so much
more; because he realized that this was as close to reality
as he would probably ever come. He was no fool. He knew

that in making it possible for Polly to go he was freeing her for a destiny that could never include him. Yet lest he weaken in his original resolve he must blind himself to that certainty.

Later they always went to the farm, and as they clattered over the wooden planks of the bridge, swerved up the lane and saw the big white house sleeping in majestic serenity, a glad excitement that was a sense of ultimate homecoming quickened in Polly. She loved this place and everything that went with it, even Kit who could be so patronizing and so lovely, even sullen, strange little Martin Chase! She wanted to embrace the land and the barns and the people with a frantic sweep of her arms. She wanted to hold them close and never lose them. And with a little inner cry of protest, she always remembered, walking across the damp grass toward the door, that this too was under the whip of her particular demon.

They had one week of halcyon days there toward the end of the summer after Dan, to Sam's gloating delight, had given up trying to sell cars in Gem Lake and gotten on mending roads. Sam was not delighted when Polly announced the concurrent vacation she had wangled out of George Walcott, but he was powerless to prevent her taking it. When he got home one night she was simply gone.

Polly awoke mid-mornings deliciously rested. More rested, she mused, stretching lazily on the good bed, than she could remember ever having been before.

Dan would have been up for hours, down at the culvert driving a team of mules and dumping big hunks of dirt with a shiny scoop affair. She would halloo and wave at him from the bridge, and he would look up, his teeth a white flash in the burned mahogany of his face. Then she would half leap, half scramble down, the concrete scraping her legs, and be caught in the sweaty strength of his arms. And his lips would be cracked and dusty, his chin like sandpaper, but their kiss a savage glory in the singing morning air.

"Love me darling, even dirty? Lord, you smell so sweet, you look so fresh!"

"I should, I feel wonderful. I slept the sleep of death. Kiss me again, then we'll eat."

While the mules nibbled grass they would sit in the shade of willows along the bank and eat the breakfast Dan's mother had packed—scrambled egg sandwiches, peaches, doughnuts, and coffee from a thermos jug. Then she would lie beside him while he smoked, one arm behind his curly head, the other around her, and she could feel the sound of his heart and of his breathing. The stream went by in liquid gabblings. The sky was hot and very blue. And there was a bird that every day about this time sang its wild little heart out in a nearby tree.

Finally she would rise and go from him to be with his mother, canning, cooking, talking woman talk. Or she would romp the fields in hoyden abandon with the children and their fat spotted pony, Twinkle, a terrifying creature which always bucked her off. But all day she would think of Dan, marking time till sunset when he should come up the lane, ravenous for food and her love.

After a great smoking supper they would sit on the porch with the family, talking, watching the night come down. Or they would walk up to the grove and back. Then when everyone else had gone to bed, when the stillness of sleep wrapped the whole farm gently, Dan would spread a blanket on the lawn and they would lie together on the hard earth. They lay upon the hard curve of the earth, and kissed each other until they dared not kiss again.

And Dan told her, "It's because I love you that I won't, my darling. You don't understand that—neither do I maybe, but that's the way it's got to be."

"But life's so short and time's so—crazy. I'm going away. What if something should happen? What if I never came back?"

"Or met somebody else? I've thought of that often enough, God knows!" He rolled over on his back. One hand, holding a burning cigarette, was across his eyes. What he said next was perhaps the most difficult thing he had ever said. "In that case I wouldn't want you to have any regrets. You—mustn't feel tied to me in any way." There was a long silence, and then suddenly he sat up. "But listen, you be careful! I'm no prize, but you won't meet other men like me. Anybody who could be here with you feeling the way I do at this moment and—and not—"

His face was tormented. "Oh hell! But you be careful, do you hear? You won't run into love like I've got for you twice in a week.

"Oh Polly—Mona—Kvasir—I do love you! I want to marry you and have children by you, a whole flock of them who'd look and be exactly like you, but it wouldn't matter if you couldn't have 'em or if you got fat and frumpy tomorrow because I love you—the wild little whatever-it-is that makes you you!"

It rained, their last night. For a long time they sat on the porch watching the lashing downpour. At length the wind changed, driving them indoors. Dan dumped some clean red cobs into the kitchen range.

"A fire at this hour?" Polly asked.

"I like a kettle on. Makes it cozy. Coffee?"

"No. Milk, I think."

The teakettle began to whine and sigh softly. In the pantry they found sardines and crackers and a thick-frosted cake. He split the fish, plastered them with mayonnaise and made clumsy cracker sandwiches. He portioned out the cake.

When they were finished, he stepped into the downstairs lavatory and ran water upon a soft new cloth. He smoothed her hair behind her ears, tilted her chin and washed her face and sticky fingers.

"Just what do you think you're doing?"

He kissed her lightly. "Getting you ready for bed."

From her perch on a tall stool she put her arms around his waist and pressed her cheek against the hard whiteness of his shirt. How fiercely beat a man's heart!

"Polly listen," he said, "we've been happy, but we've had so little time." He was smoothing her hair, making her drowsy. "Come sleep in my arms. No, don't look at me like that—I haven't changed, I just want you close to me, to feel your warm little body clinging to me one night of my life, that's all. Will you?"

"But—how could we?"

He led her to the door. It was a typical off-kitchen bedroom. Tiny and fitted only with a narrow steel bed and chair. Here Dan's mother snatched an hour or two of rest when she decided to cold pack corn into the night.

She put her fingers to her throat. "I don't want them to think I'm—terrible."

"They couldn't. They think you're the sweetest thing God ever put breath into. And my folks are funny maybe about things like this. Even if things were different between us, I think they'd understand. It's our last night, honey. It would be the perfect way to end it."

Three minutes marked the rain, the singing kettle, and the clock.

"Yes," she murmured, "it would be."

Suddenly she darted ahead, kicked off her slippers and held out her arms to him. He came into them, gathering her close, kissing her eyes as though she were a sleepy child. From the foot he pulled a soft blue comfort, knotted with white yarn, like stars.

The kettle sang. The rain laughed softly.

Once, much later, she stirred at the cautious touch of lips upon hers. She opened her eyes and smiled.

"Comfortable?" he whispered.

She nodded and went back off to sleep, knowing that he was right. Never again would she be loved like this.

CHAPTER TWENTY

LYDIA WIPED HER hands over and over on a dishtowel. It was hard to breathe, hard to think these days. "What do you intend to do this winter, Dan?" she asked.

"Work for the county until cold weather," Dan said cheerfully, shaking tobacco into a cigarette paper. "I can make twice as much that way as selling cars right now. Then Martin says he can get me in at the court-house issuing auto licenses. After that—well, I may have to pitch in and help my folks save their place."

"Save their place?" Lydia said incredulously. "You don't mean they're in danger of losing that lovely home?"

"It's become too much of a burden. They've come to the point where they think it'd be easier to just let it go. Maybe they're right, but I hate to see it. We were all born there, you know."

"Well, that's a shame. Your poor mother! That certainly is a shame." Lydia's eyes went dim in genuine sympathy, and an unreasonable feeling of personal loss. However little Dan had, there had been the comforting reassurance that anyway his folks were well fixed. She and Sam had even bragged about that Over Home, where the gods of estate held sway. And now—now the danger of Polly's marrying him was diminished even more, only—

"It just doesn't seem right," she said vaguely. "No, and

180

it doesn't seem right for you to be doing this for Polly when they need your help—when you need things yourself!" She watched him jerk the little bag shut with his teeth and tuck it into the neatly mended pocket of his shirt.

"Sam's making good money now, but it takes so long to catch up and—and then too—" Lydia hesitated. Some of Sam's inventors were kicking, demanding results. "This may not last long either. Nothing ever seems to last!"

Dan smoked thoughtfully for a minute, then opened the lid of the range and tossed in the unfinished cigarette. Lydia saw that there was no cheer on his face, that there was a kind of sickness in his eyes.

"Oh now Mom Andrews," he said in a falsely bright tone, "we wouldn't want it to, would we? Things have to change. It's best that they do." Or was it? Was it best that Polly go? Was this what Polly really wanted? But he knew that whatever the disillusionments in store for her, whatever regrets she was sure to have in scorning her other facile talents, she would never be content until she had at least taken a plunge at this more difficult thing. Only then could he hope to have her.

"I wish I could have gotten the money sooner," he said, "but it took longer than I expected for the loan to go through."

"Well that's a good thing, really. It wouldn't have done much good if the job had fallen through or something. I guess the poor kid still is skeptical of things working out." Lydia sat down by the table, her eyes staring toward the afternoon dazzle of the lake. "I—I get cold chills when I think of actually producing the money. I don't think she believes yet that I could have saved it. As for Sam, I may have to just tell him. If I handle him right he may understand."

"I hope so," said Dan. "I wouldn't want to buy his regard, but maybe he'd understand why I haven't appeared quite as affluent as I'd like to, or why I haven't gotten her a ring."

"I'm sorry about—about the way things have been this summer," Lydia groped. "Sam doesn't mean to be harsh, it's just that he's so worried all the time."

"I know. I don't blame him for the way he must have

seen things. But if you do tell him about this, don't let him think for a minute there are any strings attached. There's no debt of any kind, Mom. You know that."

He smiled and his tone was casual, but the shape of suffering was on his mouth. Lydia suddenly couldn't bear it. Tears darted down her nose. "You're—wonderful, Dan," she said thickly. "So much finer and bigger than we are—than any of us! She'll never find anyone else like you!"

"She'll never find anyone who's crazier about her," he admitted with a half smile. "You'd better tell her about the money tonight."

The lake was scarlet with sunset as Polly trudged home from work that night. Her arms ached from the sack of groceries Lydia had telephoned her to bring, but sight of the water put the old pounding glory in her throat. If you go or if you stay, there is always the lake. The lake always there, fulfilling itself in beauty. If she didn't escape, not even this time—and even now she could not honestly believe that she would—there would still be the lake. She had that of this town!

How little else. How few friends. Even as a child, a scared little too-bright runt, afraid of girls, quailing before boys, shabby and ashamed, taking refuge in a shining asylum of dreams: Sam would sell an invention; they would become fabulously rich; she and Jean would somehow have long curls and bicycles and velvet dresses and friends. Mother would move with quiet grace through a tall brick house flung up on a cliff of the lake. Or—she would grow up and be a great actress, a renowned poet, an artist whose pictures splashed across the covers of *The Ladies' Home Journal*. They would all fête her when she came briefly back, they would claim to have been her chums.

A panic of futility gripped her. Why couldn't anything be? Ever! Why had she been cursed with talent only to butt her head against a wall! This bait of a job, this fantasy of Lydia's funds—to what avail? At the last minute something would happen. She wouldn't believe again. And she wondered if she even wanted to. A lawyer. My God, what glory in being a lawyer? What did she want, where was she headed, anyway?

Lydia met her as she came across the sagging porch.
Lydia's eyes were dark with excitement. "Here, let me
take that sack. Goodness, I didn't know there'd be so
much to carry, but I was out of everything. Come—come
on in!"

Lydia set the sack down upon the open lid of the old
secretary, snatched a white envelope from one of the
cubby holes. "I've got the money for you, honey," she
whispered. "I drew it out of the bank."

Peering inside, Polly saw the neatly clipped green packet
of bills. Money! Why didn't I have you long before? Why
not that first time when I was all ready to go, sure of
what I must do—before Dan? She thought of him with
a sudden agony of realized loss. Dan was right. There
would never again be a man who loved her so unswervingly, in whose eyes, shabby and pretentious though she was,
she would still be the godhead, in whose arms, desired but
untaken, she could lie the night long.

Suddenly, fiercely, she regretted what had not been; he
should have planted her with his seed—settled the thing
so that they would have had to marry, had to fight their
way together. She was afraid—she had to face it—after
his constancy, his help, she was afraid of the long fight
ahead, alone.

"Honey, aren't you glad?" Lydia asked anxiously. "I—
thought you'd be so tickled. I thought I was doing the
right thing for you, I've always tried to do the best thing
for all you kids, but I don't know, I don't know why it
is that—that it's always wrong!"

And that, curiously, settled it. Oh, Mom, Mom, sad,
passionate, well-meaning failure of a darling! I'll go, it's
best that I go, that I escape, find something decisive in
this mad tumble of a driven but aimless life. I've got to
bring some pattern of accomplishment into the jumble,
the mad poverty-lashed people that we are!

"Of course I'm glad!" Polly cried. "It would be insane
to be anything else."

The car door slammed.

Lydia said, "Come on in awhile, Dan. You don't have
to go right back, do you?"

"Yeah," said Sam, blowing his nose. "Stick around
a few minutes. I gotta git back out on the road

now and hustle, so it'll be kinda lonesome for Mama."

Dan said nothing. But he turned and went toward the porch. His silent acquiescence irked Sam. "Sure, he'll probably hang around here all day mopin' and belly-achin' while me, her own father, has to get out and dig!" he fretted to Lydia when the screen door had closed.

Lydia glared at him. "Isn't it hard enough?" she demanded. "Isn't it *ghastly* enough without you starting that? I wish—" her voice was thick with a coming sob—"I wish now we'd let them, I wish we'd said to go ahead and get married and persuaded her to stay! To have her back— I—I'd give anything to have—her—back!"

"Yeah, and she'd of stayed too and then where'd she been at? We'd had a flock of grandkids to feed besides." Sam was grinning, attempting to be facetious. He tweaked his wife's nose, hauled her down from the top step and hugged her. "Snap out of it honey, she ain't dead or nothin'. This is what she wanted, ain't it? A lot better'n getting married and not amounting to a tinker's damn. Cheer up and tonight I'll take you to a picture show."

Inside, Dan stood looking helplessly about the Plain Room. Nothing had happened to it. It was the same. The worn linoleum, the knobby secretary with the lid flopped forward; the home-made book shelves and library table— unchanged. He crossed the register into the Swell Room, stood upon its brightly flowered rug. The davenport was placidly ready to be sat upon, its team mate the big chair, was open-armed. Kindly, stupid things that had held her, known her from childhood, only sat thus with blank good will, waiting. Waiting for voices and quarreling and laughter and all the myriad moods of her—or anyone. They couldn't care.

An hour ago she had been here and now she was gone. Every trace of her, bags and trunk and purse and upturned red hat, and her big eyes eager and half scared, and her tremulous mouth that had clung and yet been impatient to be gone. *An hour ago.* She had said, "Time goes so fast—I'll soon be back." And as in a dream, he had crazily tried to clutch time—the flesh of her body, the husk of her voice, the fleece of her hair, that was all of time and life to him, only to know with a snap of reality that she who was breath to his being was not to be held.

He knew now what she had meant, prattling her puzzle of time, place and awareness. When is *Now?* What are we doing *Here?* What is there about *This Moment* that makes it different from all the rest? He had not been able to answer. She had been close then and it had seemed merely an amusing figment of her fancy. Now he had the answer—his answer, anyway. For him *she was* time, place, and awareness. These unchanged rooms were no longer his Place. Time had stopped at ten o'clock of a September morning.

"Well," bellowed Mrs. Ashbaugh from the ramparts of her cement porch, "she's on her way."

"Yep," agreed Sam, "and so am I. Gotta make a livin' even if the kids do go off and learn a lotta folderols that'll probably make 'em too good for the old folks."

Lydia had gone into the house. She couldn't bear to talk to Mrs. Ashbaugh right now. How could Sam be so idiotic? She was angry and very lonely as she stood gazing with sad surprise about the cluttered rooms. She too had expected to find them changed in some sympathetic fashion. Where was Dan? Comforting him would have helped to salve her own wounds; it was disappointing and rather annoying not to find him here. Was she the only one who really cared? Men—they just barged off and left a woman alone to grieve.

And then she heard the balky starting of the car and visualized Sam jogging alone all day over country roads. Guiltily she darted across the room, lifted the curtain at the bay window and waved to him. He waved back. She laughed, to please him, dropped the curtain, and plunged back to the davenport for a good cry.

It came to her now that Dan was up in Polly's room. The poor boy! Poor Dad! Poor Ken, away from home! If only she could love and comfort them, make them happy forever.

At length Dan came downstairs. At sight of his face she begged, "Don't take it so hard, Dan. She'll come back to you. To all of us." He covered his eyes and turned his back quickly. "Don't—cry, son," she said. "Some day she'll be yours to keep!"

"God Mom, I wonder!" he said. Suddenly he kissed her and was gone.

CHAPTER TWENTY-ONE

THE CAR AT the curb choked away, and Lydia went tiny-stepping toward the porch. Indignation grimmed her lips and made her eyes flash. Mrs. Bateman made her tired! The very idea hinting that about Sam when her own puny husband was nothing but a bricklayer! Yes and he made eyes at the girls; believe me she could tell Mrs. Bateman a thing or two if she wanted to be mean—how Vee and Jean called him Paw Paw and Snuggle-up! How would *that* sound at Ladies Aid?

In spite of her anger, a wicked snicker broke her lips as she paced into the dusky interior of the house. But it was no wonder the ladies were hearing things—not with the way that hypocrite of a Clete was doing, putting the blame on Sam when those inventors got mad. *What's* going to become of us? I declare I don't know. If only he'd listened to me, not gone in with that pussyfooting crook in the first place. But no, he knew better.

Poor Sam! He'd struggled so desperately all these years, experimenting, never satisfied, always thrusting ahead, cocky, hopeful—and in the inevitable defeat consoling himself with the blatant boast, "Well that's that, but by hellsky nobody can say Sam Andrews ever beat a guy."

But now—driven to the wall, befogged by the alliance with a former Senator, vaguely conscience-smitten but glorying in the thrill of paying up old debts— Oh, it was all a mess! Of course, she reasoned as she tossed her white hat on the bed and ran a comb through the black muss of her hair—there was nothing those inventors could *do*. When grown men forked over money they should know what it's for. *We* never went around yelling for sympathy when we got beat. Then she corrected hastily, but Sam didn't beat a one of them! It's Clete! His end of the business is to sell those patents, it's not Sam's responsibility, all he agreed to do was enroll them.

She was lying down, wishing Jean would get home from Vee's and suggest what the dickens to have for supper, when there were steps on the porch and voices—Kenneth's, and the honeyed bubble of a girl's. Lydia began pawing under the bed for her shoes, calling, "Ken? Wait, I'll be right out! My, I'm so glad—"

But Kenneth, in dusty white linen, with a white hat on the back of his head, rushed into the bedroom, plunked his suitcase on the floor, and grabbed his mother.

"Listen Mom," he murmured, "Cele's had a row with her folks and the show's just closed. She's gonna stay here with us for a while. Okay?"

"Why yes, yes of course, honey," Lydia panted. "Just wait'll I get my shoes on and I'll go out." Flustered, she went forth to greet Celeste Lindell, the petite ingénue of Sullavan's show. "Take off your hat!" she babbled. "Sit down. Kenneth, why didn't you ask her to sit down? Haven't you any manners?"

"Heck, she ain't tied and there's plenty of chairs."

"*Ken*neth! Oh well, I guess you're used to his ways. Ken, take her bags upstairs and put them in Polly's room. My, it'll seem good to have somebody up there now that she's gone. I can hardly bear to pass that empty room."

"I'll bet it is lonely for you," Celeste sympathized. She was a honey-haired girl who toe-danced and sang lyric soprano. Offstage, she discarded her theatrical wings and became merely a pretty girl, easy to know. Lydia, still somewhat in awe of show people, was relieved.

Was she Ken's latest heart interest? Lydia wondered. How lucky it wasn't that slinky dark "heavy"! Celeste would be like one of her own girls. Yes, she was glad Ken had brought her home, even if Dad did raise the roof

—though maybe this time he wouldn't if only they both paid in a little.

If only— If only there weren't any more calls from irate inventors. If only Old Lady Henniper stayed away. If only Uncle John didn't come whining around. If only Jean didn't get balkish. If only Sam could get a regular, respectable salaried job on the road again.

If only—!

Lydia sat beaming, but her hands twisted convulsively in her lap.

When Sam extricated himself from the complications of the patent business he had fifty cents and a million-dollar idea. Ironically, this was destined to be his last great brainstorm, his final contribution to civilization, one that was very real, practical, and soon to be in widespread use. He knew it. Knew it with every ounce of his fat little being, with a conviction that ran electrically through his bones, leaving him charged and almost sick with hope.

One of the absurdities he had encountered in his snoop for patented treasure was a remarkably ugly doll whose eyes were red buttons of self-illuminating glass salvaged from a junked automobile. Sam had no interest in the toy, he even regretted having to take its creator's money. But the principle it involved, the wicked red glass gleam of its eyes haunted Sam's fertile brain. That glass was magic stuff. Why couldn't it be used for roadside signs?

He went to the junkyard and got himself a pocketful of the gleaming pebbles. There he encountered Simon Griffith, the great Welsh saint of the church, a man with the face of a gargoyle, the slow sure brain of a craftsman, and the often quite foolish generosity of a truly religious man.

It would have been the same had Sam run into the town's most notorious scoundrel. Fortunately it was Simon Griffith whom he buttonholed. "What d'you think of it, Simon, y'ole devil you?" he concluded, tossing the grease-crusted pebbles from palm to palm.

"Brother Andrews," Simon averred in his soft slow brogue, "you have hit upon something that will revolutionize advertising in this country."

"Y'really think so, huh?" Sam asked humbly, filled

with a flooding hope. Somehow this manifestation of faith
from Simon meant more than the too glib marvelings of
fellas like Judge Bellamy and other big guns to whom he
had trotted for confirmation of genius so frequently in
the past. He thought of how Simon, with a family of his
own to support on meager earnings as a plasterer, had
helped Jean go to conference, offered Polly money for
college, and often, when Andrews' fire and food were low,
insisted that they go home with his brood for Sunday
dinner. Sam suddenly wanted to share his coming wealth
and fame with such a man.

"Say, how'dja like to get in on it?" he blurted. "How'dja
like to help me figger it out?" His tone became assured.
"Make some models, get a big outfit like Dutro-Corbett
of Chicago interested in it, get some backing, I tell you
we'd make a killin'." He blew his nose. "You've been
damn' good to us, Simon, and by golly if I can put you
into something big why shouldn't I? What d'ya say?"

Simon wiped his streaming face with a blue handkerchief, studied it a moment, and then repocketed it. "Brother Sam," he said with his grave smile, "you can count on
me to help you in any way I can."

For two weeks they worked in the Andrews basement,
bending old tin into shape, gluing and screwing, drawing
their wobbly letters with a pencil, Sam fretting, "Damnit,
wish Polly was here to do the printing for us." A stomping
that shook the floor above came down to him, the beat of
Ken's foot at the piano, and the unmelodic plinking
thunder of his hands. "Ken!" he bellowed up through the
register. "Cut out that Goddamn' racket and get down
here, see if you can't be some help to us!"

"Oh, for cripe's sake," Ken snarled, shrugging up from
the bench. "No peace around here at all. If I'd known
he was gonna be home all the time messin' around I'd
never have brought you here, Cele. C'mon, give papa a
hug, you sweet little hoofer!"

"But Ken you should help," Celeste always pleaded.
Her eyes were like great blue flowers. Her lips were full
and red, tremulous and sweet.

Kenneth loved her, and it was unlike anything he had
felt for the Kitty-darlings of the past. He believed that if
he were to lose her he would die. And that he was in

constant peril of losing her, he knew. There were things
she hadn't told him; her eyes held troubled secrets she
refused to share. She had created for him an acute problem. He must—and soon—get a job so that he could
afford to marry and provide for her. He wanted her for
himself, out of this house where Sam begrudged their
every bite, where Lydia went around anxious and misty-
eyed and Jean (as if *she* ever turned her hand to help!)
mocked "home-again-Ken," fought cattishly with Stew,
and hooted vulgarities.

He was sorry he had brought Cele here, but he had
been afraid to let her go elsewhere lest the thing he feared
would keep her forever from him. So overpowering was
this concern, so zealous the change she had stirred in him,
that he was actually spending a part of every day apply-
ing for jobs. It filled him with frustrate despair to learn
that there were no jobs to be had, and if there were, he
had slight chance of getting one. These business men who
had known him all his unstable life could not realize the
love-wrought miracle. That now, since Cele spoke of
leaving the stage anyway, he was willing to plod along
in some dull estimable niche of small town citizenship.

His father's voice raged up again, and he went below
to lend a hand to hammer and brush, screw driver and awl.

At last it was done. After much experiment and dis-
carding, the thing was finally finished. Simon himself lent
Sam the money to go to Chicago with their ugly duckling
of a swan of a sign. It said, mundanely enough, BUY AT
BROWN'S, in crudely affixed, quavering rows of gems,
but in the black of the basement, licked by the white
tongue of Ramey's Boy Scout flashlight, BUY AT
BROWN'S became a flaming message.

Into Chicago Sam chugged. Into the offices of the
Dutro-Corbett glass company he strode, straight into the
private sanctum of Camden Corbett, himself. There he
was graciously, even cordially received, a circumstance
which neither surprised nor particularly impressed Sam.

"Course I got it covered," he lied smoothly this day to
the pink-faced man behind the desk. "Got the patent
applied for—"slapping his knee—"but if you people are
interested—"

Early in the days of his genius he had actually taken

this precaution and suffered a constant vigil lest someone steal his idea. As far as he knew, no one had ever even tried. Now such wariness seemed to him but the mark of the amateur. Honest to God veteran inventors like himself knew better than to fork over patent fees until they had a bite or two.

The Dutro-Corbett people were interested, as he had known they would be. Big men were always interested in his ideas. Seldom to the point of parting with any cash, but—interested. This time, however, things happened with whirlwind rapidity. When, three hours after his interview, Sam found himself escalating streetward with his newspaper-wrapped sign in one hand and a check for five hundred dollars in the other, he was jubilant.

"Well by God," he chuckled. "By hell and—and by damn, they didn't waste no time! Yes sir," he breathed, trotting trance-like into the street and pausing a moment, his ruddy little face uplifted to gray stones—and stars— "there's an outfit that's gone places because they saw what they wanted and grabbed it. An outfit that's goin' places bigger yet 'cause I showed 'em the way—'cause I'm gonna take 'em there!"

He glanced again at the check, and stuffed it in his pocket. He'd start home tonight, take Lydia a new dress, tell her to start building that house on the lakeshore 'cause when he got those new models built with the right kind of tools and metal and stuff that Cam Corbett had advanced him the money for, well by the great gallopin' Jehoshaphat, they'd have the world by the tail with a downhill pull! They could have any damn' thing they wanted. Yes, and Simon Griffith could too!

The rent was again past due, the utilities company threatening disconnection, winter blowing its first chill down their backs. Mr. Timmet, whose prices were so high that only the rich, and the very poor who must have credit, could trade with him, now took their grocery orders with an uneasy insuck of breath. Crouching across the counter he would wheeze at Ramey or the angry Jean, "You tell your papa to come see me, will you? Tell him I wanta have a little talk." Old Lady Henniper came almost daily, prowling their premises, shaking her hooded

head over the state of the garden, the lawn, the several
clumsily patched windows, and—ears pricking to the saw's
rasp and the joyful or despondent curses in the basement
as Sam wrestled with his angel—suspiciously prodding,
"Hain't Mr. Andrews working?"

"Yes, Mr. Andrews is working!" Lydia informed her
testily, eyes furtive toward the stairs lest Celeste come
down.

"Then it seems he oughta pay me something, times is
hard."

"As if we don't know that!" Lydia muttered. "Mr.
Andrews is working on something that will keep him home
for a while, but you'll get your money, don't worry."

Yes, and your wreck of a house too!—she thought with
triumphant asperity. Oh to get out of this miserable place.
To have a home of their own. To not have to go through
this time after *time*! But it did seem as if Sam could have
taken a little of that money to salve their creditors, to
spare her this.

"We-ell," the crone gnawed dubiously at her drooping
lip, "your boy home again and with a girl too, I hear, and
that daughter—Molly—"

"Polly!" Lydia corrected in disgust.

"Her off at law school, it don't seem right, none of your
children working, and taking outsiders too when a poor
old lady like me—"

"Oh you don't know a thing about our affairs!" Lydia's
voice shook with indignation. "You have no idea, simply
no—no con*cep*tion of our problems and no idea of our
plans!" She whirled and snatched up the broom that sloped
against the piano. Her knuckles gripped white about the
hard wood of its handle. She began to sweep. "You'll get
paid!" she panted, hacking vigorously at the rug. "You'll
get your money!"

When the spectre had vanished Ramey came in, munching bread and peanut butter. "Old Faithful been spouting
off again?" he grinned.

Lydia laughed. "Oh she makes me so mad! She makes
me sick!" She lowered her voice and frowned toward the
ceiling, "I hope Cele didn't hear. The poor kid, Dad makes
it miserable enough for her as it is."

"Yeah," said Ramey, picking up his tarnished second-hand trumpet, and blowing a few mournful toots, "I like ole Cele. Wish she'd marry Ken. Wish she'd quit hearin' from that other fella."

"What—what other fellow?" Lydia asked.

"Oh some bozunkus she gets letters from from home." He blared forth, *I ain't got no-boody and no-b-b-b-ooody cares for me!* "Gets 'em down at general delivery, I seen her. Heard her and Ken fightin' about it one night. Guess that's why he's so boo-hoozit half the time."

Oh, thought Lydia—oh—dear! That—that wasn't fair of Celeste. Not when they were keeping her and all. Poor Ken! He and Sam were quarreling so violently now too. Poor Sam, confident and yet so agitated, so fatally sick with apprehension lest this enterprise fall through. Poor— yes, poor Cele! She loved the girl, and Cele did everything she could to help. Who could tell what the child had been—and was going—through? . . . And poor Jean— Jean and Stew, quarreling whenever he came up from that Illinois bank on weekends, not laughing, playing their idiotic pranks any more—Stew had changed; Jean staying home, with scorn on her lips and secret, disconcerting stars in her eyes—Jean, why do you sometimes weep at night? I have passed your door and heard the bitter choke of your tears. . . . Poor Dan, who came no more. And Polly —poor lost Polly—out there. Drinking what black potion of disillusion and despair? Her letters were strange with an unspoken sickness of spirit. She was frightened and there was none to comfort her. Lydia knew—she knew! Oh Father which art in heaven, be with us, give us hope and harmony and strength. And there in the shabby sunlit room she wept, Lydia wept for her children.

Through it all—through a thousand tribulations and furies—Sam worked. Worked with fanatic zeal and wom-anish particularity, with hopes and misgivings whose mer-ciless flagellations surpassed any he had ever endured. This his *opus magnus,* his *nonpareil.* He had too long chased the apples of Hesperides not to know when he was at last within range of them. No zig-zag lettering now. He hired a sign painter. No clumsily affixed junkyard buttons, but quivering snakes of refulgent glass. And lest BUY AT BROWN'S fail to prove a worthy handmaiden of such a goddess as this new patron saint of all signs would be, he sweat over a hundred slogans and at length whimsically decided upon a tribute to the store which had so faithfully fed them during all their periods of want:

IT'S TIME TO TRY TIMMET'S
Green Goods
Fresh Fruits
Choice Meats
Nuts

The day of his departure they all were at the windows, Jean, Lydia and Ramey bunting against each other at the bay window in the Swell Room, Ken and Cele together on the lower landing of the stair. Simon carried the royal sign to the car, gingerly turning and guiding it into the back seat where it was wrapped in a ragged patchwork quilt. The family would have gone outside too to call their "Good lucks" from the curb, but it was a blowy gray day and Sam had said, "No sense in all of you catchin' your death of foolishness. 'Bye Liddy, 'bye kids, damn ya, never did like ya very good anyway!"

He looked nice now. He had borrowed Uncle Mac's overcoat. "I wish he'd gotten a new hat," Lydia fretted. "That thing's so greasy and out of shape."

"Maybe he will when he gets to Chi," Ramey said. He thumbed his nose at his father and waggled sign language for "Bring home a box of candy," squaring his hands and rubbing his middle.

"Ramey stop it," Lydia nagged uneasily. She fumbled in her pocket for a piece of torn sheet with which she wiped her eyes. "Well there he goes! I—I wish he had a heater in the car."

"Lord, he might come home in a Packard," Kenneth grinned. "Be just like him," he chuckled, "if the deal goes through."

"Yes. Yes, it would too!" Lydia laughed breathlessly. "I'll never forget the time he sold the fly paper holder and brought that thousand dollars home in cash—in one dollar bills. You should have seen us, Cele, we thought we were millionaires. Oh kids, do you suppose that—that this time—?"

Celeste bent to pick up last night's papers. Folding

them neatly together she said, "I believe so, Mrs. Andrews. This is such a splendid idea, and he's waited for it so long. I believe you folks are going to have everything you want."

Ken's deep-socketed eyes challenged her mockingly. "Everything? Then you'll have it with us, understand? Dad's a different guy when he's in the money." He became urgent. "He'd give every darn' one of us kids whatever we asked for if he could. Cars, set us up in business —wouldn't he, Mom?"

Lydia nodded, pleased, hopeful. "Yes! Yes Cele, he would."

"If this deal goes through we can get married, quit the show business, build us a house! If this deal goes through—"

"If the deal goes through!" Jean mocked lazily from the davenport. "My gosh I wish I had a nickel for every time that's been said around here. Not a dollar, mind you, a nickel—I'd still be rich." She flopped over on her stomach, smoothed the rumpled funnies into shape. "When's this family gonna wake up, get wise, quit believin' in fairies? They ain't no Santa Claus. They ain't no Easter bunny. They ain't no man in the moon!" She scratched her fluffy head, turned to wink wickedly. "Don't let 'em kid you, Cele."

With quivering droop they stared at her. Their eyes were resentful, protesting, but impotent before the truth: Dreams are their own fulfillment. Only the mad ask more.

CHAPTER TWENTY-TWO

THE DUTRO-CORBETT glass company were being very kind to Sam. Very courteous. More than fair. They were no longer interested in his self-illuminating sign, but they expected no portion of the five hundred dollars returned. They had, it seemed, a working fund for the encouragement of worthy ideas. The new model was not quite what they were looking for, but perhaps some time in the future—

And with the same abracadabra speed with which he had been given encouragement, Sam now found himself discouraged out. It was as if velvet-gloved hands had crammed back down his throat all his confidently rehearsed assertions, explanations and plans before they could emerge. As if these same unctuous paws had lifted him bodily, and pitched him down a greased slide to the street.

He stood there a moment, attempting to get his bearings. To grope through a labyrinth of words and events to the door of some understanding. He felt dazed, struck a blinding thump with those gloved fists. But it didn't hurt yet. He felt nothing but the chill mist on his shaven cheek, the cold bite of the walk through the holes in his carefully shined shoes, the nip of the lake wind down his newly trimmed neck. He stood, all freshly barbered and polished, as if he were about to enter the building, and time telescoped with wishful bewilderment so that, for an instant, he imagined he had not yet gone in. The conference was yet to come, the contracts soon to be drawn up, and images of wealth, glory, and success were immediately to become firm golden realities in his hand.

But the only reality he grasped was the sign, the now somewhat ludicrous sign which people stared at curiously as they passed. He advertised Timmet's grocery on Michigan boulevard in Chicago with his sign.

Finally he began to move down the street toward the car, his knees whacking the metal as he walked with the sign gripped awkwardly before him. It was too big to simply tuck under his arm. He gazed interestedly into show windows, buying things with his mind. He paused a moment before a display of furs, silken things that swathed the snobbish wax models in a smoky sheen. And now, recalling his absurd notion to take Lydia home a fur coat, the pain struck, wracked him, and lacerated his soul. His clutched sign cut into his palms. His face did not change, but desolation was in his eyes. He tromped on fiercely to the car.

Damnit. Goddamnit t'hell if a man just had the capital to ever do anything for himself! If he didn't have to go wriggling on his belly to somebody else for backing. Again he pondered the incomprehensible circumstance of the morning. They'd gotten het up about it—now they'd cooled off. He wondered that he could himself have expected anything else, recalling the myriad enthusiasms and renegings of Big Business to his ideas before.

They'd staked him to five hundred dollars. That still seemed appalling. And yet what was five hundred to those boys? Nothing. While to him—to him— His eyes narrowed, a smile played at his set mouth, he stomped on the gas vengefully. To him it meant his models and patent fees. He'd go ahead with this thing himself, he'd show 'em! Then when they came crawling back it'd cost 'em a hell of a lot more than five hundred dollars, he'd tell 'em that right now! He wasn't licked yet, not by a long shot! Maybe this was a damn' good thing.

I ain't gonna be a peddler *all* my life. This is still a big thing. We'll have that big house yet—I'll tell Liddy—

He began to rehearse what he'd say about how he'd put the D. C. people in their place. Damnitall though she'd be disappointed and he couldn't blame her. He guessed he'd better take home a box of candy to cheer her up.

He skidded around a corner and suddenly his headlights plucked DRINK CHEERUP POP! out of the night. Sam fairly stood on his not very good brakes. He had to back up to direct the full astonishment of his gaze upon the offending scarlet letters. A self-illuminating sign was beaming at him from the roadside. He got out and walked over to it, stared up, shook it and felt a choking swell in his throat, though his face was absolutely calm. A self-illuminating sign. Not his sign. Not the ornate, carefully hammered-out sign he and Simon had worked on with their few tools. This was a professional sign, finely conceived and beautifully made. It didn't even remotely resemble his sign—except for the self-illumination.

He whistled softly. "Well I'll be damned!" he said. "I'll be damned plum to hell and back again for a sucker! But they can't do this to me! Oh, no! They can't do this to Sam Andrews!"

Sam stalked into Walcott's office the next day, Simon Griffith lumbering in tow, and further declaimed his wrong. "Here's that proof of invention I had you notarize way last summer. Here's Simon, the man that helped me work it out. Here's the dope I got back from the patent office when I sent 'em five dollars to see if they was anything on the market like it. That outfit stole my idea!" he said in a voice of seething calm. "They stole it when I went in there that first time and by God I don't intend to sit back on my rumpus and let 'em get away with it!"

George Walcott hunched farther back on his. "And," he said with an arch smile, "I suppose you want me to sue —for half of what I can get?"

"Exactly!" said Sam. "They've got millions. We can clean up!"

"Well Sammy I hate to contradict you," Walcott grinned condescendingly, "but you haven't got a suit in a bushel basket. That affidavit isn't worth the paper it's written on. That junk from the patent office don't mean anything— even the patent itself wouldn't mean too much. And just because you run onto a sign utilizing your principle after you've been chump enough to hand that principle over to a concern that's likely to use it—that doesn't necessarily mean they did. They could incorporate under a thousand different names. And even if you were able to trace your idea back to them, you took money for it. You took five hundred dollars, which ain't pin money. And I bet you signed some papers you were too excited to read—or didn't understand, like those dopes you and Clete take advantage of!" George Walcott tipped back his head and roared. "Chickens come home t'roost, you know. No Sammy, you haven't got a chance! I wouldn't touch it with a ten foot pole."

Sam slapped his knee, sat staring out of the window for a minute or two. Then he shrugged, "Guess maybe you're right. The little fellow never has got a chance. I had a big idea there—the biggest fish I ever hooked and he got away." He stood up, looking around for his hat. He had been sitting on it. He punched it into shape, jammed it on. "Well Simon, c'mon. You'll go back to plasterin' houses, I'll go back to buyin' chickens."

Walcott bit at a fresh cigar. "Why don't you stick to it this time? What's the idea of monkeying around with crazy ideas that never get you anything but set-backs?"

Sam whirled on him. "Hell!" he snapped. "I had an idea that a million dollar corporation thought worth stealin', didn't I? Don't that prove something? You and the rest of the country will see my signs on every fence post. And I put 'em there, George Walcott! I may never get any credit for it, but I put 'em there!"

Simon planked a big hand on his shoulder. "You're right, Sammy. Money isn't everything. And you'll figure out something else just as good. I'll help you. I haven't got the ideas, but I've got tools and a pair of good hands. I'll help."

"Sure," Sam said. "Hell yes. It ain't the end of the world or nothin'."

CHAPTER TWENTY-THREE

IT HAD HAPPENED. The miracle had transpired, the dream come true. Gem Lake was behind her. She had escaped. This, the far country. These, her chosen hills.

Hills. Hills! Mornings, rushing to class in that white-pillared city, empty stomach pinned with queasy tightness to her backbone, bulging notebook clutched in her arms, her toes would grip her small scuffed oxfords in a brace against the terrific down-rush to the bottom. Nights, plodding up the last cruel slope, it seemed as if it would be easier to simply claw and knee her way to the top. It was like an old nightmare of crawling up a dizzily paved slope with some nameless terror in pursuit. All existence was now like that. All existence in the hills. And there was no escape.

Escape? My God—she would lift her face from the ponderous tome she was trying to sop into the dry sponge of her brain—this *was* escape! Wasn't it? Where next? If this, the long anticipated, could prove so barren, so lacking in every splendid glory with which her eager brain had garnished it—comfort and culture, friendships, learning—glib, stirring knowledge that would unlock all doors to success—if these, the confidently sought, were not here, where then? Toward what other peaks could she hurl her frantic rope of dreams?

She was a little mad with homesickness, longing for Dan, and the demands of a new job. She was starved of body and soul. When the girls of the office went off together to the Top Hat tearoom for eighty cent lunches and dollar dinners, Polly sneaked into an A. & P. store for a can of soup and a pint of milk. She cooked on an electric grill in her room. An orange crate was her cupboard. She spread a paper napkin on a corner of her study table and crouched there before her cup, plate and spoon, forcing a dribble of food toward the tightness of her stomach. From below would come the smoking odor of fried potatoes, beef and onion, the spiced fragrance of a fresh pie; laughter, voices. She could not eat.

It was no better when she recklessly joined the girls. Their fur coats were humiliating contrast to the shiny navy blue twill suit she still wore, though bleak November winds moaned. "I should think you'd freeze!" they often scolded, and though her shoulders would be hunched into muscled knots, she would claim brightly, "I'm warm-blooded. Why if I was home I'd still be going swimming in the lake." Anything to postpone wearing that brown wreck of a coat with its mothy collar, its tangled web of lining.

But sometimes, desperate for company, she would shiver downtown with these sorority girls who worked with her and who, surprisingly, liked her. In the shops they would pause to buy hose or gloves or hats while she stood rather defiantly by, bare hands rammed into pockets, her beret perched with gamin carelessness over one ear. In the tearoom they would slide out of their silk-lined furs (it was as if the female of the species sprouted this sleek flattering fur with the first frost on this campus, as if failure to do so marked one with the pox of the dread secret sickness, the disease of loneliness Polly was trying so passionately to conceal). They would sit casually in their black crêpe dresses or their good woollen sweaters, toying with wooden beads as they studied the menu and said, "Damn that diet, it's me for a steak. How's about you, Poll, what're you going to have?"

"Me?" she gulped, eyes craven before the staggering prices on the bill. "Why, I—I'm not very hungry. I think I'll just have a salad." And that ornate creation of curly leaf and raw tomato cost her fifty cents and left her stomach yawning. She could have filled up on Wheaties a couple of days for that!

No, she was better off away from the girls, though it stirred her to believe that for the first time in her life cozy doors of friendship stood wide to her, and all she need do was walk in. She was better off avoiding them, scuttling away from the lockers while they still dawdled with poised lipstick and laughter, ducking like a small furtive cockroach herself into a store, padding the long upward stretch buoyed only by the promise of mail.

Her letters would be lying on the newel post, one in Mom's dear scriggles, always one, often two in Dan's tall hand. They sustained her, kept her alive. They proved that somewhere on earth, and it seemed far, far as Asia, there were people to whom a person named Polly Andrews mattered. Fantastic as it seemed, they cared about her!

Despite the barriers thrown up by her want and her own fierce sense of inferiority, Polly laid strange claim to one person here. One day in a class in Bills and Notes, a young man bowed to her with a faintly puzzled frown on his dark, heavily-browed forehead. She could feel him watching her, and when the class was dismissed, he galloped through the swarm to extend a cordial hand.

"Sa-ay! Aren't you the little gummywozzle I met once up in a law office in Gem Lake? Now wait, don't tell me your name, see if I don't remember." His keenly fixed glance out of alert green gold-flecked eyes, his breadth of shoulder in the tweed suit, his booming, democratic cocksureness as he shouted, "Andrews! Polly Andrews!" made her gulp with gratitude.

Yet she was conscious of her devil's snigger, whether for herself or for him she didn't quite know. He was so blatantly just right. Everything about him—the neat gold clip which held his flamboyant tie, his jeweled fraternity pin, the gold football and several honor keys which dangled casually across his sturdy athlete's chest, proclaimed and attested one fact: He was Wonderful, and he knew it, in a manner so gracious, hearty, yet almost self-effacing, that he seemed curiously funny, and so—pathetic, somehow. Polly was attracted by him, and repelled by him. At one dizzying stroke she knew that she admired him immensely—and felt vaguely sorry for him. Merely to see him was to recall scowling sports page images of him, or beaming likenesses as he accepted cups and scrolls as token of being Representative this or that. *College Humor's* Hall of Fame had featured him as a wealthy youth who worked his way through undergraduate school, Polly recalled. There had been a sizzling controversy about it. He had been condemned as violently as he was admired. "Taking jobs away from kids that need 'em!" his critics cried. That's it, Polly thought—he's Big. He's grotesquely Big, so big he's embarrassed by it, he goes around hiding under a tent of bigness, wanting people to understand. He reminded her of someone, but she couldn't think who it was.

"How come you're here?" he demanded, lifting a finger in salute to the "Hi, Jud"s and "How they goin' Masters?"s that echoed from all sides as the male mass swept by. "In a third year class, I mean. Isn't this your first crack at jurisprudence?"

"Well not exactly. That is—" she hugged her battered note book against her chest as they swung into step down the cool tiled hall, "I've been learning a good deal from my boss up home. Studying his case books like—like you suggested!" she blurted, suddenly remembering. "That day you came up and sold me some magazines!"

Jud Masters halted abruptly. "Sa-ay, I did at that! Well what d'ya know? Well I'll be dogonned!" He stared at her, his mouth twisted into a wondering grin of pride. "Well! Since I'm practically responsible for you being here guess I better look after you! How do you like it here?" he boomed, as if beginning his duties as host then and there.

"Why I—like it fine!" she chirped.

"Got a nice place to stay?" He whipped out a notepad. "Where d'you hang your hat?"

"Oh yes, lovely." She gave him the address.

"Sa-ay, I know them, the Liebsch's! Fine people, fine. Well look, I got your phone number, I'll call you up sometimes. And if you ever need anything, books or stuff or advice, just yell for Uncle Jud. I live at the Commons." He glanced at his wrist watch and extended a hairy paw. "Look pal, I gotta trot—meeting of the *Review* staff, but I'll be seein' you. G'bye."

On that day, and those ensuing ones when they met in class, when he lent her books and bent over her chair in the law library, the scent of good fabric and shave cream mingling to remind her nostalgically of Dan, his magnanimity was something to cling to. It assuaged the pain of finding that even here where all was to have been so different she was again the diffident girl among ignoring men. Men who this time knew more than she did! Who vaguely patronized and resented her, rode rough-shod over her few cheeped opinions, dismissed her as competition because she was here not for a degree, but to scrape and patch together enough knowledge to supplement what she already had and pass the state bar examinations—an eventuality in which few of them, if they considered it at all, could believe. Men who snubbed her socially, to whom it apparently never occurred that she could laugh, swim, dance, or make love under the moon.

These things didn't occur to Jud Masters either, but he didn't seem to have romantic interests in any girl. Now and then she saw him in the company of some suave campus queen, but on these occasions Jud only looked uncomfortable and the girl bored. That's because he's such a man's man—Polly thought with the loyalty of her gratitude. He's too Big to be romantic; for all his dominant assurance, the poor guy just doesn't know how! And again she felt a twinge of pity for him, a foolish, fierce little passion to shield and defend.

Once, to her excitement, he stopped at the office to leave a copy of Magill's *Cases on Civil Procedure* with her. Polly returned to her desk self-consciously flushed.

"New campus conquest, Poll?" asked Maida Frazier, a pretty thing, who was sorting graduate cards at a near file.

"No," she admitted. "He's just sort of being nice to me."

"Trust old Jud!" Maida laughed—and Polly winced. What was this undercurrent thing that made girls mingle rebellion and amusement with their admiration for him? Was it that he strove a little too valiantly to share the lot of the common herd?

"Who's he taking to the Phi Delt dance?" Maida asked.

With a stupid stab of hope, Polly wondered. Jud was president of Phi Delta Phi, that snobbish upper crust of the legal fraternities. He'd have to go. He'd have to take

a sorority girl. But she sat staring blankly over the typewriter a moment, crazily dreaming. He liked her. The way
he'd like a homeless mongrel pup. He was at ease in her
presence because she did not doubt his greatness or hold
it against him. He was happier with her—she knew it in
a sudden, ironic, triumphant burst—than with anyone
else! Then why—why couldn't she have this break? To
have something dazzling, tremendous like that to write
home about—just once! Something to convince them she
was doing all right, they mustn't worry; to take the sting
of defeat out of these bleak months.

And oh, she wanted to go! She ached to dress up and
hear music, to feel a man's arms about her and to dance
again. She wanted a date!

Her room, that night, was intolerable. When she had
done her dishes, she got into her raincoat and charged out
into the damp wind. It was the old childish rush away
from loneliness and a self that could not be escaped. Cars
went by, tires sputtering, their tail lights penciling the
wet pavement. From the long lighted halls laughing
couples emerged, and bright spills of girls. The little figure
scudding by feasted her eyes, she filled her ears with the
lilting flakes of conversation and music that slamming
doors would suddenly cut off.

She wanted to belong. She wanted to cut back and
literally be her age. She was no older than most of them.
She wanted to be eighteen, perhaps, and an undergraduate
away at the *U.,* living in a dorm or a sorority house,
gabbling of ten o'clocks and parlor dates and spreads.
Vista—she thought of it with the same ache of pride and
shame she felt for her family. Its febrile little "locals"
whose rushing and pledging had been of such marvelous
import. Its few bleachers before which inconsequential
"Iowa Conference" games were fought with the mad frenzy
of the Big Ten. She felt cheated of the proper sort of
college just as she felt cheated of a proper family, yet
lashed to both with ties of shared need, some primitively
loyal affection.

And—though not for the first time tonight—she was
brought up sharply to the way it was about Dan too.
Was every phase of her life, including marriage, to be a
falling short, a compromise? Dan, for all his fineness, was

rooted in the old way of things. He didn't belong there, neither of them had willed or could help it—it was simply, unalterably so. Why couldn't she have met him here? Why couldn't he have been the same poised, intelligent Dan who loved her so much, but with a future to match her own, a college man?

And she thought with wry amused sadness of their dream of how she should first gobble success and then pass the platter to him. It was grim and tough and she'd be lucky to get by at all. Thinking then of the brief on which she should be working, she turned back toward the Liebsch house.

But there was to be no work that night. A special delivery letter lay on the carpet beneath her door when she returned.

Polly dropped to the bed and read it without removing her wet coat. Then she stared blindly at the walls of her room. Jean—married! Jean—Stew! And she had a sudden horrible, ribald picture of a pair of quarreling cats, rolling over and over each other, clawing, snarling, making love. . . . After that first blithe period of pranks their love had risen to such furies of hate. Stew was too much the suave young sophisticate for jealousy, but he was proud. He loved his dignity. It had incensed him to play the cuckold to Jean's brazen flittings-about. There had been a gladiatorial battle every time he came, Stew managing always to be the aloof, slightly cynical martyr; Jean hurling her bitter lance of words, shielding, defending herself with the claim that he neglected her, he didn't care, he was ashamed of her, else why didn't he take her home to meet his folks? And now these bloody, battle-scarred lovers, these wild young cats had mated, curled up together—for better or for worse!

She spread out the pages again and read Lydia's excited scribble through blurred eyes: "It was right after you went away, that time they went to Omaha. They decided to keep it secret on account of Stew's folks who think he's too young to get married, he says, though I'm afraid there's more behind their opposition than that. The first we knew about it was yesterday. The milkman had seen the notice in a bunch of old Omaha papers. It certainly knocked the pins out from under me, I can tell you! Jean didn't deny it, so I got in touch with Dad and he came home and a big bawl was had by all.

"I won't pretend I wasn't hurt. Dad and I wouldn't have tried to stop them and I did want all my children married at home. We're announcing it right away so people won't talk. Some of them are going to be disappointed when they find there's no *reason*. You know how anxious some people are to think harm of a girl, especially anyone as popular as Jean has been."

Now Lydia waxed philosophical. Polly could see the eye dimming, hear the hysteric sighing—"Shocked as I was at first, all I want for any of you kids is your happiness. Stew's a wonderful boy who's going far. He'll make her a fine husband, and it isn't as if she were leaving us right away. She's going to stay here until Stew can patch up things at home and find a house."

Polly folded the letter and put it back in its envelope. Then she went to stand at the window, gazing out into the wet black night. Jean married! She still tried to comprehend the fact of it.

Though Polly had often hoped for this very thing, now she was stricken with a sense of loss, a sharp and nameless panic more dreadful than anything she had yet known. She felt, literally, as she stood there at the window looking down, down into the black cliffs below, as if she had clawed her way to the top of a steep wall and now could only dangle there, without the strength to pull herself over, and in terror lest she lose her grip and fall back. Back—to what? Even the distorted unity of the family was shattered now. And Dan seemed some far lost image of the past, a figure with open but empty arms. No, there was nothing to fall back to! She had to hang on here. She mustn't get too bitter or too tired.

At length she yanked herself from her broodings and sat down to write to Jean. Now, through the power of words as hysterically emotional as Lydia's, she was proud big sister, pouring out love and joy. "I'll send you something as soon as I get my next check," she wrote—and thought extravagantly of electric toasters and coffee tables and puffy satin spreads. Jean probably wouldn't get much. Poor kid, eloping like that, knowing there couldn't have been a wedding at home. And the relatives would probably ignore this as they had Jean's graduation. Polly recalled, angrily, how Jean had surveyed the pittance of her presents as they were "displayed" atop the bookcase on that occasion—a pair of cheap teddies, a scrapbook, and some wash rags spread out separately to look like more; how Jean's lip had quivered as she shrugged, "Oh well, the announcements probably took 'em by surprise. I don't s'pose they ever figured I'd pull through school!"

She wanted to fling fierce, protective arms about Jean, who spurned all protecting; to shield that cool lovely body with her own hot small one, keep it safe from the cruelties she knew would come stabbing. Stew's folks. The brow-liftings and whisperings, the anticipatory watching of the whole town. And oh please, please!—Polly was somewhat shocked to find herself praying even as she wrote—*don't let them be right!*

She had sealed her letter and was getting into her coat again when the telephone rang. She stood tense, listening, telling herself with ironic pretense that it might be for her.

"Miss Andrews!"

Incredibly, it was. She raced down, heart thumping.

"Hi, Gem Lake! Know who this is?" The cordial boom, the jovial good-guyness.

She gripped the receiver, chirped a bright little, "But of course. How—are you, Jud?" (If this was just about another brief, a book, a bit of business—she thought wildly—she'd kill him!)

And then it was happening. He was asking her. Jud Masters, the great and godly, was asking the shabby little misfit-nobody for the pleasure of her company at the Phi Delt dance.

CHAPTER TWENTY-FOUR

DAN WORKED FOR the county, up before daylight harnessing his mules, lunching out of a bucket at noon, heading back up the lane only when dusk was too thick for further seeing. Infinitely weary, he ate supper, smoked the third cigarette of his day's allowance, bathed, wrote to Polly, and tumbled into bed. Reluctantly, when cold weather came, he had to give up the long lucrative hours of road mending to go into the county treasurer's office at Crescent, where his curly head bent all day over columns of figures.

He had to dress up now and drive back and forth and the pay was small. This necessitated new economies. He ate a candy bar for lunch and spent the noon hour contacting life insurance prospects, some of whom he was able to sell before returning to the farm at night. He subsisted on two cigarettes a day. His stockings wore out and his mother darned and redarned them. His shirt collars were turned and carefully stitched. He was always immaculate, but threadbare and a trifle shiny. Because he was handsome and instinctively gallant, women smiled upon him; the crowd of sleeks with whom he had once danced and drunk were disgruntled at his refusal to come back and accused him of going irreparably to seed. He only half-heard, half-cared. Before him was but one image and one goal.

Despite the audacious boasting of Polly's letters, he knew that she was suffering, that she had encountered things which she could not combat. He guessed far more than she ever told him. He was honest in his desire for her happiness, yet this unaccounted-for misery that ran through all she wrote had in it a note of comfort for him. Surely now she realized how much greater was the kind of love he could give her than anything she might find there. And that, he had come to know, was what she needed—bolster to her ego, constancy, the kind of worship that made her God in her own eyes. Not facile fruition from her many little talents, not recognition or financial reward or even actual greatness. She only thought she must have them because of the peculiar malnutrition of her life. If she understood now, or could be made to understand, that her long pursued visions were but mirages that could lead her on mercilessly, never quenching her thirst; that her only hope for happiness—not satisfaction, but a kind of buoyant content—lay in turning her back upon them for his deep devotion; if she realized, as surely she must, that she was essentially and more truly a creature of hot blood and supple flesh than one of mental accomplishment then there was but one solution, one fulfillment.

He had few illusions as to what marrying her would mean. She would revel in frustration, she would be condescending often, and there would be that constant drain and source of turmoil, her folks. *His* folks, he thought with tender impatience, no matter how they might treat him. Vulgar, pretentious, lost and wild though they were, he couldn't despise or even resent them greatly. They were too much a part of Polly. He could blame them for the petty snobberies and violent contradictions of her nature; but for all that was fine and generous and rather magnificently, if mistakenly, ambitious in her, he knew that he must thank them too.

Of course Sam would raise hell. But by then he hoped it would be too late to matter. And it would be best. She would have had her little fling at greatness. She would be ready—at least so the frantic undertones of her letters led him to believe—to come gratefully and forever into his arms.

To that end he was saving. He would marry her at Christmas.

The thought was appeasement for the days when her letters failed to come. Stomping into the back hall at night, half frozen, he would glance anxiously into the kitchen, where his mother would have propped the envelope beside his plate. If it wasn't there he cuffed back disappointment sharply, and thought of tomorrow when it would be there for sure. Drying his hands, he would stand in the door visiting with his mother, speaking of everything else, yet comforted by knowing—although she seldom spoke of it either—that she understood.

She would poke the fire, dump in a few more of the clean red cobs, rinse her hands at the sink and shove kettles and pans to the front of the stove. His lone place at the table would be as attractive as possible on these nights, the chandelier with its scalloped shade shining down on his white napkin, the newspaper neatly by, the cut glass dishes of crisp green pickles and ruby jam and butter within easy reach. His mother would fuss over his food, keep refilling his coffee, expressing in swift tidy little attentions words that she couldn't speak, and that he wouldn't want her to.

But one night when he was especially tired she pressed his shoulder and remarked in a tone careful not to sound too concerned, "Goodness, it's been nearly a week now, hasn't it, son?"

That sprung the locks of his reserve. In assuring her that Polly was just busy, he found confirmation of this in his own mind. And because he needed that confirmation so much, he was suddenly confiding what he hadn't meant to broach to anyone but Polly, herself.

"I know it would be best, Mom, if I can make her see it. And I've been thinking—it wouldn't be as if I were deserting you folks either. We could fix up the tenant house. It's better than—" He was about to say "what she's used to at home," but substituted, "lots of places. I could work in town until time for spring plowing, then take over for Dad. If we had a good crop year we'd pay the interest and maybe a little on the principal and come out all right for another year, anyway."

He needed a haircut, his mother noticed. His curls grew so thick and riotous. He looked like a curly-maned young stallion in which there surged some untapped strength. He looked young and proud and hopeful and a little desperate, and she prayed that this one last thing on which he had set his heart would work out.

"I wish to God I'd seen it like this before," he said. "She said something about it once herself, but I just couldn't picture her on a farm. Now—well, I can't picture her in a law court either."

"Neither can I," his mother agreed. "I think she'd like the earth once she got some of it on her hands. I don't think it would beat her or subdue her talents at all, the way so many writers lead you to believe. If anything, it might stimulate them. I think something genuine like a farm is what she needs. I'd help her with the work, and oh—" she exclaimed suddenly, "I'm so glad!"

Dan felt happier after that. There was reassurance in discussing his plan with someone who didn't doubt, and who seemed so pleased. Kit's cool queries about Polly's progress and his own stopped rankling so much. He ignored Martin Chase's patronage. It even stopped hurting so much to go to Kay's where the quiet warmth and goodness of the home Doc had given her was an almost intolerable reminder of what he had hoped—in the first glory of loving his girl—that he would provide for her. How he had wanted to rescue her from shabbiness. The knight in armor! Siegfried! Lohengrin! He grinned a trifle wryly. He'd bungled, spent too lavishly, loved too inordinately, gotten out of step somehow with the grim and stringent times.

And she had had ideas about rescuing herself!

The letter finally came, on the last day of a week that had grown insupportably long and dark. He came in late that Saturday night, took his usual miserable look, and there it was, propped miraculously by his plate. The world swung back into perspective. He drew a deep breath and grinned his relief as he washed.

"Goodness Danny, how you spatter," his mother scolded, coming in with fresh towels.

He hugged her, picked her up by the elbows and kissed her hard on the mouth.

A teakettle was singing on the glowing stove. Dan felt ravenous. He helped himself to a hot roll from under the dishcloth that covered the pan and split its steaming middle. He didn't touch the letter, but consciousness of it filled him, together with the humming warmth of the room, the food's fragrant smell, the radio's throaty murmur and the click of Kit's and Martin's cards as they played double-sol' in the sun parlor.

Kit came in. "My goodness, all this time and you haven't even bothered to see what she's got to say!" she exclaimed.

That brisk touch and the frail spicy scent of her filled him somehow with a furious resentment. He sprang up, not finishing his pie, and took the letter with him upstairs.

He flung himself face down across his bed, lit his cigarette, and ripped open the envelope, smiling at the paper on which she typed. The little miser, cutting off the tops of spoiled office pages or using the backs. There was always something touching about those odd sizes and filled-up margins, something peculiarly Polly. And she knew it would be all right with him if she scribbled on paper sacks.

"Dan dear," he read—and felt a sharp instant apprehension. What, after all, was that but an inversion of "Dear Dan?" He read on swiftly.

Presently his eyes slowed and he looked up, stared at the wall. Physical pain had been gathering within him at every word; now he knew that he must pause, get his bearings a minute or something—he didn't know just what —might happen. He must remember that this was—Polly. Exaggerating, bragging, flaunting her little triumph as if it were something immense, yet glossing it over with affection, making its bitterness easier to take. "And darling I told him all about you while we danced. . . . It was so beautiful there in the fraternity house, *your* kind of house, honey—slick and smooth and so exactly the sort of place you ought to be that I simply ached—" That—of all the pitiful little barbs of ecstatic romanticizing—that bit deepest, hurt the most. A law fraternity house, while he—he had been buoyed up at thinking they both belonged on a farm!

It went deeper than that though. This Jud Masters who seemed to be the Lord's anointed—there was something staunch and hard and competitive about the sound of him. In his very name. It did little good to recall the innumerable past loves of which Polly had often prated. They had been nothing to worry about. He had despised and resented them, known an acid distaste at Polly's bothering with them, but then despite the inner seethings of jealousy he had been armored in his own superior strength.

Now he felt the piercing shatter of that armor. As if he were actually going to pieces somewhere inside. He rolled over, reached out blindly to turn off the lamp, and lay a long time in the cold darkness, smoking one cigarette after another and trying to reason away his suffering. What had the letter been, after all, but a long, probably fancy-gilded account of a dance? She'd be bound to get excited over going to a fraternity party with a man she described as "handsome and popular—the type I know you'd have been down here, Dan. In a way he reminds me of you—I guess that's why I couldn't resist going—" Oh God, if only she wouldn't make those comparisons!

He recognized too, though all that was chivalrous in him tried not to, the cheap pretension back of that "couldn't resist going." He'd told her when she left to have a good time—and he'd meant it. He had actually wanted her happiness, whatever the painful emotional cost to himself. But her passionate letters of love and loneliness, implying innumerable rejected dates, had hoodwinked him into believing. Now he saw the garish transparency of it all. Her almost defiant persistence in thinking he would esteem her "popularity" and that old silly notion she'd had about being inferior in his eyes, to Jean. The letter was as if she were now offering jubilant proof of things long pretended to.

"Couldn't resist going—" My God, she'd jumped at the chance!

A helpless anger shook him. He got up and began to rip off his clothes, letting resentment bloom bitterly, a stark hot jealousy flare. In being furious with her he could postpone a little while the grim steeled looking at the truth: Polly had found the man who could take her away from him.

CHAPTER TWENTY-FIVE

POLLY AWOKE WITH a jar. "Gem Lake next stop." The conductor was taking up the scrap of cardboard clipped on the coach wall. Frantic with the haste of the untraveled, she tugged on her galoshes, dragged her suitcases down from the rack overhead, and sat tense and ready on the edge of the seat. It was still dark outside with the blinding snow. A dim blur of light that was the town of Springs, whisked past. Only a few miles more. She could feel the train slacken speed. There was a dim ghost-whistling far ahead. The conductor took her bags and she staggered down the aisle after him. Then there was the grinding stop, the jerk, the cold brace of air, and Ken's and Ramey's sniveling faces looking up.

They kissed briefly and pushed against the wind to the car.

"Your train was late," Kenneth accused.

"Yes, on account of the storm. We had a long wait in Waterloo."

"Jeebers cripes, get a guy up at six o'clock to meet ya and then have to stand around and wait an hour!"

"Hey Poll, what'dja bring me for Christmas?" Ramey fidgeted from the back seat.

"A pair of goggles."

His face brightened, then sagged. "Aw, whatja tell me for?"

"I didn't, I knew you didn't want to know. Gosh, you've grown!"

"You oughta be home," Ken said. "You're bleeding us all to the bone down there."

"What have I ever cost *you?*"

"Well it ain't fair, Mother sticking dollar bills in her letters and sending you boxes of grub when the rest or us hardly've got enough to eat half the time."

"You're exaggerating, Ken. Besides, Mom did the same thing for you when you were gone. Cele still staying at our place?"

"Yeah."

"How does Dad like that?"

"Oh he raises hell, like he always does."

Ramey beamed wickedly. "What makes Ken sore though is 'cause she still gets letters from her other fella."

"Shut up!" Kenneth barked.

So that's it—Polly thought.

They waded up to the snow-banked porch. The hall's unchanged smell of dust, old varnished wood and strong coffee turned back the wheels of time. Here no glamorous homecoming—she simply had never been gone. The door rattled open and Lydia rushed upon her exclaiming, "Why Polly! Why honey, here you are! I didn't hear you come and I've been watching for you too!" She felt thicker to Polly's hugging arms. She looked the same, only in the long absence Polly had forgotten what that was. Now that she saw, she remembered the black silvering hair, the long sensitive nose, the dusky skin and passionate beautiful eyes.

"Oh Mom!" she choked. "Oh Mother, I—I've been so homesick for you!"

"Poor kid, up all night, you're tired," Lydia said. "Don't bother with your galoshes. Get in here over the register where it's warm."

A faint wave of heat was struggling up from below.

"Dad'll be right up. He's fixing the furnace. Poor Dad," she confided in an undertone, "he's been awfully worried lately so don't feel hurt if he seems a little cross. He's had an awful burden to carry."

Celeste came out of the kitchen. She was wearing an old gray sweater of Ken's, out at the elbows. Her pretty nose was rosy. "Welcome home, Polly," she smiled without waiting to be introduced. "Hungry? I've got breakfast ready."

Polly looked at this toe dancer in the ragged sweater and it struck her suddenly how very like them, like the tattered silver paper pattern of their lives, she was.

"Grand. I'm starved. Where's Jean?"

"Where'd you suppose she'd be?" Kenneth growled. "In bed, of course. Getting married hasn't changed her any."

They progressed into the kitchen. "Why it is a kitchen, isn't it?" Polly marveled. "I haven't been in one for months!"

"Then you can have a good dose of dishwashing while you're home," Kenneth said.

"No sir, Polly's going to have a good rest!" Lydia surveyed her anxiously. "You're awfully thin, you've been working too hard, I can tell by your eyes. Have you had your blood tested lately?"

"Oh, I'm all right." She squeezed into her old place by the sink. "I see we still eat here."

"Yes," Lydia apologized. "It's just too much trouble carrying things back and forth from the dining room. Sit down and eat, Cele, I'll pour the coffee. I've had mine."

"No, Mrs. Andrews, you drink another cup with Polly."

Sam came banging out of the back hall, wiping his nose on his shirt sleeve. "Hell of a fine job you did building the fire before you left!" he snorted at Ken. "Damn' thing went out and I had to start it all over again."

"Dad, aren't you even going to speak to your daughter?" Lydia prodded.

"Oh hello, Polly." He bent toward her lifted mouth. "How d'you like it down there?"

"It's all right," she said. "I like it fine." Polly set down her cup. "I'm too tired to eat. Anybody care if I go to bed?"

"Of course not," Lydia sympathized. "You go crawl in with Jean. That's where Cele sleeps now. Your room is like an icebox."

"I'll sleep better in my own bed if you can scare up the covers."

"I can take some blankets off from Kenneth's bed, but it worries me to think of you up there without a bit of heat."

They shivered up the steps, began the assembling of ragged quilts, frowzy blankets and a few old coats, while Lydia told her, "Things have been under an awful strain this winter with Jean pulling the stunt she did—" she smiled quaveringly—"and Cele staying here and all. Of course," she declared in sudden passionate conviction, "it *is* best about Jean, I don't care what the neighbors or relatives say or how Dad and I felt at first! We're rid of the worry of Jean's running around, for one thing—and she and Stew are happier. They don't fight nearly like they used to when he comes. Dad doesn't think that's often enough or that Stew gives Jean enough money. It does seem as if with what he's making and his father's being so well off and all, he'd leave her more than five dollars every couple of weeks. And honestly Polly, it—it doesn't seem quite fair for us to—well, it sounds hideous even to say—but it's true that we shouldn't have to support her now that she's his wife."

"No, I guess not," Polly said wearily. The old chant. The unchanged scrabble for harmony. And she had come back to it with such nostalgic surge! Where was the tender homely beauty, the ancient love-beat beneath their ranklings that she had thought would ground and reassure her? Out There hadn't been what she had dreamed of; and Here—this wasn't as she had dreamed either. Where *was* fulfillment and love and stability? In Dan?

"Then too, Cele's being here hasn't helped matters any," Lydia continued, pushing with her shoulder against the stuck door of Polly's icy cubicle.

The garishly painted furniture—like a woman who's gotten herself up wrong and realizes, too late, her tawdry taste. And the dusty droop of dance programs, so pridefully displayed across the mirror top. And her still cluttered makeshift desk, all the facilely drawn caricatures and smart, empty little foamings of verse— Polly saw it all through shocked, sick eyes. At least I've grown up enough to know how shallow I am, she thought; at least I've gotten the right perspective on that!

"Poor Cele," Lydia went on, "she's broke and her folks won't send her a cent and she swears she won't go home. I made an awful mistake when I invited her to stay here with us last fall. Dad resents it so, but what can we do? I can't drive the girl out. She's so lovely, not a bit of trouble, and she does earn her board just by helping me. You know Jean never was much of a hand around the kitchen. She and Jean get along fine, thank goodness—she's been helping Jean with her dancing. Jean may get up a class of her own after Christmas." Lydia's eyes flashed in dark challenge, "I guess that will show people she didn't have to get married!"

"I suppose that is what a lot of them think."

"Of course it is, the old scandal-mongers! Honestly Polly, sometimes I feel like getting up at Ladies Aid or Over Home and screaming what I *know*—that she's all right, she hasn't missed a month! I'd like to see Mrs. Kessler's face, and Aunt Chick's. I honestly believe they'd be disappointed. But you just can't."

Polly crawled gratefully between the blankets. Her mother kissed her. "Have a good sleep sweetheart, and don't get up till you feel like it. I'll try to keep the kids quiet. Warm enough?"

Polly burrowed deeper into her slowly warming den and thought with drowsy confusion of how Jud had put her on the train that had brought her home to Dan. "Well 'bye pal—wish I was goin' with you!" Ah, her devil snorted as she felt the feathery prick of the pillow—if he only had!

Toward noon Polly was awakened by a faint but horrible noise of crying in the next room. She sat up, listening. Ramey bellowed loudly—it must be Ken. Now what world-shaking doom was his? she wondered impatiently, snatching up her clothes.

Jean was in the bathroom, kneeling on the stool lid probing its clanking depths with a hairpin.

"Jean!"

"Poll!"

They kissed. "Sorry I can't hug ya, kid," Jean said, lifting a slender dripping arm. "I'm trying to get this darn' thing fixed before my husband—" Polly caught the childish lilt of pride—"puts in an appearance."

"Gee, what a glamorous job for a bride!"

"Ain't it though?" Jean shrugged and poked her bright head again over the churning abysm. With a kind of guilty fascination Polly studied her—the little pointed breasts asway in the good blue wool sweater, the graceful curve of hip under her nubby tan skirt, the long sheer-hosed legs and pointed feet in their shining tall-heeled pumps. Jean, no longer a little girl—or had she ever been? Jean broken, taken, married. Polly was seeking, reluctantly, some mystic evidence of change, some secret alteration.

"With this thing rattling and Ken bellyachin' we'll make our usual delightful impression on the guys."

"What's the matter with Ken this time?"

"Cele's gone," Jean announced, fitting the top lid back so that the liquid dirge was muffled. "This Verne Bailey she's been corresponding with—they've been secretly married, kid, all the time she's been here living off'm us!"

Polly gasped. "How do you know?"

"He came after her today. A good looker too and I don't mean perhaps! Said he'd come to take her home for Christmas. I think she knew it all along but she hadn't said a word to us. It sure burns me up when I think of what a hard time we've had to keep enough potatoes in the skillet for our own family!"

Polly thought of Lydia's criticism of Stew. That, she supposed, was different. "Was Ken here?"

"Yes sir. He and this Verne visited while Cele packed her suitcase. Then Ken excused himself and came upstairs and I heard Cele go into his room and talk to him quite a while. Thank goodness Mom and Dad were down cellar bottling that poultry medicine Dad's been making, so I entertained him."

"You would!"

"Then Cele came down and told the folks and all of us good-bye, Merry Christmas, nice as you please, and said she didn't know for sure whether she'd be back. Then we heard Ken bawlin' and Mother went up to see what was the matter, and he said Cele had told him she'd married this boy friend from home last spring just before she went on the show. This summer I guess she fell for Ken and didn't want to go back at all."

"Gosh, that is a mess!"

The two girls stared at each other, groping toward the significance of this thing. It affected each of them, they sensed—but how? Jean's bed was already made, and as the saying vulgarly went, she would lie in it. And yet if she remained apart for any time from Stew, no telling what might befall. As for Polly, protestingly, she felt its warning. Oh why did all this have to happen now, muddling her own swiftcoming hour with Dan?

"Well nitzo, you're dressed," Jean said briskly, gathering up her rings from the bowl, "let's go see what brand of fits the folks are having by now."

Lydia, they found, had reached the benevolent stage. "I tell you my heart aches for that poor girl!" she declared, perched sadly on the piano bench. "To make a mistake like that—she couldn't have known her own mind, and now—now she'll be so miserable!"

"Oh, I donno'," Jean said, "I wouldn't call Ken such a prize."

Lydia's eyes flashed. "That'll do! He's hurt, hurt to the quick and I won't *have* you quarreling, making things any worse than they are!"

"Yeah Jean," Polly begged, "please. Good Lord—" her voice rose to match her mother's, "the first day I get home, I should think—!"

"Please!" Lydia sobbed. "Please, girls, please!"

"Well hark the herald angels sing!" Jean jeered lightly. "A gal can't even make a remark around here!" She slammed through the hall doors and returned with a coat over her arm. "C'mon Poll, let's go downtown to do our Christmas shoplifting. Maybe that'll pep everybody up." She jabbed a long imp finger beneath her mother's trembling chin. "Whatcha want this year, Mom? I'll charge it to Stew!"

"All I want is for you kids to get along, that's all I want!"

"Well we'll ask Santa Claus if he thinks there's any hope for us. Poll, go see if you can persuade old fat chicken-medicine Santa down-cellar to let us have the car, it's freezing outside."

Sam's entire income for several months had depended upon his poultry remedy which he brewed upon an old oil stove in the basement. Stewing, spilling and strewing, he bottled, congratulated himself, and cussed. The medicine had worked surprising cures. He had had excellent luck selling it, had even several agents working for him, one of them Uncle Glen who, despite past treachery in circulating the formula during Sam's first venture, had come blubbering of bills and swearing promises. Now to the family chorus of "I told you so" Sam complained that Glen was hogging the territory, cutting the price, and threatening to go into competition with him. With the approach of the holidays, however, farmers' wives were disposing of their poultry and finding other things more alluring than the huge wine-colored bottles of Sam's Happy Hen Tonic.

Roads were impassable. The car hid its hand-painted portrait of a beaming hen in the garage. Sam was having one of his mean streaks. Cele's departure today hadn't helped.

He was primed to bursting with this foul injustice when Polly came groping through the cave of the coal room. "Me hustlin' like hell to feed my own and then her, a married woman not even one of the family livin' off'm us! I've never been madder about anything in my life!" He jabbed a rusty funnel into the top of a vinegar jug. "By God I got a notion to make out a bill and send it to that guy and if he don't pay up bring suit. They'd do it to us quick enough, don't you know they would? Never notice nobody handin' us anything, not by a long shot!"

Polly saw the futility of asking for the car. "No, I guess not, Dad. Unless," she couldn't help adding as she retreated, "it was a creditor who couldn't help it."

Sam trotted after. "Well I ain't gonna get caught with my pants down again. Stew's gonna kick in his share for Jean after this—a rotten shame his folks bein' so high and mighty, not even writing her or us when I'm the one that's feedin' her! Don't you go marrying Dan unless you know damn' well he can support you, understand?"

"Don't worry," she said testily, "I won't!"

"No you don't, missy!" Sam shot at Jean, who was

poking through vases and drawers in search of the car keys.

"Don't *what?*"

"Don't take that car out today. Not on these slippery streets and gas what it costs. Not on your grandmother's hind leg!"

"Who said I was? C'mon, kid."

Grinning, Sam slyly reached into a pocket and produced a handful of change. "Here." He tossed her a quarter. "Get me a couple cigars, and a little candy for your mother. Hell, it's Christmas, ain't it?"

Lydia, who had been staring blindly out of the frosted window, said resentfully, "You don't act like it! Why not let them take the car? Cold day like this and all those groceries to carry."

"Have 'em sent out. Nope Liddy, can't do it." He jingled the car keys tantalizingly. "Ain't safe on these streets, and I gotta save every drop of gas for when I can get back to work." He yawned, trotted across the room and kissed his wife's neck. She jerked her head away.

Jean whirled toward both of them. "Now don't you two turtle doves get owly! We wanta walk, don't we, Poll?"

"If you see Ramey tell him to pick up some more tires at the junkyard," Sam instructed. "I cut up the last one today."

"Tires?" Polly asked.

"Yeah," said Jean. "You know—yule logs!"

"Member how we used to lipperty-lip playing Peter Rabbit on this stretch going to school?" Polly said as they crossed the tracks and descended the slope toward town.

"Yeah, I remember. Lord how we've come up in the world. Those days we had to burn Shunk by Shunk's wood. Now we're burning tires—and Lordy how they smell—from the junkyard! And a big fight every time Ramey has to go get 'em. Thank the Lord—" Jean clutched her small veiled hat, "I'm getting out of it! Just as soon as Stew finds us a place to live."

"Jean, was that why you got married—to escape the way things are at home?"

"Escape?" Jean's laugh was brittle. "I haven't left yet, have I? And I ain't likely to until Stew can persuade his folks I won't contaminate their company. Stew's weak,

Poll, bein' the only child and all, he's weak where his folks are concerned. And there was this girl back home they were hell bent on him marrying—she's more up their social avenue, I guess. And us fighting all the time. We figured it was either break up or tie up—and we were there in Omaha where it'd be so easy to get married and keep it a secret.

"I wish we hadn't kept it secret, though. I wish we'd told right away, especially Stew's folks. Now no tellin' when they'll come around. And all the old hens here are counting their fingers, especially the mamas of the gals that hoped to hook Stew themselves!" Her tone changed, became tinged with proud defiance. "I got the smartest, swellest guy in Vista college and they're so jealous they stink. I guess the dumb bunny of the Andrews outfit didn't do so bad for herself, after all. Stew's got a swell education and a swell set-up in his dad's bank and boy am I gonna have everything I want! Me darling, a banker's wife —can you tie that?"

The lyric patronage—the lilting bluster. First evidence of change, all this, yet essentially Andrews. The sting of it was like the cold sneaking up under Polly's skirt, gnawing at her bones under its cheap thinness. Jean looked already so trig and expensive in her new coat of some thick tweedy powder blue stuff; above its flattering blue fox collar Jean's small bright head set proudly. Well —Polly knew with an oddly painful sense of something lost—she needn't worry about Jean's clothes any longer. Even if Stew only gave the family five dollars every two weeks, thank heaven Jean did look so well turned out. Let her have that little much. Let her sad little banners fly.

For there *was* something wistful, intolerably sad about Jean's marriage. Not to have a wedding or a honeymoon —the "big shebang" which Jean had always so grandiosely planned when they were little girls. Not to be accepted by her husband's people. Unshowered and unfêted, to be only jealously watched by those she knew. But there was something more. Something that in spite of the agony Polly had endured from her own uprooting, she herself had gained. A period, whether bitter or beautiful, of living alone, becoming an entity apart from family or possessive man; a life-space, no matter how brief, utterly and forever yours because you had "stood on your own." And whether you did this bravely and triumphantly, or with sick knowledge of your own failure, it was something you should have, a memory of escape and trial without which you would never be quite complete. Even Ken had had that. Even girls who went away to clerk in dime stores or wait tables. But Jean would never have it, just as she would probably never have the dancing class of which Lydia had spoken. Jean would probably have babies!

Incredible as the thought of Jean's svelte body's thickening, the swelling of her star-like breasts, she was of that elastic strength that is surprisingly fecund. And beneath her lazy wit, her disdain, her quicksilver intrigues, there was a kind of cool maternal common sense. *She* would not protest, at least not savagely, being bound before she had ever a chance to fly. But in her very indifference, in asking and getting—however smug her pratings—so little, she moved Polly to compassion.

Yet Jean, she realized, actually felt sorry for her!

It was four o'clock when they came back across the snowy porch. The house was chill and Sam snorting.

"Seen anything of Ramey?" he demanded. "Sent him away from here three hours ago and he ain't back yet!"

Ken had come downstairs. His eyes were red, but an acrid good humor, the result of an hour's philosophizing with Lydia, had returned to him. "Give him time, give him time," he jeered. "Maybe Junky's all outta tires and he's gotta sneak some off the mayor's car."

Lydia, shuddering in from the kitchen, signaled the girls to carry their holly-wrapped bundles upstairs, but Sam was alert.

"Never mind, I see 'em!" he barked.

"Ah-ah," Ken mocked, "Santa Claus don't come to little boys that peek!"

"If that don't beat hell—spendin' money for Christmas presents when we ain't got coal to keep your mother warm. Well I know what I'll do. I'll have Stew get us some when he comes, that's what I'll do!"

"He will too," Jean worried. "Oh Poll, don't let him!"

They had reached the landing window. Polly clutched her sister's arm. "Jean, look!"

Ramey was coming across the yard, stooped with the weight of the tire hung around his neck, but happily dragging a large evergreen in the snow behind. Clad only in a skimpy mackinaw, he looked chilled to the bone, but catching sight of his sisters, he grinned, pointed with pride to his tree, and rid himself of several grotesque antics with which he had been bursting all the way home.

"Poor kid," Polly said. "Wonder where he got it."

Then they both gasped, "Oh ye gods—Stew!"

A snowball from Ramey thudded against the window; another struck Stew's sedan as it pulled up at the curb. With a little shock of joy and anxiety, Polly saw that someone was with him. It couldn't be Dan—oh not yet, please not yet! she thought frantically. The old sweet fear of him, the frenzied humility and shame of what she was and what she felt passionately she must hide from him, made her knees weak, her throat pound.

But it was Dan. She saw him stoop out of Stew's long low car. She saw the white flash of his teeth as he called to Ramey, scooped up snow, and drew back his arm to throw. She saw that he was not the far lost prince of her lonely dreaming, but—like the house, the folks—wonderfully and regrettably the same. He was the same Dan the family had milked and finally snubbed. He was the same, stamping with the old eagerness up the walk ahead of Stew; and yet upon his face, the set of his shoulders, and defying his swinging stride, there was—something; a false confidence, a too desperate hope, frightening her still more. Oh why, she wondered wretchedly, must he come like this, so soon? There had been no time to gather up and sort her thoughts, to get emotionally or mentally prepared for this reunion that should have been so perfect, and would be such a hideous flop!

"If Ramey'd only get in here, give Dad that tire, get the fire going!" Jean was cursing softly. "Oh damnit, Polly, damnit!"

"Why kid, what's got into you?" Polly asked. "You and Stew always got a kick out of things like this before."

"Well I'm sick of the same old joke. And now that Stew's in the family it ain't funny any more. Oh well, c'mon." Jean whisked around. "Let's get rid of this junk and go see what we can do to spread a little peace on earth good will t'men around here."

They dumped their packages on Jean's bed, slapped powder on their noses and clattered back downstairs. Ramey was just dragging his tree through the door, leaving a snowy trail behind. "Junky let me cut it!" he elated. "Ain't it a dinger though? Biggest we ever had."

"Well brush it *off!*" Lydia fretted. Then with nervous, effusive surprise, "Why Dan, you stranger, hello! Stew! Girls, girls, here's your boy friends! Jean—Polly!" she shouted.

"Only one tire?" Sam fumed. "How in hell d'you think we'll keep warm over Christmas on only one tire?"

"What's the idea?" Stew frowned. There was something commanding, important and impatient in his tone. The successful young executive in his excellent coat, his neatly knotted white silk scarf and Stetson hat. The Grand Duke of Ephesus. The Son-in-law. "You folks out of coal?"

Jean bent over the bannister to kiss him. "Naw, we're gonna make tire swings out of 'em! Hi Dan!" She flung out her arms and embraced him too.

Polly scudded down and was in Dan's arms. He was kissing her with naked lost hunger. It could not be helped; their drive together was natural, unthinking and not to be stopped, but again Polly was sorry that it had to be like this, with Ramey ogling up and Sam's wrath watching and Lydia's vague hysteric concern. As if—oh God, she thought with murderous fury, as if we hadn't the right! While Jean and Stew because of the circumstance of a job, a little money, a ceremony—!

"But if you folks haven't got coal in the house let's go get some!" Stew was saying concernedly. "How about it, Dan?"

"Why yes, sure," Dan said.

"No," Lydia moaned, "you boys don't need to do that! Sam, tell them they mustn't!"

"Why not?" Sam muttered glumly, half ashamed. "Hell, we gotta keep warm."

"Sure, everything's gonna be swell!" Ramey whooped. "I got a Christmas tree and Polly's home and the guys'll get the coal, Merry Christmas folksies, yippee!" He straddled his tree and rode it into the house.

Now for a moment a grip of silence came over them, the strangeness of their being here together like this after the months of change. They all felt it—that it should somehow be different. The cold and the want, the old pattern of anger and mocking jibe and holiday emotions gilded to tarnished tinsel pitch—why all this? How could it be?

"Well," Stew said again, "let's go, Dan."

Dan's free hand plunged into his pocket. But it emerged with a groping motion. His other hand gripped Polly tighter against him as he said self-consciously, coloring because he was so poor at dissembling. "Look, it's been so darn' long since I've seen my girl—mind going without me? I'll settle up later."

"But you could go along, Poll," Jean offered cruelly. "I'll stay help Mom get supper."

"Thanks," Polly muttered, "but I'd rather stay. It's so cold."

Sam snorted and tromped on through the clattering doors. "Well don't lollygag all day," he flung over his shoulder. "Your mama wants to see you too, you know."

They stared at each other dumbly when they were alone. And when their mouths desperately, fumblingly met, it was wrong—all wrong. Dan parted his lips as if to say something, then tightened them. "No, I guess maybe I better not," he said finally.

"Better not what, honey?" Polly whispered. She put her arms around him, up under his coat, laid her head against the dull familiar thud of his heart. "Tell me what you were going to say."

Real, Dan—real! She was pounding it into her senses. Not far away, but here, a hard curve of body beneath her arms, a man whose love for excellent ress and generous gesture and honest directness had met with such humiliating compromise. She hid her eyes to clutch him close in some meager, agonized comfort for both of them.

"It isn't the time nor the place, Polly. And I guess maybe it wasn't such a good idea anyway," he said humbly.

And that was worst of all. She could bear anything but

that. Her own sense of guilt and defeat, the family's captiousness—anything but Dan's humility, that resigned, beaten tone in his voice.

"*What* wasn't such a good idea?" she demanded sharply. "Honestly Dan, I don't get you! You're not the way I expected you to be at all! Nothing is! What are you driving at? Are you just trying to arouse my curiosity, or what? Oh Dan—Dan what's the matter with everybody anyway?" she blurted as a hot shame of tears broke.

"No Polly don't," he begged miserably. "Please don't cry. I'll tell you." He gathered her a little tighter, as if there might yet be a chance as he said, "I was going to ask you to marry me before you go back. Or marry me and not go back at all."

"Oh—no!" she cried instantly, startled that out of all her blind confusion that much should be so clear. Was this quick negation a shield for her own weary longing, or the grim logical outgrowth of Ken's experience—and Jean's? She had to go back, keep going back, this time and the next until—until somehow she had triumphed over everything that this bleak day represented. *Everything!* And to compensate, because she could not bear that inevitability—losing Dan, not only as he once had been, but as he was, hungering hopelessly against her now—she kissed him frenziedly and said, "It isn't that I don't love you, honey—you know that! It's just—just—"

"I know what it is," he interrupted quietly. "I know a hell of a lot more than you think I do!"

CHAPTER TWENTY-SIX

THE FINANCIAL STATUS of the Andrews family was again so bad that the gas company had disconnected services, but they could brag truthfully that they had an oil burner attached to their furnace. Unable to get credit, and desperate for fuel, Sam had concocted it out of odds and ends of pipe and a valve which fed the furnace dribblings from a tilted tank of crude oil. It worked. Smokily, malodorously, it worked. As the first trickle of heat choked up through the register, the three bundled figures huddling over it backed away, blinking at the fumes, but beaming excitedly at each other. Dad had come through again!

"Let there be heat, and there was heat!" Jean proclaimed.

"Sam!" Lydia yelled, irritation naturally dominating her relief. "It's smoking!" She coughed demonstratively.

"Have to get used to that," Ken answered, his voice echoing up through the grate below.

"Well can't you fix it? We can't stand this! Tell Dad to do something."

"Dad is doing something." There was a devil of good humor in Ken's voice. The contraption had been partly his doing and it had worked. "Dad's connecting up the gas!"

231

"Now looky here," Lydia sputtered to her unseen opposition. "You tell him I said not to!"

"Aw he probably ain't really," Ramey comforted.

"Why, that'd be stealing!"

There were banging noises from below. The smoke gradually evaporated and diminished.

Ken strode in from the direction of the kitchen, greasy-faced but grinning. Sam followed, waggling a wrench triumphantly at Lydia and twitching with guilty pride.

"Sam, you didn't!" Lydia tragically reproached him.

"You're damn' right I did. A twist of the wrist with the monkey wrench and there she was. Got all three burners goin' strong right now. Just go see. We'll show this town they can't freeze us out. Cuttin' off gas in the middle of winter, not lettin' a man have coal. We'll show 'em!"

"H'ray for Dad!" Jean whooped, giving him a kick in the rear. "Now I can make some candy!"

This cleared the gloom from Ramey's brow. He bounded after, shouting, "And popcorn, Jean! Let's pop some corn too!"

"I tell you it's stealing!" Lydia declared, wringing her hands. "Stealing gas from the gas company that's what we're doing!"

"Heck, they got plenty more," Ken said, filling his pipe and handing the tobacco can back to his father. "It ain't as if it was bread or coal or stuff like that. Gas— what's gas? Just a lotta hot air. I got plenty myself!"

"Hell yes, Liddy," Sam solaced. "We ain't depriving anybody else of anything. They'll never miss it, never know the difference."

"Well I suppose I'll have to let you if you're sure," she compromised uneasily. "And I tell you right now this depression has made a difference. A difference in the moral code of people. Almost a difference in right and wrong. Things look different when you're cold and half-starved!"

There was drama in this and in her own voice saying it. Her spirits were rising with the warmth of the room. The fragrance of bubbling fudge and popping corn floated in. She stood up. "We'll get along! Dogonnit, we'll pull through somehow!"

But there were often times when they doubted it.

Once when they nearly lost. The pails of oil as brought from the filling stations were gummy thick with cold. They took to setting them over a low gas flame to warm and thin.

Kenneth had been down for a new supply before breakfast one morning. Now they were crowded about the kitchen table, frittering away time over coffee and corn flakes, the two men dreading another day of chasing the elusive dollar.

Suddenly there was a burbling glug. Lydia screamed as a single mouth of flame swallowed the warming oil can and sent long tongues licking up the wall paper, leaping with demon speed across the ceiling. Sam's fat stomach was wedged between the sink and the table, but he gave one powerful shove which freed him, crossed the room, and seized the can of boiling oil and was out the door which Ramey already held open. He pitched the mass into the nearest snowbank, and slapping at his shirt with seared hands was back in the kitchen where Kenneth was frantically dousing pails of water at the walls and ceiling.

"Your hands!" Lydia shrieked.

"Nev' mind my hands." He snatched a wet towel from her and began to fight the fire.

They worked silently, swiftly, and with as much uniformity as a trained brigade, Jean handing Ken the pails as they were filled at the faucet of the sink, he standing atop the wreck of the table pitching them accurately at the worst spots of conflagration, Sam, Lydia and Ramey soaking towels in the overflow and beating out the nearest flames.

It was conquered as suddenly as it had attacked. Shaking, soaked, singed of hair and eyebrow, they crept out of the drenched black mess that had a moment ago been breakfast in the kitchen, and collapsed on chairs in the front of the house.

Ramey began to struggle with a window.

"Ramey, don't!" Lydia said. "The neighbors—!"

"Neighbors hell," grunted Sam. "I gotta have a little air."

"Yeah Mom, Dad's gotta have air. He's sick. Look at his hands."

"Oh Sam, Sam, your hands!" Lydia sobbed hysterically. "Go right to the doctor!"

"We can't have a doctor," Sam snorted. "Want the whole town to know about us using the gas when we ain't s'posed to? Get some vaseline. I'll be all right."

Jean produced the salve and a strip of torn sheet. "I think you had better go to a doctor," she said in an undertone.

"No, slap the stuff on. That'll do the trick. I'll be all right, I'm tough, I can stand a little cookin'."

Now they were hunched in a frightened unit of despondency. How would they heat the oil hereafter and so continue to keep warm? How would they ever patch up and repair the wrecked kitchen to keep Old Lady Henniper, the neighbors and the gas company from knowing? An exciting near-death had stalked down upon them and they had met and conquered it with valor; how could they endure the torment of not being able to tell?

"Well," said Jean at length, "we ain't gettin' anyplace sittin' here like a bunch of scarecrows. Mom, you go lie down, you look all in. Ken, c'mon, help me mop up." She turned to her father who was staring grimly at his swathed paws, wondering how he would work with their gnawing pain growing more intense. "Dad, please go see a doctor. Tell him—tell him—" inspiration flashed across her face. "Tell him you did it on the car, that the radiator boiled over on you!"

He looked up. "By God, that is an idea. Liddy, where's that insurance policy I took out when I was trying to sell it? You know—the one that protects you from any accident that happens around a car."

"Why somewhere among your papers I suppose. But Sam, you can't! It wouldn't be right!"

"Right, hell! If I can get twenty-five bucks a week outta bein' laid up I'm a gonna do it. Jean go find it, will you?"

"I doubt if it's good yet," she reminded him, "but I'll look."

"I hope it *has* run out!" Lydia insisted tearfully. "When our family gets so desperate we'll deliberately steal gas and cheat an insurance company—"

But she waited anxiously on Jean's rummaging, and

the announcement, "How's this for a close call? It's dated the twentieth and this is about the fifteenth—that makes it five days to go!" brought Lydia a torment of relief and anxiety. A hundred dollars a month would seem a fortune. They could buy coal, pay up the gas, fix the kitchen, eat, see a movie! And Sam could rest while his hands healed. The brave old darling. And after all, she reasoned, the oil had been hauled *in* a car, and been obtained at a place where cars are serviced so that—actually when you figured it all out, they had the right—almost.

Sam, trudging up the rubber mats of the doctor's stairway, felt his courage ebbing as the pain in his hands increased. He hated to lie. He hated to cheat. He had loved his lifelong brag, "By God we may not have much, but I've always done right, don't y'know I have? It never got us a brick house along the lakeshore like Judge Bellamy and those birds, but it's worth something knowing you've been decent. Ain't that what you say, Liddy?" They had been often desperate, but seldom quite so poor or so desperate as these last two years. His association with Clete Parrish had been the beginning. Sam's crimes since had been ridiculously few, absurdly trivial, harming no one. But despite bombast and damnings, he loathed them and loathed himself for stooping to them. More than all else he would loathe sitting across from the honest spectacles of old Doc Gregg and telling this preposterous thing.

No, damned if he could do it! But how could a man work with his hands burned to the bone? How could he drive and wrangle with people who clutched their remaining money and refused to buy any of the devices he had put together and must somehow sell? How could he put the devices together in the first place without his hands? *How?*

Those were the questions he asked of the doctor as his wounds were dressed. The friendly, "Hi Sammy," of this man to whom he owed hundreds of dollars for the delivery and upkeep of his family, put the truth, grim and frantic, on his lips. He told about the oil, even about the gas.

"As I see it, you were just borrowing gas until you got on your feet again, eh Sammy?" asked the doctor with a comic lift of shaggy white brows.

Sam agreed that he was. Of course he intended to pay for it, when he could!

"I don't see why in hell this burn couldn't been off'm the car," Sam complained. "Then I could've collected on an accident policy I took out. Just my luck. A rich cuss like George Walcott sprains his ankle stepping off a running board and pinches his thumb in the car door and I donno' what all and cashes in, but with all the drivin' I do I even get burned in the kitchen where it don't do me no good!"

"Well supposing we just suppose this did happen in the garage, my ingenious friend Sammy," Doctor Gregg said, unscrewing the cap to his fountain pen and picking up the policy which Sam had slapped disdainfully to the desk.

Sam gripped his shabby hat with his crippled hands. A thick surging crowded up his throat. It was his way of crying, silently, without tears.

"I wouldn't do this for George Walcott," the doctor said, "or any of the spineless leeches on relief. But a man who'll think up a contraption like that, a man who'll snatch a pail of hot oil with his bare hands and hustle it out where it can't blow up his family, an honest, indomitable fighter like you, Sam Andrews, deserves a professional lie, well-told." He stood up. "Sign here, if you can. I'll mail this in. You go home and take one of those pills and go to bed."

"Thanks, Doc," Sam blurted. And as he trotted out his head was low.

Fear and failure had brought them unity. Jean had been blithe, sending her cheer into the chill dark corners of the house, steering off Lydia's despondency, manipulating meals out of nothing, gentle even with Ramey. Ken had cooperated, gamely drowning pride in a raucous kidding as he steered into a filling station, tooted imperiously and commanded, "Fill 'er up! Crude oil in my crude oil can, my crude oil man!"

But with the arrival of the insurance checks which seemed at first a blessed fortune, their exceptional harmony was shattered. The cry changed from "Will we live?" to "Will I get my share?" "I've gotta have shoes!"

"I need 'em worse!" "Dad, can I get a haircut?" "Cigarettes—" "Well I can't cook without lard, can I?" "Coal, by God! And we've gotta do something to the kitchen!"

The state of the kitchen was their sorest trial. The blackened walls made a sorry setting for their meals and screamed evidence of what had happened. They went sick with apprehension whenever Old Lady Henniper's prying cane tapped up the walk, and they kept her out of the kitchen by every conceivable ruse. But it was impossible not to invite Mrs. Ashbaugh in when she came beating on the back door with a steaming kettle of noodles or a platter of doughnuts.

"My kids can't get away with it!" she would roar. "And I hate to throw it out!" Her massive hips overflowing a chair, she would exchange riotous vulgarisms with Jean and Sam—this lady, this president of clubs—ignoring the condition of the room with a kindness so complete that Lydia would weep when she was gone:

"I tell you they don't come often like that woman! I don't care if she is a Presbyterian, she's a saint. And won't this soup taste good? Sam, surely—you don't suppose she suspects we *need* it?"

"Hell no, and what if she does? We gotta eat." Then at his wife's angry distress, he would slap her behind, kiss her sullen mouth and laugh, "Course she don't suspect. Why, the neighbors think we're the Rockafellers. Besides, ain't she been bringing stuff in here for years?"

CHAPTER TWENTY-SEVEN

JUD MASTERS was wonderful and he knew it, in a manner so childishly proud of himself, yet so cleverly beribboned with democracy, that Polly couldn't figure him out. She didn't exactly want to. He had stridden across her horizon in such dazzling regalia that to go probing the trappings for the man beneath would be, she had sense enough to realize, sheer folly. He was important, splendid, and he paid attention to her. What girl in her right mind would ask more?

And yet Polly, who demanded so much of everything, would go prying. At first his being nice to her had been but part of his "policy" of being nice to people. She had known that baldly. Even in her wild flutter of preparing for that first tremendous date, even consoled by the fact that he liked her, she had suspected him of magnanimous motives. "My pal Poll, see? I'm giving her a break and I want you guys to be nice to her." It had been the only gall in the whole event and she had been willing to swallow it to gain the larger glory. But later, in the blue velvet regality of the fraternity's lounge, she hadn't been so sure. She had felt curiously at home—far more so, she marveled, than ever at Gem Lake dances or Vista affairs. And Jud had been big and protective and proud, and his brothers had traded dances quite as if they wanted to, and it had all been so very Cinderella that, in trying to write of it to Dan, she had been taken aback because the truth needed so few embellishments!

And yet when she stripped the truth clean she was perturbed to find that there *were* gross elements of exaggeration in Jud himself. It was such common knowledge that he was popular that no one else took the trouble to observe that actually he wasn't particularly sought after. It's that he's too big for most people, she told herself again. He goes around doing so much good that they shy from him! He tries terribly not to, but in the very trying he makes people feel insignificant. And that part of him—its baffled loneliness of spirit, its confused and secret shame—she understood and for it she felt sympathy.

But what she could not understand or become reconciled to was that his democracy often had a political smack and a smug after-beat.

"Y'know that guy'll do just about anything for me," he would remark with a grin. "Yes sir—" as the eager nonentity raced off to do his bidding "—he may not rate with the big boys but I've found it pays to lend a hand to podunks like that."

Yet it was invariably they who lent the hands, or more accurately their voices to laud his praise, their humble but valid votes when it came to elections. He was president of his fraternity, a member of Coif, one of the twelve Senior A. F. I. men, an editor of *Law Review,* and headed for that superscoop of all legal honors, the Supreme Court Day arguments. And yet what was there about him that invited skepticism, that rang him false? He reminded Polly of someone; some hauntingly familiar person not to be recalled at once because perhaps never seen except in a dream.

Jud Masters her dream man? Her devil howled. Yet why did she wait with such terrible intensity for his calls? Why did her own little destiny seem to hang now in the balance of his regard? Why, when she often felt a fierce protest that he should walk the earth so neatly stocked with all the affluence, pomp and glory that it would be such heaven for Dan to have—why did she know such blind jubilance at times in his presence, feel always as if with one sweep of his hand, one chuckle announcing, "There, Scrub, there it is!" he would dump the whole thing in her lap. All knowledge. All power. All human success. For Jud had the combination. One touch of his fingers and the bolts would be unbarred.

The illusion was heightened by the cultural aspects of university life. Using his own student activities ticket and borrowing another, Jud took her to lectures, plays and concerts. They "dressed," he in his tuxedo, she in one of her two formals—the blue taffeta which she had picked up, slightly soiled, at a closing-out sale, or the rose crêpe which Jean had made out of a pair of curtains and some gold braid originally intended for trimming a lampshade.

They sat in the vast marble auditorium awaiting the coming of the Great who was to bring the Message: Elmer Rice, still raw from a round with the critics; Edna St. Vincent Millay in a medieval gown and haircut to read bewildering enchantment from a very modern loose leaf notebook; William Beebe plunging them under the sea for a breathless peep at a world of flashing scale and fin; winsome little Lorado Taft, kneading clay as deftly, lovingly as housewives knead dough; and that white-haired prince, Norman Thomas, converting them (Polly at least, and passionately) to Socialism.

Or they would await the liquid sweep of gold-fringed curtains for the spun delight of the Play. Or—and this oddly moved Polly most of all—they would wait for the Concert. They would hear the anxious plaint of tested fiddle string, like a small voice pleading to hasten—hasten. And the rich, globe-like sound of a piano key—ripe, ready, pluck me—pluck me. And the jubilant hurt of a smooth cry torn from a horn. She never heard the horn without remembering Ramey, young eyes rolled to the ceiling, as he lifted his adored second-hand trumpet for a wild little hope-cry at the world. They brought her the family, these anxious pre-tunings. And then the moment of awed silence, the delicate spread of the director's hands, the baton's dipping down-swoop—and glory.

Except on the radio, Polly had never heard a symphony before. Now she discovered that it was like poetry unwritten but groping down the labyrinths of her brain in a ghost semi-sleep, like the pictures she hadn't yet painted, but would—but would!

She would feel it all coursing through her in a stinging winy flood.

She would dig her nails into Jud's wrist sometimes, as she exclaimed, "Gee! Isn't it grand? I mean—that last piece—it sort of said everything, didn't it?"

He would grin tolerantly and agree, "Yeah, that bird Beethoven sure could write a mean opus. Y'ever hear *Missa Solemnis?* Boy, there's a grand thing!" And he hummed a few notes. *"Missa Solemnis,"* he would repeat reverently. "Don't hear it often, but I calls it the best thing that old misanthrope ever did." Casually, "Studied up on composers and all that stuff. Nothin' like a little music to round off your personality, eh Smidgin? My grandfather sure could handle a fiddle, and I've got an aunt in grand opera. Rose Linscott, she's sung with Tibbett and all those boys. Y'know I could've been a musico myself if I hadn't been so busy with stuff like football and presiding over the destiny of the proletariat." He laughed and shook his black head. "I played the trombone in our high school band though."

"My brother plays the trumpet."

"Zat so? And once darned if I didn't wade into an opera. *The Eagle Flies High,* I called it—it was about the Boy Scouts and it sure would've been a honey! Yeah, old Jud ain't all just ambassador at large!" he crowed softly. "Never can tell what's underneath the side a guy shows the world. Man can't live by bread and beans alone. Of course," he added jokingly, "I wouldn't be averse to the royalties if I ever get the thing finished and published."

"That's the real job, isn't it?" she ventured. "Reaching a willing publisher for anything?"

"Yeah," he said with a bitterness that attested baldly to some past failure, "they all play favorites. The unknown can't break in. But Gran's got faith in my work. She raised me, you know. She'd back anything I went in for. They can't keep some of us down, can they kid? We'll show 'em!"

He nudged her playfully, encompassed her hand with

his meaty dry one. They didn't look at each other; they sat for a moment locked in a brace of shared longing. *The Eagle Flies High!* Polly thought. Dear God! She wanted to laugh. She wanted to cry. He was so marvelous and so pathetic, so bungling and misguided in his search for adulation. That was the night she felt deeply akin to him.

She did not like him so much the night of the lecture by Stephen Vincent Benét. "Boy, ain't he the fleabite babbler?" Jud scoffed as they left the hall. "If I couldn't make a better talk than that—!"

"But gosh," Polly said, "anybody who could write *John Brown's Body* doesn't need to be an orator."

"Why he lisps!" Jud jeered, smacking a big hand on her shoulder and giving her a tender shake.

"Not in his verse," she insisted stubbornly.

" 'The moon is a white nut peeled of its husk!' " Jud quoted with farcical eloquence. "Nuts! 'Roll your hands in the honey of life'—and get stung, I'd say. That's from one of his earlier poems. He published his first volume when he was about seventeen—ever know that? The boy genius they called him, but I bet there was pull someplace." He snorted in derision. "Heck, if all you gotta do to be famous is put pretty words together, we're a cinch, Poll. Y'oughta see some of my pomes!"

"Yours?" She wrenched away. "Gee, I didn't know you wrote too."

"Oh, there's quite a few things you don't know about me, pal, but you will!" Casually, "I write sonnets mostly. Editor of our paper used to run one about every Saturday night. Gosh, I bet I got enough for a book."

"What are they about?" she asked suspiciously.

"Oh, life and America and democracy and junk. Poet laureate of Mastersville, that's me, kid!" he joked in generous self-satire. Then a shy earnestness coming over his leonine face, "I—wrote one about love once too."

"When, Jud?" she asked with an eager show of interest, though she didn't know just what she hoped. Spring, after all, paced with soft urgings beside them. And she had sat fasting at this perpetual Youth Conference table so long. "Who for?"

"Oh, for somebody you wouldn't know!" he teased.

Jud Masters giveth and Jud Masters taketh away, she thought angrily. Blessed be the name of Jud Masters! And suddenly, to her own astonishment, she was blurting, "Who cares who it was for? You—you great big sure-of-yourself Mr. God!"

"Why—Poll! Why, why Smidgin'!" He clamped both hands upon her shoulders, hauled her up against his starched shirt front. "Since no man knows himself, as the poet says— Well gee, I know a sense of humor and a serious moment don't always mix, but look Poll," he said bluntly, desperately, "you've got something I want!"

She stared at him, amazed.

"Oh dogonnit, I'm a man's man, Poll, I never had any sisters." There was something touching in the way he scowled that. "And I never made love to a girl before in my life. But you—you're so cute and crazy, you're so smart and ambitious we—we'd go places together, y'know it?"

She didn't grasp at once what he was driving at, what he was trying to say, but with a revealing blow, she recognized the elusive person with whom she had sought to identify him. In his thirst for knowledge, his illimitable ambition, even in his pseudo-popularity, in characteristics countless and revealing he reminded her of—*herself!*

Was he, for all their difference in taste and breeding, male counterpart of Polly Andrews? Was he meant to complement her talents, by his skill in handling people, his solid financial background, his prestige, fated to take her places she could never go alone?

He could! There was no doubt of it. Gazing into the stricken intensity of his great handsome bullish face, she realized with a shock that he wanted to! In his crudely smooth, self-protective way, Jud Masters was trying to inform her that he loved her!

"But there's someone else, Jud," she finally said. "Back home."

For an instant he looked incredulous, pained. Then ego came to the rescue. "Attagirl, you sense an advantage and you take it. You know competition just whips me on! Of course," he added quietly, "I wouldn't poach on another man's territory—wouldn't be playing ball, not playing the game. But I know you wouldn't be buzzin' around with me, letting me learn to—care," he blurted unhappily, "if you weren't really free."

Free. The word had a clean and naked sound. Free! You fought your way up and out of things. Clean and high as a beaten rock, you stood alone and were free. Free to choose.

But you had to be careful. "Freedom's a hard-bought thing." You had to be sure.

"I'm sorry, Jud," she said. "I thought we were just friends. I didn't dream that you—" and she too used the silly word—"cared!"

"But you Poll," the man begged in what she sensed was the most painfully humble moment of his life, "you don't think I'm so—bad, do you?"

The distortion. The grotesque anguished mask of hope and challenge. The dumb brute, the Campus Leader, the high-flown Eagle now dashed bitter-low!

"I think you're about the most stupendous person I've ever met," she said sharply, carefully, not looking at him. "And we could go far together, plenty far. But I wasn't kidding. There is someone waiting."

"But you ain't engaged or you'd say so!" Jud bellowed jubilantly, catching her arm and galloping her up the slope. "He's had his chance, now it's mine. And as I say, I relish a little competition. Such as it is."

Thus Jud Masters disposed of Dan Scott.

He circumspectly waited to kiss her until they were in the shadow of her doorstep, but there he did so soundly, if not expertly. And rushing dizzily upstairs later she despised herself because her starved and sentient flesh actually thrilled. But maybe that was best too, she realized, lashing about her room—if it were going to be this way.

If it—were. She thought miserably of her passionate promises to Dan. But she had been blind then, love-drugged, sick with the anguish of wanting. She was rudely awake now, and almost regrettably clear-headed. You had to be, in this world where the weak went down, where you fought for your identity and honor, where you saw with pitiless clarity your own shortcomings, your appalling lack, and with a kind of panic that time is short and already the world is a lap ahead of you. You have to keep in the race by whatever means at hand, you have to watch for a chance to dart ahead and beat the world to the post.

The world. The world of girls going their gay indifferent way without you; of sweetly patronizing club women; the world of Uncle Mac refusing oh so neatly even to endorse your college note; the world of contemptuous sales people and stupid teachers and little pink rabbit registrars who have seen you sweating and gulping in apology for your past due bills. You must show the world! Beat the world! Climb on top of the world and lacerate it with your tall and shining heels!

Out of a blaze of pent-up bitterness came the cold white stone of calculation. Jud Masters could bring all this to pass.

CHAPTER TWENTY-EIGHT

JUD TAUGHT POLLY things like tennis and paddling a canoe, and what there was exciting about baseball. She listened, she learned, quickly but not too adroitly, which was excellent because it allowed her to admire his skill. Nor did Jud skip that pleasant if puzzling essential, sentiment. Once aware that even a female who has something to "offer" lusts after romance, Jud cheerfully began to provide the proper sets, props and lines with all the diligence that he employed in "studying up on composers and all that stuff." Hand in hand and often sighing, they strolled the moonlit avenues tradition-dedicated to campus love. Equipped with blankets, portable phonograph, sandwiches and the books Jud was stripping in preparation for Supreme Court Day, they canoed to an island far up the river and sprawled beneath floating cloud and lacy tree, studying, laughing and making Jud's singular brand of love.

This last consisted in cuffing Polly about like a Great Dane pawing a puppy, picking her up with one hand or tossing her to his shoulder with gleeful Tarzanic shouts. He was very proud of his physical prowess and she was the perfect vehicle for demonstrating it. But when she whimpered that he *hurt,* he would be instantly contrite, hastening with all Boy Scout chivalry and aptitude to render first aid. "Gee, of all the clumsy cyclops!" he'd scold himself. "Why, I wouldn't hurt my little sweet for all the jools of India! Guess I'm just a brute that don't know my own strength. Gee little pal, I'm dopey about you," he would joke mournfully, kissing her with vast respect. Then frowning serious, chafing her hands, "I didn't know a self-sufficient guy like me could get so crazy about a girl. It—it's enslaving, dogonnit!" And he would quote poetry—good substantial stuff like Browning or Scott.

For all his bombast, his often irritating impeccability, he was, Polly knew, a genuinely nice person with a great deal of sincerity, insight, and personal charm. That he was astute enough to use these qualities to best advantage she could have no objection. She was even beginning to profit by it. As Jud Masters' girl she enjoyed a pleasant new prestige in classroom and office, for although Jud the Great had never particularly attracted girls, neither had he sought them; she for whom he had finally fallen was certain to attract some notice. This last factor was as disturbing as it was flattering. Jud, like Dan, was a one-woman man, and he did not take defeat lightly. Already she had let him "learn to care," as he said. What— she sometimes wondered in guilty confusion and a kind of appalled fear—was she getting herself into?

She felt deeply indebted to him. Not only had he rescued her from loneliness, he had patched up many a gap in her knowledge, drilled her in notes, torts, principles of proof, attachments and executions, pleadings and procedure—a myriad of things that had been mistily vague to her. "By golly you'll pass the bar exams when I do this summer or not at all!" he warned her, and gradually, wonderfully, she began to believe. With the shrewd super-scholar, the opportunist, politician, omnipotent Jud Masters, to coach her to the finish, it could, must and would be!

And after that? Beyond that she didn't dare think.

In exchange for Jud's excellent coaching Polly drudged like a little slave on the Brief and Arguments he and his colleagues were preparing for Supreme Court Day. She tagged them cheerfully to the library and wormed through dusty files digging up reports which they studied, outlined and argued about, sometimes honoring her by turning to her for an opinion. When the titanic sheafs and drafts were finally assembled, she did an enormous stint of the typing. And when the copy was back from the printers, she proofed and page proofed until her shoulder muscles were knotted and her eyes bleary, and was rewarded by Jud's jarring backslap, his marveling, "Gee pal, I didn't think there were dames like you! Instead of helping a man, all most girls think about is clothes and how pretty they are and how much money you spend on 'em. Why—" he declared triumphantly, "do you realize that I haven't spent more'n about ten dollars on you altogether?"

Astonishingly, Polly realized that this was so. She didn't know whether to be offended or amused; she thought wistfully for an instant, and yet impatiently too of Dan's extravagance for love. Dan, who had so little.

"No," Jud averred solemnly, "it's wonderful to find someone like you who—who could be a real helpmate to a man." His face was almost brutishly intense, yet childishly hopeful too.

"Just think, mugwump, an office of our own some day, huh? You digging up the dope like you have for us guys (they think you're swell too, by the way) and me turning on the heat in court. I'm sort of a blunt bloke offstage, but don't think I can't be eloquent under fire! Gosh, you should've heard me in the prelims when I was a freshman and then a junior! Me and my partner won every round. He'd studied twice as hard as I did, but when it came to the showdown it was my arguments that won the petticoated pancake. Gee—" he grinned, pleased eyes low as he admitted, "all the guys and profs'n everybody said they never heard anything like it even in real court. Don't think your side-kick won't do you proud when the great day comes. Just you wait!"

Busily and gratefully Polly waited. Jud Masters did not rush into anything, and she needed time, desperately, to make up her mind.

There was so much to be considered. The folks were having a bitter time of it still. The very valiance of Lydia's letters, her determined cheer, so unlike the spasms of melancholy she had in person when things were bad—

were proof enough. I deserted them, Polly often thought wretchedly; I took their money. They're looking to me to succeed. Their faith in me, their hope, is back of all that ghastly cheerfulness Mom writes. I've got to make good! I'm the only one. Ken won't now, and Jean's marriage is a disappointment after all—its secrecy, Stew's folks still unreconciled and working on Stew, upsetting him—and Jean pregnant already, to the town's delight. (Only she *didn't have* to get married! She didn't! They'll see!) I've got to pass those exams. I've got to go on from there. And Jud can help. Jud was the only answer. It would take several hundred dollars even to start practicing. A partnership with Jud would solve everything.

And he wasn't—so bad. Ye gods, she told herself angrily—he's wonderful! He's made to order for me; we fit perfectly; we're alike. And we're crazy about each other really, we get along swell—and if we despise each other a little too, well, maybe that's healthy, that's all right.

Of course there was the difference in background. Stew had been democratic too—before marrying Jean. And there was Dan.

Dan. Here she would halt in her savage pacing, she would stand very still in the silence of her room, and suddenly plunge her face in her hands. Dan! But he might have taken me and he didn't. And she would deliberately flagellate herself with that repulsion, as if to justify and compensate. I'm free. He freed me, himself! I've come this far, but I can't hold up forever. It's only far enough to get my bearings, look about, and make my choice.

But though she fought it through hours on end, she could reach no definite conclusion. It was too much. I'll wait, she finally thought wearily, surrendering to a consoling fatalism. It's coming. One of these days Jud's going to ask me, and then surely I'll know what to do!

The Supreme Court Day arguments were held in the House Chambers of Old Capitol building on a May afternoon. The entire body of the law school attended, plus a liberal sprinkling of parents. There were too, professors, attorneys and district judges, shaking hands and occasionally whooping with rich male laughter; laughter sprung from some dark shining well of favored fortune. You filed the world in metal cabinets; you thumbed the tabs of the world's troubles and told the world what was what; you pointed the sly and secret path that must be taken; you guided and hustled the errant world on its way; you made the laws and you read them, you were crafty and big-mouthed and shrewd, growing fat on the world's ignorance and guile—for you were a lawyer, Lord-God of the universe!

And yet somehow today as always they seemed to Polly a bunch of enviable, vaguely to be scorned, bright and bossy little boys, no more worthy of the power invested in them, than—Ramey! Her own secret delight at finding herself in such a *godely companye* was none the less keen for the observation. She only knew a little more certainly where she stood with this super-circle. She had scrabbled up from a clan expressly created for the badgering of lawyers; with dog-like humility she had served. Now, though they didn't know or care, she was here, triumphant, on the platform of special privilege with them. And she would go on, surpass them. Precisely how she didn't know, but it had to do with her bevy of artistic talents, which she felt few of them possessed, at least in such degree; and with Jud. Jud, the all powerful, who could bring anything to pass!

He strode in now, followed by his partner, a shy, dark little man who seemed more shadow and bodyguard than equal for Jud's ebullience. Polly, however, knew Upton Towne to be fierce, and dependable, that in the brown eyes brooding behind those spectacles lurked a demon of wit and fire. Yes, Jud would be well fortified against the attack of the appellees, now being seated at their table. William Buckley and Harmon Graves constituted the enemy. Both these men Polly knew to be stringent competition, as indeed Jud would wish them, the better himself to shine.

And what of the object of her proud affection? Polly surveyed him with meek trust not untinged with anxiety. His jaw was jutted, there was about him a scowling earnestness that presaged no good for the opposition. Glancing about the room, he grinned with his winsome admixture of bashful but unquestioning assurance, as if to say, "Ain't it the limit? Here I go again!" Catching Polly's eye, the grin twisted into that tugging wink of secrecy. "We know, don't we, kid? We'll show 'em, eh pal?"

Her heart swelled. She hoped so, frantically!

Now in marched with swift and solemn tread the nine black-robed justices. And instantly Polly gulped back her satiric mockings. God, but they looked wise and kind and terrifying! Humility washed over her in a sepulchral flood. Would she ever be half so great as one of these? And Jud —could even he bear up? *Wouldn't they see through him?*

The bailiff rapped, the audience arose; and it was like obeisance in a priested chapel, waiting for the gravely rustling squat of nine bony old rumps upon their elevated bench. Then, hear, ye! Hear, ye! The Supreme Court was now in session!

The chief justice announced the case with all the dignity attendant upon a genuine issue. Indeed neither Polly, nor scarce anyone present, now retained the slightest recollection that anything but a matter of import was to be weighed here this day.

Jud spoke first, and thus it was that almost from the first, as he had subtly predicted, the show was his. Calling into play all the hearty good-fellowship at which he was past master, he scooped the audience up in his palm and held them there. There too he deftly stroked each of the venerable Solons by airing his knowledge of their political and economic status, and addressing them each by name. Polly was at first taken aback by this technique, as plainly were the other members of the quartette, who had approached the tremendous hour less craftily equipped. "Yes, Justice Turner, you as a good Democrat, interpret my remarks correctly. . . . But Justice Dillahunty, had I been counsel for the railroad company I can only hope and assume I'd have framed the interrogatory in much the same manner you framed your opinion in the famous Weishaupt case—" (These offered in such a slyly humorous, boyishly self-effacing tone that the whole court laughed, and pleasure touched the grim old poker faces on the bench.)

When it was all over, the flashlight pictures and the

movies, the reporters hustling up, the handshaking, Polly met Jud in an adjoining chamber, as he had asked her to.

"Well gummywozzle, what'd you think of Papa Jud?" he grinned, bursting with pride in himself as he mopped his brow and jammed data into his cowhide briefcase.

"Oh Jud, I'm speechless. I'm—overwhelmed!" She was. It was a trifle dismaying. "You were wonderful!"

"Yeh—" He knocked her chin playfully with a big smooth fist. "You weren't any too sure of me. You had doubts, I could tell!"

She gasped and sputtered, secretly astonished that he had known.

"But I guess I showed my little sweety pal," he gloated. "I guess now she knows who'll be announced winning duo at the banquet tonight!"

"Yes." She was beaming, willing to wallow in humility, her pride and delight in him were now so great. "Yes, there's no doubt of it. Even Buck and Harmon know they're licked."

"Then you'll marry me?" he blurted. "If we do win—" he was scowling, eyes low, as he fumblingly tugged at the straps of his case—"you'll marry me, pal?"

Polly stood very still for an instant, staring at him. It had come. How like him to sneak up on her at an auspicious moment like this and blurt it out. She stood waiting, in a blind and frigid tension, for her own answer to form. And it was as she had trusted; now there seemed no doubt.

"Yes," she said levelly, "I'll marry you, Jud."

CHAPTER TWENTY-NINE

LYDIA SAT ON the piano bench in the Swell Room, writhing through one of the most distressing conferences of her life. In the first place, she had been "caught dirty." She had gotten up this morning with a dizzy headache, and had scarcely touched the house. This afternoon she had lain down without first getting cleaned up, and it would be just her luck to have somebody come. Somebody special.

It was. Facing those three gracious ladies who emerged from the shiny car and came up the walk, smiling and cordially inviting them in, taxed her hospitality to its limits. Snatching at papers, straightening her mussed hair, apologizing in a voice nervously loud, she seated them, Kit and Mrs. Scott on the davenport, Kay in the big chair. So cool they were, so exquisitely dainty in their summer chiffons and white gloves, while here she perched in her most faded, ragged old house dress, smiling until her jaws ached and trying to keep her voice steady as she evaded their inquiries about Polly.

"We're so disappointed at not finding her here," Kay said. "We thought we'd take her home with us and surprise Dan. School is out, isn't it?"

"Well it's over," said Lydia, clearing her throat. "But she hasn't come home yet. She went home with a friend to visit for a few days before going to Des Moines to take her oral bar examinations."

"And then when do you expect her?" Mrs. Scott leaned forward.

"It will be another week or so at least," Lydia said. She drew a deep tight breath. "Hasn't she—hasn't she let Dan know?"

"Oh surely she must have!" Kit said. "It's just that he hasn't let *us* know. I just can't understand Dan any more. He's so reticent about everything these days."

Suddenly an embarrassing silence was upon them. Lydia, gripping the edge of the piano bench, heard Ramey tramp into the kitchen, get a drink and leave the faucet trickling; then the door's slam, the raucous little boy bellow as he shouted down to a friend. Children had so little consideration! she thought in confused rebelliousness. Oh why—why did Polly have to do a thing like this? . . . Not that it wouldn't be best in the long run—surely. But to make this decision in such haste, to go off down there visiting that fellow's grandmother, instead of coming home first to explain. (When Lydia was *so lone*some for her too now that Jean, in spite of her condition, was off on that foolish trip with Stew! Stew's folks couldn't come up *here* to meet their daughter-in-law, now that they'd finally decided to be forgiving, oh no! Stew probably didn't even want them to, she thought bitterly. Instead, when the high and mighty Volds beckoned, the culprits had to trot! Children—parents—her mind groped in its distress. Just no consideration at all! But Scotts, on the contrary, were *so* nice.) Oh, why had Polly been so headstrong, unfeeling—not even telling Dan apparently? Leaving Lydia in a spot like this!

"Law!" Kay exclaimed presently. "It's hard to imagine Polly a lawyer. I suppose because she's so little. And she will be, after these examinations, won't she?"

"We hope so," Lydia said, breathing deep. "Of course she's had it pretty hard, trying to qualify with just a year at the university. But she seems to have passed the written ones all right."

"Has she made any plans to actually practice?" Kit asked. She sounded slightly incredulous. They all did. There was a quality of unreality about the immediacy of

Polly's career. A year ago she had been but an energetic girl with a curious dream. Now the dream was coming true and they couldn't get used to the idea. They weren't quite sure they liked it—Lydia now least of all.

"Yes. Yes, she has," Lydia acknowledged. "I'm not exactly free to discuss it yet but—she may enter a partnership."

There was a second of silence as this took effect. Lydia found that she was trembling absurdly, that it was hard to breathe. That she was evading an issue, hiding something, was obvious, though these polite ladies gave no indication that they noticed. They just sat there smiling their vaguely puzzled smiles, but wondering. And they were so charming, so exquisitely groomed. They made her feel inferior and on the defensive, reminding her somehow that Dan was quality, that if anything it might have been they who were concerned about *his* marrying Polly! But instead they had come here in simple eager kindliness to offer their hospitality, which must only be rebuffed.

"A partnership," Mrs. Scott murmured. "That's nice. Here?" she asked.

"No, I'm afraid not. I'm afraid that if she—accepts this offer—she'll be leaving us for good." Lydia's eyes were uncontrollably wet. At the moment she desperately meant the words that rushed out. "But maybe she'll change her plans. Maybe she—she won't even be admitted to the bar, after all! I tell you I don't know—I just don't *know* what's best! She needs a rest. She's worked too hard. I wish she'd stay home, just be with us awhile, all of us—you folks as well as us. I—I wish she'd marry Dan and just stay close to home!"

And now that it was said, she did! From the first Lydia had been upset about that man Polly was writing home about. Nobody could be that perfect and not be downright horrified at the Andrewses! Jean's marriage rose before her like a stark warning; thus far it had brought only misery to Jean, Stew, all of them. But this plan of Polly's was even worse. When Lydia considered Jud's money, his background and prestige, all that would be expected of his relatives, she was terrified. If Polly had tried to camouflage and change them on Dan's account, what would be in store for them if she ever brought Jud Masters home? Only, she knew with deep stifling pain—Polly had changed, she was harder and wiser now. She might not even risk it, she might not even bring him home with her! And oh, it was so unfair, all of it—so tragically, confusingly unfair to Dan.

"We all do," Mrs. Scott said. "But I'm afraid that now—"

She looked questioningly at Kay, who began to pull on her gloves. "They'll work out their problem," Kay said. "After all, Dan wanted her to go. He must have anticipated this."

"Yes." Lydia was crying with apologetic little gulps. "Yes, he wanted her to go. He knew what to expect." Somehow, recalling that helped to mitigate her own pained sense of responsibility. "But oh—he's such a good boy!"

"Yes, he is," Mrs. Scott agreed without apology. "He just hasn't found himself and it's our fault, really—the fault of us parents who have had to depend on our children because of the times. But times will change. Times are bound to get better, even if it takes a war to do it," this quiet little woman said astonishingly, pulling on her gloves.

CHAPTER THIRTY

POLLY WAS A mouse every minute she spent in Grandmother Masters' gloomy old mansion in Mastersville, Iowa. When she spoke she squeaked. Perched miserably on one of the many ornate and hideously uncomfortable Louis XIV chairs, she kept her hands folded. She had, she felt, in some strange spell cast by stained glass windows and velvet portières, changed to a sickly blue-gray hue. She nibbled at the food which a housekeeper as old as Grandmother Masters herself set before her on Dresden china, sterling silver, and thick cut glass. She nodded in agreement with Grandmother Masters' declaration that Edgar A. Guest was the only poet of insight since Oliver Wendell Holmes—with the exception, however, of a certain Masters' cousin by the name of Jenny Blake, whose privately printed works Polly could aspire to own when she entered the family. Inwardly sniffing but uttering silly squeals of delight, Polly examined the leather-bound doggerel which she wouldn't be caught dead reading, let alone possessing!

She cheeped and mewled false admiration for the monstrosities which Grandmother Masters had dragged home from all parts of Europe and America in the name of art. An Italian marble fireplace, resplendent with cherubim, seraphim and dove, eighteenth century French urns,

Chinese gongs, fancily dazzling buhl work tables, plus a clutter of remarkably ugly and "unique" statues, lamps and clocks. Peeping, "A feather mattress, how lovely!" she crept into the black walnut four poster which Gran assured her had cost a thousand dollars, and nearly smothered.

She loathed being a mouse. She despised herself in the role so utterly that even her devil was too disgusted to jeer. But she dared not risk offending this generous old lioness, Jud's grandmother, by whom Jud's law practice was to be financed. And so she went pitty-patting about the Persian-carpeted, velvet-draped tomb, unutterably bored, acutely miserable, and wildly anxious to get home. Home to the lake and Mom and Dan.

Grandmother Masters' idea of a good hostess was to be a good monologuist. Her guests need never strain to make conversation. She *was* conversation. She made a mouse of nearly everyone she met. For this reason she was considered something of a tyrant in this small city which had been named for her husband and which owed its very existence to her washing machine factory. Sycophants she had in plenty, men aspiring to jobs or advancements, their wives courting favor to that end—but few friends. She was a very lonely old lady who, now that travel was burdensome, strove to bury a lifelong lack in an avalanche of words. All that had ever concerned her and hers became through the resonant trumpet of her voice, signal and to be marked with awed respect by those lesser clans which comprised society.

She did not begrudge these outsiders their accomplishments, she simply ignored them. All persons allowed to slide down the toboggan of her tongue landed adequately clad in coats-of-arms, or at least waving credentials. The great were Masters' intimates, the near-great Masters' friends, the superior Masters' associates, and the inferior objects of Masters' charity.

On this ladder toward Masters recognition Polly found no rung to which she could cling.

As—the night at dinner when Grandmother Masters was extolling Jud's genius. "He was a very precocious child," she bragged with a nod of her overcurled white head. "He skipped a whole grade in school, mind you! A whole grade, Polly, what do you think of that?"

Polly had opened her mouth and was groping for words that would subtly put over the thought that the skipping of one might be excellent, but the skipping of three—as she knew from experience—could be downright brutal, when Jud cut in, "And gee were those other blokes sore! Thought it was pull or something."

"Pull!" his grandmother snorted. "Just because his uncle was president of the school board. Jealousy, that's all it was. There are drawbacks to everything, Polly. The bigger the man the bigger the target, as Senator Masters used to say. And as you'll find out when you're Jud's partner. A man's wife is blamed for his success just as much as he is!"

"Say Gran that's good," Jud laughed. "That's sure a crack at the proletariat, ain't it, Poll?"

Polly laughed too and mousily agreed that it was, thus furthering her standing with Grandmother Masters, whose approval was daily growing for a girl of such attainments as Jud had described who could yet be so modestly in good taste, so enthusiastically Masters-conscious when in the Masters household. So pleased in fact was Grandmother Masters with her own wit and the appreciation of it by her prospective relative, that she was moved then and there to do something about it. She leaned forward, chuckling to herself. The candlelight shone rosily on her white bob of hair which sat absurdly like a doll's wig above the gaunt sharpness of her face.

What a homely old crone she is! Polly thought. She laughs like water going down a clogged sink.

"Now children," said the old woman impressively, "I have a surprise for you."

Polly and Jud exchanged glances. This, they hoped, the long awaited signal that Gran was ready to talk finances. She knew and approved of their plans but thus far, to Polly's mystification and suspense, nobody had even mentioned money.

"If you'll come into the library with me—" She arose with a flashing gesture of gemmed hands. Jud gave her his arm. Polly trotted along behind.

Thank heaven! This thing settled, maybe she could get out of staying on here until after the orals. Maybe she could think of some excuse to go home. Home—Home to Dan. What she would say to him, how tell him, she didn't yet know. Only that he could turn the sense of loss and bitterness incorporate in her very triumph, into a riot of pain, deep and good.

Without the healing dignity of that hurt, this step—a crass marrying for money, advantage, like some trite picture-show formula, would be intolerably shallow and absurd. Dan—even the fact of his anguish at giving her up—could fortify her for the future. And selfish, distorted though she knew the attitude to be, it was something she could not help.

A gas log hissed bluely in the library grate. They sat down before it on a purple and gold striped settee whose six cloven hooves perched upon six shiny purple globes. Tonight Grandmother Masters was too intrigued by her generosity to remind them, as she generally did, that they were sitting upon a fortune. She arranged the lace ruff at her wrinkled neck, folded her hands, and smiled into the poorly concealed anticipation of their faces.

"Children," she announced, "you're going to be married right here!"

"Gran!" Jud whooped. "D'you mean it?"

"Oh but we couldn't!" Polly cried feebly. She was alarmed. This thing was rushing toward consummation too fast. And she was offended. Weren't brides usually consulted about such things?

"And," Grandmother Masters continued, blithely ignoring the protest, "Polly is going to wear my wedding dress! The one your own mother wore, Jud."

At once Jud became very solemn. He put his arm around her and the two of them gripped hands in true Masters' expression of grief, their faces stoical as they recalled the tragic run-away in which Jud's mother had broken her neck and his father been fatally trampled in an attempt to stop the horses. Four-year-old Jud had landed unhurt in the mud.

"I never had a daughter to wear it," Grandmother Masters informed Polly, "so I determined that as long as I lived the brides of my sons and grandsons should be married in it. You'll be joining distinguished company, my dear, when you don that old Venetian lace. Rose, the

prima donna I spoke of, she wore it when she married
Jud's Uncle Hervey. Blanchard, my son who's now an
Episcopal bishop, saw his wife come down the aisle in it.
And you'll have the honor of being the first granddaughter
to wear it!"

She drew back, pleased, proud. Polly did her best to
look impressed. But suddenly, to her own amazement, she
heard her own devil-prodded voice inquiring, "But isn't
it customary for a girl to be married in her own mother's
wedding dress?"

The instant the words were out, she was aghast. That
was rude! she thought. And how in the name of heaven
could I wear that old moth-riddled suit affair Mom senti-
mentally showed me once? What's come over me? She
sat with her hands locked tight, half-pitying the old
woman's obvious consternation, half enjoying it.

Grandmother Masters was baffled only for a minute.
"No, it is *not* customary," she declared adamantly. "Not
when they are married in my house!"

"But—but maybe I'd rather not be married here!" Polly
said. She was striving to keep her voice sweet, but there
was a defiant trembling behind it. She felt, in a sudden
stupid and awful panic, as if she were going to cry. "Maybe I'd rather be married at home!" Home. Ken hammering a wedding march on the out-of-tune piano, Ramey
tooting accompaniment to the prima donna's solo, the
good bishop perching on Dad's crutch chair! Her devil
howled with laughter. Her throat choked tight.

"Well gee, Poll," Jud said concernedly, "we—well, we
didn't know you felt that way!"

Polly kept her eyes low. I've got to get control of myself! I mustn't be a fool. "I'm sorry," she managed. "I
didn't mean to sound ungrateful. Only most girls are
married in their own homes. Their—their parents sort of
expect them to be. I mean—there's no reason why I
shouldn't be too!" she declared with sudden passionate
conviction, looking up. "And—and it would be so much
trouble for you."

"Trouble!" Grandmother Masters snorted, affronted.
"I can hire things done, can't I? I've staged weddings fit
for a king, and on shorter notice than this too! I could
have the invitations out, the caterers hired, this place

decorated inside of a week or two. No sir," she declared vehemently, "I've never seen Jud act this way about a girl before, but I always swore that when he did, no matter *who* she was, I'd see that he married her properly, and without wasting time!"

"Aw now Gra-an!" Jud colored with embarrassment. He was acutely troubled by the unexpected feud between these two. Grinning and cajoling, he grabbed Polly. "Say, ain't Gran swell though, huh?" he demanded. "You don't realize what she can do. And y'know what I been thinking? Why couldn't we pull the big show the same day we get admitted to the bar? It'd sure make headlines, and the papers playing up the romantic angle wouldn't hurt a coupla kid barristers just getting started. Why, I bet—"

Just then, to Polly's infinite relief, the old housekeeper labored in. "Pardon me," she puffed, "but long distance is calling. For the young miss."

Puzzled but grateful, Polly broke free. She couldn't have stood much more.

It was Lydia's voice which came trembling down the wire. "Polly, you've got to get home right away. Jean's been taken to the hospital! She's—awfully bad."

"But I thought she was off on that trip with Stew."

"They just got back and she—she—" The receiver vibrated with wrenching sobs.

"Don't cry Mom, please! There isn't time. What happened? What's wrong?"

"She's had her baby. A baby boy—premature, but they think he'll live. Now—you—come!"

"Yes. Yes Mother, I'll come right away, as soon as I can."

For a moment after Polly had hung up, she stood in the hall, trying to control the sudden violent trembling of her limbs. Jean having her baby—already? It didn't make sense. Nothing did. Her own being here in this nightmarish house! She swam up from the blind gulf of living and saw the African mahogany hall tree grown there beside her like some horrible jungle plant; the eagle on the convex mirror clutched her distorted reflection with talons of gold. My God, who is that, who am I? What am I doing here? And the loss of identity, the magnificent distortion became symbolic of the indignity Jud expected her to placidly accept, all the intolerable humility and shameful denying of her own kin that would always be expected of her.

Grandmother Masters got unsteadily to her feet when Polly returned. It was evident that she resented this intrusion upon her plans, though she managed to look concerned when Polly told them, "My sister's awfully sick. Mother wants me to come home."

"That's too bad," the old woman said irritably. Then sharply inquisitive, "What's the matter with your sister?"

"Why, she's—" For some obscure reason Polly resented having to admit the truth. "She's had a baby. Things don't seem to be going well."

"Oh—that!" The old woman waved a jeweled claw. "You young girls don't seem to be able to stand things nowadays. Too much soft living, I guess. Why, when I had mine—"

Jud had looked acutely uncomfortable from the moment of Polly's announcement. Now he interrupted, "Gran, look—I wonder if you'd excuse us? Polly and I have got some things to talk over. Okay?" Before she could answer, he hurried Polly back into the gloomy, chilly hall.

"Gee pal I'm sorry about this," he said, frowning. "You think you've really got to go right now?"

"I'm afraid so, Jud. Mother says Jean's pretty bad."

"Well that's a shame," he condoled bigly. "Just—just when we were hitting our stride on our plans too." But it was evident that something even more than that was bothering him. Polly waited tense, and with an unhappily suspicious little grin, he blurted it out. "This sister—ain't she the one that got married last winter?"

"Fall!" Polly corrected indignantly. "But they didn't announce it until later."

"Oh yeah. Yeah, that's right," he agreed a trifle too quickly. He still wore that troubled grin. "Well, I just wanted to get you out of there before Gran got to checking up. Y'see, smudge, I understand about these things. Understand perfectly. Golly, what kind of a liberal would a guy be if he didn't? But Gran—"

"Gran what?" Polly blazed suddenly. She felt weak and sick and furiously strong. She wanted to claw him, this handsome young paragon. She wanted to kick and scream and bloodily bite. "What about Gran? And you—what've you got to be so damn' smug and liberal about?"

"Why Poll! Why—why, Smidgin!"

"My sister's a good girl, do you hear? A hell of a lot better than I am, if you want to know it!"

"Poll—" He looked faintly ill. "You don't mean—"

"Oh, I'm a virgin, if that's what's bothering you. But I wouldn't be, if a certain man I know hadn't been so darned swell!"

This was crazy! What was the matter with her? Then she was clutched by a calamitous impulse to laugh. For Jud's first aghast stare had changed to an almost tenderly pleased expression. He thought—there was no doubt of it—that she meant him!

"Why honey, I didn't dream it was—hard for you! I didn't know!"

He tried to take her in his arms, but she twisted away, covered her face with her hands. She mustn't laugh— mustn't! He was too funny—and insufferably pitiful, grimacing with emotion like that.

"All right," he said quietly, "I won't touch you. I know you're under a strain. But now more than ever I hope we needn't postpone our marriage long. And if you'll forgive me for saying so, this means a great deal to me. You've never told me you love me, you know. And this proves it. Doesn't it?" he whispered hopefully, bending close.

As suddenly as she had been stricken with laughter, she was crying. She felt so guilty, so mean and all mixed up. "Oh—I—I don't know! It—it just makes me so mad to have anybody think my family isn't everything it should be! I—I just go nuts!"

"I'm sorry, honey. I apologize. Of course you come from a fine family! Why, I bet—"

"No, I don't," she interrupted impatiently, dabbing at her eyes. "That's the funny part. You've got an awful surprise in store. My folks are—" Even yet she couldn't force the word "poor." "We aren't well-off, and we're all crackpots—like me, I guess. But I love them. I won't hurt them or cheat them for anybody alive! Not even your grandmother, Jud." She looked at him steadily. "And since I've been in your home, found out that even our wedding would have to be hers—the Masterses—I've been wondering if I wasn't a fool to say I'd marry you at all."

"Polly, listen." He took both her arms. There was nothing grotesque in his face now. "You're going home now, but you've got to come back for the exams. Meet me in Des Moines that day. Or I'll drive up after you. Anyway, we're going to take those orals together and go away some place together and be married. Just you and I, Poll, regardless of what Gran wants."

CHAPTER THIRTY-ONE

SAM STOOD ON the brick platform looking up as Polly's heels ticked down the iron steps of the train.

"Hi, Dad!"

"Hi, Polly."

She kissed him briefly on the lips. The stubble on his ruddy cheek and the hairs curling up at the throat of his dark blue shirt were surprisingly white. Otherwise, he was unchanged.

"This all you got?" He kicked her bag with a crippled shoe.

"I checked the rest." She handed him the stubs. "Want me to go along?"

"Not unless you want. The car's parked right over there."

Peering at the pasteboards, he went trotting across the platform, behind the creaking baggage cart. It was early. The sky was still faintly ribboned with dawn and the air was chill. Polly shivered in her thin suit as she went over to the cindery parking section where the car stood. The fenders were rusting. The Happy Hen painted on the door was beginning to peel.

She got in and leaned her head against the worn upholstery. The little town was just beginning to wake up. Across the street, a man in coveralls came out of the filling station and began to hose the drive. The smell of coffee came faint and aromatic from a near-by lunch wagon. People were beginning to straggle past on their way to work, whistling, jingling keys. Polly huddled lower, eyes closed. She didn't want to speak to anyone just yet.

Sam tromped up with the bags. Unlocking the trunk that made the rear end of the car protrude like that of a duck, he energetically shoved them in. He came around and fitted his stomach under the wheel.

Polly sat erect and asked the question that hadn't seemed expedient until now. "Dad, how's Jean?"

"Well she ain't any too good, but she'll pull through." He backed up with a jerk. "Mama and I ain't lost any of you kids yet and we don't intend to start now!"

It was almost funny in its grim ultimatum. Sam, the boss, the super-salesman, was telling the Lord just how far He could go.

"When did all this happen?"

"Yesterday afternoon, right after she and Stew got in from that trip to see his folks. We tried to get her not to go in the first place, but you know how she is—can't tell her a damn' thing!"

"Dad, please don't talk that way. Not now."

"Hell, a man's gotta say what he thinks. Everybody else will. They'll say she had to get married, like they been wanting to think."

"Yes. Sure they will."

"Mama and I know better, don't you know we do? But there ain't a way you can prove a thing like this, not a way in the world. I'm so fightin' mad already I can hardly see straight, but I might as well go jump in the lake for all the good it'll do."

"That's right," Polly said. "We've got to forget how it looks. The main thing now is Jean." They were passing the ancient ivied brick shambles of the college. Beyond it, already flaked with sunlight, lay the lake.

They bumped to a stop at the curb. And the reality of the old familiar scene—the great trees arching the walk with their lacy shade, Ramey's ball glove drooling horse-hair on the sagging front step, the bright crooked patches on the rusty screen—struck like a comforting fist, dulling the possibility of this thing. Jean would come yawning and writhing down the stairs, kiss her sister with long red mouth, jeer some gaily lewd remark as she flounced past.

It was Lydia who came downstairs. Polly could see her mother's feet on the steps; then her body in a rumpled crêpe dress, lace collar awry; then her stricken face, the eyes tragic in a way that made the most impassioned tears of the past seem slight.

"Polly!" It was a little croak. Lydia came into Polly's arms and wildly, softly cried. Dry-eyed, Polly held her close in small firm arms.

"Don't cry, Mom."

"No, Mother, please," Sam said wearily. "Hell, she ain't dead yet."

"Sam!" Lydia glared at him. "How can you? How *can* you?"

Now Kenneth swung around the landing, a look of grave importance on his handsome face. "Yeah Dad, for Lord's sake. Remember Mother's been up all night."

"C'mon, Liddy," Sam said humbly, patting her shoulder. "Let's go see if Ramey's got breakfast ready. Polly's prob'ly hungry."

The kitchen smelled bitterly of boiled-over coffee and scorched egg. Ramey, a dishtowel around his waist, was pitching silverware onto the oilcloth as they came in. "Hi, Polly Woggy!" He hugged her clumsily; he had grown inches again. "Glad t'see you back in front, old top!" He slapped the appropriate places. Then in a seriously grown-up tone, "Gosh, ain't it awful about Jean?" He snuffled loudly.

"All right, Ramey—all right!" Ken hushed him. "How about something to eat?"

And it was the same, every intonation, every move; how could anything more cardinal than a lost job or a threat of dispossession be wrong? But a new solemnity was upon them that squelched even their appetites. Presently they shoved aside their plates, got up and filed into the Swell Room, where Sam recited the facts. Against the wishes of the doctor and the family, Jean had taken that trip to meet her in-laws.

"But I should think Stew would have known better!"

"He did. He didn't want her to go, and you can't blame the guy, damned upsetting for everybody, his folks suddenly yelling for him to bring her home after all this time, and her in the family way!" Sam chewed gum vigorously and slapped his knee. "But that just egged her on. 'I'm not ashamed if you're not!' she told him. 'We ain't got anything to be ashamed about!'"

"And they haven't!" Lydia seethed. "That's what makes it so hideous, so ghastly—what people will say!"

"I guess they treated her all right, but she was sicker'n hell by the time they got back. Only she tried not to let on. The kid's got spunk, don't y'know she has? She even joked."

Ken turned from the window, tamping his pipe. "Yeah, when Mom finally pinned her down about what was wrong, she said, 'Frankly folks, I feel like I'm going to have pups!'" He tipped back his head and the whoop of his laughter washed the room clean.

Holding their sides, feeling that they mustn't, that it was wrong somehow, they broke into laughter, and found the rich tearing hurt of it wholesome and good.

"No!" Polly gasped. "And wh—what did Stew say?"

"Well, you know how Stew is," Kenneth grinned. "For a minute Stew looked disgusted, then in that dead-pan way of his, he said, 'For Lord's sake, woman, hold it! A premature baby's bad enough, but premature pups—ye gods!'"

And they were off again.

"That's what the poor little tike looks like too," Sam said, when he had subsided to a chuckle. "A little blue hairless pooch. They weren't going to let Mama and me see him!" he announced indignantly. "Us, his own grandparents, don't that beat hell? But I guess we fooled 'em, didn't we, Mama? We snuck in the nursery when nobody was lookin' and if they don't roast him in that contraption they got him in it'll be a wonder. Believe me when I get a chance I'm goin' to tell that young Doc Lansdale a thing or two!"

"Lansdale?" Polly asked. "Why didn't she have Dr. Gregg?"

"Well, Jean sort of hated to go to Dr. Gregg," Lydia said. "You see, we haven't got Ramey paid for yet!"

They went to the hospital later that morning. Polly was startled to find that her palms were cold and her throat tight as she and Lydia waited for Sam to bully the nurse into letting them in.

"What's the matter, Polly—you sick?" Lydia whispered.

"I'm all right. Just tired. And I couldn't eat much breakfast."

Sam muttered in his resonant undertone, "Beats hell her own family can't get in without all this red tape."

"Now, Sam, it—it's for her own good."

The nurse returned to tell them they could go in for a few minutes. "But please don't talk to her. She mustn't be excited in any way. She's been hemorrhaging, you know."

They nodded gravely and stole past the No Visitors screen which barred the door. The room smelled of ether, disinfectant, and spicily of the red carnations on the dresser, the only spot of color in this sterile white cell.

Jean lay in the high iron bed, her body scarcely making a ripple under the spread. It *was* Jean, Polly recognized with a sense of shock. Her deep-set eyes seemed to have been pushed even deeper into her head. The big mouth was colorless and drawn down a little at the corners. Only her bright hair, spilling like a fountain of light upon the pillow, and her hands fisted across her breast as she had slept for years, seemed the same.

As they stood at the foot of the bed, she stirred and opened her eyes.

"Oh, we woke her up!" Lydia panted in soft anxiety.

But Sam trudged forward, bent over. "How you feel, kiddo?"

Jean focused her tired gaze on him and weakly grinned. "Hi, Dad. Who's that with you?"

"That's Mother," he said loudly. "And Polly. Polly's home!"

"Oh. Hi, Mom," Jean whispered. "Hi—Poll." Her head rolled over on the pillow and the sisters regarded each other. Then one hand dragged itself up the covers to Jean's drawn face. Lying at death's door, Jean feebly thumbed her nose.

The nurse returned and told them they must go. They crept out and down the hall, past the mystery of other rooms whose doors stood slightly ajar.

"She—looks pretty bad," Polly said. Now for the first

time she felt the reality of this. That last idiot gesture so typically Jean, made it true as nothing else could. "But as long as she can do that—"

Lydia nodded. "I feel as if I should be right there with her," she worried, "but they—they don't want you to. They don't even want you to stay here and wait."

"They are pretty damn' independent out here," Sam whispered to Polly. "But after all, there ain't anything you can *do*."

Before the door marked, *Nursery. No Admittance,* Sam paused. "Wanta see him?" There was something touching about the generous importance of his tone—like his emollient offering of candy and picture shows to "take their mind off it" when he had lost a job.

"Oh no, Dad, not now!" Polly said, alarmed.

"Well, I just thought I might fix it." He jammed on his hat. "Guess the little devil'll be better lookin' in a few days at that. Yeah," he sighed as they went down the lobby steps and out into the hot blue brilliance of the day, "we mustn't worry. Jean's gonna be okay."

At the foot of the cliff upon which the hospital stood, the lake was ablaze. The air smelled loamy and grassy, of the delicate bitterness of nasturtiums, and freshly of fish and water and sand. It was good after the aseptic gloom inside. They pulled it into their aching throats and headed toward the car.

Several other cars were parked on the curved drive. Two people emerged from one of them, a man and a tall woman in yellow linen and a garden hat, her arms filled with flowers. They were face to face with the little trio before eyes met and recognition dawned.

"Dan! Why—*Dan!*"

"Hello, Polly," he said without surprise. "When did you get home?"

"Just now! Just this morning."

They stared at each other, made no move to come together. His head seemed unduly large with its thick burden of curls, and long hours of plowing had burned his skin an almost apricot red. But there was a dignity about him that belied the dumb hurt in his eyes. There was still the old poise that was so confusing, that had always made her feel angrily humble and ill at ease.

"I'm sorry about Jean," Dan said. "I'm sorry it—had to be this that brought you home."

"Yes." She could scarcely breathe. She was conscious of the perspiration on her upper lip, and the stifling crash of her heart. "Yes, so am I," she said inanely.

Kay had spoken to Sam and Lydia in low, sympathetic tones. She turned now to Polly, extending a slender hand. "It's good to see you, Polly, but we're so worried about Jean! Vee Jordan's call last night came as quite a shock."

The corners of Sam's mouth tightened with quick truculence. "I suppose it'll shock a lotta people. I suppose they'll all be saying she had to get married."

The anguish on Lydia's face deepened. She emitted a little moan.

Kay looked mildly taken aback. "Oh, my goodness," she protested, "I didn't mean to imply—"

"I know *you* didn't, Mrs. Teele." Sam folded his arms and chewed delicately on his gum. "Bein' a doctor's wife and all, you understand about things like this, but a lot of people'll be tickled to death to think that secret marriage was 'cause she was already in the family way!"

"Look Kay," Dan interrupted deftly, "let Polly and me take those flowers on in." The eyes of brother and sister touched briefly. For an instant too Kay glanced at Polly with an expression of tenderness and concern, as if asking her to realize that they understood. Then Dan took Polly's arm and they went together up the concrete walk and through the heavy doors.

Polly's head was low. Her eyes blurred and her throat felt strangled. "They won't let us see her," she muttered.

"No. Sure not. I'll give these to the floor nurse. Wait here." In a moment he returned and stood looking at her. "Polly, don't honey!" he begged. "Not this first day you're home. Don't look so harsh and defiant. No one's blaming your dad, just as no one's blaming Jean."

She said nothing. She stood in savage silence letting the familiar wound of family pride and shame and Dan's love cut through the mousiness, falsehood and failure of all these past months.

"Kay and I came because we love you and your folks. All of you. That won't ever change, Polly, no matter what you think. No matter how much you change, yourself."

She put her hands over her face. Down the hall an infant wailed. She was going to make a scene. She didn't care. They must be used to scenes here.

"I haven't changed," she said thickly. "Oh Dan, I—I haven't changed at all!"

"Here," he said. "In here." He guided her around a corner into a small waiting room. He kissed her. After Jud's clumsy, half-playful kisses, the grave touch of Dan's mouth was like coming alive after death. "Polly," he asked, "are you going to marry that guy?"

She drew back. For a long startled moment she studied his face. Not like this. She hadn't planned it to be like this! Freeing herself from his arms, she went and stood by the window that overlooked the lake. "I don't know," she said.

"You've got to tell me, Polly." His voice was more desperate than she had ever heard it. "I—I can't go on like this. I've got to know!"

She stood there, tugging at the ball fringe on the curtain, watching the cranes cutting the sky like white boomerangs. When she spoke it was as if she had not heard him, although she had heard plainly. She spoke cruelly, out of some blind resentment that he was so much finer and more honest than she. Out of the frantic miserable groping of her heart. "I don't know," she repeated. "I owe you so much."

"Owe me?" he asked in a sick whisper. *"Owe* me? My God, Polly, what are you driving at? What do you mean?" He was actually trembling. "If that's all that's keeping you back, a sense of responsibility, of duty to me—!"

"No, that's not all. But you've been so swell—so big about the folks, so wonderful to me. And I've treated you abominably. Even loving you, I've been hideous to you, I don't know why. I should make it up to you instead of hurting you more!" she cried wretchedly. "And Jud's not like you. I thought he was, a little, but he's not. He'll never understand the family, I found that out. But Dan —he does understand me! He knows what I want out of life and he can help me get it. He already has. Oh, I know it sounds crazy, like something out of a movie, to marry for—for advantage, but why not be brutally crass and admit that's what it is? And then again it—it's more than that, a set of circumstances that seem created especially for me. And he is smart—about the smartest man I've ever met, and good—wonderfully good. Oh, Dan, I'm so mixed up!" She turned suddenly to face him and found him looking at her with an expression that startled her.

It was a harsh expression. An expression of disdain.

"You said you hadn't changed. Why, you little fool, you're not the girl I thought I loved at all!"

She gasped. She had an actual sensation of falling. Dan couldn't stop loving her! That was one thing that mustn't change. It was the only permanent, stable thing she had ever known. It—had to go on!

"Dan," she whispered wildly, "Dan, I am!"

"When I first met you—when you left here last fall— you had dreams and ambition and pride. They came between us often enough, God knows, but I loved you for them, I wanted to help. Now what ambition you had has become a rotten scheming thing I don't recognize as yours, Polly. Don't worry about making anything up to me," he said bitterly. "You couldn't! Not now. C'mon, let's get out of here."

"Dan!" She clutched at his shoulders, but he struck her hands down.

"I said let's get out of here." His face looked more stricken, more sickly lost than hers. "For good!"

CHAPTER THIRTY-TWO

JEAN ANDREWS VOLD, to the delight of her enemies and the disgust of many relatives, did not die. Both she and her impatient son lived, rather shamelessly, to "disgrace the family" as Aunt Chick put it. Even Stew, the poised, harbored an unconscious grudge at his wife, not so much for her misfortune in delivering the child of their secret marriage early, but for brazenly living through it!

His honor was secure enough during that week when Jean was the principal actress in what seemed a deathbed scene, and he was in honest anguish at the thought of losing her. People spoke to him in voices respectfully hushed. There were flowers and innumerable kindnesses. Had Jean graciously spoken her last weak words and let the curtain fall on her beauty, the climax would have been too exquisite for malicious tongues to mar. But such placid and accommodating an act was not for Jean.

"Thought I was a goner, didn't you?" she beamed one day at the anxious huddle about the bed. "Well we fooled you, me and this little puddle puppy!" She kissed the dark fuzz that was visible above the downy blue bundle of blanket.

"Hell no!" Sam denied, slapping his knee and chuckling in the first genuine rejoicing he had known since Lydia's terrified message summoned him home. His unwavering bedside manner was to "jolly" the patient, convalescent or dying. "No sense goin' in there lookin' like we're ready to bawl," he always whispered to Lydia, though his lips were grim and his soul sick with apprehension. Now the warmth of his relief spread a rosy glow over his face and his shiny bald head. He grabbed a grimy wad of handkerchief, behind which he coughed and blew his nose. "Hell, we knew you were just playin' off. Why, you'll be up going to a dance tomorrow!"

Jean thrust a slim bare foot from under the covers and wiggled her toes. "Boy, would I like to! I bet that's why old Mr. Spitbox here got in a rush. Him knowed him was keepin' him's muzza from makin' whoopee!"

"Jean!" Lydia protested. *"Are* you going to start out calling that helpless tike such dreadful names?" How wonderfully good to be able to scold Jean again!

"Yeah, give the kid a fair break," ordered Stew with his lopsided grin, half-important, half-bemused. "Don't ruin his speech before he even gets any!"

Jean twisted her big mouth to a pout. "Hear that, wet pants? Your ma must be doin' okay the way everybody's bossing her!" But her eyes, gazing down, were hazy with happiness.

Of Jean's immediate family, Ken alone harbored doubts. "I don't care which guy you choose," he informed Polly, "but don't pull the stunt Jean did. I'm takin' plentya razzing over this premature baby gag!"

"You're her brother, you should stick up for her!" Polly bristled. "Even if she hadn't been married long enough. However, I know she has!"

"I suppose—" Ken grinned maddeningly, pulling a gray hat carefully over one eye and turning his head from side to side to survey the effect in the bookcase mirror— "you were along every time they were together?"

"Oh, you—you whited sepulchre!" Polly panted. And for a second she shared Lydia's passion to scream denial from the housetops. As if it really mattered.

But it was Sam, who had always predicted just such a "John's girls" performance from Jean, who was now her self-appointed champion. With difficulty Lydia restrained him from starting slander suits against his erstwhile partner in the patent business, the entire Ladies' Aid, and his own shocked and indignantly blustering clan.

When the prospect of Jean's demise had been imminent, Grandma Andrews had wept softly, "Poor little thing! Ooooooh, that poor, poor little thing!" Aunt Chick, whose visits were rare, had bounced into her car and run over every day to ask with rich solicitude, "How is she? Now if there's anything we can do—"

But now that Jean was convalescing and the baby thriving, now that there was to be no funeral to hush doubts in proving that since mother and/or child had died this must have indeed been one of nature's errors, the relatives felt definitely duped and their ire ran high.

"It's this damnable age we're living in!" Grandma raged, stamping her cane. "Ooooh, I tell you things like this didn't happen in my day! Ooooooh, I can't bear it, my own granddaughter—ooooh, why did this have to happen to me?"

"She's disgraced the family," Chick reiterated to the buzzing group in the smoke-filled room. "Disgraced us all! Even Mac feels it down at the bank. I tell you, we'll never live this down!"

"Aw, Gawdamighty, Chick!" guffawed Glen, wagging his cigar with a shower of ashes. "Christ! This ain't the first kid that its mama and papa had to hurry to the preacher's for fear of foaling on the way. Why, I think it's a hell of a good joke, by Jesus, after Liddy making Sam and them kids go to church like she always has!"

Herbert, on a visit from Cedar Rapids, placed one fat paw upon either knee, great belly hanging between. "You may laugh," he declared in evangelical tones, "but it's disgraceful! Positively disgraceful!" Then Herbert, the celibate, met the sly grin and broad wink of Glen, the sexlessly married, with an uncomfortable frown. "I repeat," he said, "it's—on the surface, it's disgraceful. Of course it's possible that she *was*—er—secretly married."

"A secret bride has a secret to hide," Glen's wife recited with vigorous mechanical toy noddings of her sterile blonde face.

It was here that Sam stomped in. Mac had been lying on the davenport with a paper over his face, feigning sleep to hide his amusement at the virulence of his in-laws.

Now he sat upright, snickering audibly. This was going to be good!

Glen's wife stopped chewing her gum; one hand froze to her beads as Sam challenged in a voice impressively controlled, "All right, Gert! Since you seem to be the authority around here on such things I'll just let you be first to read this paper!" He shook a document at her, rapped it sharply with his finger. "Then I want you to pass it around and let everybody else read it themselves. It's Jean's wedding certificate, and if you wanta look up the records in the Omaha courthouse you'll find the license dated the same. Here, Herby, you pure old bachelor, take a look at a birth certificate. I had 'em make me an extra copy for this very purpose. See where it says *premature* —right there! Pass that around too. And if you still have doubts, ask Doc Lansdale—he'll tell you all right how they been cookin' the little cuss in an incubator and I donno' what-all!"

Sam was panting. He mopped his brow and bellowed, "I'm here to tell you right now I've taken all the slander I'm goin' to! Gert, you eat your words about Jean or I'll tell that adopted son of yours where he came from! Mac, you and Chick do the same or by God I—I'll start a run on your bank! Glen, if I ever hear of you making another filthy remark about either of my girls I'll beat you to a pulp! Herb, I want you to personally see that every other member of the family gets a letter giving them the dope about this thing once and for all!"

In a silence broken only by Grandma Andrews' sobs, the documents went the rounds. Chick was the last to receive them. With only a perfunctory glance, she thrust them at Sam. Then with a little snort, she retreated upstairs, her plump feet spanking each step. The fact still remained that Jean had disgraced the family.

Now that the intense strain was over, Polly was lost, confused, and bitterly lonely. Her own plans had been rushing toward a consummation which seemed as imperative to her life course as that first grim march she and Lydia had taken across the Vista campus, two frightened women in two cheap voile dresses, who, knowing they had only Sam's precarious job for backing, had yet gone to see the dean about enrollment. "I'll go with you, honey," Lydia had said, drawing a deep worried breath. "It's all I *can* do." And summoning her curious reserve of regality and charm, Lydia had turned the trick. The man had given Polly a partial scholarship and allowed her to sign a note.

And just as then Polly had not questioned, "Can I make it? Will I be happy in this?" (she hadn't been, she was much too young and damned with brains to fit) so later, deciding on law school, there had been only the fierce determination, "Here I go. I must!" The same clutching out at the sure, immediate next rung upward that had led her to agree to marry Jud.

Jean's illness was as though in her swift, sightless climb she had pitched over a precipice and the blow had stunned her. She could not comprehend quite how to regain her footing, or precisely what had happened. More than all else, she could not realize that she had lost Dan. It was inconceivable. Yet he had gone from her at the hospital and not returned, not even called.

"But honey, what can you expect?" Lydia asked. "He knows you were going to break up anyway."

"I know but—but it shouldn't *be* like this!"

Lydia sighed and dusted at the piano. "Well I don't know, I don't understand you, honey. Dan doesn't deserve to be hurt any more. Last fall after you left, I tell you he looked like—like he'd been shot! And yet he wouldn't have had you not go. Dan's the most generous, unselfish person I've ever known!" Never had she been more tempted to tell about Dan's giving her the money. If Polly knew— Perhaps Polly *should* know. But Lydia's brain scuttled in fright from the revelation. No telling how she might react. She might not marry Jud. And—and maybe that *was* best, after all. Or she might be furious at both Lydia and Dan! That pride of hers—pride that wouldn't let the poor baffled, bungling child call Dan even now—

Polly watched her mother, annoyed by the secret hinting frenzies of her face. What—as Jean would say—was eating her now? She was sorry she had confided in Lydia, but she had been unable not to. The helpless loquacity of the Andrews tribe! The need to take all the wild sick burden of their troubles and dump them on the shabby but receptive family hearth.

But this time it hadn't eased her or lightened them at all. The very presence of her people only augmented Polly's stunned loneliness. She was not of them any more. "Not the girl I thought I loved" . . . the phrase crawled its painful way through her brain again, recalling all her startled agonies of protest. How could Dan have said a thing like that to her? *Dan!* But she *had* changed. Even her family repelled her. The little things Lydia did— wiping cake batter from a spoon with her finger, tapping her gold tooth while she talked, her throat-clearings, eye-blearings and nose-blowings grated Polly into silent frenzy. And it was all she could do to listen to Sam's cocky, get-rich-quick schemes in which he still placed time, faith, and money. His cussings, braggings and jokings were scarcely to be borne. She snapped at him sometimes and was instantly the sufferer. . . . The ring around his baldness was white now; he was fatter and redder and wearier, and there was an undertone of desperation in his boasts and in his humor. Impregnable though he had always seemed, she knew now that he was like a little rubber ball, bouncing back from every throw, but getting bruised and battered from the impacts. Why must she too hurl him from her?

Proud as she had always been of Ken, his superior condescension riled her. She was an outsider to the circles in which, though penniless, he still moved. The big cars still swept to the curb and tooted their imperious summons. The girls who clung to his arm were younger now, many of them little sisters to those who had courted him in vain and gone off at length to college or to marry. But even these youngsters were sophisticated to a degree which ignored Polly. Brag about his sister Kenneth might, but accept her as his social equal, never.

Even Ramey, Polly's private pet, she now saw as an untamed colt. He talked with his mouth full, called for what he could not reach by pointing and demanding, "Gimme!" He made vile faces and had tantrums. Torn between Lydia's lenience and Sam's vituperations, he did practically as he pleased. He was still sweet and earnest and eager, but hopelessly spoiled.

You have no one! her devil jeered. You have let yourself grow beyond the honest madness of your people. You have cut away the man whose idolization made you God. You are no one now. You haven't even one friend. . . . Frantically she thought of girls whom she might call up or go to see, but in all Gem Lake there was only Vee, who had been adopted by a swift new crowd and changed in some indefinable way. No, said the voice of her fears, there is no one. . . . But there's Jud! she reminded herself, half defiantly. He had been writing her, threatening to come to Gem Lake unless he heard from her, yet his letters had more the ring of a man who fears defeat than one in love. However desperately Jud might "care," it could never be more than an extension of his own self-regard.

"But Poll, you said those orals are the fifteenth, and here it is the twelfth," Jean said one day, sitting up in bed, manicuring her nails. "You ought to be making plans. What about that Jud guy? What're you going to do?"

Below the window the waves rolled in. There was rhythm to their very inanity, Polly thought—a recitative of unaccomplishment. She turned back to Jean.

"I don't know. Sometimes I wonder if I could even pass them."

"You mean you're actually thinking of quitting now, not going through with it after all that *work?*" Jean shook her amazed head. "Honestly Poll, you may be educated, but you get screwier all the time!"

"I don't know *what* I want!"

"Well it's high time you're making up your mind. What about that partnership? What about getting married there in the prima donna's castle, or whatever it was? Are you going to marry the guy or not?"

"That's what he's wondering. Also his grandmother."

"But what do you tell them?"

"Nothing." A wicked grin flitted across her face. "I haven't written either of them since I left, isn't that awful?"

Jean's mouth popped open. She surveyed her sister in a second of mute dismay. "After them having you down there and her wanting to give you that high-powered wedding and all? Why, Poll! They'll think you're just plain ignorant!" But suddenly Jean giggled. "I bet this is the first time anybody ever had the nerve to give any of that outfit the cold yawn."

"It's not so much nerve as—as—"

"I know," Jean added cryptically, returning to her nails. "It's Dan. Kid, don't be a fool."

"But he's never acted like this before!"

"Don't worry, he'll live. Or maybe that's what is worrying you." Jean bit at a hangnail with tiny doll's teeth. "You wanted a tearful farewell with Dan promising to be true to the red white and blue, never looking at another woman and all that ap-cray while you team up with somebody else, ain't that right? And because he had enough guts for once to walk off the stage saying he didn't give a damn', thanks, you'd actually throw over everything you've slaved for and practically got! You're a mess, Polly. You're no different from the rest of us, after all. You're just a dim-wit emotional mess, and if you aren't careful it's going to throw you for a whale of a loss."

"I know it," Polly said miserably. "But I can't help it."

"Can't help it!" Jean's voice was scornful. "Good Lord, Polly, you're the only one of us that ever could help anything. Look how you've had jobs, and went to college on your reputation, and moved hell and highwater to go study law. We've been so proud of you, kid, we've—counted on you sort of to—well help put the family back on its feet. I don't mean financially. I can do that someday maybe myself, just from marrying Stew. I mean—" She filed her nails absently, agrope for a way to phrase this abstraction of which Polly was already so inescapably aware. "I mean to cancel out things like—like this dumb stunt I pulled but couldn't help!" She gestured with a bewildered expression about the narrow white room. Married. A mother. For Jean too it failed to make sense. "Polly please," she said, leaning a little forward. "Don't let us down. Don't be like Ken. Don't just—come home!"

CHAPTER THIRTY-THREE

DAN WAS UP at dawn that morning. His mother heard the
back door slam, the clank and plod of harness and hooves.
She hallooed breakfast from the porch, but again as usual
he only shook his head. She frowned and stood for a
moment looking out over the rolling land that had been
theirs so long and now was precariously close to not being
theirs. A white smoke of mist was running before the sun.
Trying to keep ahead. She was not a woman to philoso-
phize, but she felt the breath of something destroying as it
bore down on the racing heels of her life. She could run,
had been running all her life, from stove to table, from
crib to bed and back again, with zest and the assurance
that all was well. But now she was running without that
assurance, and she couldn't help panting a little.

Of course, she told herself, it wouldn't be so dreadful
losing the land if somehow before that—happened—the
children were all provided for, settled happily. The girls
were all right, Kay with Doc, and Carol with Glen and
their boys, and Kit teaching and eventually perhaps she
and Martin—though of course that was indefinite, but it
would be nice—he'd been so good to June. She shut her
eys and thought of June, the homely little curly-head
who'd looked so much like Father; June, their first blessing and their first loss. Losing the land would not hurt

half so much as losing June. But there were still the others, pleasantly taken care of, except Danny. Their baby, their long-coveted only boy. They had planned to do such splendid things for him. Ironically enough for him alone their plans had gone awry. All of them had gone east to school and the girls—except June, who'd gotten homesick and come back to marry Martin—had finished. But the elements had conspired to deprive Dan of what he should have had. Fire, death, the tired land, had called him back after only two years at military academy. Young as he was, he had put his strong shoulder to the wheel and helped bring order out of chaos. His money as well as Father's had gone into the fine new house. Time went skidding and suddenly he was older and too proud to return to school. He had not seemed to care a great deal, but had run wild for a time, drinking, though she knew he had always been a good boy otherwise. And then, blessedly, he had found that nice little Andrews girl and executed a complete about-face.

If only things were not so complicated now. If only they were in a position to help him instead of being a drain upon him again. It was a shame, Father's having to let the hired men go, but Danny had insisted that he wanted to help, particularly as there was nothing to do elsewhere. Poor lad, he'd tried so hard, working and saving until there was no more work to be had and nothing more to be saved.

She had expected Polly's return to drive the weary loneliness from his eyes, to bring back the old joyously concocted plans for living. That had been stupid too—just wishful thinking, for she had helplessly known how things would be now that Polly was so near her goal. Only why must it have happened so soon? Why couldn't they have had a few final days together, instead of the swift cutting apart that must have taken place when Dan went over that day with Kay? Dan hadn't been the same since then; even on those nights when he'd come in and not found a letter, he hadn't been like this—aloof, silent, or when he did speak, with a false unconcern in his voice, an alien bitterness at the corners of his mouth. He still arose early, worked doggedly all day, ate, stumped up to bed. But not to sleep, she anxiously knew. She sometimes awoke in the far spaces of the night to hear the tramp of his feet. And she could not reach him, go to him; there was nothing she could do. That child—Polly—she had never understood her, never would, but because Dan so terribly wanted her, she felt a helpless desolation at being his mother and yet powerless to take the one life important to her son and make it his.

Toward ten o'clock she filled a thermos jug with hot coffee, packed some sandwiches and fruit into a basket, and walked out across the pasture toward that silhouette of man and horses against a white cloud. The team drew up to the fence and stood bluttering and shaking themselves as Dan climbed down from the cultivator and parted the fence wires to crawl through.

"Aha, Mammy, lunch for your little farmer boy!"

He was being deliberately cheerful, to repay her for walking out. They sat down on the prickly pasture grass. Beside them the sun-silvered corn rattled and whispered in a restless shimmering dance. While Dan ate, his mother gazed out across the green and golden fields. The sun had licked up the last shred of mist; it was warm here and the soil smelled good.

She smiled reflectively. "I'll never forget how your father tried raising cotton and tobacco when he *fust came nawth*."

"You knew better. Why didn't you talk him out of it?"

"I was in love with him. I thought he knew everything. Girls are like that."

"Not any more." Suddenly the pain smote him again, a disintegrating blast. He could not hold the cigarette he had been rolling; the shreds of tobacco spilled to the ground and the wisp of paper floated away. Quickly, instantly, he moved his hands to cover the grimacing distortion of his face.

His mother sat for a few moments watching the curly bowed head, the uncontrollable clench and quiver of muscles under the perspiration-streaked shirt. Even as a child, Dan hadn't cried. She couldn't bear it. She got quickly to her feet.

"This isn't like you, son."

Turning a little away from her, he got a handkerchief from his trousers pocket. When he looked up his eyes were wet, but his face was calm. "I haven't been like myself for too long."

"But—isn't there something you can do?"

Do? Yes, he supposed there were things you could do. Get tight. Take a woman. The traditional things that were supposed to make a man forget—though his mother hadn't meant that. But he knew that such would offer no appeasement; he had grown beyond all that. It would be like Polly's frantic, puerile dating binges of a year ago—cheap and futile, with the ugly taste of self-disgust. No—and his eyes roved the hills with a kind of bitter calculation, a look of challenge and possessiveness that had grown steadily since the beginning of this other loss—self-destruction, temporary or permanent, could accomplish nothing. The only thing to *do* was to hang onto what you had. To just go on living and fighting your lonely fight, but by God, hanging on! He could. He would. This was his portion of earth, just as Polly was still his woman. He had been gentle with Polly, and he had lost her—but he would not be gentle with the land. He would wrest every drop of productivity from it; he would plant it with his blood and seed and make it bear enough to save itself. He might grow old and queer here, like Crazy Mitch across the hill, but no one should take it from him. For it held not only a portion of himself and his own people, but of her —as she had been. He would live on here with her in memory. He knew, as his mother must know, that he did not want to forget.

He shook his head. "No, there's nothing anyone can do."

For a moment more his mother hesitated. Then she stooped and gathered up the lunch things and turned toward the house. He was right. There was nothing anyone could do, except Polly herself.

Polly left the hospital and walked swiftly through the hot drowsy noon. Overhead, trees clutched each other in leafy embrace. The air was pungent with the rich smell of gardens; onions had shoved above the surface of the earth, like fat white pearls held upright by their stems of silvered green; there were blood-streaked beet tops in shaggy rows, and ferny forests of tomato vines in which nested the scarlet globes of fruit. From open windows of neat bungalows came the click and bubble of canning jars, the clatter of dinner dishes, and in Mrs. Courtney's, the pleasant babble of voices at a luncheon bridge. And it was all orderly and right, but not for her. She had never fit into such patterns. She never would, no matter what she made up her mind to do.

"Don't just come home!" She shuddered. Jean was right. She couldn't do that. And wouldn't going back to Dan, if he would have her, be just—coming home too? Wasn't that what Jean had meant? Home. Homecoming . . . ! Suddenly such an awful wave of homesickness for the farm struck her that she halted there on the walk and her eyes went blind. That's what I need! she thought. To—*go home*. Just once more. Even if it's for the last time. Suddenly she began to run.

Stew, in white ducks and polo shirt, was in the kitchen with Lydia when Polly came in. They were just finishing a lunch of lettuce sandwiches, lemonade and bakery pie.

"Why, I didn't hear you come in!" Lydia gasped. She twisted about to get another plate from the cupboard. "We'd have waited only we—we never know just when to expect you these days."

"Thanks, Mom, I don't want anything to eat, just something to drink—it's so hot." Polly accepted the squat glass Lydia handed her. "Stew, what would you take to let me use your car?"

Stew looked up. "What for?" he asked in the fondly kidding tone he used for all the family.

"I thought I'd drive out to Dan's."

An anxious look came into Lydia's eyes. "Honey, what are you going to do?"

"I've got to see him. I—I can't go down there and take those exams wondering about him. If I did that I might as well stay home. Of course," she added with a wry smile, "I may not get to go anyway, if the finance company won't let Dad out of town with the car!"

Lydia set down the pitcher with its clopping ice. For a second there was no sound but the buzzing of a fly. Lydia groped at her apron pockets for a handkerchief and cleared her throat. "Well, I don't know how to advise you," she said in a voice of bleak defeat. "All my life

I've hoped that when times like this came I'd be ready, that I could help, but now you—you seem to have grown beyond me, all of you! All I can say is—do what will make you happy."

"And who knows what that is?" Gratefully Polly caught the keys Stew tossed her. She kissed her mother's damp cheek with its tormented eyes, and ran.

She headed Stew's car along the lake road. Change had come upon the town in even the little time she had been gone. The lake road no longer curved the water like a caressing arm, but had become a harsh white highway whose markers pointed the straightest, quickest route to Crescent and Sioux City. No more was it the road of escape for two mad, poor, rich young gods in love to flee a father's wrath. It was now a humming highway, a tongue of coldly burning stone that licked across the hills, spurning even the cool brilliance of the lake.

She turned off from it presently, choosing the narrow gray alleys of the country roads that would take her to the farm. They stretched over the green ridges beyond like a soft dark carpet upon a stair. The trees made them cool and lovely, mysterious with slant purple ladders of shadow. Drowsing chickens in weeded gullies sprang up to dart across her path. And it was all dear and familiar —the summer chant of cricket and pigeon and rustling corn, the scent of clover and sweet baking grasses and dust, the crazy-quilt pattern of peeled black earth and yellow blowing barley and green pasture and sky; sweet, nostalgic, a something she must make a part of herself forever, because it was of Dan.

Now that she had made up her mind, it was as if all things led unswervingly and with a kind of singing serenity to him. Her heart, beneath its blind determination, was curiously quiet, like a still bright pool glimpsed in the dusk of a grove. Wise or foolish, generous or the most selfish thing she had ever done, this was simply something she had to do.

But when she at last swung into the shady upslope of the Scott lane, saw again the giant barns, the brick silos and the great house at the top of the hill, courage drained from her. The realness of this place was like a stab; it leaped alive at her in beauty as it had not even in her dreams. Mrs. Scott's flowers, like banners of colored smoke against the house; the lawn, mown smooth, and that forgotten grindstone where she had once proudly pedaled a hatchet sharp for Dan! This place was lovely; it held happiness and peace. And suddenly, sweeping upon it so, seeing it anew, she had a bleak sense of loss and estrangement. She belonged here no more. Wouldn't they think her audacious to come like this, knowing—as they must—that she was no longer Dan's girl?

But it was too late to turn back. The dogs had heralded her approach and now the children came racing, shrilling her name. They were taller, freckled. Marilyn had lost a tooth. The child proudly exhibited the hole as Polly climbed out.

"Uncle Dan pulled it with a string. He made it turn into a dime!"

"Is Uncle Dan home?"

"He's down on the south eighty," Skippy volunteered. His brown fists were rammed into the pockets of his turned-up coveralls. "But we can have fun, Polly, I'll go get the pony, I can harness her up myself!"

Mrs. Scott came scuttling down the back steps. "Polly! Oh Polly my dear, I'm so glad you've come!"

Propelled by relief and joy, they embraced. She smelled delicately of starched gingham and lavender. Polly felt the crinkled softness of her cheek, the press of her small work-happy hands as they turned, to the children's disappointment, toward the house.

"Aw Grandma, we want to show her our turtle!"

"Hush now." Mrs. Scott was beaming and Polly knew that she was beaming back. "Later, children. Maybe Polly is—is going to stay," she said. It was a flat little statement of hope, so simple, so trusting that Polly averted her eyes.

The kitchen was winy with the scent of blubbering jam. Grapes bobbed like shiny purple marbles in a dishpan on the table, and squat glasses of the finished jelly were garnets jeweling the window. Upon the cabinet stood several tall brown loaves of bread.

"You'll have to excuse the clutter, Polly, I've been both baking and canning. Sit down and try some of my jam, won't you?"

Still smiling, but feeling tearful, Polly perched quietly

upon a stool while Mrs. Scott prepared her lunch, as Dan had so often done. The fresh crust crackled and flaked under the sawing knife.

"Here. I want you to sample both the jam and jelly. I'll get you a glass of milk," she said eagerly. "My, it's good to have you here!"

Polly's gaze strayed to the tiny off-kitchen bedroom, whose door stood wide. The blue comfort, knotted with stars—the single pillow, fat and wide and clean— For an instant she couldn't swallow. Then she gulped at the cold milk.

Her fingers were sticky when she had finished. "You'll have to wash upstairs," Mrs. Scott said. "Dan's been meaning to fix the drain down here, but I declare with all the work that boy's had to do now that we've let the tenants go—"

Polly hesitated, tempted to ask about the farm. But this afternoon she didn't want to think anything but that this place was and always would be—Scotts', a part of Dan and of herself. Yes, her own! If just once—even though he claim to hate her—she could bend Dan to her will, persuade him to give and take a final something for themselves, to bind the roots of memory here upon this place they loved, that would make it forever theirs—

She turned and ran up the hard polished stairs. How many times she had washed amid these spacious tiles, she thought, drying her hands. How often wallowed in the enormity of that tub, emerging to use Kit's talcum and Dan's own expensive brand of toothpaste neatly rolled from the bottom in its fat white tube. Despite her shabbiness and lack she had always felt at home here, while at Jud's— She shuddered. She couldn't imagine herself touching anything belonging to Grandmother Masters or Jud! Of course there, she recalled with a mocking snobbery, she had had a private bath.

She went into the hall on tiptoe, and stood by the open door of the room that had been hers. After the ugly luxury of Jud's it did not seem so splendid. Smiling, she remembered how she had at first been unable to sleep on the innerspring mattress, and how she could never get enough of admiring her body in the beveled mirror on the

closet door. Lord, what a dumb, scared little tramp had
first come home with Dan!

The door to Dan's room was closed. Dan! She thought
of him in a terrible crying whisper. She turned the glass
knob and went in. It came as an afterthought that Lydia
had said Dan had gone to her room that day she first left
home. What had he felt, standing in the center of her
deserted things as now she stood among his? What if,
rooted here beside the mute white tidiness of his bed,
surrounded by his combs and brushes and ties, it was to
know he would not come back? She covered her face;
something raw and grinding tore at her chest.

Suddenly, acting on an impulse she could not restrain,
she stole across the room and opened Dan's closet door.
Two suits hung there. Yes, the same, the only two. Not
worn exactly. Not yet out of date. But so nearly so. Silent,
unaccusing, sturdy and clean. To see them hanging so
was to see what she had done to Dan. He had been so
debonair when he had first come dashing up in the old
Buick, so jaunty a cavalier. The rough touch of that fabric
made palpable every denial, every moment of suffering
and retrogression he had known because of her.

Now as never before, she realized that she must have
driven him over the final brink, extorted the last drop of
sacrifice. And she knew that to see her again, hold her,
make final and real the intention that had brought her
back today, would be cruelest of all. Not a gift, a benediction, not even mutual completion born, distortedly, of
estrangement—but damnation renewed and intensified.
No, she couldn't do that to him too. She dropped the
sleeve she had held, quietly closed the door and crossed
the room.

Dishtowel in hand, Mrs. Scott was twisting the lids of
jars as Polly came down. "There! That makes twenty-nine
quarts," she said proudly. "Tell Dan he can tighten them
for me tonight. It's quite a walk out to where he is, but
you can wear Marilyn's straw hat." She looked up then
and saw Polly's face. Mrs. Scott brushed small trembling
blue-veined hands across her apron. "You *are* going out
to him, aren't you?" she asked in a breathless little voice.
"Or you'll wait until he comes in? You—you did come
to see him!" she argued.

"Maybe I didn't," Polly whispered. She was staring outside. "Maybe I just came to see you—the kids, the place. I've been so happy here!"

"You could always be," Mrs. Scott said in a voice quiet with desperation. "Dan's made headway already—not much, but a little. I know that with you he could save this place. I think he has a notion of trying to anyway, but with you— Polly, please don't think me a meddling mother," she burst out then, "but you two can't break up like this! Goodness, child, don't you realize what you *have* in that boy?"

"That's it. Maybe I just now do—realize. I don't deserve him. Certainly I shouldn't make things any harder for him."

"Oh, don't be silly!" Mrs. Scott snatched up her dishcloth and began to wipe the table. "How do you think he'll feel if he finds you were here—and ran off?"

"Relieved, maybe."

Mrs. Scott made a little sound of impatience. She felt like shaking the child. "Dan worships you," she declared. "That doesn't happen to many women, Polly, and when it does it's often so selfish. Dan has never been selfish about anything—even you, you know that! Oh, of course he's my son, I'm prejudiced, I want him to be happy—I suppose that's why I—I seem to be quarreling with you," she said in a shocked little tone, "because I want him to be happy, but—but they don't come any finer!" she cried shakily, rubbing at the spotless table.

She was so lovable and so daintily indignant that spontaneously, Polly flew across the room and hugged her in her arms. "Oh, Mrs. Scott!" she laughed softly. "I didn't know you had it in you! I shouldn't be glad, but I am—terribly glad you have. Where's that hat?"

In the yard she encountered the children and the nodding black and white pony, stepping primly on its high heels.

"Hey Polly, c'mon and ride!"

"No thanks, I'm going to find Uncle Dan."

"Aw nuts. Well get back for sure so as we can sit by you."

"Yes, darlings. Yes, I'll be back," she cried.

The gate by the barnlot was fastened. She could not

cope with its intricacies, and so she scrambled over, dropping to the rutted ground below.

And now leaping from stone to stone across the flashing creek, and up the sunny sweep of the pasture hill. She whipped off her hat and the sun was hot upon her blowing hair. She was Venus, born of a sea of rippling pasture grass, she was Daphne, child of the morning, and Iduna who owned the Apples of Youth, and Frigga, queen of the sky! All the world was at her feet.

Across the rolling wave-like hills she saw the neighboring farms, their buildings doll things in the singing light. And out across the silver lakes of corn, she saw a plodding silhouette of team and man that would be Dan.

"Dan!" she yelled, and waved her hat and ran. A ground squirrel dropped from its erect pencil-perch. A jack rabbit bounded wraith-like beside the fence. "Dan!"

The silhouette turned and was lost in the lanes of corn, but presently it emerged and was coming toward her, growing larger and more real with every thunking step of heavy hooves. She could see only the shaggy, bobbing heads of the horses. She waited, stomach tightening, in a sudden agony of fear. She could not see Dan's face.

Then he was beside the fence, reining the horses to a halt. But he did not climb down and come to her. He just sat there regarding her with his burned and blackened face.

"Why have you come?" he asked.

"Why, I—I—" She colored. "I don't exactly know!" she gasped.

The corn clattered and whispered. From far down the hill a dog barked, a lonely quavering sound. Dan sat there. Finally he said, "I don't get it. If things are finished between us they're finished, that's all."

"But they weren't finished!" Polly said passionately. She was angry and hurt. She felt foolish standing there behind the fence like a criminal—and confused.

Dan looked up. There was a small stabbing hope in his voice. "You mean you'd changed your mind?"

Now it was her turn to hurt, to punish and deny. It seemed, out of her humiliation and resentment, that she must. "Maybe. But if I had it's certainly changed back again!"

Pride told her now to turn and fly. To beat a quick, face-saving, somehow triumphant retreat. But what if he did not follow? No, she dared not risk this last hour before it was even begun. She stood there stubbornly and shamefully waiting, and in a moment, to her relief, he twisted the reins and crawled through the fence.

They sat down on the hot needling grass. "Sorry I was rude," Dan said. But his manner had not changed. It was as if he were cloaked in some proud insensibility that she could not penetrate. He took off his hat and wiped some of the dust and sweat from his face. "Why did you come, Polly? This time don't lie. You hadn't changed your mind, had you?"

"No," she acknowledged in a wretched whisper. "It's too late for that now. There's no going back to what we once were. If you'd married me, even made me *have* to marry you before I left—! But you didn't. I did too good a job of convincing you I wanted to go."

"And pretty soon—day after tomorrow isn't it?—you're going again, so you've come to tell me good-bye? To feel sorry for me. Probably to beg me not to—finish myself off!" He laughed dryly. "Well you needn't have bothered. Even you aren't that important to me, Polly. I found out months ago that I can go on living without you. Ever since you began writing home about that—that damned stuffed shirt, that God damned rich-bitch of a Boy Scout! And I've survived. I will survive!" he said in a quietly desperate burst. "Damn you, I won't kill myself for you, gratifying as that would probably be to your pride!"

"Oh Dan, stop. That's not it! You know that's not it!"

"Then why did you come?" he demanded, abruptly facing her. He was breathing hard. His eyes smoldered with a challenge that would destroy anything but the truth.

For a long sick moment she stared back. "All right, I'll tell you," she said. "I came because I wanted something to take along! I came thinking you might give the changed me, the despised me, something you wouldn't give the girl you respected and loved. As much as we've meant to each other it doesn't seem right that anyone else should—I mean—" She paused, suddenly drained of courage, then whispered fiercely, "Even hating me, Dan, I wanted you to be first!"

He ducked his head. "Oh, Polly—Polly, for God's sake, don't!"

"Well, you asked for it!" She got to her feet, knowing how grossly she had blundered. Yet she felt relieved of a tremendous torment. At least she had told the truth.

Automatically she turned to go, but Dan had sprung up and stood before her; she was suddenly in the hard and terrible grip of his arms.

"Dan, don't—don't!" she cried in panic. "My God, Dan, you mustn't—not now!"

"Be still! Shut your ugly damned little witch of a face and kiss me! You're mine, you've always been! You belong to me."

"Not now! Not like this! Not now!" The sky wheeled, hotly blue; she felt the hard curve of the earth beneath her back. "Dan, let me go!"

"I'll never let you go, Polly," he said firmly, but more quietly. "I'll never be that big a fool again. You didn't come to me today thinking I'd give you something to take along on that idiot's course you've set yourself. You came hoping I'd make you stay!"

"I didn't!" she sobbed. "Oh darling, I can't—I mustn't —I can't!"

"It was the reason you came. Maybe you didn't know it, but it was. You don't want to marry that guy and go on with your career, but you're afraid to admit it. After all the fireworks you're ashamed to admit it's me you want, and a good dull decent life with me, after all!"

"Oh, Dan—" she pushed him a little away and her wet eyes begged him to understand—"no matter why I came —can't you see that now—now it's too late? I've fought so hard and gone so far, I've taken so much from everybody—the folks—"

"The folks, hell!" he said bitterly. But he sat up. He moved quickly away from her. He did not want to be tempted, in his desperation, to tell her whom she really owed; he must never want her enough to use that. And he knew, with a dazed sense of defeat, that he had just been yelling in the dark—he could never break Polly as he could break the land, he could never take her or keep her against her will. With hands that shook, he rolled a cigarette. "I'm sorry," he said. "You're right. Your folks would never be reconciled to your throwing yourself away on me."

For this there was no answer. She lay upon the hot pasture grass, one hand flung across her eyes. She could smell earth and tobacco and sweat and leather and foaming hide . . . and the wild sweetness of clover . . . and in its lust for life, the pungent loveliness of the growing corn. And such desire was born in her that it consumed her, she could not move. She lay in a bath of longing so intense that her whole body was quick to things she could not see —the shadow of a cloud that traveled her limbs, the circling hope of a hawk—and the look that had come into Dan's eyes.

Now she withdrew her hand and for a long moment they gazed at each other in the shameless nakedness of their loss and love and need.

Then he flung away his cigarette and came to her.

CHAPTER THIRTY-FOUR

POLLY SPENT THE night at Scotts'. It was dusk when she and Dan arose and walked, a little apart, up across the hills to the house, but it seemed much later. It was as if a lifetime had been lived since she had waved to him from the hilltop. With a slight sense of shock she saw Stew's car standing where she had left it, and lights burning in the kitchen. Should not she and Dan alone, of all creatures, all things, through the miracle of love, the triumph of youth, have survived the vast diuturnity and emerged unchanged?

But this was not true. She knew that they alone were different. They had found their united and completed selves, and they were changed—bigger somehow in their gain, but smaller in their realization of dependence, their immense and terrible loss. Before, there had been some hope for them. Now there was none, apart. And standing a moment, dreading to go in lest the stamp of their alteration would be blatant in the light, it had seemed somehow tragic and false. A mistaken attempt to destroy some barrier that could not be destroyed, that was too big for them, that had gone on rising too long. So that, though they were leashed by a tenderness so sufficient they need not even touch hands, they were alienated too by this realization of defeat. This was infinitely worse.

But as Polly had drifted to unconsciousness in the simple goodness of the room where she had thought never to sleep again, it began to seem quite different. A sense of delight, of absolute fulfillment, had clasped her close all night. Now it wakened her, lifted her up on a wave of incredible wonder. I am changed! she thought, gazing down the slightness of her body, half expecting some sign. I am not as I was. No matter where I go or what I do, I have had Dan.

Dan! Scotts'! Being here at all after the anguish of the past weeks was like a dream from which she was reluctant to weaken. A cool breeze billowed the curtain and touched her hair. Just below her window there was a creak of pails as Mr. Scott passed with the milk. . . . Then sniffing the fragrance of bacon and coffee that floated up from the kitchen, she was instantly ravenous. She sat up and flung back the covers, leaped out of bed in the panties and brassière in which she had slept. And it was then that the reality that had hovered darkly over the rim of her happiness pounced. This was her last day of grace. The examinations were tomorrow! She would have to make up her mind about what she was going to do.

She flung herself back on the bed and buried her head in the pillow, but the drowsy comforts of happiness no longer muffled her. She could not shut it out. To go on at all, even alone, would be to leave Dan behind. They had come to a point where they could not compromise.

Presently she arose again, and pulling a quilted robe of Kit's about her, pattered on bare feet into the hall. Dan was just leaving the bathroom. His curls were blackly wet, riotous from the shower. He had dressed, but his rumpled pajamas were over his arm.

They halted in an instant of a new, curiously sweet embarrassment. Then they came together, and he held her and kissed her mouth. He had shaved. And beneath the smoothness of the fresh white shirt his muscles rippled hard. They kissed, and laughed together at themselves, and held each other with a strange sufficient lightness, for the memory of their completion was bright in their eyes.

"All dressed up?" With a careful finger she touched his starched collar point.

"Why not?" he cried. His voice was jubilant. "I'm not

working today. You and I, young lady, are going on a binge!"

"Grand!" Though she knew better; it was as if she must lift her voice, join him in some brief, necessary chant of joy.

"Sioux City. Shows, dances, eats—"

"Bells, whistles, trains!" she cried.

He snatched her close and kissed her again. "Oh, Mona-Kvasir, I love you so terribly, I've waited so long for you to come home."

To come—home. She struck aside the dark reality, the devil-reminded thing that she should be worrying about.

"We can go in style. Kit's offered us her car. Oh Polly, isn't it wonderful—aren't people—I mean—?"

He was seldom at a loss for words, but he held her a little away from him, and she knew what he meant because it was frantic on her own heart, the goodness of everything, the glory! The homely shining happiness that made all things significant—her bare feet upon the polished floor, the fruity morning smell of the country, the cheerful click and rattle of pans below. And Kit's being so nice. It was almost too much. The gold and the ring and the Tarnhelm—all at once!

"Oh Dan, I love them," she whispered, and her eyes brimmed. "All of them. They are my people!"

"They want to be," he said.

And now she knew his intention. Perhaps Kit's intention, too. If they took this trip today they would be married. She would never go to Des Moines for the examinations, or do any of the things she had planned. She would marry Dan and stay here on the farm, because he was young and strong in her love and he had the power to save it. "I've waited so long for you to come home." She was home now! Here, by her own testimony, among her people.

"Dan!" She swayed a little forward and he caught her and kissed her again. But she couldn't get married today, she was thinking in a sudden idiotic struggle with practicalities. She hadn't any clothes—only that rumpled blouse and skirt she'd worn yesterday. She'd have to go home first, get something, take Stew's car back. . . . And once she got home—

Downstairs, monotonously every so often the telephone had been ringing, but in the country you become alert only when it is Your Ring, the electric signal, the magic code of call. Now, even as Polly realized she could not go, they heard it—the long drill and two sharp short stings. They stopped kissing to listen, they held each other a little tighter, but they knew the spell was broken, that they had been kidding themselves, that they must have known.

They heard the snap of the receiver hook, Mrs. Scott's voice, and in a second her steps toward the stairway. "Polly, are you up? Gem Lake is calling."

Polly and Dan looked at each other. "Polly, don't answer it!" he said desperately. "Don't go!"

"I've got to answer," she said. She made a little motion of protest and resignation. "I—I can't go with you today, Dan. I've got to get Stew's car back. There's—so much I've got to do!"

"Then you are going ahead with those exams?"

She put her face in her hands. "It would be so crazy not to! Oh, I don't know—I don't know!"

"Polly?"

"Yes, I'm coming."

Dan released her. "You'd better have something on your feet." He went mechanically into her bedroom and returned with her pumps. Clutching the robe, she ran downstairs and took up the black cylinder which stood on the shelf of the wooden wall telephone.

"Polly? For God's sake what's the idea staying out there, not lettin' your mama know? Now get the hell home here —Stew needs his car, don't you know he does? And—" Sam's voice became wickedly secretive—"you got company."

"What?" Polly cried, suddenly petrified. "Who?"

"Oh, a son of a seacook hell's too good for," Sam chuckled. His voice faded, she heard him ask, "Here she is, wanta talk at her, Jud?"

"Dad, no—don't!" Polly protested. But Jud's voice, its rich bantering good-fellowness strangely thin over the country wires, was saying, "Hi, Smidgin. How'sa girl?"

"H-hello, Jud!" she cried shrilly. At the stove Dan's mother fried bacon, politely trying not to listen. Polly heard Dan cross the kitchen swiftly and go outside. "Wh-what are you doing up here?"

"Why, you little gummywozzle, I've come to get you, to take you to our exams."

"Oh!" Then in a rude burst, "Oh for Lord's sake! I—I'll be right home!"

She hung up and turned to the tiny woman so intent upon forking those curly ribbons of bacon, so earnest about ignoring this latest stupidity, this gross humiliation Polly had unwittingly heaped upon her and her house. She wanted to say something to cancel it out, make amends, but there were no words for her stricken regret. She could only mutter, "Please don't wait breakfast for me. I've got to go right home."

"Oh? Then you won't be going to the city with Dan?"

"No, I guess not. I—didn't have anything to wear, anyway."

"That reminds me. If you have company you'd better let me press your things."

"No, thank you. It's no one that matters!" Polly insisted curtly. She hesitated, furious with self-contempt, abject before the need to explain. Jud, the almighty, over there now—! In all the drug-eyed frenzy of early rising, breakfast—and oilcloth and egg, and Sam's cussing and Ramey's probably bare behind! How explain the ludicrous immediacy of her need to fly? How possibly unravel the snarls and loopings of her life for this woman whose own existence had been so balanced and serene? "But I've got to hurry!" she said somewhat sharply, as if Mrs. Scott's very kindness were keeping her. "I—I've got to go!"

In a few moments she came downstairs washed and combed and fully dressed. Dan stood on the back porch, smoking, and looking across the hills with embittered eyes. He roused himself as she came out the door. He looked at her a minute and then he moved down the steps with her and across the yard and opened the car door.

"Well good-bye, Polly," he said.

"Dan—" She clutched the wheel. "I don't want to go, you know that, don't you? It's Jud!" she told him unnecessarily. "Jud's come for me! I haven't written him so he got worried, he's over there now. Now!" she cried impatiently, as if by the very frenzy in her voice he must recognize what that meant. That she must race there to smooth it all out, to protect them from Jud's—Jud's—my God, how *would* he treat the family?

"So you've got to go," Dan said bitterly. "Even now the Boy Scout blows his tin whistle and you run! You're going through with it then?"

"Who says I'm going through with anything?" she cried angrily. She stepped on the starter. "Only I've got to go home, I've got to get Stew's car back."

"And you've got to see Jud!"

"Yes. Yes, I've got to see Jud!" And now that the words were spoken, they seemed alarmingly true. As yesterday she had had to see Dan, today she must see Jud. No decision could be positive without that. She had fought so fiendishly for success, extorted such sacrifice from them all, it wouldn't be fair even to Dan for her to toss the palm away without a showdown.

She backed around with a frantic twist of wheels, but Dan sprang to the running board. "You love me, Polly," he said in desperation. "You'll never be happy with any other man and you know it. Don't go, darling, come with me today, marry me! It's what you want, you know it is! Polly, I won't let you go!" he cried, clinging to the door as she drove down the lane with the dogs bounding crazily after.

At the foot of the hill, on the rough planks of the bridge, she stopped.

"Don't be a fool, Dan," she said breathlessly, clenching the wheel. "Can't you see I've got to? That it's the only way I'll be sure about—about any of it? You—me—the whole business?" she begged, searching the dark torment of his face.

"I see that I let you go once before—against my own good judgment if you want to know it—and lost you. Now I've got you back. You're mine, Polly, and by God I know what's best for you. I'm not going to let you make a mistake again!"

"And just what do you intend to do?" she demanded. She was trembling all over. She was also somehow afraid. She knew now how deeply and fundamentally Dan had changed. His mother had been wrong. Dan no longer regarded her as the privileged princess of God. He could be harsh and disdainful. He could send the fist of his love smashing through her smug preenings, her self-dramatizations, and her most fatalistically followed plans. It was wholesome somehow, it was thrilling and right; but it was distorting, wrong and terrifying too.

He stepped down. "You'll see," he said. But as she just sat there with the engine running, staring at him, he made a motion of dismissal. "Go on, beat it!" he said. "What are you waiting for?"

Polly was home in half an hour. She drove swiftly, sending the whole golden brilliance of the morning up behind her in an explosive cloud of dust. She was running away from happiness and she knew it, and she wanted to leave it behind her fast. Dan hadn't stopped her! There was triumph in that, but there was also consuming disappointment. She had *wanted* him to pit his strength against hers, yet for all his new severity, it was the way it had been before. He had let her go. And now, though her original motive today had been reasonable enough, the passion of her secret disappointment flared. Now again the blind hurtling on, even to her own destruction.

Swinging around the lake corner and up toward the college, she noticed with Andrews satisfaction the shining, hearse-sized car at the curb. It had been against Jud's principles to have a car at school, but otherwise he took considerable pride in driving Gran's Packard. He must have been on the road all night. If only he'd let them know! She sprang out and raced up the walk.

In the hallway she halted abruptly, and suddenly she wanted to weep, whether for gratitude or pity at the sad valiance of the spectacle—breakfast in the dining room! —she didn't know. The black Sunday linen tablecloth, the Post Toasties fancy in a green glass serving dish, a tarnished silver teapot pressed into service for coffee, the alien gleam of borrowed glasses and gold-rimmed cups— Mrs. Ashbaugh's, she supposed; and at one end a little blue vase in which had been stuck some brazen dandelions! Oh, pride, oh, hope, oh anxiety to please!

Oh, Mom, in your brave new housedress, with your waved hair still anet, your beautiful dark and anguished eyes so eagerly bright. "Polly!" she shouted, half rising. "There you are! I didn't hear you come in—"

And Sam, uncomfortably shirted and tied, but abark and abellow, daring any—even the great Jud, himself—to dash his precious suzerainty. Oh Father, my lord, my liege, my tyrant cock-afly! Oh, little bald-headed Dad, tired-eyed and adamant, breaker of images, believer in dreams, perched there on your fat rump, with a crumb on your chuckling mouth and egg on your tie. "Time you're gettin' home, damn ya! How you gonna explain to Jud here, stayin' out all night?"

"Dad, pipe down," Kenneth growled. He was gaunt-eyed from the early rout from bed, but dipped in thespian disdain, quite willing to pose, to aid. With daintily curled finger he drank his coffee from a cup instead of over bread.

"How's she gonna explain about my car, you mean?" Stew challenged, half-kidding, droll, correct in his sports shirt and sweater of good tan wool, but running a hand across the blue beard on his cheek.

Ramey, the untamed, crammed his mouth full of yolk-smeared toast. "Yeah Poll, whatcha got t'say for yourself?"

With eyes that went dim with proud defiance, Polly looked at Jud.

He had risen and pushed back his chair, and God, how mountain-big he was! She had forgotten. Now his tremendous shoulders in their excellent tweed, his black bull's head and thrusted chin seemed to crowd the room, to dwarf to insignificance all the preening Lilliputians in it. He was Gulliver, breaking their silly little ropes of effort with a single motion; she could feel them quaking, as if he were about to lift an annoyed thumb and mash them out.

But when he placed his hands soberly upon her shoulders and looked down into her face, she saw there such an astonished plea for help, such a sorrowful, accusing hurt, that it was suddenly he for whom she wanted to laugh and weep. Jud needed her as never before. Jud, the plutocrat, the politician, the handler of foolish little people, had found the family too much for him!

"Hey, you little mugwump, what's the idea?" he demanded heartily, managing a sick ghost-grin. He shook her in an attempt at the old playfulness. "Here I come five hundred miles to see you and you ain't even home!"

"But I didn't dream—if you'd let me know—!"

"Sa-ay, don't you read my letters? I been threatening to show up if I didn't hear from you. How come some of you didn't make this little whoozit write to the lawyer in her life?" he turned jovially to the table to ask.

But something was wrong. Polly felt it. They all did. That he was straining too hard, talking down to them, patronizing a little to compensate for—something. Perhaps for his surprise at what they were; perhaps for the disadvantage he was under at finding Polly away at another man's home. No, you could hardly expect Jud to relish that!

"Why—why—" Lydia stood up and began feverishly to scrape plates—*"didn't* she?" she gasped, though she knew the facts perfectly. "Well, you see with her sister sick and all—"

"That's right, I'm sorry." And hugging Polly, he inquired with a dash too much generous understanding, "That's the sister that had the premature baby, isn't it? How is she, by the way?"

"Why, she's getting along all right. She's getting along fine!" Lydia shrilled. She signaled with her eyes for the others to leave the table, and they obediently got up and filed into the Swell Room.

Now from his shirt pocket Sam produced one of the two ten cent cigars he had been saving for this moment. "Here Jud, smoke that, damn ya!" he offered grandly, hitching at his pants.

Jud shook his head in half-apologetic negation. "No, thanks. Never use 'em."

"Fine, fine, smoke 'em myself then!" declared Sam, the invincible. But there was something remotely forlorn about the way he put the other one back.

"Have a Lucky then, Jud," invited Ken, diving into his pocket for one of his rare packs. Polly had never seen him quite so willing to please.

Jud shook his head again, grinning in his vaguely embarrassed, vaguely lofty way. "Thanks, fella, but I don't smoke at all."

"Me neither," Ramey claimed—and it was difficult to tell whether he was being impish or sincere. "I signed a pledge!"

"As a matter of fact, so did I, Ramey," Jud said in his best Scout Leader tone, hauling Polly down beside him on the davenport. "And I've never regretted sticking to it. Of course," he added affably, for the benefit of the three men who stood uncomfortably puffing, "all my buddies smoke! Gosh, I never hold it against a guy that does," he magnanimously informed them, *"if* he can afford it. But you'd be surprised how many of even my fraternity brothers are downright moochers."

Stew snorted audibly and looked at Ken, who colored. And suddenly, unreasonably but violently, Polly felt sorry for him. She wrenched out of Jud's loosely pawing grasp.

"There are worse things!" she snapped.

"Yes. Yes, there are!" Jud agreed with exaggerated tolerance. He grinned and winked slyly at Sam, but there was no camouflage for the stunned pride, the deep and baffled hurt in his voice. "Engaged girls staying out all night for instance, eh, Mr. Andrews?"

"Just call me Sam! All the girls' fellas do!" Sam blustered, but nobody laughed; the joke fell flat. "Yeah, yep that's right, Masters. But you see these people are old friends of the family—own four or five sections of land," he cajoled. "Polly's been going out there to—to see the girls for years, ain't that right, Polly?" he demanded brazenly.

Polly's eyes were low. Don't, Dad—don't drive me or beg me or want this so much! Don't cringe before his patronage like that—not you!

"Well gee, why didn't somebody *say* so?" Jud whooped with boisterous triumph. In clumsy glad relief he began to knock Polly about. "Of course—" his tone lowered, he began to reëstablish his prestige before the circle of surprised eyes, "I *knew* it was something like that. I just wanted to get a rise out of old punkin-face here. I knew she was being true to her own personal Supreme Court all the time!" Then, "Ain't that right, pal?" he bent low to plead.

Polly stood up. She felt choked with a blind and weary anger, strung on a rack of outraged loyalties—for the family, subtly snubbed and condescended to; for Jud himself, touting a confidence no fool could feel; for Dan, whom they were asking her to deny, but who hadn't stopped her, who hadn't come!

"Oh shut up! Stop it, all of you!" she cried. And there were tears in her eyes. "What are you trying to pull, anyway? What's the big idea making me the feature attraction in a sideshow? Ye gods, I didn't know he was coming, did I? Why shouldn't I go out to Dan's? Yes, and—and stay all night!"

Lydia had come to stand in the dining room door. "Polly, control yourself," she begged.

"Yeah, Polly, for God's sake," Sam said, "nobody's accusing you of anything!"

"Why gee, pal, *no!*" Jud assured her, flushing. "I didn't mean to barge in on you like this and cause trouble. I just wanted to make sure you were coming to Des Moines and take those exams with me and—and go on together, pal," he blurted miserably.

"Sure, that's it, and she's gonna too," Sam said. "Ain't you, Polly?"

"I don't know!" She crossed to the window and drew back the curtain. "Maybe I wasn't cut out to be a lawyer. Maybe I couldn't even pass those exams—not now."

"Hell, what're a few questions?" Sam joked enormously. "If you get stuck tell 'em to go ask the old chicken medicine man! I might barge into the Senate Chamber and tell 'em what's what myself!"

"Give 'em a dose of Happy Hen Tonic, Sam," Stew grinned.

"Aw, he won't even be there. The finance man won't let him out of town with the car!" Ken jeered.

"Well it takes more'n a bunch of black nightshirts to scare me, I can tell you that! No, you ain't got anything to worry about, kiddo, with a smart cuss like Masters here back of you, you'll get by all right, won't she, Jud?"

"Why sure! Gosh, Smidgin, you'll do us all proud," Jud blustered. "I know most of those judges, and with my experience in that Supreme Court Day business," he mentioned casually, "why we—we'll go to town!" He got up and went to stand behind Polly, shaking her playfully with his big hands. "I figured we could drive back to

Mastersville this afternoon, get in a little reviewing tonight and drive on over tomorrow. And after that—"

She had tensed under his touch. She whirled about,
looked up at him with strangely shining eyes. "After that
what?" she asked urgently. "What then?"

"Well then we—we could go back to Gran's. Or—" he
swallowed, "come here, if you insist. But Gran's pretty
swell, she's still willing and anxious to let us be married
there, and if your folks don't care too much—I mean—
after *all*—!"

"After all what, Jud?" she prodded instantly. "What *do*
you mean?"

"Sa-ay, what is this?" he laughed unhappily. "What's
she drivin' at? You folks'll have to let me in on how to
handle this gal!" he invited cordially. "She's got more
quirks than a psychology prof!" He went on talking, but
suddenly he stopped, for he realized that they were not
listening, that their eyes had shifted with a single surprised
and somehow grateful motion, to the door.

"Dan!" Ken whooped. "Well, I'll *be*—!" He threw back
his head and the yell of his laughter filled the room. "Enter
at your own risk, Sam's all set to beat up on you for
keeping Polly out all night!" he panted with happy malice,
glancing at Jud. "Gimme a cigarette, darn you, I ain't had
a decent smoke since you deserted the dump!"

"Hi, Ken," Dan said. He nodded to them all, but his
eyes were steady upon Polly.

"Hey, don't let that lug bum cigarettes, he's got a pack
of his own," Stew warned, grabbing Dan's hand. "Where
you been for the last month of Sundays, anyway?"

"Yeah, Dan," Sam grumbled, "for God's sake what's
happened to you?" And then with a reluctant surge of
welcome, "C'mon in, damn ya, never did like ya very
good anyway!" He coughed and blew his nose and held
out his hand.

Dan crossed the room. "Hi, Sam. Hi—Mom."

"Oh, Dan!" Lydia's eyes were wet. "It's so g-good to
have you back! Mr. Scott meet Mr.—Mr.—oh, good
heavens," she gasped, "I've forgotten your last name!"

"Quite all right. Masters," Jud supplied, whipping forth
his politician's hand. "Glad to know you, Scott."

"Whose bus you driving, Dan?" Ken shouted with demon glee. "That ain't the usual wreck!"

"No. That's Kit's," said Dan.

"Jud drove his gramma's Packard!" Ken marveled. "Big as a train!"

"Yep, Dan, a—a Packard! See it out there?" Sam chuckled, slapping his knee. He didn't know himself what he was laughing at, but he seemed about to burst with some ridiculous relief.

"But it's not Gran's Packard," Jud corrected in proud, vaguely challenging apology. He grinned at Polly. "Guess I haven't told you, pal, that it's ours now. With Gran's compliments! Guess that's not such a bad start for a coupla kid barristers, huh? I guess we'll get by pretty good, won't we, pal?"

And for a moment the grotesquerie of it all was too much. His foolish, bitter determination to win even now against the odds that she didn't love him, and her impossible family. The blind, ferocious *need* to win to compensate for some poverty of spirit deeper than anything they in their direst need had known. Something which none of these others could comprehend—the handicap of your own advantages, and that odious, pitiable, damning power to make little ones feel littler and so, by some fabulous distortion, Bigger than you! Gazing up into the sad challenging superiority of his face which seemed to dare her not to let him down, she pitied him as never before. For an instant it seemed necessary to make the vital sacrifice he asked, if only to consume the horror of that pity, stamp it out.

"You see, Poll and I are going to be law partners," Jud informed Dan condescendingly.

"Are you about ready, Polly?" Dan asked.

She nodded. "I've got to change. I—I've got to get some clothes."

"Polly!" Lydia cried in frantic anguish. "What are you going to do?"

"Why, we're going to Sioux City and be married," Polly heard herself saying simply, with a kind of surprise, as if they should have known.

"Why, you're crazy!" Sam bellowed. But there was no conviction behind the spontaneous roar. "Crazier'n hell!"

"That's right. Crazier'n hell, like the rest of you!" It sounded wonderful. She regarded them all with pleased, excited eyes.

"Oh, I don't know what to say!" Lydia wailed. "I just want you to be happy. All of you! I—I don't want to see anyone hurt!"

"Here now, don't worry about *me!*" Jud's jaw jutted. "I don't need anybody to help *me* along! Naturally I hate to see Poll give up her career, especially after I've boosted and coached her along, but if somebody else can offer more of a future—" he was claiming tritely, tragically, and with heavy sarcasm as Polly dashed upstairs— "why —why may the best man win!"

In a few moments he was gone.

She yanked open the stuck drawers of the old orchid dresser that teetered comically on its broken casters. She dumped things into the lone gray bag she had managed to salvage for herself from those Dan had given her. She pawed the closet hooks for a clean slip and found one with a broken strap and hitched it together with a safety pin. *It beggar'd all description . . . O, rare for Antony!* Was her hair all right? she wondered, poking at it. She patted the little coat of the cheap white suit she had been saving for tomorrow. Did she look like a bride? If only Jean were here! . . . and she remembered the uptilted face under the bathroom light, Jean's fingers stenciling lipstick and patting rouge, the magically made-over clothes, a little rag-bag marvel, chiqued by Jean's deft hands.

Oh, Jean! Oh, Mom! Oh, Ken and Dad and Ramey. Oh, rickety little room—cell of my imprisoned self where I so often wept!

She sat down upon the hard bed. Her throat choked tight.

Downstairs the voices, the weeping and the laughter, the sound of a slamming door. And in the hall a quick, a panting step.

"Mom! Please don't cry, Mom!" She sprang up, she held the hot quavering shoulders in their bravely ruffled gingham. "I won't if you don't want me to! I'll stay home.

With you and Dad forever!" she claimed thickly, desperately. "Please don't cry!"

"No—no, it isn't that. I want you to be happy. You've got to leave—for the last time now. You've got to escape us all."

"But I don't want to escape you! That's why I'm doing this. Why I gave up Jud and all he represented. He'd have changed me, he'd have stifled and ruined and broken us all. Dan loves us—he'll let us be ourselves!"

"I know, I know." Lydia wiped her eyes. "I'm sorry. I guess it's partly that I did want one of you girls married at home," she said forlornly.

"We will be!" The blind abysmal pity—the need to comfort— "We'll wait if you want us to!"

"No. No, you go on, you've waited long enough. And we couldn't—we couldn't do it here very well anyway," Lydia said sadly. She gazed for a moment bleakly into the cherry tree.

And now from below came leaping and blaring an insane melody. *Here comes the bride—here comes the bride!* Browbeaten from the ancient tuneless piano under Ken's thumping hands, torn in golden jubilance from the throat of a second-hand horn.

Lydia's face changed. She laughed with a little choke. "Well! If music be the food of love—! You'd better go, honey." Her eyes flashed in one of her sudden wild and unreasonable bursts of proud exuberance. "And it's best this way, darnit, it's best, it's all right! We'll pull through somehow, and so will you and Dan! You won't live happily ever after—who does?—but you'll get along!"

They laughed and kissed each other and wiped their eyes and walked together down the hall. "Now honey, you come back in a few days," Lydia went on, still in her tone of high, defiant exultation. "I'll have a shower for you and Jean both! We'll have Vee and some of the girls and the ladies of the Aid, and something good to eat and —and everything lovely, everything just the way you want it!" she promised eagerly. "You come back!"

"Yes. Yes, Mom, I'll come back."

Dan was standing at the foot of the stairs, looking up, waiting and watching for her to come down, as he always had. He reached up and took her hand.

"Good-bye, Mom. Good-bye, Dad." Polly kissed the prune-fat mouth that wasn't chuckling now, that was tautly grim. "Good-bye, folks!" they said.

They went out the door and across the L-shaped porch and down the walk. Polly could feel, rather than see, the family crowded at the bay window, bunting each other a little, looking out. She looked up and waved Sam's own foolish little fat paw child's wave at them.

ABOUT THE AUTHOR

MARJORIE HOLMES (Mrs. Lynn Mighell) writes the popular column "Love and Laughter" for the WASHINGTON STAR. She is the author of seven novels and has contributed to numerous magazines, including MCCALLS, READER'S DIGEST, BETTER HOMES AND GARDENS, and TODAY'S HEALTH. She has also taught adult education writing courses at Catholic, Maryland and Georgetown universities, and has been on the staff of the Georgetown Writers Conference since its beginning. She is the mother of four children and grandmother of three. She lives in suburban Washington, D.C., and summers at Lake Jackson, Manassas, Virginia, where she swims, canoes, and water skis.

Heartwarming Books
of
Faith and Inspiration

☐	THE GOSPEL ACCORDING TO PEANUTS Robert L. Short	3800 •	$ .75
☐	NEW MOON RISING Eugenia Price	5466 •	$ .95
☐	I'VE GOT TO TALK TO SOMEBODY, GOD Marjorie Holmes	6566 •	$1.25
☐	PATRICIA Grace Livingston Hill	7247 •	$ .75
☐	LOVE AND LAUGHTER Marjorie Holmes	7348 •	$1.25
☐	THE WOMAN AT THE WELL Dale Evans Rogers	7366 •	$ .95
☐	MINE EYES HAVE SEEN THE GLORY Anita Bryant	7380 •	$ .95
☐	LIGHTHOUSE Eugenia Price	7382 •	$1.25
☐	THE LATE GREAT PLANET EARTH Hal Lindsey	7575 •	$1.25
☐	WHO AM I GOD? Marjorie Holmes	7608 •	$1.25
☐	HOW TO TALK TO GOD WHEN YOU AREN'T FEELING RELIGIOUS Charles Smith	7712 •	$1.25
☐	THE TASTE OF NEW WINE Keith Miller	7809 •	$1.25
☐	THEY CALL ME COACH John Wooden	8046 •	$1.25
☐	SILVER WINGS Grace Livingston Hill	8202 •	$ .95

Buy them at your local bookstore or use this handy coupon for ordering:

Bantam Books, Inc., Dept. HF, 414 East Golf Road, Des Plaines, Ill. 60016

Please send me the books I have checked above. I am enclosing $_____
(please add 25¢ to cover postage and handling). Send check or money order
—no cash or C.O.D.'s please.

Mr/Mrs/Miss_____

Address_____

City_____State/Zip_____

HF—2/74

Please allow three weeks for delivery. This offer expires 2/75.